THE ZINZOLIN BOOK OF OCCULT FICTION

EDITED AND WITH AN INTRODUCTION BY
BRENDAN CONNELL

THIS IS A SNUGGLY BOOK

Anthology and Introduction Copyright © 2022
by Brendan Connell.
All rights reserved.

ISBN: 978-1-64525-098-2

THE ZINZOLIN BOOK OF OCCULT FICTION

Brendan Connell was born in Santa Fe, New Mexico, in 1970. His works of fiction include *The Architect* (PS Publishing, 2012), *Lives of Notorious Cooks* (Chômu Press, 2012), *Miss Homicide Plays the Flute* (Eibonvale Press, 2013), *Cannibals of West Papua* (Zagava, 2015), and *Against the Grain Again: The Further Adventures of Des Esseintes* (Tartarus Press, 2021). As editor he has worked on various projects, including *The World in Violet: An Anthology of English Decadent Poetry* (Snuggly Boos, 2022), and *The Neo-Decadent Cookbook* (Eibonvale Press, 2020), which was co-edited by Justin Isis. As translator his efforts include *Alcina and Other Stories* (Snuggly Books, 2019), by Guido Gozzano, which was co-translated by his wife Anna.

SNUGGLY BOOKS

CONTENTS

INTRODUCTION

THE current volume, the first in a planned series, concerns itself primarily with the occult revival of the British Isles, as it manifested itself in fiction produced under that impulse from 1888-1911.

Occult thought has, of course, always found fertile ground to flourish in those Isles, Great Britain itself being, we must remember, the birthplace of, among many mystical others, the famous Hermetic philosopher John Dee. Certainly in foreign parts those places were associated with the presence of witches and wizards, sorceresses and necromancers—with Merlin and Morgan le Fay; Gwydion and Hellawes.

The period which this volume concerns itself with, though long-past such legendary days, was, as much as any, one in which occult activity in the British Isles was especially rich. *Séances* had reached the level of a fad; mediums abounded; ritual magic was rampant; and the production of spirit photographers was brisk.

In 1878 the London Lodge of the Theosophical Society had been founded, one of the main aims of which was to promote esoteric thought, one of the methods coming to include the Theosophical Publishing Society, which, under H.P. Blavatsky's guidance, from 1887 onward, put out the journal *Lucifer*, which was replete with pieces on such subjects as Rosicrucianism, the Kabbalah, and talismanic magic. A great many of the occultists of the day contributed to its pages, including the coroner William Wynn Westcott and Mac Gregor-Mathers, these two being the founders of the Hermetic Order of the Golden Dawn, one of a number of occult secret societies which existed at the time and which attracted many noteworthy members, including Aleister Crowley, Arthur Machen, and Florence Farr, who became the Chief Adept in Anglia, that is to say, the leader of the English branch of the Order.

The two main trends in occultism in the British Isles were, therefore, the Theosophical movement, which drew heavily from Buddhist and Hindu sources, and the various initiatic occult societies, which were generally inspired by the Western mystery tradition, Rosicrucianism, and the magico-sexual theories of Paschal Beverly Randolph. Though these two strands are often presented as having been in a rivalry, the truth is considerably more complicated, since firstly, the initiatic occult societies were also frequently at rivalry among themselves, and, secondly, the members of these same societies had often contributed their writings to Theosophical publications, had been Theosophists themselves, or would later become Theosophists, as was the case with Florence Farr, who, subsequent to her deep involvement with the Hermetic Order of the Golden Dawn, joined the Theosophical Society of London. The interests and aims of those two spheres, after all, though certainly not identical, intersected at a great many places.

The bulk of what the reader will find in *The Zinzolin Book of the Occult* should be seen, therefore, as having been created against the aforementioned background.

※

The contents of this book are arranged chronologically. I have presented the various pieces, as much as possible, in a format that aligns with their original publication, though an infrequent correction has been made where an obvious error was present, and seldomly an adjustment to a spelling or bit of punctuation has been made for the regularity of the volume.

I have, furthermore, felt compelled to take a broad enough view of the word "fiction" to allow the inclusion of the wonderful piece by the indispensable occultist Florence Farr.

I would like to conclude by thanking Damian Murphy, Daniel Corrick, Justin Isis, Quentin S. Crisp, and my wife Anna, for allowing themselves to be occasional sounding boards in my quest for a more perfect anthology.

—Brendan Connell

THE ZINZOLIN BOOK
OF OCCULT FICTION

THE ENCHANTED WOMAN

by Anna Kingsford

THE first consciousness which broke my sleep last night was one of floating, of being carried swiftly by some invisible force through a vast space; then, of being gently lowered; then of light, until, gradually, I found myself on my feet in a broad noon-day brightness, and before me an open country. Hills, hills, as far as the eye could reach,—hills with snow on their tops, and mists around their gorges. This was the first thing I saw distinctly. Then, casting my eyes towards the ground, I perceived that all about me lay huge masses of grey material which, at first, I took for blocks of stone, having the form of lions; but as I looked at them more intently, my sight grew clearer, and I saw, to my horror, that they were really alive. A panic seized me, and I tried to run away; but on turning, I became suddenly aware that the whole country was filled with these awful shapes; and the faces of those nearest to me were most dreadful, for their eyes, and something in the expression, though not in the form, of their faces, were human. I was absolutely alone in a terrible world peopled with lions, too, of a monstrous kind. Recovering myself with an effort, I resumed my flight, but, as I passed through the midst of this concourse of monsters, it suddenly struck me that they were perfectly unconscious of my presence. I even laid my hands, in passing, on the heads and manes of several, but they gave no sign of seeing me or of knowing that I touched them. At last I gained the threshold of a great pavilion, not, apparently, built by hands, but formed by Nature. The walls were solid, yet they were composed of huge trees standing close together, like columns; and the roof of the pavilion was formed by their massive foliage, through which not a ray of outer light penetrated. Such light as there was seemed nebulous, and appeared to rise out of the ground. In the centre of this pavilion I stood alone, happy to have got clear away from those terrible beasts and the gaze of their steadfast eyes.

As I stood there, I became conscious of the fact that the nebulous light of the place was concentrating itself into a focus on the columned wall opposite to me. It grew there, became intenser, and then spread, revealing, as it spread, a series of moving pictures that appeared to be scenes actually enacted before me. For the figures in the pictures were living, and they moved before my eyes, though I heard neither word nor sound. And this is what I saw. First there came a writing on the wall of the pavilion:—"This is the History of our World." These words, as I looked at them, appeared to sink into the wall as they had risen out of it, and to yield place to the pictures which then began to come out in succession, dimly at first, then strong and clear as actual scenes.

First I beheld a beautiful woman, with the sweetest face and most perfect form conceivable. She was dwelling in a cave among the hills with her husband, and he, too, was beautiful, more like an angel than a man. They seemed perfectly happy together; and their dwelling was like Paradise. On every side was beauty, sunlight, and repose. This picture sank into the wall as the writing had done. And then came out another; the same man and woman driving together in a sleigh drawn by reindeer over fields of ice; with all about them glaciers and snow, and great mountains veiled in wreaths of slowly moving mist. The sleigh went at a rapid pace, and its occupants talked gaily to each other, so far as I could judge by their smiles and the movement of their lips. But, what caused me much surprise was that they carried between them, and actually in their hands, a glowing flame, the fervor of which I felt reflected from the picture upon my own cheeks. The ice around shone with its brightness. The mists upon the snow mountains caught its gleam. Yet, strong as were its light and heat, neither the man nor the woman seemed to be burned or dazzled by it. This picture, too, the beauty and brilliancy of which greatly impressed me, sank and disappeared as the former.

Next, I saw a terrible looking man clad in an enchanter's robe, standing alone upon an ice-crag. In the air above him, poised like a dragonfly, was an evil spirit, having a head and face like that of a human being. The rest of it resembled the tail of a comet, and seemed made of a green fire, which flickered in and out as though swayed by a wind. And as I looked, suddenly, through an opening among the hills, I saw the sleigh pass, carrying the beautiful woman and her husband; and in the same instant the enchanter also saw it, and his face contracted, and the evil spirit lowered itself and came between me and him. Then this picture sank and vanished.

I next beheld the same cave in the mountains which I had before seen; and the beautiful couple together in it. Then a shadow darkened the door of the cave; and the enchanter was there, asking admittance; cheerfully they bade him enter, and, as he came forward with his snake-like eyes fixed on the fair woman, I understood that he wished to have her for his own, and was even then devising how to bear her away. And the spirit in the air beside him seemed busy suggesting schemes to this end. Then this picture melted and became confused, giving place for but a brief moment to another, in which I saw the enchanter carrying the woman away in his arms, she struggling and lamenting, her long bright hair streaming behind her. This scene passed from the wall as though a wind had swept over it, and there rose up in its place a picture, which impressed me with a more vivid sense of reality than all the rest.

It represented a market place, in the midst of which was a pile of faggots and a stake, such as were used formerly for the burning of heretics and witches. The market place, round which were rows of seats as though for a concourse of spectators, yet appeared quite deserted. I saw only three living beings present,—the beautiful woman, the enchanter, and the evil spirit. Nevertheless, I thought that the seats were really occupied by invisible tenants, for every now and then there seemed to be a stir in the atmosphere as of a great multitude; and I had, moreover, a strange sense of facing many witnesses. The enchanter led the woman to the stake, fastened her there with iron chains, lit the faggots about her feet and withdrew to a short distance, where he stood with his arms folded, looking on as the flames rose about her. I understood that she had refused his love, and that in his fury he had denounced her as a sorceress. Then in the fire, above the pile, I saw the evil spirit poising itself like a fly, and rising and sinking and fluttering in the thick smoke. While I wondered what this meant, the flames which had concealed the beautiful woman, parted in their midst, and disclosed a sight so horrible and unexpected as to thrill me from head to foot, and curdle my blood. Chained to the stake there stood, not the fair woman I had seen there a moment before, but a hideous monster,—a woman still, but a woman with three heads, and three bodies linked in one. Each of her long arms ended, not in a hand, but in a claw like that of a bird of rapine. Her hair resembled the locks of the classic Medusa, and her faces were inexpressibly loathsome. She seemed, with all her dreadful heads and limbs, to writhe in the flames and yet not to be consumed by them. She gathered them in to herself; her claws caught them

16

and drew them down; her triple body appeared to suck the fire into itself, as though a blast drove it. The sight appalled me. I covered my face and dared look no more.

When at length I again turned my eyes upon the wall, the picture that had so terrified me was gone, and instead of it, I saw the enchanter flying through the world, pursued by the evil spirit and that dreadful woman. Through all the world they seemed to go. The scenes changed with marvellous rapidity. Now the picture glowed with the wealth and gorgeousness of the torrid zone; now the ice-fields of the North rose into view; anon a pine-forest; then a wild seashore; but always the same three flying figures; always the horrible three-formed harpy pursuing the enchanter, and beside her the evil spirit with the dragonfly wings.

At last this succession of images ceased, and I beheld a desolate region, in the midst of which sat the woman with the enchanter beside her, his head reposing in her lap. Either the sight of her must have become familiar to him and, so, less horrible, or she had subjugated him by some spell. At all events, they were mated at last, and their offspring lay around them on the stony ground, or moved to and fro. These were lions,—monsters with human faces, such as I had seen in the beginning of my dream. Their jaws dripped blood; they paced backwards and forwards, lashing their tails. Then too, this picture faded and sank into the wall as the others had done. And through its melting outlines came out again the words I had first seen: "This is the History of our World," only they seemed to me in some way changed, but how, I cannot tell. The horror of the whole thing was too strong upon me to let me dare look longer at the wall. And I awoke, repeating to myself the question, "How could one woman become three?"

KARMIC VISIONS

by H.P. Blavatsky

Oh, sad no more! Oh, sweet *No more!*
Oh, strange *No more!*
By a mossed brook bank on a stone
I smelt a wild weed-flower alone;
There was a ringing in my ears,
And both my eyes gushed out with tears,
Surely all pleasant things had gone before.
Low buried fathom deep beneath with three, NO MORE.
—Tennyson ("The Gem" 1831)

I

A camp filled with war-chariots, neighing horses and legions of long-haired soldiers. . . .

A regal tent, gaudy in its barbaric splendour. Its linen walls are weighed down under the burden of arms. In its centre a raised seat covered with skins, and on it a stalwart, savage-looking warrior. He passes in review prisoners of war brought in turn before him, who are disposed of according to the whim of the heartless despot.

A new captive is now before him, and is addressing him with passionate earnestness. . . . As he listens to her with suppressed passion in his manly, but fierce, cruel face, the balls of his eyes become bloodshot and roll with fury. And as he bends forward with fierce stare, his whole appearance—his matted locks hanging over the frowning brow, his big-boned body with strong sinews, and the two large hands resting on the shield placed upon the right knee—justifies the remark made in hardly audible whisper by a grey-headed soldier to his neighbour:

"Little mercy shall the holy prophetess receive at the hands of Clovis!"

The captive, who stands between two Burgundian warriors, facing the ex-prince of the Salians, now king of all the Franks, is an old woman with silver-white dishevelled hair, hanging over her skeleton-like shoulders. In spite of her great age, her tall figure is erect; and the inspired black eyes look proudly and fearlessly into the cruel face of the treacherous son of Gilderich.

"Aye, King," she says, in a loud, ringing voice. "Aye, thou art great and mighty now, but thy days are numbered, and thou shalt reign but three summers longer. Wicked thou wert born . . . perfidious thou art to thy friends and allies, robbing more than one of his lawful crown. Murderer of thy next-of-kin, thou who addest to the knife and spear in open warfare, dagger, poison and treason, beware how thou dearest with the servant of Nerthus!"[1]

"Ha, ha, ha! . . . old hag of Hell!" chuckles the King, with an evil, ominous sneer. "Thou hast crawled out of the entrails of thy mother-goddess truly. Thou fearest not my wrath? It is well. But little need I fear thine empty imprecations . . . I, a baptized Christian!"

"So, so," replies the Sybil. "All know that Clovis has abandoned the gods of his fathers; that he has lost all faith in the

---

1 "The Nourishing" (Tacit. Germ. XI)—the Earth, a Mother-Goddess, the most beneficent deity of the ancient Germans.

warning voice of the white horse of the Sun, and that out of fear of the Allimani he went serving on his knees Remigius, the servant of the Nazarene, at Rheims. But hast thou become any truer in thy new faith? Hast thou not murdered in cold blood all thy brethren who trusted in thee, after, as well as before, thy apostasy? Hast not thou plighted troth to Alaric, the King of the West Goths, and hast thou not killed him by stealth, running thy spear into his back while he was bravely fighting an enemy? And is it thy new faith and thy new gods that teach thee to be devising in thy black soul even now foul means against Theodoric, who put thee down? . . . Beware, Clovis, beware! For now the gods of thy fathers have risen against thee! Beware, I say, for . . ."

"Woman!" fiercely cries the King—"Woman, cease thy insane talk and answer my question. Where is the treasure of the grove amassed by thy priests of Satan, and hidden after they had been driven away by the Holy Cross? . . . Thou alone knowest. Answer, or by Heaven and Hell I shall thrust thy evil tongue down thy throat for ever!" . . .

She heeds not the threat, but goes on calmly and fearlessly as before, as if she had not heard.

". . . The gods say, Clovis, thou art accursed! . . . Clovis, thou shalt be reborn among thy present enemies, and suffer the tortures thou hast inflicted upon thy victims. All the combined power and glory thou hast deprived them of shall be thine in prospect, yet thou shalt never reach it! . . . Thou shalt . . ."

The prophetess never finishes her sentence.

With a terrible oath the King, crouching like a wild beast on his skin-covered seat, pounces upon her with the leap of a jaguar, and with one blow fells her to the ground. And as he lifts his sharp murderous spear the "Holy One" of the Sun-worshipping tribe makes the air ring with a last imprecation.

"I curse thee, enemy of Nerthus! May my agony be tenfold thine! . . . May the Great Law avenge. . . ."

The heavy spear falls, and, running through the victim's throat, nails the head to the ground. A stream of hot crimson blood gushes from the gaping wound and covers king and soldiers with indelible gore. . . .

II

Time—the landmark of gods and men in the boundless field of Eternity, the murderer of its offspring and of memory in mankind—time moves on with noiseless, incessant step through aeons and ages. . . . Among millions of other Souls, a Soul-Ego is reborn: for weal or for woe, who knoweth! Captive in its new human Form, it grows with it, and together they become, at last, conscious of their existence.

Happy are the years of their blooming youth, unclouded with want or sorrow. Neither knows aught of the Past nor of the Future. For them all is the joyful Present: for the Soul-Ego is unaware that it had ever lived in other human tabernacles, it knows not that it shall be again reborn, and it takes no thought of the morrow.

Its Form is calm and content. It has hitherto given its Soul-Ego no heavy troubles. Its happiness is due to the continuous mild serenity of its temper, to the affection it spreads wherever it goes. For it is a noble Form, and its heart is full of benevolence. Never has the Form startled its Soul-Ego with a too-violent shock, or otherwise disturbed the calm placidity of its tenant.

Two score of years glide by like one short pilgrimage; a long walk through the sun-lit paths of life, hedged by ever-blooming roses with no thorns. The rare sorrows that befall the twin pair, Form and Soul, appear to them rather like the pale light of the cold northern moon, whose beams throw into a deeper shadow all around the moon-lit objects, than as the blackness of the night, the night of hopeless sorrow and despair.

Son of a Prince, born to rule himself one day his father's kingdom; surrounded from his cradle by reverence and honours; deserving of the universal respect and sure of the love of all—what could the Soul-Ego desire more for the Form it dwelt in.

And so the Soul-Ego goes on enjoying existence in its tower of strength, gazing quietly at the panorama of life ever changing before its two windows—the two kind blue eyes of a loving and good man.

III

One day an arrogant and boisterous enemy threatens the father's kingdom, and the savage instincts of the warrior of old awaken in the Soul-Ego. It leaves its dreamland amid the blossoms of life and causes its Ego of clay to draw the soldier's blade, assuring him it is in defence of his country.

Prompting each other to action, they defeat the enemy and cover themselves with glory and pride. They make the haughty foe bite the dust at their feet in supreme humiliation. For this they are crowned by history with the unfading laurels of valour, which are those of success. They make a footstool of the fallen enemy and transform their sire's little kingdom into a great empire. Satisfied they could achieve no more for the present, they return to seclusion and to the dreamland of their sweet home.

For three lustra more the Soul-Ego sits at its usual post, beaming out of its windows on the world around. Over its head the sky is blue and the vast horizons are covered with those seemingly unfading flowers that grow in the sunlight of health and strength. All looks fair as a verdant mead in spring. . . . . .

IV

But an evil day comes to all in the drama of being. It waits through the life of king and of beggar. It leaves traces on the history of every mortal born from woman, and it can neither be seared away, entreated, nor propitiated. Health is a dew-drop that falls from the heavens to vivify the blossoms on earth, only during the morn of life, its spring and summer. . . . It has but a short duration and returns from whence it came—the invisible realms.

> "How oft'neath the bud that is brightest and fairest.
> The seeds of the canker in embryo lurk!
> How oft at the root of the flower that is rarest—
> Secure in its ambush the worm is at work. . . . . ."

The running sand which moves downward in the glass, wherein the hours of human life are numbered, runs swifter. The worm has gnawed the blossom of health through its heart. The strong body is found stretched one day on the thorny bed of pain.

The Soul-Ego beams no longer. It sits still and looks sadly out of what has become its dungeon windows, on the world which is now rapidly being shrouded for it in the funeral palls of suffering. Is it the eve of night eternal which is nearing?

V

Beautiful are the resorts on the midland sea. An endless line of surf-beaten, black, rugged rocks stretches, hemmed in between the golden sands of the coast and the deep blue waters of the gulf. They offer their granite breast to the fierce blows of the north-west wind and thus protect the dwellings of the rich that nestle at their foot on the inland side. The half-ruined cottages on the open shore are the insufficient shelter of the poor. Their squalid bodies are often crushed under the walls torn and washed down by wind and angry wave. But they only follow the great law of the survival of the fittest. Why should *they* be protected?

Lovely is the morning when the sun dawns with golden amber tints and its first rays kiss the cliffs of the beautiful shore. Glad is the song of the lark, as, emerging from its warm nest of herbs, it drinks the morning dew from the deep flower-cups; when the tip of the rosebud thrills under the caress of the first sunbeam, and earth and heaven smile in mutual greeting. Sad is the Soul-Ego alone as it gazes on awakening nature from the high couch opposite the large bay-window.

How calm is the approaching noon as the shadow creeps steadily on the sundial towards the hour of rest! Now the hot sun begins to melt the clouds in the limpid air and the last shreds of the morning mist that lingers on the tops of the distant hills vanish in it. All nature is prepared to rest at the hot and lazy hour of midday. The feathered tribes cease their song; their soft, gaudy wings droop and they hang their drowsy heads, seeking refuge from the burning heat. A morning lark is busy nestling in the bordering bushes under the clustering flowers of the pomegranate and the sweet bay of the Mediterranean. The active songster has become voiceless.

"Its voice will resound as joyfully again tomorrow!" sighs the Soul-Ego, as it listens to the dying buzzing of the insects on the verdant turf. "Shall ever mine?"

And now the flower-scented breeze hardly stirs the languid heads of the luxuriant plants. A solitary palm-tree, growing out of the cleft of a moss-covered rock, next catches the eye of the Soul-Ego. Its once upright, cylindrical trunk has been twisted out of shape and half-broken by the nightly blasts of the north-west winds. And as it stretches wearily its drooping feathery arms, swayed to and fro in the blue pellucid air, its body trembles and threatens to break in two at the first new gust that may arise.

"And then, the severed part will fall into the sea, and the once stately palm will be no more," soliloquizes the Soul-Ego as it gazes sadly out of its windows.

Everything returns to life, in the cool, old bower at the hour of sunset. The shadows on the sun-dial become with every moment thicker, and animate nature awakens busier than ever in the cooler hours of approaching night. Birds and insects chirrup and buzz their last evening hymns around the tall and still powerful Form, as it paces slowly and wearily along the gravel walk. And now its heavy gaze falls wistfully on the azure bosom of the tranquil sea. The gulf sparkles like a gem-studded carpet of blue-velvet in the farewell dancing sunbeams, and smiles like a thoughtless, drowsy child, weary of tossing about. Further on, calm and serene in its perfidious beauty, the open sea stretches far and wide the smooth mirror of its cool waters—salt and bitter as human tears. It lies in its treacherous repose like a gorgeous, sleeping monster, watching over the unfathomed mystery of its dark abysses. Truly the monumentless cemetry of the millions sunk in its depths . . .

"Without a grave.
Unknell'd, uncoffined and unknown . . ."

while the sorry relic of the once noble Form pacing yonder, once that its hour strikes and the deep-voiced bells toll the knell for the departed soul, shall be laid out in state and pomp. Its dissolution will be announced by millions of trumpet voices. Kings, princes and the mighty ones of the earth will be present at its obsequies, or will send their representatives with sorrowful faces and condoling messages to those left behind. . . .

"One point gained, over those 'uncoffined and unknown',"
is the bitter reflection of the Soul-Ego.

Thus glides past one day after the other; and as swift-winged Time urges his flight, every vanishing hour destroying some thread in the tissue of life, the Soul-Ego is gradually transformed in its views of things and men. Flitting between two eternities, far away from its birthplace, solitary among its crowd of physicians, and attendants, the Form is drawn with every day nearer to its Spirit-Soul. Another light unapproached and unapproachable in days of joy, softly descends upon the weary prisoner. It sees now that which it had never perceived before. . . .

VI

How grand, how mysterious are the spring nights on the seashore when the winds are chained and the elements lulled! A solemn silence reigns in nature. Alone the silvery, scarcely audible ripple of the wave, as it runs caressingly over the moist sand, kissing shells and pebbles on its up and down journey, reaches the ear like the regular soft breathing of a sleeping bosom. How small, how insignificant and helpless feels man, during these quiet hours, as he stands between the two gigantic magnitudes, the star-hung dome above, and the slumbering earth below. Heaven and earth are plunged in sleep, but their souls are awake, and they confabulate, whispering one to the other mysteries unspeakable. It is then that the occult side of Nature lifts her dark veils for us, and reveals secrets we would vainly seek to extort from her during the day. The firmament, so distant, so far away from earth, now seems to approach and bend over her. The sidereal meadows exchange embraces with their more humble sisters of the earth—the daisy-decked valleys and the green slumbering fields. The heavenly dome falls prostrate into the arms of the great quiet sea; and the millions of stars that stud the former peep into and bathe in every lakelet and pool. To the grief-furrowed soul those twinkling orbs are the eyes of angels. They look down with ineffable pity on the suffering of mankind. It is not the night dew that falls on the sleeping flowers, but sympathetic tears that drop from those orbs, at the sight of the GREAT HUMAN SORROW. . . .

Yes; sweet and beautiful is a southern night. But——

> "When silently we watch the bed, by the taper is flickering light.
> When all we love is fading fast—how terrible is night. . . ."

VII

Another day is added to the series of buried days. The far green hills, and the fragrant boughs of the pomegranate blossom have melted in the mellow shadows of the night, and both sorrow and joy are plunged in the lethargy of soul-resting sleep. Every noise has died out in the royal gardens, and no voice or sound is heard in that overpowering stillness.

Swift-winged dreams descend from the laughing stars in motley crowds, and landing upon the earth disperse among mortals and immortals, amid animals and men. They hover over the sleepers, each attracted by its affinity and kind; dreams of joy and hope, balmy and innocent visions, terrible and awesome sights seen with sealed eyes, sensed by the soul; some instilling happiness and consolation, others causing sobs to heave the sleeping bosoms, tears and mental torture, all and one preparing unconsciously to the sleepers their waking thoughts of the morrow.

Even in sleep the Soul-Ego finds no rest.

Hot and feverish its body tosses about in restless agony. For it, the time of happy dreams is now a vanished shadow, a long bygone recollection. Through the mental agony of the soul, there lies a transformed man. Through the physical agony of the frame, there flutters in it a fully awakened Soul. The veil of illusion has fallen off from the cold idols of the world, and the vanities and emptiness of fame and wealth stand bare, often hideous, before its eyes. The thoughts of the Soul fall like dark shadows on the cogitative faculties of the fast disorganizing body, haunting the thinker daily, nightly, hourly. . . .

The sight of his snorting steed pleases him no longer. The recollections of guns and banners wrested from the enemy; of cities razed, of trenches, cannons and tents, of an array of conquered spoils now stirs but little his national pride. Such thoughts move him no more, and ambition has become powerless to awaken in his aching heart the haughty recognition of any valorous deed of chivalry. Visions of another kind now haunt his weary days and long sleepless nights. . . .

What he now sees is a throng of bayonets clashing against each other in a mist of smoke and blood; thousands of mangled corpses covering the ground, torn and cut to shreds by the murderous weapons devised by science and civilization, blessed to success by the servants of his God. What he now dreams of are bleeding, wounded and dying men, with missing limbs and matted locks, wet and soaked through with gore. . . .

VIII

A hideous dream detaches itself from a group of passing visions, and alights heavily on his aching chest. The nightmare shows him men expiring on the battlefield with a curse on those who led them to their destruction. Every pang in his own wasting body brings to him in dream the recollection of pangs still worse, of pangs suffered through and for him. He sees and *feels* the torture of the fallen millions, who die after long hours of terrible mental and physical agony; who expire in forest and plain, in stagnant ditches by the road-side, in pools of blood under a sky made black with smoke. His eyes are once more rivetted to the torrents of blood, every drop of which represents a tear of despair, a heart-rent cry, a lifelong sorrow. He hears again the thrilling sighs of desolation, and the shrill cries ringing through mount, forest and valley. He sees the old mothers who have lost the light of their souls; families, the hand that fed them. He beholds widowed young wives thrown on the wide, cold world, and beggared orphans wailing in the streets by the thousands. He finds the young daughters of his bravest old soldiers exchanging their mourning garments for the gaudy frippery of prostitution, and the Soul-Ego shudders in the sleeping Form. . . . His heart is rent by the groans of the famished; his eyes blinded by the smoke of burning hamlets, of homes destroyed, of towns and cities in smouldering ruins. . . .

And in his terrible dream, he remembers that moment of insanity in his soldier's life, when standing over a heap of the dead and the dying, waving in his right hand a naked sword red to its hilt with smoking blood, and in his left, the colours rent from the hand of the warrior expiring at his feet, he had sent in a stentorian voice praises to the throne of the Almighty, thanksgiving for the victory just obtained! . . .

He starts in his sleep and awakes in horror. A great shudder shakes his frame like an aspen leaf, and sinking back on his pillows, sick at the recollection, he hears a voice—the voice of the Soul-Ego—saying in him:

"Fame and victory are vainglorious words. . . . Thanksgiving and prayers for lives destroyed—wicked lies and blasphemy!" . . . .

"What have they brought thee or to thy fatherland, those bloody victories!" . . . whispers the Soul in him. "A population clad in iron armour," it replies. "Two score millions of men dead now to all spiritual aspiration and Soul-life. A people, henceforth deaf to the peaceful voice of the honest citizen's duty, averse to a life of peace, blind to the arts and literature, indifferent to all but lucre and ambition. What is thy future Kingdom, now? A legion of war-puppets as units, a great wild beast in their collectivity. A beast that, like the sea yonder, slumbers gloomily now, but to fall with the more fury on the first enemy that is indicated to it. Indicated, by whom? It is as though a heartless, proud Fiend, assuming sudden authority, incarnate Ambition and Power, had clutched with iron hand the minds of a whole country. By what wicked enchantment has he brought the people back to those primeval days of the nation when their ancestors, the yellow-haired Suevi, and the treacherous Franks roamed about in their warlike spirit, thirsting to kill, to decimate and subject each other. By what infernal powers has this been accomplished? Yet the transformation has been produced and it is as undeniable as the fact that alone the Fiend rejoices and boasts of the transformation effected. The whole world is hushed in breathless expectation. Not a wife or mother, but is haunted in her dreams by the black and ominous storm-cloud that overhangs the whole of Europe. The cloud is approaching It comes nearer and nearer . . . Oh woe and horror! . . . I foresee once more for earth the suffering I have already witnessed. I read the fatal destiny upon the brow of the flower of Europe's youth! But if I live and have the power, never, oh never shall my country take part in it again! No, no, I will not see——

"'The glutton death gorged with devouring lives . . .'

"I will not hear——

"'robb'd mother's shrieks
While from men's piteous wounds and horrid gashes
The lab'ring life flows faster than the blood!' . . . ."

IX

Firmer and firmer grows in the Soul-Ego the feeling of intense hatred for the terrible butchery called war; deeper and deeper does it impress its thoughts upon the Form that holds it captive. Hope awakens at times in the aching breast and colours the long hours of solitude and meditation; like the morning ray that dispels the dusky shades of shadowy despondency, it lightens the long hours of lonely thought. But as the rainbow is not always the dispeller of the storm-clouds but often only a refraction of the setting sun on a passing cloud, so the moments of dreamy hope are generally followed by hours of still blacker despair. Why, oh why, thou mocking Nemesis, hast thou thus purified and enlightened, among all the sovereigns on this earth, him, whom thou hast made helpless, speechless and powerless? Why hast thou kindled the flame of holy brotherly love for man in the breast of one whose heart already feels the approach of the icy hand of death and decay, whose strength is steadily deserting him and whose very life is melting away like foam on the crest of a breaking wave?

And now the hand of Fate is upon the couch of pain. The hour for the fulfilment of nature's law has struck at last. The old Sire is no more; the younger man is henceforth a monarch. Voiceless and helpless, he is nevertheless a potentate, the autocratic master of millions of subjects. Cruel Fate has erected a throne for him over an open grave, and beckons him to glory and to power. Devoured by suffering, he finds himself suddenly crowned. The wasted Form is snatched from its warm nest amid the palm groves and the roses; it is whirled from balmy south to the frozen north, where waters harden into crystal groves and "waves on waves in solid mountains rise"; whither he now speeds to reign and—speeds to die.

X

Onward, onward rushes the black, fire-vomiting monster, devised by man to partially conquer Space and Time. Onward, and further with every moment from the health-giving, balmy South flies the train. Like the Dragon of the Fiery Head, it devours distance and leaves behind it a long trail of smoke, sparks and stench. And as its long, tortuous, flexible body, wriggling and hissing like a gigantic dark reptile, glides swiftly, crossing mountain and moor, forest, tunnel and plain, its swinging monotonous motion lulls the worn-out occupant, the weary and heartsore Form, to sleep. . . .

In the moving palace the air is warm and balmy. The luxurious vehicle is full of exotic plants; and from a large cluster of sweet-smelling flowers arises together with its scent the fairy Queen of dreams, followed by her band of joyous elves. The Dryads laugh in their leafy bowers as the train glides by, and send floating upon the breeze dreams of green solitudes and fairy visions. The rumbling noise of wheels is gradually transformed into the roar of a distant waterfall, to subside into the silvery trills of a crystalline brook. The Soul-Ego takes its flight into Dreamland. . . .

It travels through aeons of time, and lives, and feels, and breathes under the most contrasted forms and personages. It is now a giant, a Yotun, who rushes into Muspelheim, where Surtur rules with his flaming sword.

It battles fearlessly against a host of monstrous animals, and puts them to fight with a single wave of its mighty hand. Then it sees itself in the Northern Mistworld, it penetrates under the guise of a brave bowman into Helheim, the Kingdom of the Dead, where a Black-Elf reveals to him a series of its lives and their mysterious concatenation. "Why does man suffer?" enquiries the Soul-Ego. "Because he would become one," is the mocking answer. Forthwith, the Soul-Ego stands in the presence of the holy goddess, Saga. She sings to it of the valorous deeds of the Germanic heroes, of their virtues and their vices. She shows the Soul the mighty warriors fallen by the hands of many of its past Forms, on battlefield, as also in the sacred security of home. It sees itself under the personages of maidens, and of women, of young and old men, and of children. . . . It feels itself dying more than once in those Forms. It expires as a hero—Spirit, and is led by the pitying Walkyries from the bloody battlefield back to the abode of Bliss under the shining foliage of Walhalla. It heaves its last sigh in another form, and is hurled on to the cold, hopeless plane of remorse. It closes its innocent eyes in its last sleep, as an infant, and is forthwith carried along by the beauteous Elves of Light into another body—the doomed generator of Pain and Suffering. In each case the mists of death are dispersed, and pass from the eyes of the Soul-Ego, no sooner does it cross the Black Abyss that separates the Kingdom of the Living from the Realm of the Dead. Thus "Death" becomes but a meaningless word for it, a vain sound. In every instance the beliefs of the Mortal take objective life and shape for the Immortal, as soon as it spans the Bridge. Then they begin to fade, and disappear. . . .

"What is my Past?" enquires the Soul-Ego of Urd, the eldest of the Norn sisters. "Why do I suffer?"

A long parchment is unrolled in her hand, and reveals a long series of mortal beings, in each of whom the Soul-Ego recognizes one of its dwellings. When it comes to the last but one, it sees a blood-stained hand doing endless deeds of cruelty and treachery, and it shudders. . . . . . Guileless victims arise around it, and cry to Orlog for vengeance.

"What is my immediate Present?" asks the dismayed Soul of Werdandi, the second sister.

"The decree of Orlog is on thyself!" is the answer. "But Orlog does not pronounce them blindly, as foolish mortals have it."

"What is my Future?" asks despairingly of Skuld, the third Norn sister, the Soul-Ego. "Is it to be for ever dark with tears, and bereaved of Hope?" . . .

No answer is received. But the Dreamer feels whirled through space, and suddenly the scene changes. The Soul-Ego finds itself on a, to it, long familiar spot, the royal bower, and the seat opposite the broken palm-tree. Before it stretches, as formerly, the vast blue expanse of waters, glassing the rocks and cliffs; there, too, is the lonely palm, doomed to quick disappearance. The soft mellow voice of the incessant ripple of the light waves now assumes human speech, and reminds the Soul-Ego of the vows formed more than once on that spot. And the Dreamer repeats with enthusiasm the words pronounced before.

"Never, oh, never shall I, henceforth, sacrifice for vainglorious fame or ambition a single son of my motherland! Our world is so full of unavoidable misery, so poor with joys and bliss, and shall I add to its cup of bitterness the fathomless ocean of woe and blood, called WAR? Avaunt, such thought! . . . Oh, never more. . . ."

XI

Strange sight and change. . . . The broken palm which stands before the mental sight of the Soul-Ego suddenly lifts up its drooping trunk and becomes erect and verdant as before. Still greater bliss, the Soul-Ego finds *himself* as strong and as healthy as he ever was. In a stentorian voice he sings to the four winds a loud and a joyous song. He feels a wave of joy and bliss in him, and seems to know why he is happy.

He is suddenly transported into what looks a fairy-like Hall, lit with most glowing lights and built of materials, the like of which he had never seen before. He perceives the heirs and descendants of all the monarchs of the globe gathered in that Hall in one happy family. They wear no longer the insignia of royalty, but, *as he seems to know*, those who are the reigning Princes, reign by virtue of their personal merits. It is the greatness of heart, the nobility of character, their superior qualities of observation, wisdom, love of Truth and Justice, that have raised them to the dignity of heirs to the Thrones, of Kings and Queens. The crowns, by authority and the grace of God, have been thrown off, and they now rule by "the grace of divine humanity," chosen unanimously by recognition of their fitness to rule, and the reverential love of their voluntary subjects.

All around seems strangely changed. Ambition, grasping greediness or envy—miscalled *Patriotism*—exist no longer. Cruel selfishness has made room for just altruism and cold indifference to the wants of the millions no longer finds favour in the sight of the favoured few. Useless luxury, sham pretences—social and religious—all has disappeared. No more wars are possible, for the armies are abolished. Soldiers have turned into diligent, hard-working tillers of the ground, and the whole globe echoes his song in rapturous joy. Kingdoms and countries around him live like brothers. The great, the glorious hour has come at last! That which he hardly dared to hope and think about in the stillness of his long, suffering nights, is now realized. The great curse is taken off, and the world stands absolved and redeemed in its regeneration! . . .

Trembling with rapturous feelings, his heart overflowing with love and philanthropy, he rises to pour out a fiery speech that would become historic, when suddenly he finds his body gone, or, rather, it is replaced by another body. . . . Yes, it is no longer the tall, noble Form with which he is familiar, but the body of somebody else, of whom he as yet knows nothing. . . . Something dark comes between him and a great dazzling light, and he sees the shadow of the face of a gigantic timepiece on the ethereal waves. On its ominous dial he reads:

"NEW ERA: 970,995 YEARS SINCE THE INSTANTANEOUS DESTRUCTION BY PNEUMO-DYNO-VRIL OF THE LAST 2,000,000 OF SOLDIERS IN THE FIELD, ON THE WESTERN PORTION OF THE GLOBE. 971,000 SOLAR YEARS SINCE THE SUBMERSION OF THE EUROPEAN CONTINENTS AND ISLES. SUCH ARE THE DECREE OF ORLOG AND THE ANSWER OF SKULD. . . ."

He makes a strong effort and—is himself again. Prompted by the Soul-Ego to REMEMBER and ACT in conformity, he lifts his arms to Heaven and swears in the face of all nature to preserve peace to the end of his days—in his own country, at least.

A distant beating of drums and long cries of what he fancies in his dream are the rapturous thanksgivings, for the pledge just taken. An abrupt shock, loud clatter, and, as the eyes open, the Soul-Ego looks out through them in amazement. The heavy gaze meets the respectful and solemn face of the physician offering the usual draught. The train stops. He rises from his couch weaker and wearier than ever, to see around him endless lines of troops armed with a new and yet more murderous weapon of destruction—ready for the battlefield.

WAS HE MAD?

by Charles E. Benham

I

"THE senses," said the Professor as we were sitting over the fire one evening, "are of course our only messengers from the world of existence. They five are the only travelers on whose accounts we have to rely for our information concerning the Is-ness of the Universe. And they five are each acquainted with a different aspect of the Universe. Just as different facts and observations impress variously different voyagers to new lands, so each of these our five messengers comes to us rendering his peculiar version. If there had been one less of these messengers, we should have had a very different notion of things. Now the most important of the senses is of course . . ."

"The sense of sight," I interposed.

"Certainly not," he said. "No, the most important undoubtedly is the sense of touch. This is not only because all the senses are but modes or forms of the sensation of touch, but for other reasons. The sense of sight is the sense of touch awakened by the impinging of a wave of ether, just as hearing is the touch of a wave of air. Taste and smell too are the results of touch in the glands and tissues and nerves of the body itself. But the importance—the super-importance of touch is more apparent when we consider that by it we become aware of the three dimensions of matter. I am speaking of touch in its ordinary sense now, apart from its operation in sight, hearing, taste, and smell. Were it possible to imagine ourselves bereft of the power of touch while retaining our other senses, we should imagine ourselves in a condition in which we could not possibly have any evidence of such a thing as we now call thickness. It would not enter into our experience, nor consequently into our imagination."

"Stay a moment," I said. "Surely you are going a little too far. I follow you when you say it would not enter into our experience—at least, I think I follow you, though it is exceedingly difficult to clear one's mind of this notion of the three dimensions of space, after being from the dawn of consciousness accustomed to it. It is, I say, very difficult to imagine oneself without it. You might as well try to rid your mind of the idea of time, and then conjecture what manner of ideas would then remain in the mind. It cannot be done without long and deep thought. But even granting that you are right and that all our ideas of perspective and of the threefold dimensions of matter are not due to the stereoscopic effect of our binocular vision, but that they accompany that stereoscopic effect as associations of the results of experiments in the sense of touch, I am still at a loss to understand how that can preclude imagination from picturing to itself so extremely simple a condition of matter as a cube. Nay, I can hardly think imagination could avoid falling into the idea, for space itself must have three dimensions—no more and no less—to fill it."

"We had better stop there," said the Professor, as I was just about to explain myself at further length, "as you are already slipping into a good many fallacies. Let us look at this matter a little more closely before our ideas become more complicated and therefore confused. You do not see why imagination cannot picture things that are not stored in memory by experience. This is your fundamental fallacy. Very little thought would show you clearly that imagination could only combine and arrange in fresh forms the materials that it finds in the memory. Can you imagine a color not in the solar spectrum? Why surely all the shades of which this compound color is made up exist in the rainbow. No; I say, tell me if you can picture in your mind a new tint altogether—a simple color not compounded of nor resembling any tint you ever saw? You cannot; no, certainly not; of course not. Not because there are no such colors, for it happens there are, but because there are none in your memory. Blind from birth, a man can imagine neither light nor color because they are not in his experience. The fact that imagination arranges and does not originate thoughts—analyses, synthesizes, classifies, sub-divides, re-combines and so forth, the various materials in the storehouse of the memory, but creates them not, is well known to every beginner in philosophy. It is almost an axiomatic doctrine."

"This is true enough," I said, as I felt myself getting wedged into a corner, though I thought I could still see a loophole of exit. "But you cannot deny that many things have been imagined that have never had any existence in experience at all, or how could a novelist or a dramatist originate such characters as a Hamlet or a Touchstone or even a Pickwick or a Sam Weller?"

I saw the absurdity of my remark as I spoke. How often has it happened to me that the very utterance of a false argument seems to invoke the spirit of its refutation? Especially has this been the case in my talks with the Professor. Often enough when I have laid before him difficulties that I have puzzled over all my life, the solution has burst forth upon me while I spoke—like a lightning flash darting across the cloud of my doubt. I fancy the explanation so uppermost in the Professor's mind that its "sphere," as he calls it, extends into my understanding even before he utters it forth in language. And on this very occasion, I felt my argument answered by a silent forerunner of the Professor's reply.

"Surely," he said, "these very instances that you quote are as good witnesses as could be selected for the truth of what I was just saying. Shakespeare and Dickens were above their fellows in two things; they observed better and could put their observations more aptly into language than others."

Still I was unwilling to allow myself to be completely vanquished.

"But how about Shakespeare's Julius Caesar," I said. "You cannot pretend that he observed the doings of a man who died centuries before?"

"Why not?" replied the professor, and in a moment I again felt within me the mysterious precursor of his reproof.

"Can we not observe the dead," he continued, "when we have their lives and actions before us in black and white? Can we not . . ."

"Enough!" I cried. "You are right, and my whole interruption was uncalled for. Proceed. You were telling me, and I see it now, that but for the power of touch we should not, even in imagination, conceive of a third dimension."

"No, we should not," he said. "I am glad that is quite clear, because that is the fundamental statement on which rests all that I am about to remark. If, indeed, some one among us, or some man in past times, or some being of superior intelligence, were to give us an account of a third dimension of space, which with our four senses (supposing we had only four) we could not of ourselves have discovered, we should still find ourselves unable to attach any very clear meaning to his words. We should but be like men, blind from their birth, listening to an account of the wonders of light. We could take it on faith, and if we had reasons for giving credit to the revealer of this unknown and unimaginable dimension of matter, we should probably do well to trust him for this declaration of a third dimension, although we should not be able to understand. It would be faith—not knowledge. Now what I want to arrive at is this: If the addition of one sense provides us with such a different aspect of the whole universe, is it not a little more than probable that, were yet another superimposed upon the five, we should have an altogether fresh view compared with which the cube itself would be but a superficies?"

"Now," said I, "you are beyond my depth. That I cannot at all comprehend. The cube fills up all space as it seems to me, and compare it with what you will, it cannot appear to be a superficies."

"I see," he remarked, in a tone of evident disappointment, "that you have missed the purport of all that I have been trying to say."

He was wrong, for I saw more than I pretended to see. But I disliked metaphysical theories about a possible fourth dimension, and did not wish to drift off into surmising about the Unknowable, a course that has always seemed to me unscientific and unprogressive.

"How can I put it to you in a clearer light," he added presently, after pausing for a while and looking intently into the fire. "Look here," he exclaimed, as though he had suddenly found the key to my understanding. "Do you believe that there is a Spiritual World?"

"Yes," I said slowly, wondering into what corner this admission would drive me. "Yes, I don't think physical phenomena are at all explicable without some sort of postulated metaphysical."

"Good expression," he said in a satisfied way, which made me think I had really said a clever thing. "You think," he continued, "that a spiritual world exists, but of its nature you know nothing."

"Exactly," I answered.

"Well, what is the difference between believing in a spiritual world—a postulated metaphysical, as you neatly express it—and in believing that the three dimensions are not the all in all of being?"

I paused, feeling confused and uncertain and hardly knowing where we were. "Do you mean that," I said hesitatingly, "a spiritual world and the fourth dimension are identical?"

"Why not?" asked the Professor, with extraordinary emphasis and earnestness.

"What a strange fancy," I said. "But it pleases me, I must confess; and though the idea is so new to me that I cannot on the moment pronounce any definite opinion upon it, yet certainly I think I have never heard any theory of spiritual existence that seems more possible and more reasonable. The notion is nevertheless enshrouded in vague clouds of doubt that prevent me from accepting it at once, but it is full of suggestions of its own truth."

"Think it over," said the Professor, looking at me steadfastly as he rose to take his departure, "and if when I next call you are confirmed in the opinion, I shall make you my confident for strange disclosures." With a firm grasp of the hand, he bade me good night and left.

For more than an hour after he departed, I sat over the dying embers of the fire reflecting deeply upon this singular idea; and the more I thought it out the more reasonable and the more possible it appeared, and something made me feel it must be true.

II

It was two weeks before the Professor and I again found an occasion for a quiet chat alone, though we met once a few days after at the house of a friend. It was a singular fact, which I had often noted with surprise, that the Professor would never enter into a philosophic vein of talk except when we were alone together. We frequently met socially, but no matter how small and select our circle, he would never rise above the most commonplace conversation in the presence of a third person. Indeed, he would always appear a man with very little to say for himself, for it was his maxim that people should argue on general matters only occasionally, on political matters very rarely, and on religious matters never. So that with these three channels of converse barred and philosophy vanished, there was little opportunity left for him to show the real depth and fertility of his intellectual nature. If anyone introduced any abstruse subject, he would turn the drift of conversation promptly and skillfully, edging off the deeper question as though it were something too sacred to be allowed in the social circle. To me, of course, who knew him more intimately, he was a very different being; in fact, I might say I knew, or seemed to know two Professors—one the learned metaphysician, and the other the easy-going, inoffensive *sine qua non* of certain dinner parties. I once asked him—the metaphysical one—why he kept up this dual nature, allowing himself to be so needlessly underestimated by all except myself.

"I have a purpose to serve," he answered, "in making you my Elisha, and the real fact is that I have no special desire for unnecessary confinement in a madhouse, which might be my lot were I to say publicly some things that I know. Of course, I might guard my most advanced and difficult utterances, but when certain mysteries are daily present to me, it is not easy in speaking of them, to keep within bounds, and I should run the risk of my supposed insanity being certified by the infallible decrees of orthodox medical science. Even if I were not actually made to suffer physical restraint, there is little doubt I should be branded as a harmless lunatic, a consummation I naturally object to, not only personally, but because it would be a serious blow to my mission in the world."

This reply it was that first roused my suspicions, not, indeed, as to the Professor's sanity. I knew him too well not to be fully convinced that his mental faculties were of the highest order, but as to what his "mission" might be, and I began to fancy he had some discovery or secret with which he was thinking of entrusting me. And I was not altogether wrong.

On November 7, 1886, just a fortnight after the conversation narrated in the first chapter, I was alone with him again, sitting as before over my fire. It was about eleven o'clock at night, and after a rather dreary pause, he again referred to his anxiety that the world should not be permitted to ridicule and misjudge his advanced notions.

"Now, candidly," he said, "what do you yourself suppose an ordinary businessman would think of such a conversation as we had a fortnight ago?"

"I should expect him to smile, and put us down as two rather over-inoculated patients of M. Pasteur," I said.

"Good," he answered, laughing. "That is to say, they would suppose that we had taken into our systems such a lot of his hellish virus that we had gone stark, staring mad."

"That puts it more plainly still," said I. "We should no doubt be reckoned mad—harmless madmen. In fact, it was but the other day I was speaking to a friend of mine—one of the shrewdest men I know, and he began talking about the very matter that we were speaking of—a possible fourth dimension of space. How such a subject crept up in our conversation I forget, but I know his remark was that he always considered that a man who could believe in such damned nonsense as that must have a tile loose."

The Professor turned impatiently in his chair, and gave the fire a vigorous and vindictive dig with the poker.

"The shrewdest man you know," he exclaimed sarcastically. "And you—what did you say to this shrewdest man?"

"Well, I hardly knew what I ought to say. I could not find courage to confess that I was at least half a believer in this very folly that he was deriding. Moreover, I felt that I knew so little about the matter that I certainly could not give any lucid reason for the half-faith that I held. Therefore, though I blush to say it, I gave way to a strong temptation that beset me to change the subject, and no doubt my friend believes at this moment that I have as much contempt as he for such wild notions."

"There is no need to blush because you carried out the scriptural precept not to cast your pearls before swine," said the Professor. "Your shrewd man was not the kind of man to be able to comprehend the possibility of anything existing that could not be made manifest to his five senses. Because his five fingers each touched one point of the great universe, there was no room for a sixth point. That would be his style of logic! What end, then, could be served by talking to such a man of things that were as far beyond the scope of his mind as heaven is above earth? Your silence was commendable. But enough of him. Let us now have a little serious talk. I have some remarkable disclosures to make to you if I find you in a due state of receptivity—as I have reason to suppose I shall find."

I wondered what he could mean.

Presently he went on. "I have made up my mind," he said, "to show you some very wonderful experiments that I cannot demonstrate to the world at large, simply because, like your 'shrewd' friend, people would only think me mad, and would not believe even if I showed them the experiments before their own eyes. For the generality of men do not believe a thing because it is shown to be true, unless it is orthodox—unless any of the rulers have believed in it, and, above all, unless it is what they want to believe. But first of all you must make up your mind that nothing that I am about to show you shall alarm you, however strange and unusual it may be. And now look here!"

III

. . . As he spoke, a heavy book that was lying on the table rose without any apparent cause, turned itself about, stood on end, leaped into the air, glided along backwards and forwards, and after further mysterious evolutions proceeded, as if lifted by an invisible hand, from the table to my lap, where it lay tranquilly.

All this time, the Professor sat almost motionless—merely exhibiting a slight twitching of the right hand and a convulsive, strained expression of countenance as he watched the movements of the volume. His calmness astounded me, for I never for a moment attributed the uncanny manifestations to him, and expected them to strike him with the same cold horror as I was experiencing.

For my own part, the unutterable sensation of dread that seized me is beyond all words to express. Now that the absurd feeling has passed away, I cannot recall my sensations, but I know that my hair stood on end with fear, and I shook and trembled from head to foot. My head whirled, and I fancied it must be all a dream. Gradually, a dawning conviction came over me that the Professor was responsible for this eerie piece of business and that this was the secret with which he was going to entrust me.

"Good heavens," I cried. "What on earth is this uncanny power? Is this a trick to frighten me, or have you been studying witchcraft?"

The Professor was calm and unmoved.

"You can believe or disbelieve," he said. "You have seen with your own eyes. If you believe, we will go further; if you disbelieve, it would be no use to do so, and there must be an end of it."

As he spoke, a fearful sensation of horror was creeping over me. It is impossible, I feel sure, for the reader of this narrative to enter into the feelings that take possession of one when in a moment all one's ideas of the "Is-ness of things" are uprooted. I fancied—it was the only solution, however terrible—that I must have gone from my mind and that all around me was imagination or fantasy. Yet surely not so—there sat the Professor, unmistakably real, and there lay the book motionless in my lap.

"In the name of all that is good and true," I began, but I could say no more. My head swam, my eyes closed. I felt myself falling to the ground in a swoon. I remember no more until I came once more to consciousness, and found the Professor standing over me looking anxious and concerned. Gradually, as I "came to myself," the recollection of what had happened unfolded itself.

"It is only as I feared," said the Professor, after I had become restored.

"The sudden disclosing to the mind of laws that subvert our previous notions of the operations of force, as manifested in the environment, is a terrible shock, and is the secret of the terror that inspires children and the vulgar at the apparition, whether real or imaginary, of bogeys and phantoms. The eyes of the intellect are dazzled, the brain is overpowered, and the senses are intoxicated. You must rest your thinking faculties as far as possible for a week or two, and you will then find yourself able to return to our experiments, not only without discomfort or without fright, but also even with keen interest; and now I will leave you to follow out my advice in this respect. Goodnight, old fellow. Go straight to bed, and think no more about what has happened until I come and see you again."

With these words, he shook hands and said farewell. I was still too overcome to reply, and could not even see him to the door. I merely muttered a confused farewell, and crept off to bed with a sick and despondent heart.

IV

The next day, my miserable frame of mind had by no means left me. To dismiss the events of the previous evening from my thoughts, as the Professor had advised, was an utter impossibility. On the contrary, these recollections dismissed all other ideas, and I found myself unable to give attention to the ordinary affairs of life. Everything seemed unreal; my surroundings appeared to be a mere phantasmagoria, a projection of fantasies on my brain as unsubstantial as the images projected by a magic lantern on a screen to amuse children. A horrid suspicion haunted me that I was going from my mind. I felt no confidence, no reliance in any one of my senses. I think that no one who has not been through a similar state can have any idea how implicit, and how constant, is the trust that we all of us place in the infallibility of natural effects that experience has tested and never found to fail. When I walked, I ceased to retain any faith in my muscles or organs, or in the earth as a support. If I laid anything on the table, I felt constrained to watch it for some seconds to make sure it would not bound off to the ceiling or glide away to the ground. As for the Professor, I felt towards him one passion only—that of inveterate hatred. Or was it fear? At any rate, it was an indescribable antipathy. I would not go near him at any price; I even took the precaution to keep the latch of my front door fastened so that it could not be opened from the outside, for he was in the habit of walking in unannounced. Even with this precaution, I was far from feeling safe, for who could tell whether he could not, with his hateful witchcraft of fourth dimensions and spiritual hands, stand on the doorstep and calmly undo the door on the inside.

So things went on for a week, when at length I found relief. It was exactly as the Professor had said. My brain had been overpowered and my senses dazed. Gradually my mind regained its normal strength, and within a fortnight, I was able to think with pleasure and even to theorize upon the singular phenomenon that had caused me so much horror and wretchedness. I became deeply interested in it, and so far from disliking the Professor, I began to long for another visit and further experiments.

At my own request, he called. I told him all that had happened, of my dejection, my uncanny feelings, and the revival of the sway of reason in me. He seemed much pleased, and was especially delighted when I went further and gave him the crude theories that I had formed.

"I imagine," I said, "that we have a magnetic power that we only lack the faculty to exercise. You appear to have discovered and developed that faculty. Is not that so?"

"Hardly, I think," he replied. "I will first show you an experiment, and will then as far as possible explain to you the *modus operandi*, though you must bear in mind that I do not claim to fully understand the matter myself, as I am new to it. However, I will tell you all I can. Fetch down that case with the stuffed bird up there on the wall."

It was a pet canary that had died a year before. I had had it stuffed, for it was a favorite of mine, and I kept it over the mantelshelf, perched on a twig just as it used to perch and sing in its cage.

"I am going to take this bird out," said the Professor.

"All right," I said, not very pleased. "Do so if you wish, though I have been at some pains to make the case thoroughly air tight, so as to keep out insects."

The Professor smiled, and as he did so, to my intense astonishment, I saw the bird in the case, which he was holding in his hand, vibrate. And then the front of the bird disappeared as far as the legs, leaving the remainder standing as though it had been cut straight down with a keen knife.

"Watch it closely," said the Professor.

I did so. I looked at it as nearly as I could front ways, and could see that it was not cut through, for the front appeared yellow as though covered with feathers and not showing the cork with which it was stuffed.

"Watch it still," said the Professor. As he spoke, the disappearance progressed. In a second, all the body had gone, and gradually the vanishing spread to the very tip of the tail. The bird was gone.

The next thing I saw was that it was in the Professor's hand. The case remained sealed, intact. My astonishment, as may be supposed, knew no bounds. In another minute, the Professor had replaced the bird on its perch, its reappearance being the exact converse of its disappearance. First of all came the tail, and at the same moment the tail vanished from the bird in the Professor's hand, and the same process extended gradually along the body. When only the head remained outside the case, a sudden thought inspired me. In a moment, I grasped the head and endeavored to snatch it away, in order to make perfectly certain that no trick was being practiced.

It seemed to be riveted in the air. I pulled at it in vain. The Professor tried to restrain me, but I was too quick for him. A smart tug, and the headpiece of my poor canary was in my hand and the resistance ceased. At the same moment, the body portion inside the case fell from its perch. The two were severed.

I was intensely annoyed when I saw what had happened, for the damage was beyond repair.

"Your own fault," said the Professor calmly.

I was bound to admit it was, and looked very foolish as I tried to hide my concern by assuring him it was of no consequence.

"Well, now let me proceed to explain," he said. "Suppose you had a plane surface bounded on all four sides by barriers. To a person who did not know of a third dimension, who knew of length and breadth, but could not imagine thickness because it did not enter into his experience, to such a person, I say (of course a merely hypothetical and impossible individual), it would seem that it would not be in any way possible to remove that plane surface without taking away the barriers, and yet you know well enough it could be at once done by lifting the plane surface or by lowering it. To any one gifted with a sense of the fourth dimension, thickness itself is but as it were superficial. There is an aperture still open to that closed case. It is what I call the fourth dimension, or the spiritual aperture. The only reason why you could not put your hand into that aperture is because you cannot see it, and your senses do not direct you. Were the requisite sense unveiled, as it is with me, you would be able easily to do what I have done. Therefore it was that your clumsy effort wrenched the head off the bird."

I understood very little of his explanation, though now the meaning is slightly clearer, and I seem to have a dim conception of the matter.

"But," I said, "why do you not show this extraordinary power to everyone? Why make such a secret of it?"

"Your memory is very defective," he replied. "What was your own answer last time we met, when I asked you what you thought an ordinary businessman would think about a fourth dimension?"

"Oh yes, I know," said I, "but that's quite a different matter. People would ridicule the theory, but the facts they could not deny."

"You are very, very wrong, if you really think that," said the Professor. "Recollect the parable of Dives. Moses and the Prophets give the theory; the resurrection is the fact. If they will not hear the one, they will not believe the other."

"I cannot see how scientific men can deny facts that are brought before them," said I.

"No more can I," said the Professor, "and yet they do. But I will tell you what I will do, to set your mind at rest on the point. I am going up to London tomorrow, and shall probably stay a few weeks. I will get introductions to two or three of the most eminent physicians and scientific men (which I can easily manage through my friend, John Rook, the publisher), and you shall just hear the result for yourself."

"Very good," I said. "And now let us have some further experiments."

"No," he said firmly. "We have had enough for you to digest until my return. Too much food for the body gives gastric fever; too much for the brain gives brain fever. On my return, I hope to show you some still more astounding experiments, also to make you acquainted with the rather unpleasant operation that I performed on myself in order to lay open the spiritual faculty, and perhaps, if you wish it, to do the same for you. And, as a final idea for you to consider, let me tell you that only human force—that is, mental and spiritual activity—operates in the spiritual dimension, and that that aperture is only open or accessible to man. Dust cannot get into your bird-case, but I can force dust in. This is because gravitation is of no account in the spiritual dimension, where spiritual—that is human—force alone operates."

Leaving me this idea to work out, he said farewell until the time he should come back from town and perform further experiments for my edification.

V

A week after the Professor left for London, I went for a short holiday, choosing the Scotch lakes for my tour. If there is one thing I dislike when away on a holiday, it is to be worried with a number of letters forwarded on to me on business and everyday matters, which take all the pleasure from a trip away from home. I therefore took the imprudent course of instructing my housekeeper to forward me nothing that came by post, but to place all letters on my study table that I might attend to them when I returned. It was a delightful holiday to me. I forgot all cares amid the mountain scenery of the highlands, and never gave a thought to the Professor or to the fourth dimension as I reveled in solitude by the lakes and streams of old Scotland.

On my return, I took up the little pile of letters that lay on the table. After dismissing to the waste-paper basket several circulars relating to gold mine and other schemes for drawing money from sanguine investors, I took up an envelope on which I at once recognized the handwriting of my friend, the Professor.

I tore open the seal hastily, and not without a feeling of regret that this one communication had not been sent on to me, especially as it was marked "immediate and important," on the outside. But what was my dismay when I read its contents: "Come at once to Engleford Asylum, where your unfortunate friend is to be at once confined. I was fool enough to try the experiments, as you suggested, before two scientific men. The result is a certificate of my lunacy. Lose no time, or I shall verify the certificate and 'twill be too late."

Within three hours, I was at Engleford and flying to the asylum. It is a massive building of white brick, within a minute's walk from the railway station. At the gate is a bell-handle. I tugged it with remarkable energy, and a great bell clanged as though it would wake the dead. The porter came. I asked to see the superintendent on urgent business.

I was shown into a small office. The superintendent entered, and suddenly it flashed upon me that after all I hardly knew what I had come for. From the postmark, I judged the Professor had been in the asylum about ten days.

"I have come," I said, rather bluntly, as the superintendent motioned me to a chair, "to see you with regard to a rather curious case," and giving him the Professor's name, I asked whether it could be true that he had been sent to the asylum.

"Yes, poor fellow," said the superintendent. "His was a sad case, a very sad case. He seemed almost like a sane man when he entered, but his symptoms developed with remarkable rapidity, and in three days had taken a very pitiable form of monomania, under which he is, I fear, likely to remain all his days. He has a fancy that he is a canary, and that someone has beheaded him."

I sank back in my chair. It was then too late. The shock had been too much, and had unhinged his mind. I felt I could ask no more. I could not wish to see him in his pitiable plight. I merely expressed my thanks to the superintendent for the information, told him how dear a friend of mine the Professor had been and how shocked I was.

It was too late. The Professor was mad.

ZARINA!
(A VISION)

by Helen Fagg

FLOATING in the astral light of our own planet, ages and ages ago, hovered a beautiful Spirit. She, from worlds beyond our knowledge, drew near, and kept aeons after aeons watching the human races as they swept from the unseen into the seen, from spirit into matter, and from matter into spirit.

Whether she, in the ages past had been as they, I cannot tell. But after watching human life and human woe for centuries I thought I saw her resolved to become as the sons and daughters of men, to share their sorrow, for what is shared is divided and thereby lessened. She resolved to begin at the first round of the ladder, and gradually to ascend. In short, to throw herself into the whirlpool of human existence.

Ages rolled on but what were they to her? She had enrolled among the children of men, like they, she was clothed in a decaying garment, and like them she cast it off when worn out, only to assume another.

Up the eternal, spiral column of life she travelled step by step, until one morning a beautiful babe was born on the earth and the mother whispered: "The Gods have smiled on thee!"

What was the cloud of melancholy which deepened on the fair young face as girlhood stole on and deepened as girlhood faded? Alas, the consciousness of earth was beginning to return, the succession of lives to which she had bound herself must be passed. Earth began to fetter her, as she gradually realised the sad tragic truth, that although thousands pressed around her, yet was she alone! "I will be a poet", she said, "and feel for others!" And Spirits from other worlds inspired her so that man wept when they read her sonnets. For each man stands like a mournful spectre, and is alone, finding little love and little sympathy in those around. But the poet reaches every heart in its loneliness, shattering the stern walls around, to let the sunlight stream into it. She touched the hearts of men and made them better. She, clad in mortal flesh, revealed the folded page of nature and spelt out for men its mystic symbolism.

Once more she folded her earthly garment and laid it aside for a new one. And now she was born on the earth a beggar's child! the Spirits of the earth formed her robe of flesh into perfect beauty. The poet's soul was there, and she looked through it into other souls. What was there but sorrow and loneliness again in store for herself and the crowds of weeping humanity around her? If thou wouldst see the real man thou must look within. That which is within is the real, the outer is its shadow, still oftener its mask.

From childhood she grew into womanhood, and consciousness began to dawn fuller than before. Now she dimly saw forms around her, which were clothed in subtler garments than those of the flesh. Knowledge came into her heart, and she remembered what she had been before. Remembrance returned gradually, steadily, as womanhood advanced. The lives she had lived in the past ages grew like a great light of memory, and overwhelmed her. . . .

"Look," said the people, pointing at her, "look, that is Zarina, the beggar's child!"

"A beggar's child!" exclaimed a young man one day, when he heard these words. "A beggar's daughter!" he repeated to himself as in a dream, feeling a sudden wave of love for her overspread all his being.

"Ah," was the answer given by an old, white-bearded man to the youth, as he stood and gazed at the beautiful girl dressed in rags. "Only a beggar's child!"

Zarina caught the words, caught the tone. The hot blood rushed to her temples, and she fled in sorrow down the narrow street. The youth, brushing back his long dark hair with one hand, and with the other clasping tight his violin, for he was a musician, tried to overtake her. But the footsteps of wounded vanity and shame are swift, and she was gone. So he returned to the old man, and questioned him easily concerning her whom he already loved so madly.

"What would you with the beggar's daughter?" he was sternly asked. "Would you gain admittance into her humble home, and flaunt before her eyes the golden toys which turn a maiden's brain? Nay, nay, thy face is that of an honest man. . . . Know that I am a philosopher, and that heaven and earth are unveiled at my bidding? Come then, with me."

Calitzo followed the speaker silently down the narrow street and entered with him a low, arched doorway. Beyond this was a long, narrow passage, at the end of which the old man opened a door, and ushered the youth into a small, barely furnished room, where a lamp was burning, although it was still daylight,

Calitzo asked no questions. He had a strange sense of being entirely at this stranger's bidding; that he could not speak or move, or do anything, except the old man willed it.

"I know you, O poet-musician," said the old man. "Do not you recognise me? Ah, well, heaven and earth are closed books to most; the past is obliterated to you, the future unknown; and yet, poor fool, you do thirst for knowledge! Knowledge shall come, your fate is written on your brow, and your past is as yesterday to me. Your future? Youth, it is for you to make it.

So is mine. Would you know the beggar's daughter? I will tell you of her. Ages ago, she was born as a child unto me—she was a poet. She touched all men's hearts but mine, for it was hardened; and with a poet's love, she gave her life for mine, and entered into her rest. You were then a noble boy, and she loved you. But she gave you up, while giving up her life for me, and left you alone on earth. Her father, he who is now her parent, in a hot, unguarded moment, seeing your despair, killed me; yes, he took away the life she had saved by sacrificing her own.

"Oblivion wrapped all in darkness, until the sea of time washed us all to the shore once more, and we were again clothed in flesh. And now am I a philosopher and an alchemist. The keys of the past are mine; but before I can attain to the perfection of knowledge I must return four-fold into her heart that which I withheld from her, for I loved her not in the bygone ages, and made her life sad. I must also before I can help thee, accord unto him who was thy father, Calitzo, full reward for the rash deed, which caused my disembodied spirit to suffer ages in being so suddenly severed from the body. I will give her back to thee; for which purpose I must make use of powers forbidden, and thus bring on just retribution to all of us. Zarina does not know me and I dread her. Knowledge is dawning upon her, as it must upon all one day, and she begins to converse with and discern the unseen. Time must not be lost, and first of all the memory of the past must be imparted to thee. Come!"

The alchemist led the way into an inner room, where Calitzo almost fainted with the suffocating fumes. The place looked like a cave, lit with a curious, fairy-like vapour hanging as cobwebs drawn hither and thither. The various odours of chemicals making him feel quite ill, he dropped down on a rude bench, while the alchemist kept moving round and round him, until he saw that Calitzo was fast asleep. Then the old man proceeded to make some mixture, muttering all the while weird sentences, and drawing diagrams upon the floor, until the neighbouring clock struck the midnight hour. . . . "It shall be," he murmured. "Thou, Calitzo, art one to whom I shall owe a great debt of gratitude, but thou knowest it not. Zarina cannot be thine unless her father dies, and the hour that brings her here, shall bring death to him. Then will she turn to thee as her only friend, and thus fate will be accomplished." He awoke Calitzo, and made him tell him what he had seen. The youth described Zarina's home, her beggar father, and then, as one in a dream, spoke of a life, ages ago, when he and she loved each other! of her sad tragic death, and of his own rash act. " In three days," said the alchemist, under his breath, "she shall be thine, and I shall be delivered unto the evil powers, to whose aid I resort. Come to me," he added aloud, "at midnight, the third night from this. Everything shall be prepared, and she shall be thine."

Zarina sat in her father's room alone. It was the third day after the alchemist's interview with Calitzo, and she knew of the awful powers which were to be used that night, powers which she might not be able to withstand. Better than the alchemist, she knew also that her father, and even Calitzo, her beloved of old, might fall a victim to them. For two nights the mystic spells had been at work, and now on this last and fatal night she alone must counteract them. She sat thinking until half past eleven, and then, drawing a black shawl around her, silently left the house, taking her way to the abode of the alchemist. Her inspired face was rigid and sad. "This night the powers of Light and Darkness shall meet, and the alchemist must not be allowed to give himself up to powers of Evil" . . . . it is she alone, who shall pronounce the fatal words, and she alone, who shall be delivered unto the dark destiny, if anyone must be. The supernal love and power which inspire one at the thought of saving others at one's own sacrifice, pervaded her whole being. . . .

She opened the door of the alchemist's house and crept silently along the narrow curving passage; and although she had never been there before, nothing seemed unfamiliar to her in it; she passed through the first room. Absolute silence reigned around, and she heard only the beatings of her own heart. Thud! thud! thud! like a great mallet, beat that heart which was so soon to stop for ever. She placed her hand on the latch of the alchemist's sanctum and softly stepped in. The old man stood beside a table covered with vessels, and outside the circle with the curious characters in it which was drawn upon the floor, sat Calitzo on a bench. His breath came short and fast as she appeared, and the alchemist fixed his gloomy eyes upon her. But Zarina, keeping her gaze fixed upon him whom she had loved so well in her previous life, never looked after the first glance at the old man again. Evidently her visit was expected, for the old man betrayed not the least surprise and only waited in breathless silence. But now, she slowly approached the magic circle, and the alchemist began to look uneasy. Suddenly, a great cry of horror escaped from his breast, as, with the first stroke of the town-clock tolling midnight she was within the circle, and as the mists and vapour from the chemicals he had prepared arose into the damp air enveloping her as in a shroud.

Her action had been so quick and unexpected that while he was yet speaking, the phosphorescent smoke filled with filmy living creatures had entirely closed around her, and she sank within the magic circle a helpless heap. . . .

"Lost, she is lost!" cried the alchemist. "Nay, Calitzo, approach her not. Zarina is lost, lost. She has taken the curse upon herself, and her father, my enemy, still lives . . ."

Lost! Lost! the cry that escaped the old man's lips was caught up and re-echoed like a deep sigh by Calitzo's violin. It sang an old melody, a familiar dirge:—

"Saved—ah, saved! Hell loses power
Over him, who for another
Gives his life. . . .
Not lost—but saved!"

The melody grew fainter, as the mists thickened around Calitzo. Then a faintness came over him and he lost consciousness. When he awoke he found the alchemist kneeling with his head on Zarina's prostrate form and as dead and cold as his victim was. The violin was silent and daylight was stealing in, struggling with the dark shadows of the cave. With a heartrending cry Calitzo knelt down beside her and softly breathed her name. . . .

But Zarina answered not. The glorious spirit had thrown off for the last time, and now for ever, the dusty garment of flesh. It was hovering again in the resplendent light of All-consciousness.

IN THE SÉANCE ROOM

by Lettice Galbraith

DR. VALENTINE BURKE sat alone by the fire. He had finished his rounds, and no patient had disturbed his post-prandial reflections. The house was very quiet, for the servants had gone to bed, and only the occasional rattle of a passing cab and the light patter of the rain on the window-panes broke the silence of the night. The cheerful glow of the fire and the soft light from the yellow-shaded lamp contrasted pleasantly with the dreary fog which filled the street outside. There were spirit-decanters on the table, flanked by a siphon and a box of choice cigars. Valentine Burke liked his creature comforts. The world and the flesh held full measure of attraction for him, but he did not care about working for his *menus plaisirs*.

The ordinary routine of his profession bored him. That he might eventually succeed as a ladies' doctor was tolerably certain. For a young man with little influence and less money, he was doing remarkably well; but Burke was ambitious, and he had a line of his own. He dabbled in psychics, and had written an article on the future of hypnotism which had attracted considerable attention. He was a strong magnetiser, and offered no objection to semi-private exhibitions of his powers. In many drawing-rooms he was already regarded as the apostle of the coming revolution which is to substitute disintegration of matter and cerebral precipitation for the present system of the parcels mail and telegraphic communication. In that section of society which interests itself in occultism Burke saw his way to making a big success.

Meanwhile, as man cannot live on adulation alone, the doctor had a living to get, and he had no intention whatever of getting it by the labour of his hands. He was an astute young man, who knew how to invest his capital to the best advantage. His good looks were his capital, and he was about to invest them in a wealthy marriage. The fates had certainly been propitious when they brought Miss Elma Lang into the charmed circle of the Society for the Revival of Eastern Mysticism. Miss Land was an orphan. She had full control of her fortune of thirty thousand pounds. She was sufficiently pretty, and extremely susceptible. Burke saw his chance, and went for it, to such good purpose that before a month had passed his engagement to the heiress was announced, and the wedding-day within measurable distance. There were several other candidates for Miss Lang's hand, but it soon became evident that the doctor was first favourite. The gentlemen who devoted themselves to occultism for the most part despised physical attractions; their garments were fearfully and wonderfully made. They were careless as to the arrangement of their hair. Beside them, Valentine Burke, handsome, well set up, and admirably turned out, showed to the very greatest advantage. Elma Lang adored him. She was never tired of admiring him. She was lavish of pretty tokens of her regard. Her photographs, in costly frames, were scattered about his room, and on his hand glittered the single-stone diamond ring which had been her betrothal gift.

He smiled pleasantly as he watched the firelight glinting from the many-coloured facets. "I have been lucky," he said aloud; "I pulled that through very neatly. Just in time, too, for my credit would not stand another year. I ought to be all right now if——" He broke off abruptly, and the smile died away. "If it were not for that other unfortunate affair! What a fool—what a damned fool I was not to let the girl alone, and what a fool she was to trust me! Why could she not have taken better care of herself? Why could not the old man have looked after her? He made row enough over shutting the stable-door when the horse was gone. It was cleverly managed though. I think even *ce cher papa* exonerates me from any participation in her disappearance; and fate seems to be playing into my hand too. That body turning up just now is a stroke of luck. I wonder who the poor devil really is?"

He felt for his pocket-book, and took out a newspaper cutting. It was headed in large type, "Mysterious Disappearance of a Young Lady.—The body found yesterday by the police in Muddlesham Harbour is believed to be that of Miss Katharine Greaves, whose mysterious disappearance in January last created so great a sensation. It will be remembered that Miss Greaves, who was a daughter of a well-known physician of Templeford, Worcestershire, had gone to Muddlesham on a visit to her married sister, from whose house she suddenly disappeared. Despite the most strenuous efforts on the part of her distracted family, backed by the assistance of able detectives, her fate has up to the present remained enshrouded in mystery. On the recovery of the body yesterday the Muddlesham police at once communicated with the relations of Miss Greaves, by whom the clothing was identified. It is now supposed that the unhappy girl threw herself into the harbour during a fit of temporary insanity, resulting, it is believed, from an unfortunate love affair."

Valentine Burke read the paragraph through carefully, and replaced it in the pocket-book with a cynical smile.

"How exquisitely credulous are the police, and the relatives, and the noble British public. Poor Kitty is practically dead—to the world. What a pity——" He hesitated, and stared into the blazing coals. "It would save so much trouble," he went on after a pause, "and I hate trouble."

His fingers were playing absently with a letter from which he had taken a slip of printed paper—an untidy letter, blotted and smeared, and hastily written on poor, thin paper. He looked at it once or twice and tossed it into the fire. The note-sheet shrivelled and curled over, dropping on to the hearth, where it lay smouldering. A hot cinder had fallen out of the grate, and the doctor, stretching out his foot, kicked the letter close to the live coal. Little red sparks crept like glow-worms along the scorched edges, flickered and died out. The paper would not ignite; it was damp—damp with a woman's tears. "I was a fool," he murmured, with conviction. "It was not good enough, and it might have ruined me." He turned to the spirit-stand and replenished his glass, measuring the brandy carefully. "I don't know that I am out of the wood yet," he went on, as he filled up the tumbler with soda-water. "The money is running short, and women are so damned inconsiderate. If Kitty were to take it into her head to turn up here it would be the——" The sentence remained unfinished, cut short by a sound from below. Someone had rung the night-bell.

Burke set down the glass and bent forward, listening intently. The ring, timid, almost deprecating, was utterly unlike the usual imperative summons for medical aid. Following immediately on his outspoken thoughts, it created an uncomfortable impression of coming danger. He felt certain that it was not a patient; and if it were not a patient, who was it? There was a balcony to the window. He stepped quietly out and leaned over the railing. By the irregular flicker of the street-lamp he could make out the dark figure of a woman on the steps beneath, and through the patter of the falling rain he fancied he caught the sound of a suppressed sob. With a quick glance, to assure himself that no-one was in sight, the doctor ran downstairs and opened the door. A swirl of rain blew into the lighted hall. The woman was leaning against one of the pillars, apparently unconscious. Burke touched her shoulder. "What are you doing here?" he asked sharply. At the sound of his voice she uttered a little cry and made a sudden step forward, stumbling over the threshold, and falling heavily against him.

"Val, Val," she cried, despairingly. "I thought I should never find you. Take me home, take me home. I am so tired— and, oh, so frightened!'

The last word died away in a wailing sob, then her hands relaxed their clinging hold and dropped nervelessly at her side.

In an emergency Dr. Burke acted promptly. He shut the outer door, and gathering up the fainting girl in his arms, carried her into the consulting-room, and laid her on the sofa. There was no touch of tenderness in his handling of the unconscious form. He had never cared much about her, when at her best, dainty in figure and fair of face; he had made love to her, *pour passer le temps*, in the dullness of a small country town. She had met him more than half-way, and almost before his caprice was gratified he was weary of her. Her very devotion nauseated him. He looked at her now with a shudder of repulsion. The gaslight flared coldly on the white face, drawn by pain and misery. All its pretty youthfulness had vanished. The short hair, uncurled by the damp night air, straggled over the thin forehead. There were lines about the closed eyes and the drooping corners of the mouth. The skin was strained tightly over the cheekbones and looked yellow, like discoloured wax. His eyes noted every defect of face and figure, as he stood wondering what he should do with her.

He knew, no-one better, how quickly the breath of scandal can injure a professional man. Once let the real story of his relations with Katharine Greaves get wind and his career would be practically ruined. He began to realise the gravity of the situation. Two futures lay before him. The one, bright with the sunshine of love and prosperity; the other darkened by poverty and disgrace. He pictured himself the husband of Elma Lang, with all the advantages accruing to the possessor of a charming wife and a large fortune, and he cursed fate which had sent this wreck of womanhood to stand between him and happiness. By this time she had partially recovered, and her eyes opened with the painful upward roll common to nervous patients when regaining consciousness. With her dishevelled hair and rain-soaked garments, she had all the appearance of a dead body. The sight, horrible as it was, fascinated Burke. He turned up the gas, twisting the chandelier so as to throw a full light on the girl's face.

"She looks as though she were drowned," he thought. "When she is really dead she will look like that." The idea took possession of his mind. "If she were dead, if only she were dead!'

Who can trust the discretion of a wronged and forsaken woman, but—the dead tell no tales. If only she were dead! The words repeated themselves again and again, beating into his brain like the heavy strokes of a hammer. Why should she not die? Her life was over, a spoiled, ruined thing. There was nothing before her but shame and misery. She would be better dead. Why (he laughed suddenly a hard, mirthless laugh), she *was* dead already. Her body had been found by the police, identified by her own relations. She was supposed to be drowned, so why not make the supposition a reality? A curious light flashed into the doctor's handsome face. A woman seeing him at that moment would have hesitated before trusting her life in his hands. He looked at his unwelcome visitor with an evil smile.

She had come round now and was crouched in the corner of the sofa sobbing and shivering.

"Don't be angry with me, Val, please don't be angry. I waited till I had only just enough money for my ticket, and I dare not stay there any longer. It is so lonely, and you never come to see me now. It is ten weeks since you were down, and you won't answer my letters. I was so frightened all alone. I began to think you were getting tired of me. Of course I know it is all nonsense. You love me as much as you ever did. It is only that you are so busy and hate writing letters." She paused, waiting for some reassuring words, but he did not answer, only watched her with cold, steady eyes.

"Did you see the papers," she went on, with chattering teeth. "They think I am dead. Ever since I read it I have had such dreadful thoughts. I keep seeing myself drowned; I believe I am going to die, Val—and I don't want to die. I am so—so frightened. I thought you would take me in your arms and comfort me like you used to do, and I should feel safe. Oh, why don't you speak to me? Why do you look at me like that? Val, dear, don't do it, don't do it, I cannot bear it."

Her great terrified eyes were fixed on his, fascinated by his steady, unflinching gaze. She was trembling violently. Her words came with difficulty, in short gasps.

"You have never said you were glad to see me. It is true, then, that you don't love any more? You are tired of me, and you will not marry me now. What shall I do? What shall I do? No-one cares for me, no-one wants me, and there is nothing left for me but to die."

Still no answer. There was a long silence while their eyes met in that fixed stare—his cold, steady, dominating, hers flinching and striving vainly to withstand the power of the stronger will. In a few moments the unequal struggle had ended. The girl sat stiff and erect, her hand grasping the arm of the sofa. The light of consciousness had died out of the blue eyes, leaving them fixed and glassy. Burke crossed the floor and stood in front of her.

"Where is your luggage?" he asked, authoritatively.

She answered in a dull, mechanical way, "At the station."

"Have you kept anything marked with your own name—any of my letters?'

"No, nothing—there."

"You *have* kept some of my letters. Where are they?"

"Here." Her hand sought vaguely for her pocket.

"Give them to me—all of them."

Mechanically she obeyed him, holding out three envelopes, after separating them carefully from her purse and handkerchief.

"Give me the other things." He opened the purse. Besides a few shillings, it contained only a visiting card, on which an address had been written in pencil. The doctor tore the card across and tossed it into the fireplace. Then his eyes fastened on those of the girl before him. Very slowly he bent forward and whispered a few words in her ear, repeating them again and again. The abject terror visible in her face would have touched any heart but that of the man in whose path she stood. No living soul, save the "sensitive" on whom he was experimenting, heard those words, but they were registered by a higher power than that of the criminal court, damning evidence to be produced one day against the man who had prostituted his spiritual gift to mean and selfish ends.

In the grey light of the chilly November morning a park-keeper, near the Regent's Canal, was startled by a sudden, piercing shriek. Hurrying in the direction of the sound, he saw, through leafless branches, a figure struggling in the black water. The park-keeper was a plucky fellow, whose courage had gained more than one recognition from the Humane Society, and he began to run towards the spot where the dark form had been, but before he had covered ten yards of ground rapid footsteps gained on his and a man shot past him. "Someone in the canal," he shouted as he ran. "I think it is a woman. You had better get help."

"He was a good plucked one," the park-keeper averred, when a few days later he retailed the story to a select circle of friends at the bar of the Regent's Arms, where the inquest had been held. "Not that I'd have been behindhand, but my wind ain't what it was, and he might have been shot out of a catapult. He was off with his coat and into the water before you could say Jack Robinson. Twice I thought he had her safe enough, and twice she pulled him under; the third time, blest if I thought they were coming up at all. Then the doctor chap, he comes to the surface dead-beat, but the girl in his arms."

"'I'm afraid she's gone,' he says, when I took her from him, 'but we won't lose time,' and he set to and carried out all the instructions for recovering the apparently drowned while I went for some brandy. It wasn't a bit of use. The young woman were as dead as a doornail. 'If she'd only have kept quiet, I might have saved her,' he says, quite sorrowful-like, 'but she struggled so,' and sure enough his hands were regularly torn and bruised where she'd gripped him."

Dr. Burke and the park-keeper were the chief witnesses at the inquest. There were no means of identifying the dead woman. The jury returned a verdict of *felo de se*, and the coroner complimented the doctor on his courageous attempt to rescue the poor outcast.

The newspapers, too, gave him a nice little paragraph, headed, "Determined Suicide in Regent's Park. Gallant conduct of a well-known physician"; and Elma Lang's dark eyes filled with fond and happy tears as she read her lover's praises.

"You are so brave, Val, so good," she cried, "and I am so proud of you; but you ran a horrible risk."

"Yes," he answered, gravely, "I thought once it was all up with me. That poor girl nearly succeeded in drowning the pair of us. Still, there wasn't much in it, you know; any other fellow would have done the same."

"No, they would not. It is no use trying to pretend you are not a hero, Val, because you are. How awful it must have been when she clung to you so desperately. It might have cost you your life."

"It cost me my ring," he replied, ruefully. "It is lying at the bottom of the canal at this moment, unless some adventurous fish has swallowed it—your first gift."

"What does it matter," she answered, impulsively, "I can give you another tomorrow. What does anything matter since you are safe?"

Burke took her in his arms, and kissed the pretty upturned face. She was his now, bought with the price of another woman's life. Bah! he wanted to forget the clutch of those stiffening fingers and the glazed awful stare of the dead eyes through the water.

"Let us drop the subject," he said, gently. "It is not a pleasant one, and, as you say, nothing matters since I am safe"—he added under his breath, "quite safe *now*."

The carriage stood at the door. In the drawing-room Mrs. Burke was waiting for her husband. She had often waited for the doctor during the four years which had elapsed since their marriage. Those four years had seen to a great extent the fulfilment of Burke's ambition. He had money. He was popular, sought-after, an acknowledged leader of the new school of Philosophy, an authority on psychic phenomena, and the idol of the "smart" women who played with the fashionable theories and talked glibly on subjects the very A B C of which was far beyond their feeble comprehension. Socially, Dr. Burke was an immense success. If, as a husband, he fell short of Elma's expectations, she never admitted the fact. She made an admirable wife, interesting herself in his studies, and assisting him materially in his literary work. Outwardly, they were a devoted couple. The world knew nothing of the indefinable barrier which held husband and wife apart; of a certain vague distrust which had crept into the woman's heart, bred of an instinctive feeling that her husband was not what he seemed to be. Something, she knew not what, lay between them. Her quick perceptions told her that he was always acting a part. She held in her hand a little sheaf of papers, notes that she had prepared for him on the series of *séances*, which for a month past had been the talk of the town. A medium of extraordinary power had flashed like a meteor into the firmament of London society. Phenomena of the most startling kind had baffled alike the explanations of both scientist and occultist. Spiritualism was triumphant. A test committee had been formed, of which Dr. Burke was unanimously elected president, but so far the attempts to expose the alleged frauds had not been attended with any success.

It was to Mdme. Delphine's house that the Burkes were going tonight. The *séance* commenced at ten, and the hands of the clock already pointed to a quarter to that hour, when the doctor hurried into the room.

"Ready?" he said. "Come along then. Where are the notes?"

He glanced hastily through them as he went downstairs.

"Falconer and I have been there all afternoon," he explained as they drove off. "I had only just time to get something to eat at the club before I dressed. We have taken the most elaborate precautions. If something cannot be proved tonight——" he paused.

"Well?" she said, anxiously.

"We shall be the laughing-stock of London," he concluded, emphatically.

"What do you really think of it?"

"Humbug, of course; but the difficulty is to prove it."

"Mrs. Thirlwall declares that the fifth appearance last night was undoubtedly her husband. I saw her today; she was quite overcome."

"Mrs. Thirlwall is a hysterical fool."

"But your theory admitted the possibility of materialising the intense mental——"

Burke leaned back in the carriage, laughing softly.

"My dear child, I had to say something."

"Valentine," she cried, sorrowfully, "is there no truth in anything you say or write? Do you believe in nothing?"

"Certainly. I believe in matter and myself, also that the many fools exist for the benefit of a minority with brains. When I see any reason to alter my belief, I shall not hesitate to do so. If, for instance, I am convinced that I see with my material eyes a person whom I know to be dead, I will become a convert to spiritualism. But I shall never see it."

The drawing-room was filled when they arrived at Mdme. Delphine's. Seats had been kept for the doctor and his wife. There was a short whispered consultation between Burke and his colleagues, the usual warning from the medium that the audience must conform to the rules of the *séance*, and the business of the evening began in the customary style. Musical instruments sounded in different parts of the room, light fingers touched the faces of the sitters. Questions written on slips of paper and placed in a sealed cabinet received answers from the spirit world, which the inquirers admitted to be correct. The medium's assistant handed one of these blank slips to Burke, requesting him to fill it up.

It struck the doctor that if he were to ask some question the answer to which he did not himself know, but could afterwards verify, he would guard against the possibility of playing into the hands of an adroit thought-reader. He accordingly wrote on the paper, "What was I doing this time four years ago? Give the initials of my companion, if any."

He had not the vaguest idea as to where exactly he had been on the date in question, but a reference to the rough diary he always kept would verify or disprove the answer.

The folded slip was sealed, and placed in the cabinet. In due time the medium declared the replies were ready. The cabinet was opened, and the slips, numbered in the order in which they had been given in, were returned to their owners. Burke noticed that there were no fresh folds in his paper, and the seal was of course unbroken. He opened it, and as his eye fell on the writing he gave a slight start, and glanced sharply at the medium. Beneath his query was written in ink that was scarcely yet dry, "On Wednesday, November, 17, 1885, you were at No. 63, Abbey Road. Only I was with you. You hypnotised me.—K. G." The handwriting was that of Katharine Greaves.

The doctor was staggered. In the multiplied interests and distractions of his daily life he had completely forgotten the date of that tragic visit. He tried to recall the exact day of the month and week. He remembered now that it was on a Wednesday, and this was Monday. Calculating the odd days for the leap year, 1888, that would bring it to Monday—Monday the 17th. Four years ago tonight Kitty had been alive. She was dead now, and yet here before him was a page written in her hand. He sat staring at the characters, lost in thought. The familiar writing brought back with irresistible force the memory of that painful interview. It suggested another and very serious danger. Burke did not believe for a moment that the answer to his question had been dictated by the disembodied spirit of his victim. He was racking his brains to discover how his secret might possibly have leaked out, who this woman could be who knew, and traded on her knowledge, of that dark passage in his life which he had believed to be hidden from all the world. Was it merely a bow drawn at a venture, which had chanced to strike the one weak place in his armour, or was it deliberately planned with a view to extorting money?

So deeply was he wrapped in his reflections, that the manifestations went on around him unheeded. The dark curtain which screened off a portion of the room divided, and a white-robed child stepped out. It was instantly recognised by one of the sitters—a nervous, highly-strung woman, whose passionate entreaties that her dead darling would return to earth fairly harrowed the feelings of the listeners. Other manifestations followed. The audience were becoming greatly excited. Burke sat indifferent to it all, his eyes fixed on the writing before him, till his wife touched him gently.

"What is the matter, Val?" she whispered, trying to read the paper over his shoulder. "Is your answer correct?"

He turned on her sharply, crushing the message in his hand. "No," he said audibly. "It is a gross imposture. There was no such person."

"Hush." She laid a restraining hand on his arm. "Do not speak so loudly. That is a point in our favour, anyway. Mr. Falconer has proposed a fresh test. He has asked if a material object, something that had been lost at any time, you know, can be restored by the spirits. Madame returned a favourable answer. Mr. Falconer could not think of anything at the moment, but I had a brilliant inspiration. I told him to ask for your diamond ring—the ring you lost when you tried to save that poor girl's life."

Burke rose to his feet, then recollecting himself, sat down again and tried to pull himself together. There was nothing in it. If this Madame Delphine really was acquainted with the facts of his relations with Katharine Greaves she could not know its ghastly termination. He tried to reassure himself, but vainly. His nerve was deserting him, and his eyes roved vacantly round the semi-darkened room, as if in search of something. A sudden silence had fallen on the audience. A cold chill, like a draught of icy air, swept through the *séance* chamber. Mrs. Burke shivered from head to foot, and drew closer to her husband. Suddenly the stillness was broken by a shriek of horror. It issued from the lips of the medium, who, like a second Witch of Endor, saw more than she expected, and crouched terror-stricken in the chair to which she was secured by cords adjusted by the test committee. The presence which had appeared before the black curtain was no white-clad denizen of "summer-land", but a woman in dark, clinging garments—a woman with wide-opened, glassy eyes, fixed in an unalterable stony stare. It was a ghastly sight. All the concentrated agony of a violent death was stamped on that awful face.

Of the twenty people who looked upon it, not one had power to move or speak.

Slowly the terrible thing glided forward, hardly touching the ground, one hand outstretched, and on the open palm a small, glittering object—a diamond ring!

It moved very slowly, and the second or so during which it traversed the space between the curtain and the seats of the audience seemed hours to the man who knew for whom it came.

Valentine Burke sat rigid. He was oblivious to the presence of spectators, hardly conscious of his own existence. Everything was swallowed up in a suspense too agonising for words, the fearful expectancy of what was about to happen. Nearer and nearer "it' came. Now it was close to him. He could feel the deathly dampness of its breath; those awful eyes were looking into his. The distorted lips parted—formed a single word. Was it the voice of a guilty conscience, or did that word really ring through and through the room—"Murderer!"

For a full minute the agony lasted, then something fell with a sharp click on the carpetless floor. The sound recalled the petrified audience to a consciousness of mundane things. They became aware that "it" was gone.

They moved furtively, glanced at each other—at last some-one spoke. It was Mrs. Burke. She had vainly tried to attract her husband's attention, and now turned to Falconer, who sat next to her.

"Help me get him away," she said.

The doctor alone had not stirred; his eyes were fixed as though he were still confronted by that unearthly presence.

Someone had turned up the gas. Two of the committee were releasing the medium, who was half-dead with fright. Falconer unfastened the door, and sent a servant whom he met in the hall for a hansom.

When he returned to the *séance* room the doctor was still in the same position. It was some moments before he could be roused, but when once they succeeded in their efforts Burke's senses seemed to return. He rose directly, and prepared to accompany his wife. As they quitted their seats, Falconer's eyes fell on the diamond ring which lay unnoticed on the ground. He was going to pick it up, but someone caught his hand and stopped him.

"Leave it alone," said Mrs. Burke, in a horrified whisper. "For God's sake, don't touch it."

Husband and wife drove home in silence. Silently the doctor dismissed the cab and opened the hall-door. The gas was burning brightly in the study. The servant had left on the side-table a tray with sandwiches, wine, and spirits. Burke poured out some brandy and tossed it off neat. His face was still rather white, otherwise he had quite recovered his usual composure.

Mrs. Burke loosened her cloak and dropped wearily into a chair by the fire. A hopeless despondency was visible in every line of her attitude. Once or twice the doctor looked at her, and opened his lips to speak. Then he thought better of it, and kept silent. Half an hour passed in this way. At last Burke lighted a candle and left the room. When he returned he carried in his hand a small bottle. He had completely regained his self-possession as he came over to his wife and scrutinised her troubled face.

"Have some wine," he said, "and then you had better go to bed. You look thoroughly done up."

"What is that?" She pointed to the bottle in his hand.

"A sleeping-draught. Merely a little morphia and bromide. I should advise you to take one, too. Frankly, tonight's performance was enough to try the strongest nerves. Mine require steadying by a good night's rest, and I do not intend risking an attack of insomnia."

She rose suddenly from her chair and clasped her hands on his arm.

"Val," she cried, piteously, "don't try to deceive me. Dear, I can bear anything if you will only trust me and tell me the truth. What is this thing which stands between us? What was the meaning of that awful sight?"

For a moment he hesitated; then he pulled himself together and answered lightly—"My dear girl, you are unnerved, and I do not wonder at it. Let us forget it."

"I cannot, I cannot," she interrupted wildly. "I must know what it meant. I have always felt there was something. Valentine, I beseech you, by everything you hold sacred, tell me the truth now before it is too late. I could forgive you almost—almost anything, if you will tell me bravely; but do not leave me to find it out for myself."

"There is nothing to tell."

"You will not trust me?"

"I tell you there is nothing."

"That is your final answer?"

"Yes."

Without a word she left the room and went upstairs. Burke soon followed her. His nerves had been sufficiently shaken to make solitude undesirable. He smoked a cigar in his dressing-room, and took the sleeping-draught before going to bed. The effects of the opiate lasted for several hours. It was broad daylight when the doctor awoke. He felt weak and used up, and his head was splitting. He lay for a short time in that drowsy condition which is the borderland between sleeping and waking. Then he became conscious that his wife was not in the room. He looked at his watch, and saw that it was half-past nine. He waited a few minutes, expecting her to return, but she did not come. Presently he got up and drew back the window-curtains. As the full light streamed in, he was struck by a certain change in the appearance of the room. At first he was uncertain in what the change consisted, but gradually he realised that it lay in the absence of the usual feminine impedimenta. The dressing-table was shorn of its silver toilet accessories. One or two drawers were open and emptied of their contents. The writing-table was cleared, and his wife's dressing case had disappeared from its usual place. Burke's first impulse was to ring for a servant and make inquiries, but as he stretched out his hand to the bell his eyes fell on a letter, conspicuously placed on the centre of a small table. It was addressed in Elma's handwriting. From that moment Burke knew that something had happened, and he was prepared for the worst. The letter was not long. It was written firmly, though pale-blue stains here and there indicated where the wet ink had been splashed by falling tears.

"When you read this," she wrote, "I shall have left you for ever. The only reparation in your power is to refrain from any attempt to follow me; indeed, you will hardly desire to do so when I tell you that I know all. I said last night I could not endure the torture of uncertainty. My fears were so terrible that I felt I must know the truth or die. I implored you to trust me. You put me off with a lie. Was I to blame if I used against you a power which you yourself had taught me? In the last four hours I have heard from your own lips the whole story of Katharine Greaves. Every detail of that horrible tragedy you confessed unconsciously in your sleep, and I who loved you—Heaven knows how dearly!—have to endure the agony of knowing my husband a murderer, and that my wretched fortune supplied the motive for the crime. Thank God that I have no child to bear the curse of your sin, to inherit its father's nature! I hardly know what I am writing. The very ground seems to be cut away from under my feet. On every side I can see nothing but dense darkness, and the only thing that is left to us is death.—Your wretched wife, Elma."

From the moment he opened the letter, Burke's decision was made. He possessed the exact admixture of physical courage and moral cowardice which induces a man worsted in the battle of life to end the conflict by removing himself from the arena. He had taken the best of the world's gifts, and there was nothing left worth having. His belief in a future life was too vague to cause him any uneasiness, and physically, fear was a word he did not understand. He quietly lighted his wife's letter with a match, and threw it into the fireless grate. He smoked a cigar while he watched it burn, and carefully hid the charred ashes among the cinders. Then he fetched from his dressing-room a small polished box, unlocked it, and took out the revolver. It was loaded in all six chambers.

Burke leisurely finished his cigarette, and tossed the end away. He never hesitated a moment. He had no regret for the life he was leaving. As Elma had said, there was only one thing left for him to do, and—he did it.

THE LAST QUEST

by William Sharp

Death hath not yet come unto the man
who knoweth not that he is dead.
—Johannes Arbiter: *Myst.*

[As in a vision . . . the furious charge through the
smoke and across the corpsestrewn battlefield: the
neighing and sobbing of horses; the hoarse cries, the
sudden screams of men: the clang and whistle of
swords: the shrill spurting of a hail of bullets: the
bursting crash and roar of artillery: a wild rush, a
wild onslaught, and—Victory! . . . and . . .

AND as I clomb the barren and difficult steep, I yearned
for a fellow-creature, for but the hollow echo of a distant voice, even more than for escape from the twilit solitudes
of this hill whereup I toiled, forgetful whence I came and
knowing not whither I went. And it seemed to me as though
years upon years went over me in my long, ceaseless effort;
but when, with a triumph that was yet no triumph, at last I
gained the crest, I still heard in my ears the fanfare of the bu-
gles, the clash of swords, the mad rush and fury and turmoil

of the charge, while my lips quivered still with the sudden scream of *Victory*.

And when I stood upon the summit, I saw that I was in a strange land. Behind me lay a vast plain, margined afar off in the direction by which it seemed to me I had come, by obscure, impenetrable forests. Immeasurably upon this plain was ruin of ungarnered harvest. Leagues upon leagues to the east and west without end, and everywhere the grain ungathered; and nought astir save a thin dust of chaff, idly blown hither and thither by a wind that was yet too light to move the dark poppies that lay in the hollows,—too faint to bend an ear of that unlifted grain. Veiled moonlight shone upon the waste, so that even through the gloom I could see that nought moved, nought stirred: not even an owl swept with stealthy wing above the forlorn lands, not even a bat circled through the dusk, not even a cloud trailed a deeper shadow from solitude to solitude. But as I looked closer and wonderingly, and now with a great weariness of longing, I saw that every here and there the sheaves had been brought together as though the reapers had suddenly ceased from their labour and had gone to make ready for the harvesting. Yet, for the most part, the sheaves were but loosely gathered, and all untied, and with the ground near strewn with the rich grain that had, as it were, been abruptly dropped. And everywhere, far and wide, were single sheaves or small gatherings, as though the harvesters had been weary or heedless; and often sheaves that seemed as though they had been wittingly defiled or destroyed. But now all the ungarnered harvest lay silently there in the twilight; and no man came unto that which was ready for the gathering, and no man passed by that which had been idly thrown aside or ruined in wantonness. And amidst it all, this vast harvest which stretched beyond sight to the uttermost ends of the earth, there was nothing further visible but the dark-red poppies of oblivion. Of all this immeasurable toil, of all this majesty of desolation, there was nought save a thin, vanishing dust of chaff, faint as a perishing smoke over woodlands where a fire has been, but is no more.

Then as one rousing from sleep into daylight, I turned and looked beyond me. Behold, here too was a vast plain that stretched beyond the scan of mortal eyes. The sunlight lay upon it, and it was glorious to look upon. A sweet wind came out of the blue hollows of the sky, where white clouds voyaged bearing soft rains and cool shadows: and there was so wild and glad a music of birds over the illimitable savannas of golden grain, and of young corn green as the heart of a shallow sea, that I felt as though all the joy of my youth was upon me, and my heart swelled, and the blood stung in my veins. But ere long I looked with amazement, for in all that unfrontiered land beyond me I saw neither man nor woman. Yet evermore, from the east to the west, swept a gigantic shadow like unto a scythe: and where the shadow swept, the grain fell. And when I looked again I beheld a mighty Shape, clothed in the dusk of shadow as with a veil, and clad with dropping decays as with a tattered robe rent by the wind. Ever and forever the Reaper strode, with blind, oblivious eyes, with vast scythe furrowing the sunlit grain: and it seemed to me, while I watched, as though the minutes passed into hours, and the hours into days, and the days into years, and the years into the timeless wastes of eternity. Looking suddenly back upon the twilit land which first I had brooded upon, I saw that its margins were as the moving tides of ocean, and that the Reaper reaped where the grain grew by the fallen grain. And there was no rest, no end to the long sweep of the shadowy scythe. Ever, forever, the scythe swept: ever, forever, the grain fell. The sun shone, the birds sang, the world smiled; and, by the margins of the Hollow Land, where the grain rose the grain fell.

Then a terror that was of life overmastered the terror that was of death, and I strained my eyes so that I might see some living thing of my own kind. But only the rays of the sun penetrated the womb of the earth, and only the endless concourse of the grain was delivered of the unwearying mother. It seemed to me, then, as though the green corn and the golden ears were but as the multitude of lives that come forth at the rising of the sun, and are no more at the setting. And as I looked with awe and terror upon the Reaper, who reaped forever and ever where the grain rose and the grain fell, I turned and stared beyond the westering sun. And lo, I beheld yet Another. A glory of golden light he seemed, clad with ever evanishing rainbows, and crowned with the auroral flames of summer dawns.

Vast was he as the Reaper; but as he fared beyond the pathway of the sun, he was as the glory and joy of eternal youth. He, too, swayed an arm, even as the mighty scythe-sweep of the Reaper, an arm of glowing light: and therewith I saw that he sowed a living seed forever and ever. As I watched the Sower in the blinding splendour of the sunlight, it seemed to me that he moved onward as he sowed; and it was with me as though the minutes were like unto hours, and the hours like unto days, and the days unto years, and the years unto the immeasurable wastes of eternity.

Then, with a great cry, I ran down the slopes of the steep whereon I was; for my heart was fain to follow the beautiful Sower, and my soul full of dread of the Reaper that reaped forever. But when I came unto the base of the hill, and to the end of the gloomy pass that issued thence, I went no further. For over against me rose a vast wall of black basalt, and upon it, in letters of white flame, were the words of my agony. And when I read TOO SOON, I turned me in my despair, and with bitterness of grief clomb again the perilous steep.

When once more I had gained the summit, I had no heart to look where the glory of the sun fell about the Sower, sowing his living seed forever and ever. But when I looked again upon the Reaper—with mighty scythe laying low without end, without rest, where the grain rose and the grain fell—I cried aloud in my extremity of dread.

Thereafter, it seemed to me that in the Hollow Land behind me was peace. So passed I down the hill, and through the twilit waste of all that ungarnered harvest. And there was no sound there, and nought stirred, save the slow, thin fall of the dust among the hollows forever upon the dark-red poppies of oblivion.

And I know not how long I fared, or whither; but at last, weary—weary unto death of that harvest that should never be gathered—I came nigh unto the obscure forest I had seen from the hill-summit from afar. And I was glad, for I was weary of the Hollow Land.

But when I would enter the wood, I saw that the growths were intricately drawn against yet another wall of black basalt. And as I stood, pondering, I beheld two mighty portals, and betwixt them a huge mass of marble like unto the tomb. And in great letters carven thereon were the words: TOO LATE.

THE STORY OF A STAR

by A.E.

THE emotion that haunted me in that little cathedral town would be most difficult to describe. After the hurry, rattle, and fever of the city, the rare weeks spent here were infinitely peaceful. They were full of a quaint sense of childhood, with sometimes a deeper chord touched—the giant and spiritual things childhood has dreams of. The little room I slept in had opposite its window the great grey cathedral wall; it was only in the evening that the sunlight crept round it and appeared in the room strained through the faded green blind. It must have been this silvery quietness of colour which in some subtle way affected me with the feeling of a continual Sabbath; and this was strengthened by the bells chiming hour after hour: the pathos, penitence, and hope expressed by the flying notes coloured the intervals with faint and delicate memories. They haunted my dreams, and I heard with unutterable longing the astral chimes pealing from some dim and vast cathedral of the cosmic memory, until the peace they tolled became almost a nightmare, and I longed for utter oblivion or forgetfulness of their reverberations.

More remarkable were the strange lapses into other worlds and times. Almost as frequent as the changing of the bells were the changes from state to state. I realised what is meant by the Indian philosophy of Maya. Truly my days were full of Mayas, and my work-a-day city life was no more real to me than one of those bright, brief glimpses of things long past. I talk of the past, and yet these moments taught me how false our ideas of time are. In the ever-living yesterday, today, and tomorrow are words of no meaning. I know I fell into what we call the past and the things I counted as dead for ever were the things I had yet to endure. Out of the old age of earth I stepped into its childhood, and received once more the primal blessing of youth, ecstasy, and beauty. But these things are too vast and vague to speak of; the words we use today cannot tell their story. Nearer to our time is the legend that follows.

I was, I thought, one of the Magi of old Persia, inheritor of its unforgotten lore, and using some of its powers. I tried to pierce through the great veil of nature, and feel the life that quickened it within. I tried to comprehend the birth and growth of planets, and to do this I rose spiritually and passed beyond earth's confines into that seeming void which is the matrix where they germinate. On one of these journeys I was struck by the phantasm, so it seemed, of a planet I had not observed before. I could not then observe closer, and coming again on another occasion it had disappeared. After the lapse of many months I saw it once more, brilliant with fiery beauty —its motion was slow, rotating around some invisible centre. I pondered over it, and seemed to know that the invisible cen-tre was its primordial spiritual state, from which it emerged a little while and into which it then withdrew. Short was its day; its shining faded into a glimmer, and then into darkness in a few months. I learned its time and cycles; I made prepa-rations and determined to await its coming.

The Birth of a Planet

At first silence and then an inner music, and then the sounds of song throughout the vastness of its orbit grew as many in number as there were stars at gaze. Avenues and vistas of sound! They reeled to and fro. They poured from a universal stillness quick with unheard things. They rushed forth and broke into a myriad voices gay with childhood. From age and the eternal they rushed forth into youth. They filled the void with reveling and exultation. In rebellion they then returned and entered the dreadful Fountain. Again they came forth, and the sounds faded into whispers; they rejoiced once again, and again died into silence.

And now all around glowed a vast twilight; it filled the cradle of the planet with colourless fire. I felt a rippling motion which impelled me away from the centre to the circumference. At that centre a still flame began to lighten; a new change took place, and space began to curdle, a milky and nebulous substance rocked to and fro. At every motion the pulsation of its rhythm carried it farther and farther away from the centre, it grew darker, and a great purple shadow covered it so that I could see it no longer. I was now on the outer verge, where the twilight still continued to encircle the planet with zones of clear transparent light. As night after night I rose up to visit it they grew many-coloured and brighter. I saw the imagination of nature visibly at work. I wandered through shadowy immaterial forests, a titanic vegetation built up of light and colour; I saw it growing denser, hung with festoons and trailers of fire, and spotted with the light of myriad flowers such as earth never knew. Coincident with the appearance of these things I felt within myself, as if in harmonious movement, a sense of joyousness, an increase of self-consciousness; I felt full of gladness, youth, and the mystery of the new. I felt that greater powers were about to appear, those who had thrown outwards this world and erected it as a place in space.

I could not tell half the wonder of this strange race. I could not myself comprehend more than a little of the mystery of their being. They recognised my presence there, and communicated with me in such a way that I can only describe it by saying that they seemed to enter into my soul breathing a fiery life; yet I knew that the highest I could reach to was but the outer verge of their spiritual nature, and to tell you but a little I have many times to translate it, for in the first unity with their thought I touched on an almost universal sphere of life, I peered into the ancient heart that beats throughout time; and this knowledge became change in me, first, into a vast and nebulous symbology, and so down through many degrees of human thought into words which hold not at all the pristine and magical beauty.

I stood before one of this race, and I thought, "What is the meaning and end of life here?" Within me I felt the answering ecstasy that illuminated with vistas of dawn and rest, it seemed to say:

"Our spring and our summer are unfolding into light and form, and our autumn and winter are a fading into the infinite soul."

I thought, "To what end is this life poured forth and withdrawn?"

He came nearer and touched me; once more I felt the thrill of being that changed itself into vision.

"The end is creation, and creation is joy: the One awakens out of quiescence as we come forth, and knows itself in us; as we return we enter it in gladness, knowing ourselves. After long cycles the world you live in will become like ours; it will be poured forth and withdrawn; a mystic breath, a mirror to glass your being."

He disappeared while I wondered what cyclic changes would transmute our ball of mud into the subtle substance of thought.

In that world I dared not stay during its period of withdrawal; having entered a little into its life, I became subject to its laws: the Power on its return would have dissolved my being utterly. I felt with a wild terror its clutch upon me, and I withdrew from the departing glory, from the greatness that was my destiny—but not yet.

From such dreams I would be aroused, perhaps by a gentle knock at my door, and my little cousin Margaret's quaint face would peep in with a "Cousin Robert, are you not coming down to supper?"

Of these visions in the light of after thought I would speak a little. All this was but symbol, requiring to be thrice sublimed in interpretation ere its true meaning can be grasped. I do not know whether worlds are heralded by such glad songs, or whether any have such a fleeting existence, for the mind that reflects truth is deluded with strange phantasies of time and place in which seconds are rolled out into centuries and long cycles are reflected in an instant of time. There is within us a little space through which all the threads of the universe are drawn; and, surrounding that incomprehensible centre the mind of man sometimes catches glimpses of things which are true only in those glimpses; when we record them the true has vanished, and a shadowy story—such as this—alone remains. Yet, perhaps, the time is not altogether wasted in considering legends like these, for they reveal, though but in phantasy and symbol, a greatness we are heirs to, a destiny which is ours, though it be yet far away.

AUT DIABOLUS AUT NIHIL
THE TRUE STORY OF A HALLUCINATION

by X.L.

Again, I believe that all that use sorceries, incantations, and spells, are not witches, or, as we term them, magicians; I conceive there is a traditional magic, not learned immediately from the devil, but at second-hand from his scholars, who, having once the secret betrayed, are able and do empirically practice without his advice; they proceeding upon the principles of nature, where actives aptly conjoined to disposed passives will, under any master, produce their effects.

—Sir Thomas Browne: *Rel. Med.*

I

TO be ordained has been looked upon for many years in this country as the best, speediest, and safest way of "making gentlemen" of such bipeds as stand in sore need of the transformation.

As we are all by baptism spiritually cleansed of all blemish, so is the son of the tradesman, doctor, solicitor, or what not, socially regenerated by taking holy orders.

Now this bewildering wholesale social acceptation of the ninety-and-nine who positively decline to stray, finding it a much more profitable policy to stay quietly in the fold nibbling the fodder, is peculiar to Protestant communities, and we do not find the same social indulgence extended to spiritual advisers in Roman Catholic countries. In climes still fascinated by the scintillations proceeding from the Triple Crown, the priest is not received—that is, familiarly received—apart from his official capacity in society. He is, of course, ever to be forthcoming and at hand as a professional healer of souls when no other or better healer of souls can be found, and when a soul needs healing very badly; but if he be not a man of culture and refinement,—that is, if he has failed to catch the tricks, manners, and bearings of such—for the mere question of birth is, of course, of minor importance, the laying on of the bishop's hands having smoothed over all that difficulty,—the mere fact of his being a priest does not entitle him to claim any of the privileges accruing to that most elastic title of gentleman; and many a woman of social rank abroad will readily, gladly—nay, eagerly—confess to, and receive absolution from, a man whose society at her dinner-table she would not tolerate for a moment.

We cannot but think that this reserve has its advantages, and that all people of refined feeling benefit by a rule which requires from one seeking familiar social recognition the production of some other credential, save only that the postulant be a servant of the Church.

At home, we find the spiritual adviser, merely by reason of his office, entitled to lay a claim-nay, actually laying a claim-to a place at our dinner-table, to a chair at our club, to the smoking of our cigars, the drinking of our wines, the riding of our horses, the consoling of our wives, and, alas! the marrying of our daughters, when, in many instances, the social merits of the man himself would hardly justify him, under ordinary circumstances, in aspiring to a closer intimacy with us than may reasonably be expected to arise from the proper exercise of his professional duties in the saving of our souls, and the flogging of our boys.

Such a man being so received, in the event of his not being sweet and whole, will hardly think it worth his while to purify himself of his uncleanness solely for our sakes-nay, in many instances, will take a grotesque and savage delight in endeavoring to widen, by his vulgarities, the deplorable breach which, if we are to believe cynics and scoffers, already exists between St. James's Square and Mount Sinai.

Abroad, the priest who would seek to be considered a gentleman, and be received as such in society, must endeavour to imbue himself with some of the refinement innate in those with whom he would fain consort, and thus it happens that he studies with more or less success to imitate such *ad unguem facti homines* as may from time to time swim within his ken.

So it is that we not infrequently find (and oddly enough more often than not in the most exclusive social coteries like that of the Faubourg St-Germain), not only the most charming, refined, and sought-after men to be priests, but also to be men of low birth and origin, who owe, however, their social recognition and success, not to their cloth, but to the grace with which they have learned to wear it. To such a man as this we will now introduce the reader.

The career of the Abbé Girod had been an eminently successful one—successful in every way; and even he himself was forced to acknowledge such to be the case as he reviewed his past life, sitting by a blazing fire in his comfortable apartment in the Rue Miromesnil previous to dressing for the Due de Frontignan's dinner-party.

Born of poor parents in the south of France, entering the priesthood at an early age, having received but a meager education, and that chiefly confined to a superficial knowledge of the most elementary treatises on theology, he had, in five-and-twenty years, and solely by his own exertions, unaided by patronage, obtained a most desirable berth in one of the leading churches in Paris, thereby becoming the recipient of a handsome income, and being thus enabled to indulge in his rather expensive tastes as *dilettante* and *homme du monde*.

The few hours snatched from his parochial duties he had never failed to devote to study, and his application and determination had borne him golden fruit in more ways than one. He had, moreover, so cultivated and made such good use of the rare opportunities afforded him in early life of associating with gentlemen, that when now at length he found his presence in demand at every house in the "Faubourg" where wit and graceful learning were appreciated, no one would ever have suspected he had not been nurtured and bred in accordance with the strictest canons of social refinement.

But in his upward progress such had been his experiences of life that when, during the brief intervals of breathing-time he allowed himself, he would look below and above, down to where he had begun and up to where he was endeavoring to climb, he was forced to confess that at every step a belief, an illusion, had been trodden under foot; that the clouds of glory of which Wordsworth speaks had either altogether died away on the horizon, or had become so threatening and dark in aspect as to make him instinctively seek refuge under the umbrella of cynicism; and he would wonder, while bracing himself for a new effort, how it would all end, and whether the mitre he lusted for would not perhaps, after all, be placed upon a head that doubted even the existence of a God.

He was not, however, a bad man, but merely one of that class who have embraced the priesthood merely as a means of raising themselves from obscurity to eminence, and have, in their intercourse with the world, discovered many flaws and blemishes in what at one time they may have considered perfect. He was indeed only fervent in his apolausticism; and the embracing of such golden images as he might care to adore, he found dangerous to his peace of mind, in that the gilding thereof was but too apt to come off upon his lips. When at first his reason began to reject many of the dreams and fables hitherto cherished and believed in, the Abbé Girod was almost inclined to abandon in despair any attempt to discern the false from the true, and this all the more that he saw plainly the time thus spent was in a worldly sense but wasted, and that the good things of this world come to such reapers as gather in wheat and tares alike, well knowing there is a market for them both.

During a certain period, therefore, of his struggle upward—

"An infant crying in the night,
An infant crying for the light,
And with no language but a cry,"—

while his worldly ambition was aiding by sly insinuations the deadly work already begun by the destruction of his dreams, Henri Girod was nigh being an atheist.

But the nature of the man was too finely sensual for this phase to be lasting; and when at length he found himself so far successful in his worldly aspirations as to be tolerably sure of their complete fulfillment; when at length he found time to examine spiritual matters apart from their direct bearing upon his social altitude, his aesthetic sense—which by this time had necessarily developed—was struck as by a new revelation, and thrilled and entangled by the exquisite *beauty* of Christianity; and thus, as a shallow philosophy had nearly reduced him to become an atheist, so a deep and sensual spirit of sentimentality nearly reconciled him to becoming a Christian.

His Madonna was the Madonna of Raphael, not that of Albert Dürer: the woman whose placid grace of countenance creates an emotion more subtly voluptuous than desire; not she in whose face can be discerned the human mother of the Man of Sorrows and of Him divinely acquainted with all grief The Christ he adored was not the Friend of the broken-hearted, the Healer of the blind Bartimeus, He whom Andrea del Mantegna shows us hanging on the cross; but He "who feedeth among the lilies"—the Alpha and Omega of all aesthetic conception. Christianity, in a word, he looked upon as the highest moral expression of artistic perfection, and he regarded it with the same admiration he accorded to the Antinous and the Venus of Milo.

He was not, however, by nature a pagan as some men are, men who, in the words of De Musset—

"Sont venus trop tard dans un monde trop vieux";

but the atmosphere in which his early years had been passed had been so antagonistic and stifling to his warm sensuous nature, his inner life had been so cramped in and starved, that when at length the key of gold opening the prison door let in the outer air, his spirit reveled in the wild extravagance so often found accompanying sudden and long-wished-for emancipation.

His nature was perhaps not one that could have been attuned to a perfect harmony with that of a Greek or Roman of the golden days, but one rather better calculated to enjoy the hybrid atmosphere of the Italian Renaissance; and he would have been in his element in the Rucellai Gardens, conversing with feeble little Cosimino or laughing with Buondelmonte and Luigi Alamanni.

He did not trouble himself to believe in the narrative of the Bible; but its precepts and tendencies he appreciated and admired, although it must in all honesty be confessed he did not always put himself out to follow them.

In his heart he utterly rejected all idea of a future life, since it was incompatible with his conception of the artistic unity of this; but then again, he would blandly acknowledge to himself that there are perhaps, after all, things we cannot comprehend, and that beauty may have no term.

Being, however, broadly speaking, an honest man, and one unwilling to eat bread he had not earned, he assimilated so far as in him lay his duties as a priest with his ideas as a man of culture; and his sermons were ever of Love—sermons which, winged as they were with impassioned eloquence, were deservedly popular with all, from the scholar who delighted in them as intellectual feasts to the fashionable *mondaine* who was only too enchanted to find in the quasifatalistic and broadly-charitable views enunciated therein, excuses whereby her dreary and vulgar intrigues might be considered in a light more pleasing to herself and more consoling to her husband.

On the Sunday afternoon preceding the evening on which we introduce him to the reader, the abbé had departed from his usual custom, and by special request of his curé had preached a most remarkable sermon on the personality of Satan.

It is a vulgar error to suppose that men succeed best when their efforts are enlivened by a real belief in the matter in hand. Not only have some men such a superabundance of fervid imagination that they can, for the time being, provoke themselves into a pseudo-belief in what they know in their saner moments to be false, and thus fire themselves with real enthusiasm for a mere myth and shadow; but, moreover, a large class of men are endowed with minds so restless and so finely strung that they can play with a sophism with marvelous dexterity and skill, while lacking that vigorous and comprehensive grasp of mind which the lucid exposition of a hidden truth necessitates.

The Abbé Girod belonged a little to both these classes of beings; and, moreover, his vanity as an intellectual man provoked him to extraordinary exertions in cases wherein he fancied he might win for himself the glory of strengthening and verifying matters which in themselves perhaps lacked almost the elements of existence.

"Spiritual truths," he once cynically remarked to Sainte Beuve, whom, by the way, he detested, "will take care of themselves: it is the nursing of spiritual falsehood that needs all the care of the clergy."

On the Sunday in question he had surpassed himself. With biting irony he had annihilated the disbelievers in divine punishment, and then with persuasive and overwhelming eloquence he had urged the necessity of believing, not only in hell, but in the personality of the Prince of Evil.

Women had fainted in their terror, men had been frightened into seeking the convenient solace of the confessional, and the archbishop had written him a letter of the warmest congratulation and thanks.

It was a triumph which a man of the nature of the Abbé Girod particularly enjoyed. The idea of finding himself the successful reviver of an inanimate doctrine, while secretly conscious that he was in reality a skeptic in matters of dogmatically vital importance, was, to a mind so prone to delight in paradoxes, eminently agreeable; and it tickled his palate with a sharp, pungent joy to see the letter of the archbishop lying upon a volume off Strauss, and to read the glowing and extravagant praise lavished upon himself in the pages of the *Univers*, after having enjoyed a sparkling draught of Voltaire.

II

Such was the Abbé Girod, the type of a class. The Due de Frontignan, with whom he was dining on the evening this story opens, was, or rather is, in many ways a no less remarkable personage in Paris society.

Possessing rank, birth, and a splendid income, he had been blessed with more than a fair share of the good gifts of providence, being endowed, not only with considerable mental power, but with the tact to use that power to the best advantage. Although beyond doubt clever, he was universally esteemed a much more intellectual man than he really was, and this through no voluntary and willful deceitfulness on his part, but simply owing to a method he had unconsciously adopted of exhibiting his wares with their most favorable aspect to the front.

He was well read, but not deeply read, and yet all Paris considered him a profound scholar; he was quick and epigrammatic in his appreciation and expression of ideas, as men of cultivation and varied experience are apt to be; but he enjoyed the reputation of being a wit without ever having said a really good thing; and finally, having merely lounged through the world, impelled by a spirit of restlessness begotten of great wealth and idleness, society looked upon him as a bold and adventurous traveller. Only the day before we have the pleasure of introducing him to our readers, he had politely declined to leave Paris and conduct an expedition to the North Pole, but had generously volunteered to give a large sum to anyone who cared to risk his life in endeavouring to discover that inestimable boon to suffering humanity known as the North-West Passage, for which we are all so hungrily longing, and which Millais, aided and abetted by Trelawny, asserts to be the bounden duty of England to find out; at the same time promising to take care of and provide for the widows and orphans of such adventurers as might find the climate of the Pole, or the appetites of the indigenous bears, a serious impediment to their safe return and ultimate reception of the conqueror's laurels, with which we should all so eagerly greet them.

One gift he most certainly possessed, and that to an eminent degree: he was vastly amusing and entertaining, and resembled in that respect the Abbé Galiani, as described by Diderot, for he was indeed "a treasure on rainy days; and if the cabinetmakers made such things, nobody would be without one in the country."

He not only knew everybody in Paris, but he possessed that precious, rare, and extraordinary faculty of drawing people out, and of forcing them to make themselves amusing. No man, indeed, was in his society long before—often to his own great surprise—openly discussing his most cherished hobby with a new and unwonted eloquence hatched by apparent sympathy, or airily scattering as seed for trivial conversation the fruit of long years of experience and reflection. From what has been said, it may be superfluous to add that the Hotel de Frontignan, in the Rue de Varenne, was the resort, lounging place, and almshouse of all that was most remarkable and extraordinary in the fashionable, the artistic, the diplomatic, and the scientific world.

His intimacy with the Abbé Girod was one of long standing: they were bound together by one bond of union which (alas! how rarely it is forged!) is stronger and more enduring than many cemented by vows, prayers, and tears—they mutually amused each other; and while, on the one side, the keen intellect of the priest found much that was interesting in the shallow, but attractive and brilliant, nature of the layman, the duke, on the other, entertained feelings of the warmest admiration for a man who, having risen from nothing, enlivened the most exclusive coteries with his graceful learning and charming wit.

It was one of the peculiar whims of Octave de Frontignan never to have an even number of guests at his dinner-table. His *soirées*, indeed, were attended by hundreds, but his dinner-parties rarely exceeded seven (including himself), and in many cases he only invited two.

On this especial occasion the only guest asked to meet the Abbé Girod was the celebrated diplomatist and millionaire, the Prince Paul Pomerantseff.

This most extraordinary personage had for the past six years kept Europe in a constant state of excitement by reason of his munificence, eccentricity, and power.

Brought up under the direct personal supervision of the Emperor of Russia, he had escaped the emasculating influence engendered by the atmosphere of the Corps des Pages, and had learnt at an early age to rely upon himself for his virtues, while ever ready to generously extend an indulgent confidence in his friends to be ready to provide him with the requisite amount of vices. He had distinguished himself as a diplomatist and as a soldier, and had left traces of his indomitable will in many State papers, as on many an enemy's face, during the period of the Crimean war.

In London, but perhaps more especially in "the Shires," his face was well known and liked, and his method of negotiating fences was as clean and clever as the negotiator himself. Duchesses' daughters had sighed for him, but in vain; and to the "endless desolation and impotent disdain" of mothers, the continuance of his celibacy appeared to be as certain as the splendour of his fortune. Pomerantseff had, moreover,—and this is really worthy of note,—escaped altogether from that most terrible because most hopeless and incurable of maladies, ennui; and he owed this miraculous immunity from the disease which almost always overwhelms the young, rich, prosperous, and powerful, to his lucky spirit of *insouciance*, which he had carefully cultivated from early youth—from, in fact, the moment when he had met with his first disappointment.

The monotony of happiness is perhaps the most hideous monotony of all to a thinking man; and the reason of this is obvious—it is unnatural. Pleasure, with its thousand subtle perfumes, exhausts the moral atmosphere as flowers absorb the oxygen in a closed room j and we all know what the copybooks tell us about the feeling of diffidence entertained by nature as regards a vacuum. Then, again, the man who finds happiness, as it were, an inseparable accident of his life, like dining, will surely begin by fatal degrees to criticise and analyse the nature of it, as he will carefully choose the vintages of his wines. When he has reached this state he is lost; for, as Champfort truly says, "Celui qui veut trop faire dependre son bonheur de sa raison, qui le soumet a l'examen, qui chicane, pour ainsi dire, ses jouissances, et n'admet que des plaisirs delicats finit par n'en plus avoir. C'est un homme qui a force de faire carder son matelas le voit diminuer et finit par coucher sur la dure."

But Pomerantseff carefully avoided this phylloxera of the lucky: in riding to hounds he always looked at the fence he was going to take; in love he invariably ignored the heart he was supposed to be about to awaken; so that, both in jumping and kissing, he met with but few "croppers." He had, moreover, one great and precious gift, that of making himself well beloved by his friends, and healthily feared by his enemies; and the Abbé Girod, who had known him for many years, proved no exception to the general rule; for, although their friendship had never ripened into great intimacy, there was perhaps no man in the wide circle of his acquaintance in whose society the priest took a more lively pleasure.

"Late as usual!" cried the duke, as Girod hurried into the room ten minutes after the appointed time. "Prince, if you were so unpunctual in your diplomatic duties as the abbé is in his social (and, I *fear*, in his spiritual!), where would the world be?"

The abbé stopped short, pulled out his watch, and looked at it with a comically contrite air.

"Only ten minutes late; and I am sure when you think of the amount of business I have to transact, and the nature of it, you can afford to forgive me," he said, as he advanced and shook hands warmly with his friends.

"To my mind," said Pomerantseff, smiling, "dining being the most serious of our transient worldly pleasures, as it certainly is the most harmless,—for indigestion is the malady of fools, and does not concern the man *qui sait manger*,—anything that interferes with the proper enjoyment of it should be seriously punished as a crime of *lèse volupté*."

"You are right," said the duke; "and as regards that, one of the most striking proofs of Shakespeare's subtle insight into human nature is to be found in Macbeth. It is more than probable that a man so steeped in murder, and one who had contracted the rather dreary habit of consorting with witches, would, under ordinary circumstances, have treated with well-merited contempt the ghostly visitations of that utterly uninteresting Banquo; but to be annoyed at the supper-table was intolerable. This view, to my mind, gives the keynote to the latter part of the play."

"Capital! "cried the abbé. "That is quite a new idea. Fancy the Eumenides in the *pot au feu*! You cannot conceive," he continued, throwing himself lazily down upon a lounge, "you have no idea, of the amount of folly I am forced to listen to in a day. Every woman whose bad temper has got her into trouble with her husband, and every man whose stupidity has led him into quarrelling with his wife—one and all they come to me, pour out their misfortunes into my ears, and expect me to arrange their affairs."

But here the servant, announcing "M. le Duc est servi," interrupted the poor abbé's complaints.

III

"I tell you what I should do," said Pomerantseff, when they were seated at table, the Cossack coming out, as it had annoyed him to have to wait. "I should say to every man and woman who came to me on such errands, 'My dear friend, my business is with your spiritual welfare and with that alone. The doctor and solicitor must take care of your worldly concerns. It is my duty to ensure your eternal felicity, when the tedium of *delirium tremens* and the divorce court is all over, and that is really all one man can do.'"

"Very well; but suppose they should reply to me," answered the abbé, quoting his favourite Novalis, "that 'life is a disease of the spirit.'"

"By the way," broke in the duke, "talking of spiritual matters, Pomerantseff has been telling me his experiences with a man you detest, Abbé."

"I detest no man."

"I can only judge from your own words," rejoined Frontignan. "Did you not tell me years ago that you thought Home a more serious evil than the typhoid fever?"

"Ah, Home the medium!" cried Girod, in great disgust. "I admit you are right. It is not possible, prince, that you encourage Octave in his absurd spiritualism?"

But just at that moment came a whisper from a better world.

"Chateau Margaux, M. l'Abbé?" murmured the butler in his ear.

"Wait!" cried the duke, as Girod was about to smile assent; "I have some wine I want you to try." Then, turning to the butler, "Bring that Laffite Dugléré sent in yesterday, Gregoire. Now, Abbé, taste that I want your opinion before touching it myself or giving it to others. It is of the famous comet year, and of course you know the story of the sale. Dugléré sent me up a dozen yesterday as a present, with a charming note to say that he wanted the opinion of my friends, and especially of yourself. He added, that of course he could not think of charging me for it, since he bought it at such a ruinous price that no serious man would think of *buying* a bottle. He keeps it, therefore, merely as an advertisement, and to give to friends. He says, moreover, that although of course too old, it *is* still a generous wine."

The abbé looked carefully at the glass, and daintly swallowed a thimbleful; and then, after a pause of half a second, shook his head at the duke and said, smiling—

"Dugléré for once spoke the truth. It is a generous wine; far too generous, for it has given away all its best. Margaux, Gregoire."

"Capital!" laughed the duke. "I shall tell Dugléré your opinion, and he will probably sell out his stock at once. It cost him two hundred francs a bottle."

"It is possible to keep even wine too long," replied the abbé: and then added with a sweet smile, "here below all is but ephemeral and transitory, as you know."

"You asked me just now, abbé, if I encouraged our friend here in his spiritualism, did you not?" asked Pomerantseff.

"I did."

The prince smiled gravely.

"Do not you know me well enough to know that I should never dare to presume to encourage any man in anything, *mon cher abbé*?"

"But you cannot believe in it?"

"I do most certainly believe in it."

"*Mon Dieu!*" exclaimed Girod. "What folly! What are we all coming to? If men like you and Octave encourage such vulgar jugglery, it will become so paying a game that we poor priests will stand no chance against the *prestidigitateurs*. Robert Houdin will get the best of all the fathers of the Church in a week!"

"It has always struck me as most remarkable," said the duke, "that with all your taste for the curious and unknown, you have never been tempted into investigating the matter, Abbé."

"I am, as you say, a lover of the curious," replied the priest, "but not of such empty trash as spiritualism. I have quite enough cares with the realities of this world, without bringing upon myself the misery which would surely be entailed by investigating the possibilities of the next."

"That is a sentiment worthy of the Abbé Dubois," said Pomerantseff, laughing; and then the duke suddenly making some inquiry relative to the train which was to take him and the prince to Brunoy on a shooting expedition the following morning, the subject for the nonce was dropped.

When dinner was over, they repaired to the *fumoir*, which Frontignan had furnished with all the soft sensualism befitting such a temple of selfishness; and a man might, if so inclined, have not inaptly murmured to himself, on lighting his cigar and sinking into one of the voluptuous arm-chairs which embraced your limbs with a *chatterie* quite their own, "Moi seul, et c'est assez!"

But Pomerantseff strode towards the piano and opened it. "I want to sing you a rather pretty ballad a friend sent me from London yesterday," he said; "and as you both understand English perfectly, you will see that the words are rather above the ordinary level. They are written by a very dear friend of mine—a most extraordinary man—Tresilyan."

"Ah! Tresilyan is a friend of yours, is he?" said the duke.

"One of my dearest. Do you know him?"

"Hardly—although I have, of course, met him scores of times. He promised to stay with me for a few days last year at Chataigneraye"—one of the duke's places—"on his return from the leaden races; but he wrote to excuse himself. It was a bore, for I had asked two of the princes to meet him."

"Oh, of course," laughed Pomerantseff, seating himself at the piano. "One can never catch him: he has so many engagements and friends, that his life is passed in saying in that wonderful voice of his, 'Je le regrette, je ne demanderais pas mieux, mais c'est impossible!'" But one thing I will say for him: he does not pretend to be a poet; never publishes anything, and only writes for his own amusement, I am indeed one of the few men who know he writes verses at all. This thing he calls, I believe, 'Æstas Captiva.'" And the prince hummed, in a clear, true, but unpretentious baritone voice, the following:—

I

"I had thought when we met (for the year was moved
   By the tears October must always bring),
I the lover, and you the loved,
   I had said goodbye to spring.

II

"How could I foresee what I now well know.
   That you'd caught and imprisoned all summer's best?
That June, beguiled by your bosom's snow,
   Lay throbbing within your breast?

III

"That those blue-grey eyes could the sun eclipse;
   Hide him away, with his heat increased:
Though the roses peeped from your pouting lips,
   Burning to be released?

IV

"That the secret of all the sweet flowers had said,
   Only awaited one kiss of mine,
To awaken and thrill when I bowed my head,
   Where you can well divine?

V

"But thus it chanced, as we both now know,
  With a kiss from me and a kiss from you,
June lay revealed in your blushes' glow;
  Shall we keep her October through?"

"You must not think me rude," said the abbé, when Pomerantseff had got through his ditty; "but whenever I hear any sentiment of that kind I think perforce of that profound but unappreciated remark of Voltaire, 'The first man who compared a woman to a rose was a poet, the second a fool!'"

"'Il est impayable, ce cher abbé!' said Pomerantseff to the duke, with a laugh, as he rose from his seat and resumed his still-lighted cigar. "What can we do, duke, to make this wretched little pagan less material in his views?"

"Convert him to spiritualism," said Frontignan.

"Never!" cried the abbé. "It is absurd for you to disbelieve, for you know nothing about it, since you have never been willling to attend a séance, as you yourself admit."

"I *feel* it is absurd, and that is enough—for me at least."

"Certum est quia impossibile," murmured Pomerantseff, striking a match.

"I myself do not exactly believe in spirits," said Frontignan, thoughtfully.

"*À la bonne heure!* Of course not?" cried the abbé. "You see, prince, he is not quite mad after all!"

The prince said nothing.

"I cannot doubt the existence of some extraordinary phenomena," continued the young duke thoughtfully, "simply because I cannot bring myself to such an exquisite pitch of philosophical imbecility as to doubt my own senses; but, to my thinking, the exact nature of the phenomena remains as yet an open question. It is some phase of electro-biology which we do not yet understand. I have a theory of my own about it, and although it may be absurd and fantastical, it is certainly no more so than that which would have us believe that the spirits of the dear old lazy dead come back to the scenes of their human hopes and disappointments, their lives and miseries, to pull our noses and play on tambourines."

"And may I ask you," inquired the prince, with a touch of sarcasm in his voice, "what this theory of yours may be?"

"I will give you," said the duke, ignoring the sneer, and stretching himself back in his chair, as he sent a ring of smoke curling daintily toward the ceiling,—"I will give you with great pleasure the result of my reflection about the matter. You are both far more clever men than I am, and you can draw your own conclusions.

"It is my belief that the things—the tangible things—we create, or rather cause to appear, when sitting with what is now called, for want of a better name, a materialising medium, come from within ourselves, and are portions of ourselves.

"We produce them, in the first instance, generally with fingers linked; but afterwards, when our nervous organisations are more harmonised to them, they come to us of themselves, and even against our wills.

"It is my belief that these are what we term our passions and our emotions, to whose existence the electric fluid and nervous ecstasy we cause to circulate and induce by sitting with hands linked merely gives a tangible and corporeal expression.

"And after all, why should not this be so? Why, as a matter of fact, is there anything extraordinary or improbable in the suggestion? We all know that grief, joy, remorse, and many other passions and emotions, can kill us as surely and in many instances as quickly as an assassin's dagger; and it is a well-known scientific fact, that there are certain nerves in the hand between certain fingers which have a distinct and direct *rapport* with the brain, and by which the mind can be controlled.

"Since this is the case, why is it that under certain given conditions, such as sitting with hands linked—that thus sitting, and while the electric fluid, drawn out by the contact of our hands, forms a powerful medium between the inner and the outward being—why is it, I say, that these strong emotions I have mentioned should not take advantage of this strange river flowing to and fro between the conccptional and the visual to float before us for a time, and give us an opportunity of seeing and touching them who influence our every action in life?

"Nay, I will go further, and insist that my theory has a right to at least be admitted to serious discussion and investigation, for the greatest men since the death of Christ have founded their whole theory of life upon the unseen, the purely conceptional. 'Faith is the evidence of things unseen,' as the Abbé here knows well; and how terribly material have been the sacrifices made for this splendid conception! Why, then, should not a man like Loyola, for instance, have been able to really see with his earthly eyes, under certain given conditions of nervous excitement, what he was ready to sacrifice his very material body, nerves, blood, and sinews, to pay due homage to? The media through which these great conceptional realities may become tangible and corporealised should, to my mind, be thoroughly tested and examined through the lens of science before we can reject as absurd the possibility of their being so materialised.

"*Bref*, it is my belief that I can shake hands with my emotions; that Regret or Remorse, for instance, can become tangible and pinch my ears, and slap me on the back, just as surely as they can and do keep people awake at night by agitating their nervous system, or in other words, by mentally pinching their ears."

"That is certainly a very fantastic idea, Octave," said the abbé, smiling. "But if you have seen any of your emotions, what do they look like? I should like to see my hasty temper sitting beside me for a minute: I should take advantage of his being materialised to pay him back in his own coin, and give him a good thrashing."

"It is difficult," said the duke gravely, "to recognise one's emotions when brought actually face to face with them, as it were, although they have been living in us all our lives,—turning our hair grey or pulling it out,—making us stout or lean, upright or bent over. Moreover, our minor emotions, except when the medium is remarkably powerful, often outwardly express themselves to us in some unrecognisable form, sometimes as perfumes and flowers, often as mere luminous bodies. I have reason, however, to believe that I have recognised that most complex of emotions—my conscience."

"I should have thought he'd have been too sleepy to move out," laughed the abbé.

"That just shows how wrongly one man judges another," said Octave lazily, without earnestness, but with a certain something in his tone that betokened he was dealing with realities. "You very probably think that I am not much troubled with a conscience, whereas the fact is that my conscience, with a strong dash of remorse in it, is a very keen one. Many years ago a certain episode changed the whole colour and current of my life inwardly and to myself, although, of course, outwardly I was much the same. Now this episode of which I speak aroused what I am pleased to call my conscience"— bowing to the abbé—"to a most extraordinary degree; and since that catastrophe, which changed the whole tenor of my life, I have never taken part in a séance of spiritualism without seeing a female figure with a face like that of the heroine of my episode, dressed in a queer strange robe, woven of every possible colour save white, who shudders and trembles as she passes before me, holding in her arms large sheets of glass, through which dim Bohemian-glass colours pass flickering every moment."

"What a very disagreeable thing to see this weather!" said the abbé; "everything shuddering and shaking."

"Have you ever discovered why she goes about like the wife of a glazier?" asked the prince.

"For a long time I could not make out what they could be, these large panes of glass, with variegated colours passing through them, but now I think I know."

"Well?"

"They are dreams waiting to be fitted in."

IV

"Bravo!" cried the abbé; "that is really a good idea! If I only had the pen of Charles Nodier, what a charming *feuilleton* I could write about all this!"

Pomerantseff laid his hand affectionately on the duke's shoulder. "*Mon cher ami*," he said, with a grave smile, "believe me, you are wholly at fault in your speculations. Girod here, of course (naturally enough, since he has never been willing enough to attend an ordinary séance of spiritualism), thinks we are both madmen, and that the whole thing is folly; but you and I, who have been to very many extraordinary séances, and have seen very many marvellous manifestations, know that it is not folly. Take the word of a man who has had greater experience in the matter than yourself, and who is himself a most powerful materialising medium, as you know: the theory you have just enunciated is utterly false."

"Prove that it is false."

"I cannot prove it, but wait and see."

"Nay; I have given it all up now. I will not meddle with spiritualism again. It unhinged my nerves and destroyed my peace of mind while I was investigating it."

The prince shrugged his shoulders.

"Prince, leave him alone," said the abbé, smiling; "his theory is a great deal more sensible than yours; and if I could bring myself to believe that at your séances any real phenomenon *does* take place (which of course no sane person can), I should be rather inclined to accept Octave's interpretation of the matter.

"Let us follow it out a little further, for the mere sake of talking nonsense. 'Qui vit sans folie n'est pas si sage qu'il croit!' Doubtless the dominant passion of a man would be the most likely to appear—that is to say, would be the most tangible?"

"That," replied the duke, "would depend upon circumstances. If the phenomenon should take place while the man is alone, doubtless it would be so; but if while at a séance, attended by many people, the apparition would be the product of the master-passions of all: and thus it is that many of the visions which appear at séances, when the sitters are not harmonised, are often most remarkable and unrecognisable anomalies."

"I thought I understood from Madame de Girardin that certain spirits always appeared."

"Pooh, pooh! Madame de Girardin never went deep enough into the matter. The most ravishing vision I ever saw was when I fancied I saw Love."

"What? Love! An emanation from yourself?"

The duke sighed.

"Ah! that is what proved to me that what I saw could not be Love. That sentiment has been too long dormant in me to awaken to a corporeal expression."

"What made you think it was Love?" asked Pomerantseff.

"It was a white dove, with something, I cannot express in words, that was human about it. I felt ineffably happy while it was with me."

"Your theory is false, I tell you!" said the Russian; "what you saw probably was Love."

"Then it would have been God!" cried the abbé.

"Why?"

"I believe with Novalis that 'Love is the highest reality,'" replied Girod; and then, breaking forth into a laugh, he sang, pirouetting on his heel—

> "La prosperite s'en vole,
>   Le pouvoir tombe et s'enfuit;
> Un peu d'amour qui console
>   Vaut mieux et fait moins de bruit."

"Don't quote Hugo to me about love, abbé, I beg of you, for he knew nothing about it, any more than he understood a word of English, although he coolly wrote a whole volume of criticism on Shakespeare."[1]

"Where is the soul when the body is asleep?" asked the Muscovy prince.

"No, duke!" cried the abbé, laughing, and not heeding Pomerantseff's pregnant question; "what you saw was not Love, but it might all the same have been an emanation from yourself—a master-passion. I daresay it was the corporeal embodiment of your love of pigeon-shooting."

"Perhaps," laughed the duke.

"I tell you what, *mon ami*," said Pomerantsefif, rising, as he saw the abbé making preparations to depart, "I am glad that my appetite, corporealised and separated from my discretion, is not in your wine-cellar—your Johannisberg would suffer!"

---

1 I have now lying before me one among the very numerous letters which the great poet did me the honour to address to me, bearing date 20th October 1879, in which occur the following words: ". . . . . . Je ne sais pas l'anglais mais votre lettre noble et charmante m'emeut et je me ferai lire tres prochainement votre article ou je retrouveiai la delicatesse de votre esprit et l'elevation de votre talent," and so forth and so on. This will, I hope, put an end to the controversy as to whether or not the author of "William Shakespeare" understood English, for I am quite ready to produce the letter in question.—THE AUTHOR.

"Prince, you must drive me home," said the abbé. "I cannot get into a draughty cab at this hour of the night."

"*Très volontiers.* Goodnight, duke. Remember tomorrow morning at half-past nine at the Gare de Lyon," said the prince.

"Remember tomorrow night at half-past ten at Madame de Langeac's!" bawled the abbé; and so they left.

The priest hurried down the cold staircase and into the prince's brougham.

"What a pity," exclaimed the abbé, when they were once fairly started, "that a man with the brains of De Frontignan should give himself up to such wild ideas and dreams!"

"You are very complimentary," rejoined the other, smiling gravely; "for you know that, so far as believing in spirits is concerned, I am as bad, if not worse, than he is."

"Ah, but you are jesting."

"On my honour as a gentleman, I am not jesting. See here,"—as he spoke Pomerantseff seized the abbé's hand,—"you heard me tell the duke just now that I believed he had seen the spirit of Love. Well, the sermon you preached the day before yesterday, which all Paris is talking about, and in which you endeavoured to prove the personality of the devil to be a fact, was more true than perhaps you believed when you preached it. Why should not Frontignan have seen the spirit of Love, *when I know and have seen the devil?*"

"*Mon ami*, you are insane!" cried Girod. "Why, the devil does not exist!"

"I tell you I have seen him—the god of all evil, the prince of desolation! "cried the other, in an excited voice; "and what is more, *I will show him to you!*"

"Show the devil to me!" exclaimed the abbé, half terrified, half amused. "Why, you are out of your mind!"

The prince laid his other hand upon the arm of the abbé, who could feel he was trembling with excitement.

"You know my address," he said, in a quick, passionate voice. "When you feel—as I tell you you will surely feel—desirous of investigating this further, send for me, and I promise, on my honour as a gentleman, to show you the devil, so that you cannot doubt. I will do this only on one condition."

The abbé felt almost faint, for apart from the wildness of the words thus abruptly and unexpectedly addressed to him, the hand of the prince, which lay upon his own, as if to keep him still, seemed to be pouring fire and madness into him.

He tried to withdraw it, but the other grasped the fingers tight.

"On one condition," repeated Pomerantseff, in a lower tone.

"What condition?" murmured the poor abbé.

"That you trust yourself entirely to me until we reach the place of meeting."

"Prince, let go my hand! You are hurting me! I will promise to do as you say when I want to go to your infernal meeting, which will be never."

He wrenched his hand away, pulled down the carriage -window, and let the cold night air in. "Pomerantseff, you are a madman: you are really dangerous. Why the devil did you grasp my hand in that way?—my arm is numb."

The prince laughed.

"It is only electricity. I was determined, since you doubted the existence of the devil, to make you promise to come and see him."

"I never promised!" exclaimed the abbé "I only promised to trust myself to you if the horrible desire should ever seize me to investigate your mad words further. But you need not be afraid of that. God forbid I should indulge in such folly!"

The prince smiled.

"God has nothing to do with this," he remarked simply. "You will come."

The carriage had turned up the street in which the abbé lived, and they were within but a few doors of his house.

"My dear prince," said Girod earnestly, "let me say a few words to you at parting. You know that I am not a bigot, so that your words—which many might think blasphemous—I care nothing about; but remember we are in the Paris of the nineteenth century, not in the Paris of Cazotte, and that we are eminently practical nowadays. Had you asked me to go with you to see some curious atrocity, no matter how horrible, I might, were it interesting, have accepted; but when you invite me to go with you to see the devil, you really must excuse me: it is too absurd."

"Very well," replied Prince Pomerantseff, "of course I know you will come; but think the matter over well. Remember, I promise to show the devil to you so that you can never doubt of his personality again. This is not one of the wonders of electro-biology, but simply a fact: *the devil exists, and you shall see him.* Good-night."

V

Girod, as he turned into his porte cochère and made his way upstairs, was more struck than perhaps he confessed even to himself, by the quiet tone of certainty and assurance in which the prince uttered these words; and on reaching his apartment he sat down by the blazing fire, lighted a cigarette, and began calmly considering in all its bearings what he could hardly bring himself to believe to be other than a most remarkable and extraordinary case of mania and mental derangement.

In the first place, was the prince deceived himself, or merely endeavouring to deceive others? The latter theory he at once rejected. Not only the character and breeding of the man, but his nervous earnestness about this matter, rendered such a supposition impossible.

Then he himself was deceived: and yet, how improbable! Girod could remember nothing in what he knew or had heard of the prince that could lead him to suppose his brain was of the kind charlatans and pseudo-magicians can successfully bewitch.

On the contrary, although native of a country in which the grossest superstitions are rife, he himself had led such an active healthy life, partly in Russia, partly in France, and partly in England, that his brain could hardly be suspected of derangement; for an intimate and practical acquaintance with most of the fences in "the Shires," and all the leading statesmen of Europe, can hardly be considered compatible with a morbid disposition and superstitious nature.

No; the abbé was forced to confess to himself on reflection that the man who deceived Pomerantseff must have been of no ordinary ability. That he had been deceived was of course beyond all question, but it was certainly most marvellous. In practical matters, the abbé was even forced to confess to himself he would unhesitatingly take the prince's advice sooner than trust to his own private judgment; and yet here was this model of keen, healthy wisdom gravely inviting him to meet the devil face to face, and not only this, but assuring him, moreover, that it should be no unintelligible freak of electro-biology, but as a simple fact.

Girod smoked thirty cigarettes without coming to any satisfactory solution of the enigma.

What if, after all, he, the Abbé Girod, for once should abandon the line of conduct he had laid down for himself, and to satisfy his curiosity, and perhaps with the chance of restoring to its proper equilibrium a most valuable and comprehensive mind, overlook his determination never to endanger his peace of mind by meddling with the affairs of spiritualists?

He could picture to himself the whole thing. They would doubtless be in a darkened room; an apparition clothed in

118

red, and adorned with the traditional horns, would duly make its appearance, and there would of course very likely be no apparent evidence of fraud. That the farce would be cleverly played the abbé did not doubt for a moment. Even supposing some portion of the absurd theory enunciated by Frontignan to be true, and some strange thing, begotten of electric fluid and overwrought imagination, were to make its appearance, that could hardly be considered by a sane man as being equivalent to an interview with the devil.

The abbé told himself that it would be most likely impossible to *detect* any fraud; but he felt convinced that, should the prince find this phenomenon ridiculed and laughed to scorn, after a full investigation by a man of sense and culture, his faith in it would be shaken, and ere long he would come himself to despise it.

All the remarkable stories he had heard about spiritualism from Madame de Girardin and others, and which he had hitherto paid no heed to, came back tonight to the Abbé as he sat ruminating over the extraordinary offer just made him.

He had heard of dead people appearing, and that was sufficiently absurd—for he did not believe in a future life; but the devil—the idea was preposterous! Poor Luther indeed might throw his ink-pot at him; but no enlightened Roman Catholic priest could in these latter nineteenth-century days be expected to believe in his existence, no matter how much he might be forced, for obvious reasons, to preach about it, and represent it as a fact in sermons.

Yes; he would unhesitatingly consent to investigate the matter, and discover and lay bare the fraud he felt certain was lurking somewhere, but that the prince seemed to feel so provokingly certain of his consent, and he feared by thus fulfilling an idly-expressed prophecy, to plunge the unhappy man still deeper into his slough of superstition.

One thing was certain, the abbé told himself with a smile, nothing on earth or from heaven or hell—if the two latter absurdities existed—could bring *him* to believe in the devil. No, not even if the devil should come and take him by the hand, and all the hosts of heaven flock to testify to his identity.

By this time, having smoked and thought himself into a state of blasphemous idiocy, our worthy divine threw away his cigarette, went to bed, and read himself into a nightmare with a volume of Von Helmont.

The following morning still found him perplexed as to what course to adopt in this matter.

As luck (or shall we say the devil?) would have it, while he was trifling in a listless way with his breakfast, there called to see him the only priest in whose judgment, purity, and religious conviction he had any confidence. It is probable, to such an extent was his mind engrossed by the subject, that no matter who might have called just then, he would have discussed the extraordinary conduct of Prince Pomerantseff with him; but inasmuch as the visitor chanced to be the very best man calculated to direct his judgment in the matter, he, without unnecessary delay, laid the whole affair before him.

"You see, *mon cher*," said the abbé, in conclusion, "my position is just this: it appears to me that this person, whom I will not name, has been trifled with by Home and other so-called spiritualists, to such an extent that his mind is really in danger. Now, although, of course, we are forbidden to have any dealings with such people, or to participate in their infamous, foolish, and unholy practices, surely it would be the act of a Christian if a clear, healthy-minded man were to expose the fraud, and thus save to society a man of such transcendent ability as my friend. Moreover, should I decide to accept his mad invitation, I hardly think I could be said to participate in any of the scandalous, and perhaps even blasphemous, rites he may have to perform to bring about the supposed result. What do you think, and what do you advise?"

His friend walked up and down the room for a few minutes, turning the matter over carefully in his mind, and then, coming up to where the abbé lay lazily stretched upon a lounge, he said earnestly—

"*Mon cher* Henri, I am very glad you have asked me about this. It appears to me that your duty is quite clear. You perhaps have it in your power, as you yourself have seen, to save, not only as you say a *mind*, but what I wish I could feel you prized more highly, a *soul*. You must accept the invitation.

The abbé rose in delight at having found another man who, taking the responsibility off his shoulders, commanded him as a duty to indulge his ardent curiosity.

"But," continued the other in a solemn voice, "before accepting the invitation you must do one thing."

The abbé threw himself back on the lounge in disgust.

"Oh, pray for strength, of course," he exclaimed petulantly; "I am quite aware of that."

"Not only pray, but *fast*, and that for seven days at least, my dear brother."

This was a very disagreeable view of the matter; but the abbé was equal to the occasion.

After a pause, during which he appeared absorbed in religious reflection, he rose, and taking his friend by the hand—

"You are right," said he, "as you always are. Although, of course, I know the evil spirit cannot harm an officer of God's Holy Catholic Church, even supposing, for the sake of argument, my poor friend can invoke Satan, yet if I am to be of any good—if I am to save my friend from destruction, I must be armed with extraordinary grace, and this, as you truly divine, can only come by fasting."

The other wrung his hand warmly. "I knew you would see it in its proper light, my dear Henri," he said; "and now

I will leave you to recover your peace of mind by religious meditation."

The abbé smiled gravely, and his friend departed.

The following letter was the result of this edifying interview between the two divines:—

"MON CHER PRINCE,—No doubt you will feel very triumphant when you learn that my object in writing this is to accept your most kind offer of presentation to Sa Majesté; but I do not care whether you choose to consider this yielding to what is only in part whimsical curiosity a triumph or no.

"I will not write to you any cut and dried platitudes about good and evil, but I frankly assure you that one of the strongest reasons which induces me to go on this fool's errand is a belief that I can discover the absurdity and imposture, and cure you of a hallucination which is unworthy of you.—*Tout à vous,*

"HENRI GIROD."

For two days he received no reply to this letter, nor did he happen to meet the prince in society in the interval, although he heard of him from De Frontignan and others; but on the third day the following note was brought to him:—

"MON CHER AMI,—There is no question of triumph any more than there is of deception. I will call for you this evening at half-past nine You must remember your promise to trust yourself entirely to me.—*Cordialement à vous,*

"POMERANTSEFF."

So the matter was now arranged, and he, the Abbé Girod, the renowned preacher of the celebrated Church, was to meet that very night by special appointment, at half-past nine, the prince of darkness; and this in January, in Paris, at the height of the season, in the capital of civilisation—*la ville Lumière!*

VI

As maybe well imagined, during the remainder of that eventful day until the hour of the prince's arrival, the abbé did not enjoy his customary placidity.

A secretary of the Turkish Embassy who called at four found him engaged in a violent discussion with one of the Rothschilds about the belief held by the early Christians in demons, as shown by Tertullian and others; while Lord Middlesex, who called at half-past five, found he had captured Faure, installed him at the piano, and was inducing him to hum snatches from *Don Juan*.

When his dinner-hour arrived, having given orders to his valet to admit no one lest he should be discovered *not* fasting, he hastily swallowed a few mouthfuls, fortified himself with a couple of glasses of *Chartreuse verte*, and lighting a Henry Clay, awaited the coming of the messenger of Satan.

At half-past nine o'clock precisely the prince arrived. He was in full evening dress, but—contrary to his usual custom—wearing no ribbon or decoration, and his face was of a deadly pallor.

"*Mon Dieu!*" exclaimed the abbé, "what is the matter with you, prince? You are looking very ill; we had better postpone our visit."

"No; it is nothing," said the prince gravely. "Let us be off without delay. In matters of this kind waiting is unendurable."

The abbé rose, and rang the bell for his hat and cloak. The appearance of the prince, his evident agitation, and his unfeigned impatience, which seemed to betoken terror, were far from reassuring; but the abbé promptly quelled any feelings of misgiving he might have felt. Suddenly a thought struck him—a thought which certainly his brain would never have engendered had it been in its normal condition.

"Perhaps I had better change my dress and go *en pékin?*" he inquired anxiously.

The ghost of a sarcastic smile flitted across the prince's face as he replied, "No, certainly not; your *soutane* will be in every way acceptable. Come, let us be off."

The abbé made a grimace, put on his hat, flung his cloak around his shoulders, and followed the prince downstairs.

He remarked, with some surprise, that the carriage awaiting them was not the prince's.

"I have hired a carriage for the occasion," said Pomerantseff quietly, noticing Girod's glance of surprise. "I am unwilling that my servants should suspect anything of this."

They entered the carriage, and the coachman, evidently instructed beforehand where to go, drove off without delay. The prince immediately pulled down the blinds, and taking a silk pocket-handkerchief from his pocket, began quietly to fold it lengthwise.

"I must blindfold you, *mon cher*," he remarked simply, as if announcing the most ordinary fact.

"*Diable!*" cried the abbé, now becoming a little nervous. "This is very unpleasant; I like to see where I am going. I believe, Pomerantseff, you are the devil yourself."

"Remember your promise," said the prince, as he carefully covered his friend's eyes with the pocket-handkerchief, and effectually precluded the possibility of his seeing anything until he should remove the bandage.

After this nothing was said. The abbé heard the prince pull up the blind, open the window, and tell the coachman to drive faster. He endeavoured to discover when they turned to the right, and when to the left, but in a few minutes got bewildered, and gave it up in despair. At one time he felt certain they were crossing the river.

"I wish I had not come," he murmured to himself. "Of course the whole thing is folly; but it is a great trial to the nerves, and I shall probably be upset for many days."

On they drove: the time seemed interminable to the abbé.

"Are we near our destination yet?" he inquired at last.

"Not very far off now," replied the other, in what seemed to Girod a most sepulchral tone of voice.

At length, after a drive of about half an hour, which seemed to the abbé double that time, Pomerantseff murmured in a low tone, and with a profound sigh, which sounded almost like a sob, "Here we are"; and at that moment the abbé felt the carriage was turning, and heard the horses' hoofs clatter on what he imagined to be the stones of a courtyard.

The carriage stopped, Pomerantseff opened the door himself, and assisted the blindfolded priest to alight.

"There are five steps," he said, as he held the abbé by the arm. "Take care!"

The abbé stumbled up the five steps. They had now entered a house, and Girod imagined to himself it was probably some old hotel like the Hotel Pimodan, where Gautier, Baudelaire, and others at one time were wont to resort to disperse the cares of life in the fumes of opium. When they had proceeded a few yards, Pomerantseff warned him that they were about to ascend a staircase, and up many shallow steps they went, the Abbé regretting every instant more and that he had allowed his vulgar curiosity to lead him into an adventure which could be productive of nothing but ridicule and shattered nerves.

When at length they had reached the top of the stairs, the prince guided him by the arm through what the abbé imagined to be a hall, opened a door, closed and locked it after them, walked on again, opened another door, which he closed and locked likewise, and over which the abbé heard him pull a heavy curtain. The prince then took him again by the arm, advanced him a few steps, and said in a low whisper—

"Remain quietly standing where you are. I rely upon your honour not to attempt to remove the pocket-handkerchief from your eyes until you hear voices."

The abbé folded his arms and stood motionless, while he heard the prince walk away, and then suddenly all sound ceased.

It was evident to the unfortunate priest that the room in which he stood was not dark; for although he could of course see nothing owing to the pocket-handkerchief, which had been bound most skilfully over his eyes, there was a sensation of being in strong light, and his cheeks and hands felt, as it were, illuminated.

Suddenly a horrible sound sent a chill of terror through him—a gentle noise as of naked flesh touching the waxed floor—and before he could recover from the shock occasioned by the sound, the voices of many men—voices of men groaning or wailing in some hideous ecstasy—broke the stillness, crying—

"Father and creator of all sin and crime, prince and king of all despair and anguish! come to us, we implore thee!"

The abbé, wild with terror, tore off the pocket-handkerchief.

He found himself in a large old-fashioned room, panelled up to the lofty ceiling with oak, and filled with great light shed from innumerable tapers fitted into sconces on the wall—light which, though by its nature soft, was almost fierce by reason of its greatness and intensity, proceeded from these countless tapers.

He had then been, after all, right in his conjectures: he was evidently in a chamber of some one of the many old-fashioned hotels which are to be seen still in the Ile Saint Louis, and indeed in all the antiquated parts of Paris. It was reassuring, at all events, to know one was not in the infernal regions, and to feel tolerably certain that a *sergent de ville* could not be many yards distant.

All this passed into his comprehension like a flash of lightning, for hardly had the bandage left his eyes ere his whole attention was riveted upon the group before him.

Twelve men—Pomerantseff among the number—of all ages from five-and-twenty to fifty-five, all dressed in evening dress, and all, so far as one could judge at such a moment, men of culture and refinement, lay nearly prone upon the floor with hands linked.

They were bowing forward and kissing the floor—which might account for the strange sound heard by Girod—and their faces were illuminated with a light of hellish ecstasy, half distorted, as if in pain, half smiling, as if in triumph.

The abbé's eyes instinctively sought out the prince.

He was the last on the left-hand side, and while his left hand grasped that of his neighbour, his right was sweeping nervously over the bare waxed floor, as if seeking to animate the boards. His face was more calm than those of the others, but of a deadly pallor, and the violet tints about the mouth and temples showed he was suffering from intense emotion.

They were all, each after his own fashion, praying aloud, or rather moaning, as they writhed in ecstatic adoration.

"O Father of evil! come to us!"

"O Prince of endless desolation! who sittest by the beds of suicides, we adore thee!"

"O Creator of eternal anguish!"

"O King of cruel pleasures and famishing desires! we worship thee!"

"Come to us, thy foot upon the hearts of widows!"

"Come to us, thy hair lurid with the slaughter of innocence!"

"Come to us, thy brow wreathed with the clinging chaplet of despair!"

"Come to us!"

The heart of the abbé turned cold and sick as these beings, hardly human by reason of their great mental exaltation, swayed before him, and as the air, charged with a subtle and overwhelming electricity, seemed to throb as from the echo of innumerable voiceless harps.

Suddenly—or rather, the full conception of the fact was sudden, for the influence had been gradually stealing over him—he felt a terrible coldness, a coldness more piercing than any he had ever before experienced even in Russia, and with the coldness there came to him the certain knowledge of the presence of some new being in the room.

Withdrawing his eyes from the semicircle of men, who did not seem to be aware of his, the abbé's, presence, and who ceased not in their blasphemies, he turned them slowly around, and as he did so they fell upon a newcomer, a Thirteenth, who seemed to spring into existence from the air, and before his very eyes.

VII

He was a young man of apparently twenty, tall, as beardless as the young Augustus, with bright golden hair falling from his forehead like a girl's.

He was dressed in evening dress, and his cheeks were flushed as if with wine or pleasure; but from his eyes there gleamed a look of inexpressible sadness, of intense despair.

The group of men had evidently become aware of his presence at the same moment, for they all fell prone upon the floor adoring, and their words were now no longer words of invocation, but words of praise and worship.

The abbé was frozen with horror: there was no room in his breast for the lesser emotion of fear; indeed, the horror was so great and all-absorbing as to charm him and hold him spellbound.

He could not remove his eyes from the Thirteenth, who stood before him calmly, a faint smile playing over his intellectual and aristocratic face—a smile which only added to the intensity of the despair gleaming in his clear blue eyes.

Girod was struck first with the sadness, then with the beauty, and then with the intellectual vigour, of that marvellous countenance.

The expression was not unkind or even cold; haughtiness and pride might indeed be read in the high-bred features, shell-like sensitive nostrils, and short upper lip; while the exquisite symmetry and perfect proportions of his figure showed suppleness and steel-like strength: for the rest, the face betokened, save for the flush upon the cheeks, only great sadness.

The eyes were fixed upon those of Girod, and he felt their soft, subtle, intense light penetrate into every nook and cranny of his soul and being. This terrible Thirteenth simply stood and gazed upon the priest, as the worshippers grew more wild, more blasphemous, more cruel.

The abbé could think of nothing but the face before him, and the great desolation that lay folded over it as a veil. He could think of no prayer, although he could remember there were prayers.

Was this Despair—the Despair of a man drowning in sight of land—being shed into him from the sad blue eyes? Was it Despair or was it Death?

Ah no, not Death!—Death was peaceful, and this was violent and passionate.

Was there no refuge, no mercy, no salvation anywhere? Perhaps, nay, surely; but while those sad blue eyes still gazed upon him, the sadness, as it seemed to him, intensifying every moment, he could not remember where to seek for and where to find such refuge, such mercy, such salvation. He could not remember, and yet he could not entirely forget. He felt that help would come to him if he sought it, and yet he could hardly tell how to seek it.

Moreover, by degrees the blue eyes—it seemed as if their colour, their great blueness, had some fearful power—began pouring into him some more hideous pleasure. It was the ecstasy of great pain becoming a delight, the ecstasy of being beyond all hope, and of being thus enabled to look with scorn upon the Author of hope. And all the while the blue eyes still gazed sadly, with a soft smile breathing overwhelming despair upon him.

Girod knew that in another moment he would not sink, faint, or fall, but that he would,—oh! much worse!—he would smile!

At this very instant a name—a familiar name, and one which the infernal worshippers had made frequent use of, but which he had never remarked before—struck his ear: the name of Christ.

Where had he heard it? He could not tell. It was the name of a young man; he could remember that and nothingmore.

Again the name sounded, "Christ."

There was another word like Christ, which seemed at some time to have brought an idea first of great suffering and then of great peace. Ay, peace, but no pleasure. No delight like this shed from those marvellous blue eyes.

Again the name sounded, "Christ."

Ah! the other word was cross—*croix*—he remembered now; a long thing with a short thing across it.

Was it that as he thought of these things the charm of the blue eyes and their great sadness lessened in intensity? We dare not say; but as some faint conception of what a cross was flitted through the abbé's brain, although he could think of no prayer—nay, of no distinct use of this cross—he drew his right hand slowly up, for it was pinioned as by paralysis to his side, and feebly and half mechanically made the sign across his breast.

The vision vanished.

The men adoring ceased their clamour and lay crouched up one against another, as if some strong electric power had been taken from them and great weakness had succeeded, while, at the same time, the throbbing of the thousand voice-less harps was hushed.

The pause lasted but for a moment, and then the men rose, stumbling, trembling, and with loosened hands, and stood feebly gazing at the abbé, who felt faint and exhausted, and heeded them not. With extraordinary presence of mind the prince walked quickly up to him, pushed him out of the door by which they had entered, followed him, and locked the door behind them, thus precluding the possibility of being immediately pursued by the others.

Once in the adjoining room, the abbé and Pomerantseff paused for an instant to recover breath, for the swiftness of their flight had exhausted them, worn out as they both were mentally and physically; but during this brief interval the prince, who appeared to be retaining his presence of mind by a purely mechanical effort, carefully replaced over his friend's eyes the bandage which the abbé still held tightly grasped in his hand. Then he led him on, and it was not till the cold air struck them that they noticed that they had left their hats behind.

"*N'importe!*" muttered Pomerantseff. "It would be danger-ous to return; "and hurrying the abbé into the carriage which awaited them, he bade the coachman speed them away—"*au grand galop!*"

Not a word was spoken; the abbé lay back as one in a swoon, and heeded nothing until he felt the carriage stop, and the prince uncovered his eyes and told him he had reached home; then he alighted in silence, and passed into his house without a word.

How he reached his apartment he never knew; but the fol-lowing morning found him raging with fever, and delirious.

When he had sufficiently recovered, after the lapse of a few days, to admit of his reading the numerous letters awaiting his attention, one was put into his hand which had been brought on the second night after the one of the memorable séance.

It ran as follows:—

"JOCKEY CLUB, *January* 26, 18—.

"MON CHER ABBÉ,—I am afraid our little adventure was too much for you—in fact, I myself was very unwell all yesterday, and nothing but a Turkish bath has pulled me together. I can hardly wonder at this, however, for I have never in my life been present at so powerful a séance, and you may comfort yourself with the reflection that Sa Majesté has never honoured anyone with his presence for so long a space of time before.

"Never fear, *mon cher*, about your illness. It is purely nervous exhaustion, and you will be well soon; but such evenings must not often be indulged in if you are not desirous of shortening your life. I shall hope to meet you at Mme. de Metternich's on Monday.—*Tout à vous*,

"POMERANTSEFF."

Whether or no Girod was sufficiently recovered to meet his friend at the Austrian Embassy on the evening named we do not know, nor does it concern us; but he is certainly enjoying excellent health now, and is no less charming and amusing than before his extraordinary adventure.

Such is the true story of a meeting with the devil in Paris not many years ago—a story true in every particular, as can be easily proved by a direct application to any of the persons concerned in it, for they are all living still.

The key to the enigma we cannot find, for we certainly do not put faith in any one of the theories of spiritualists; but that an apparition, such as we have described, did appear in the way and under the circumstances we have related is a fact, and we must leave the satisfactory solution of the difficulty to more profound psychologists than ourselves.

THE NOVEL OF THE WHITE POWDER

by Arthur Machen

MY name is Leicester; my father, Major-General Wyn Leicester, a distinguished officer of artillery, succumbed five years ago to a complicated liver complaint acquired in the deadly climate of India. A year later my only brother, Francis, came home after an exceptionally brilliant career at the University, and settled down with the resolution of a hermit to master what has been well called the great legend of the law. He was a man who seemed to live in utter indifference to everything that is called pleasure; and though he was handsomer than most men, and could talk as merrily and wittily as if he were a mere vagabond, he avoided society, and shut himself up in a large room at the top of the house to make himself a lawyer. Ten hours a day of hard reading was at first his allotted portion; from the first light in the east to the late afternoon he remained shut up with his books, taking a hasty half-hour's lunch with me as if he grudged the wasting of the moments, and going out for a short walk when it began to grow dusk. I thought that such relentless application must be injurious, and tried to cajole him from the crAbbéd textbooks, but his ardour seemed to grow rather than diminish, and his daily tale of hours increased. I spoke to him seriously, suggesting some occasional relaxation, if it were but an idle afternoon with a harmless novel; but he laughed, and said that he read about feudal tenures when he felt in need of amusement, and scoffed at the notions of theatres, or a month's fresh air. I confessed that he looked well, and seemed not to suffer from his labours, but I knew that such unnatural toil would take revenge at last, and I was not mistaken. A look of anxiety began to lurk about his eyes, and he seemed languid, and at last he avowed that he was no longer in perfect health; he was troubled, he said, with a sensation of dizziness, and awoke now and then of nights from fearful dreams, terrified and cold with icy sweats. "I am taking care of myself," he said, "so you must not trouble; I passed the whole of yesterday afternoon in idleness, leaning back in that comfortable chair you gave me, and scribbling nonsense on a sheet of paper. No, no; I will not overdo my work; I shall be well enough in a week or two, depend upon it."

Yet in spite of his assurances I could see that he grew no better, but rather worse; he would enter the drawing-room with a face all miserably wrinkled and despondent, and endeavour to look gaily when my eyes fell on him, and I thought such symptoms of evil omen, and was frightened sometimes at the nervous irritation of his movements, and at glances which I could not decipher. Much against his will, I prevailed on him to have medical advice, and with an ill grace he called in our old doctor.

Dr. Haberden cheered me after examination of his patient.

"There is nothing really much amiss," he said to me. "No doubt he reads too hard and eats hastily, and then goes back again to his books in too great a hurry, and the natural sequence is some digestive trouble and a little mischief in the nervous system. But I think—I do indeed, Miss Leicester— that we shall be able to set this all right. I have written him a prescription which ought to do great things. So you have no cause for anxiety."

My brother insisted on having the prescription made up by a chemist in the neighbourhood. It was an odd, oldfashioned shop, devoid of the studied coquetry and calculated glitter that make so gay a show on the counters and shelves of the modern apothecary; but Francis liked the old chemist, and believed in the scrupulous purity of his drugs. The medicine was sent in due course, and I saw that my brother took it regularly after lunch and dinner. It was an innocent-looking white powder, of which a little was dissolved in a glass of cold water; I stirred it in, and it seemed to disappear, leaving the water clear and colorless. At first Francis seemed to benefit greatly; the weariness vanished from his face, and he became more cheerful than he had ever been since the time when he left school; he talked gaily of reforming himself, and avowed to me that he had wasted his time.

"I have given too many hours to law," he said, laughing; "I think you have saved me in the nick of time. Come, I shall be Lord Chancellor yet, but I must not forget life. You and I will have a holiday together before long; we will go to Paris and enjoy ourselves, and keep away from the Bibliothèque Nationale."

I confessed myself delighted with the prospect.

"When shall we go?" I said. "I can start the day after to-morrow if you like."

"Ah! that is perhaps a little too soon; after all, I do not know London yet, and I suppose a man ought to give the pleasures of his own country the first choice. But we will go off together in a week or two, so try and furbish up your French. I only know law French myself, and I am afraid that wouldn't do."

We were just finishing dinner, and he quaffed off his medicine with a parade of carousal as if it had been wine from some choicest bin.

"Has it any particular taste?" I said.

"No; I should not know I was not drinking water," and he got up from his chair and began to pace up and down the room as if he were undecided as to what he should do next.

"Shall we have coffee in the drawing-room?" I said; "or would you like to smoke?"

"No, I think I will take a turn; it seems a pleasant evening. Look at the afterglow; why, it is as if a great city were burning in flames, and down there between the dark houses it is raining blood fast. Yes, I will go out; I may be in soon, but I shall take my key; so good-night, dear, if I don't see you again."

The door slammed behind him, and I saw him walk lightly down the street, swinging his malacca cane, and I felt grateful to Dr. Haberden for such an improvement.

I believe my brother came home very late that night, but he was in a merry mood the next morning.

"I walked on without thinking where I was going," he said, "enjoying the freshness of the air, and livened by the crowds as I reached more frequented quarters. And then I met an old college friend, Orford, in the press of the pavement, and then—well, we enjoyed ourselves, I have felt what it is to be young and a man; I find I have blood in my veins, as other men have. I made an appointment with Orford for tonight; there will be a little party of us at the restaurant. Yes; I shall enjoy myself for a week or two, and hear the chimes at midnight, and then we will go for our little trip together."

Such was the transmutation of my brother's character that in a few days he became a lover of pleasure, a careless and merry idler of western pavements, a hunter out of snug restaurants, and a fine critic of fantastic dancing; he grew fat before my eyes, and said no more of Paris, for he had clearly found his paradise in London. I rejoiced, and yet wondered a little; for there was, I thought, something in his gaiety that indefinitely displeased me, though I could not have defined my feeling. But by degrees there came a change; he returned still in the cold hours of the morning, but I heard no more about his pleasures, and one morning as we sat at breakfast together I looked suddenly into his eyes and saw a stranger before me.

"Oh, Francis!" I cried. "Oh, Francis, Francis, what have you done?" and rending sobs cut the words short. I went weeping out of the room; for though I knew nothing, yet I knew all, and by some odd play of thought I remembered the evening when he first went abroad, and the picture of the sunset sky glowed before me; the clouds like a city in burning flames, and the rain of blood. Yet I did battle with such thoughts, resolving that perhaps, after all, no great harm had been done, and in the evening at dinner I resolved to press him to fix a day for our holiday in Paris. We had talked easily enough, and my brother had just taken his medicine, which he continued all the while. I was about to begin my topic when the words forming in my mind vanished, and I wondered for a second what icy and intolerable weight oppressed my heart and suffocated me as with the unutterable horror of the coffin-lid nailed down on the living.

We had dined without candles; the room had slowly grown from twilight to gloom, and the walls and corners were indistinct in the shadow. But from where I sat I looked out into the street; and as I thought of what I would say to Francis, the sky began to flush and shine, as it had done on a well-remembered evening, and in the gap between two dark masses that were houses an awful pageantry of flame appeared—lurid whorls of writhed cloud, and utter depths burning, grey masses like the fume blown from a smoking city, and an evil glory blazing far above shot with tongues of more ardent fire, and below as if there were a deep pool of blood. I looked down to where my brother sat facing me, and the words were shaped on my lips, when I saw his hand resting on the table. Between the thumb and forefinger of the closed hand there was a mark, a small patch about the size of a sixpence, and somewhat of the colour of a bad bruise. Yet, by some sense I cannot define, I knew that what I saw was no bruise at all; oh! if human flesh could burn with flame, and if flame could be black as pitch, such was that before me. Without thought or fashioning of words grey horror shaped within me at the sight, and in an inner cell it was known to be a brand. For the moment the stained sky became dark as midnight, and when the light returned to me I was alone in the silent room, and soon after I heard my brother go out.

Late as it was, I put on my hat and went to Dr. Haberden, and in his great consulting room, ill lighted by a candle which the doctor brought in with him, with stammering lips, and a voice that would break in spite of my resolve, I told him all, from the day on which my brother began to take the medicine down to the dreadful thing I had seen scarcely half an hour before.

When I had done, the doctor looked at me for a minute with an expression of great pity on his face.

"My dear Miss Leicester," he said, "you have evidently been anxious about your brother; you have been worrying over him, I am sure. Come, now, is it not so?"

"I have certainly been anxious," I said. "For the last week or two I have not felt at ease."

"Quite so; you know, of course, what a queer thing the brain is?"

"I understand what you mean; but I was not deceived. I saw what I have told you with my own eyes."

"Yes, yes of course. But your eyes had been staring at that very curious sunset we had tonight. That is the only explanation. You will see it in the proper light tomorrow, I am sure. But, remember, I am always ready to give any help that is in my power; do not scruple to come to me, or to send for me if you are in any distress."

I went away but little comforted, all confusion and terror and sorrow, not knowing where to turn. When my brother and I met the next day, I looked quickly at him, and noticed, with a sickening at heart, that the right hand, the hand on which I had clearly seen the patch as of a black fire, was wrapped up with a handkerchief.

"What is the matter with your hand, Francis?" I said in a steady voice.

"Nothing of consequence. I cut a finger last night, and it bled rather awkwardly. So I did it up roughly to the best of my ability."

"I will do it neatly for you, if you like."

"No, thank you, dear; this will answer very well. Suppose we have breakfast; I am quite hungry."

We sat down and I watched him. He scarcely ate or drank at all, but tossed his meat to the dog when he thought my eyes were turned away; there was a look in his eyes that I had never yet seen, and the thought flashed across my mind that it was a look that was scarcely human. I was firmly convinced that awful and incredible as was the thing I had seen the night before, yet it was no illusion, no glamour of bewildered sense, and in the course of the evening I went again to the doctor's house.

He shook his head with an air puzzled and incredulous, and seemed to reflect for a few minutes.

"And you say he still keeps up the medicine? But why? As I understand, all the symptoms he complained of have disappeared long ago; why should he go on taking the stuff when he is quite well? And by the by, where did he get it made up? At Sayce's? I never send any one there; the old man is getting careless. Suppose you come with me to the chemist's; I should like to have some talk with him."

We walked together to the shop; old Sayce knew Dr. Haberden, and was quite ready to give any information.

"You have been sending that in to Mr. Leicester for some weeks, I think, on my prescription," said the doctor, giving the old man a pencilled scrap of paper.

The chemist put on his great spectacles with trembling uncertainty, and held up the paper with a shaking hand "Oh, yes," he said, "I have very little of it left; it is rather an uncommon drug, and I have had it in stock some time. I must get in some more, if Mr. Leicester goes on with it."

"Kindly let me have a look at the stuff," said Haberden, and the chemist gave him a glass bottle. He took out the stopper and smelt the contents, and looked strangely at the old man.

"Where did you get this?" he said, "and what is it? For one thing, Mr. Sayce, it is not what I prescribed. Yes, yes, I see the label is right enough, but I tell you this is not the drug."

"I have had it a long time," said the old man in feeble terror; "I got it from Burbage's in the usual way. It is not prescribed often, and I have had it on the shelf for some years. You see there is very little left."

"You had better give it to me," said Haberden. "I am afraid something wrong has happened."

We went out of the shop in silence, the doctor carrying the bottle neatly wrapped in paper under his arm.

"Dr. Haberden," I said, when we had walked a little way—"Dr. Haberden."

"Yes," he said, looking at me gloomily enough.

"I should like you to tell me what my brother has been taking twice a day for the last month or so."

"Frankly, Miss Leicester, I don't know. We will speak of this when we get to my house."

We walked on quickly without another word till we reached Dr. Haberden's. He asked me to sit down, and began pacing up and down the room, his face clouded over, as I could see, with no common fears.

"Well," he said at length, "this is all very strange; it is only natural that you should feel alarmed, and I must confess that my mind is far from easy. We will put aside, if you please, what you told me last night and this morning, but the fact remains that for the last few weeks Mr. Leicester has been impregnating his system with a drug which is completely unknown to me. I tell you, it is not what I ordered; and what the stuff in the bottle really is remains to be seen."

He undid the wrapper, and cautiously tilted a few grains of the white powder on to a piece of paper, and peered curiously at it.

"Yes," he said, "it is like the sulphate of quinine, as you say; it is flaky. But smell it."

He held the bottle to me, and I bent over it. It was a strange, sickly smell, vaporous and overpowering, like some strong anaesthetic.

"I shall have it analysed," said Haberden; "I have a friend who has devoted his whole life to chemistry as a science. Then we shall have something to go upon. No, no; say no more about that other matter; I cannot listen to that; and take my advice and think no more about it yourself."

That evening my brother did not go out as usual after dinner.

"I have had my fling," he said with a queer laugh, "and I must go back to my old ways. A little law will be quite a relaxation after so sharp a dose of pleasure," and he grinned to himself, and soon after went up to his room. His hand was still all bandaged.

Dr. Haberden called a few days later.

"I have no special news to give you," he said. "Chambers is out of town, so I know no more about that stuff than you do. But I should like to see Mr. Leicester, if he is in."

"He is in his room," I said; "I will tell him you are here."

"No, no, I will go up to him; we will have a little quiet talk together. I dare say that we have made a good deal of fuss about a very little; for, after all, whatever the powder may be, it seems to have done him good."

The doctor went upstairs, and standing in the hall I heard his knock, and the opening and shutting of the door; and then I waited in the silent house for an hour, and the stillness grew more and more intense as the hands of the clock crept round. Then there sounded from above the noise of a door shut sharply, and the doctor was coming down the stairs. His footsteps crossed the hall, and there was a pause at the door; I drew a long, sick breath with difficulty, and saw my face white in a little mirror, and he came in and stood at the door. There was an unutterable horror shining in his eyes; he steadied himself by holding the back of a chair with one hand, his lower lip trembled like a horse's, and he gulped and stammered unintelligible sounds before he spoke.

"I have seen that man," he began in a dry whisper. "I have been sitting in his presence for the last hour. My God! And I am alive and in my senses! I, who have dealt with death all my life, and have dabbled with the melting ruins of the earthly tabernacle. But not this, oh! not this," and he covered his face with his hands as if to shut out the sight of something before him.

"Do not send for me again, Miss Leicester," he said with more composure. "I can do nothing in this house. Goodbye."

As I watched him totter down the steps; and along the pavement towards his house, it seemed to me that he had aged by ten years since the morning.

My brother remained in his room. He called out to me in a voice I hardly recognized that he was very busy, and would like his meals brought to his door and left there, and I gave the order to the servants. From that day it seemed as if the arbitrary conception we call time had been annihilated for me; I lived in an ever-present sense of horror, going through the routine of the house mechanically, and only speaking a few necessary words to the servants. Now and then I went out and paced the streets for an hour or two and came home again; but whether I were without or within, my spirit delayed before the closed door of the upper room, and, shuddering, waited for it to open. I have said that I scarcely reckoned time; but I suppose it must have been a fortnight after Dr. Haberden's visit that I came home from my stroll a little refreshed and lightened. The air was sweet and pleasant, and the hazy form of green leaves, floating cloud-like in the square, and the smell of blossoms, had charmed my senses, and I felt happier and walked more briskly. As I delayed a moment at the verge of the pavement, waiting for a van to pass by before crossing over to the house, I happened to look up at the windows, and instantly there was the rush and swirl of deep cold waters in my ears, my heart leapt up and fell down, down as into a deep hollow, and I was amazed with a dread and terror without form or shape. I streched out a hand blindly through the folds of thick darkness, from the black and shadowy valley, and held myself from falling, while the stones beneath my feet rocked and swayed and tilted, and the sense of solid things seemed to sink away from under me. I had glanced up at the window of my brother's study, and at that moment the blind was drawn aside, and something that had life stared out into the world. Nay, I cannot say I saw a face or any human likeness; a living thing, two eyes of burning flame glared at me, and they were in the midst of something as formless as my fear, the symbol and presence of all evil and all hideous corruption. I stood shuddering and quaking as with the grip of ague, sick with unspeakable agonies of fear and loathing, and for five minutes I could not summon force or motion to my limbs. When I was within the door, I ran up the stairs to my brother's room and knocked.

"Francis, Francis," I cried, "for Heaven's sake, answer me. What is the horrible thing in your room? Cast it out, Francis; cast it from you."

I heard a noise as of feet shuffling slowly and awkwardly, and a choking, gurgling sound, as if some one was struggling to find utterance, and then the noise of a voice, broken and stifled, and words that I could scarcely understand.

"There is nothing here," the voice said. "Pray do not disturb me. I am not very well today."

I turned away, horrified, and yet helpless. I could do nothing, and I wondered why Francis had lied to me, for I had seen the appearance beyond the glass too plainly to be deceived, though it was but the sight of a moment. And I sat still, conscious that there had been something else, something I had seen in the first flash of terror, before those burning eyes had looked at me.

Suddenly I remembered; as I lifted my face the blind was being drawn back, and I had had an instant's glance of the thing that was moving it, and in my recollection I knew that a hideous image was engraved forever on my brain. It was not a hand; there were no fingers that held the blind, but a black stump pushed it aside, the mouldering outline and the clumsy movement as of a beast's paw had glowed into my senses before the darkling waves of terror had overwhelmed me as I went down quick into the pit. My mind was aghast at the thought of this, and of the awful presence that dwelt with my brother in his room; I went to his door and cried to him again, but no answer came. That night one of the servants came up to me and told me in a whisper that for three days food had been regularly placed at the door and left untouched; the maid had knocked but had received no answer; she had heard the noise of shuffling feet that I had noticed. Day after day went by, and still my brother's meals were brought to his door and left untouched; and though I knocked and called again and again, I could get no answer. The servants began to talk to me; it appeared they were as alarmed as I; the cook said that when my brother first shut himself up in his room she used to hear him come out at night and go about the house; and once, she said, the hall door had opened and closed again, but for several nights she had heard no sound.

The climax came at last; it was in the dusk of the evening, and I was sitting in the darkening dreary room when a terrible shriek jarred and rang harshly out of the silence, and I heard a frightened scurry of feet dashing down the stairs. I waited, and the servant-maid staggered into the room and faced me, white and trembling.

"Oh, Miss Helen!" she whispered; "oh! for the Lord's sake, Miss Helen, what has happened? Look at my hand, miss; look at that hand!" I drew her to the window, and saw there was a black wet stain upon her hand.

"I do not understand you," I said. "Will you explain to me?"

"I was doing your room just now," she began. "I was turning down the bed-clothes, and all of a sudden there was something fell upon my hand, wet, and I looked up, and the ceiling was black and dripping on me."

I looked hard at her and bit my lip.

"Come with me," I said. "Bring your candle with you."

The room I slept in was beneath my brother's, and as I went in I felt I was trembling. I looked up at the ceiling, and saw a patch, all black and wet, and a dew of black drops upon it, and a pool of horrible liquor soaking into the white bed-clothes.

I ran upstairs and knocked loudly.

"Oh, Francis, Francis, my dear brother," I cried, "what has happened to you?"

And I listened. There was a sound of choking, and a noise like water bubbling and regurgitating, but nothing else, and I called louder, but no answer came.

In spite of what Dr. Haberden had said, I went to him; with tears streaming down my cheeks I told him all that had happened, and he listened to me with a face set hard and grim.

"For your father's sake," he said at last, "I will go with you, though I can do nothing."

We went out together; the streets were dark and silent, and heavy with heat and a drought of many weeks. I saw the doctor's face white under the gas-lamps, and when we reached the house his hand was shaking.

We did not hesitate, but went upstairs directly. I held the lamp, and he called out in a loud, determined voice—"Mr. Leicester, do you hear me? I insist on seeing you. Answer me at once."

There was no answer, but we both heard that choking noise I have mentioned.

"Mr. Leicester, I am waiting for you. Open the door this instant, or I shall break it down." And he called a third time in a voice that rang and echoed from the walls—"Mr. Leicester! For the last time I order you to open the door."

"Ah!" he said, after a pause of heavy silence, "we are wasting time here. Will you be so kind as to get me a poker, or something of the kind?"

I ran into a little room at the back where odd articles were kept, and found a heavy adze-like tool that I thought might serve the doctor's purpose.

"Very good," he said, "that will do, I dare say. I give you notice, Mr. Leicester," he cried loudly at the keyhole, "that I am now about to break into your room."

Then I heard the wrench of the adze, and the woodwork split and cracked under it; with a loud crash the door suddenly burst open, and for a moment we started back aghast at a fearful screaming cry, no human voice, but as the roar of a monster, that burst forth inarticulate and struck at us out of the darkness.

"Hold the lamp," said the doctor, and we went in and glanced quickly round the room.

"There it is," said Dr. Haberden, drawing a quick breath; "look, in that corner."

I looked, and a pang of horror seized my heart as with a white-hot iron. There upon the floor was a dark and putrid mass, seething with corruption and hideous rottenness, neither liquid nor solid, but melting and changing before our eyes, and bubbling with unctuous oily bubbles like boiling pitch. And out of the midst of it shone two burning points like eyes, and I saw a writhing and stirring as of limbs, and something moved and lifted up what might have been an arm. The doctor took a step forward, raised the iron bar and struck at the burning points; he drove in the weapon, and struck again and again in the fury of loathing.

A week or two later, when I had recovered to some extent from the terrible shock, Dr. Haberden came to see me.

"I have sold my practice," he began, "and tomorrow I am sailing on a long voyage. I do not know whether I shall ever return to England; in all probability I shall buy a little land in California, and settle there for the remainder of my life. I have brought you this packet, which you may open and read when you feel able to do so. It contains the report of Dr. Chambers on what I submitted to him. Goodbye, Miss Leicester, goodbye."

When he was gone I opened the envelope; I could not wait, and proceeded to read the papers within. Here is the manuscript, and if you will allow me, I will read you the astounding story it contains.

"My dear Haberden," the letter began, "I have delayed inexcusably in answering your questions as to the white substance you sent me. To tell you the truth, I have hesitated for some time as to what course I should adopt, for there is a bigotry and orthodox standard in physical science as in theology, and I knew that if I told you the truth I should offend rooted prejudices which I once held dear myself. However, I have determined to be plain with you, and first I must enter into a short personal explanation.

"You have known me, Haberden, for many years as a scientific man; you and I have often talked of our profession together, and discussed the hopeless gulf that opens before the feet of those who think to attain to truth by any means whatsoever except the beaten way of experiment and observation in the sphere of material things. I remember the scorn with which you have spoken to me of men of science who have dabbled a little in the unseen, and have timidly hinted that perhaps the senses are not, after all, the eternal, impenetrable bounds of all knowledge, the everlasting walls beyond which no human being has ever passed. We have laughed together heartily, and I think justly, at the 'occult' follies of the day, disguised under various names—the mesmerisms, spiritualisms, materializations, theosophies, all the rabble rout of imposture, with their machinery of poor tricks and feeble conjuring, the true back-parlour of shabby London streets. Yet, in spite of what I have said, I must confess to you that I am no materialist, taking the word of course in its usual signification. It is now many years since I have convinced myself—convinced myself, a sceptic, remember—that the old ironbound theory is utterly and entirely false. Perhaps this confession will not wound you so sharply as it would have done twenty years ago; for I think you cannot have failed to notice that for some time hypotheses have been advanced by men of pure science which are nothing less than transcendental, and I suspect that most modern chemists and biologists of repute would not hesitate to subscribe the *dictum* of the old Schoolman, *Omnia exeunt in mysterium*, which means, I take it, that every branch of human knowledge if traced up to its source and final principles vanishes into mystery. I need not trouble you now with a detailed account of the painful steps which led me to my conclusions; a few simple experiments suggested a doubt as to my then standpoint, and a train of thought that rose from circumstances comparatively trifling brought me far; my old conception of the universe has been swept away, and I stand in a world that seems as strange and awful to me as the endless waves of the ocean seen for the first time, shining, from a peak in Darien. Now I know that the walls of sense that seemed so impenetrable, that seemed to loom up above the heavens and to be founded below the depths, and to shut us in for evermore, are no such everlasting impassable barriers as we fancied, but thinnest and most airy veils that melt away before the seeker, and dissolve as the early mist of the morning about the brooks. I know that you never adopted the extreme materialistic position; you did not go about trying to prove a universal negative, for your logical sense withheld you from that crowning absurdity; but I am sure that you will find all that I am saying strange and repellent to your habits of thought. Yet, Haberden, what I tell you is the truth, nay, to adopt our common language, the sole and scientific truth, verified by experience; and the universe is verily more splendid and more awful than we used to dream. The whole universe, my friend, is a tremendous sacrament; a mystic, ineffable force and energy, veiled by an outward form of matter; and man, and the sun and the other stars, and the flower of the grass, and the crystal in the test-tube, are each and every one as spiritual, as material, and subject to an inner working.

"You will perhaps wonder, Haberden, whence all this tends; but I think a little thought will make it clear. You will understand that from such a standpoint the whole view of things is changed, and what we thought incredible and absurd may be possible enough. In short, we must look at legend and belief with other eyes, and be prepared to accept tales that had become mere fables. Indeed this is no such great demand. After all, modern science will concede as much, in a hypocritical manner; you must not, it is true, believe in witchcraft, but you may credit hypnotism; ghosts are out of date, but there is a good deal to be said for the theory of telepathy. Give superstition a Greek name, and believe in it, should almost be a proverb.

"So much for my personal explanation. You sent me, Haberden, a phial, stoppered and sealed, containing a small quantity of flaky white powder, obtained from a chemist who has been dispensing it to one of your patients. I am not surprised to hear that this powder refused to yield any results to your analysis. It is a substance which was known to a few many hundred years ago, but which I never expected to have submitted to me from the shop of a modern apothecary. There seems no reason to doubt the truth of the man's tale; he no doubt got, as he says, the rather uncommon salt you prescribed from the wholesale chemist's, and it has probably remained on his shelf for twenty years, or perhaps longer. Here what we call chance and coincidence begin to work; during all these years the salt in the bottle was exposed to certain recurring variations of temperature, variations probably ranging from 40° to 80°. And, as it happens, such changes, recurring year after year at irregular intervals, and with varying degrees of intensity and duration, have constituted a process, and a process so complicated and so delicate, that I question whether modern scientific apparatus directed with the utmost precision could produce the same result. The white powder you sent me is something very different from the drug you prescribed; it is the powder from which the wine of the Sabbath, the *Vinum Sabbati*, was prepared. No doubt you have read of the Witches' Sabbath, and have laughed at the tales which terrified our ancestors; the black cats, and the broomsticks, and dooms pronounced against some old woman's cow. Since I have known the truth I have often reflected that it is on the whole a happy thing that such burlesque as this is believed, for it serves to conceal much that it is better should not be known generally. However, if you care to read the appendix to Payne Knight's monograph, you will find that the true Sabbath was something very different, though the writer has very nicely refrained from printing all he knew. The secrets of the true Sabbath were the secrets of remote times surviving into the Middle Ages, secrets of an evil science which existed long before Aryan man entered Europe. Men and women, seduced from their homes on specious pretences, were met by beings well qualified to assume, as they did assume, the part of devils, and taken by their guides to some desolate and lonely place, known to the initiate by long tradition, and unknown to all else. Perhaps it was a cave in some bare and windswept hill, perhaps some inmost recess of a great forest, and there the Sabbath was held. There, in the blackest hour of night, the *Vinum Sabbati* was prepared, and this evil gruel was poured forth and offered to the neophytes, and they partook of an infernal sacrament; *sumentes calicem principis inferorum*, as an old author well expresses it. And suddenly, each one that had drunk found himself attended by a companion, a share of glamour and unearthly allurement, beckoning him apart, to share in joys more exquisite, more piercing than the thrill of any dream, to the consummation of the marriage of the Sabbath. It is hard to write of such things as these, and chiefly because that shape that allured with loveliness was no hallucination, but, awful as it is to express, the man himself. By the power of that Sabbath wine, a few grains of white powder thrown into a glass of water, the house of life was riven asunder and the human trinity dissolved, and the worm which never dies, that which lies sleeping within us all, was made tangible and an external thing, and clothed with a garment of flesh. And then, in the hour of midnight, the primal fall was repeated and re-presented, and the awful thing veiled in the mythos of the Tree in the Garden was done anew. Such was the *nuptiæ Sabbati.*

"I prefer to say no more; you, Haberden, know as well as I do that the most trivial laws of life are not to be broken with impunity; and for so terrible an act as this, in which the very inmost place of the temple was broken open and defiled, a terrible vengeance followed. What began with corruption ended also with corruption."

Underneath is the following in Dr. Haberden's writing:—
"The whole of the above is unfortunately strictly and entirely true. Your brother confessed all to me on that morning when I saw him in his room. My attention was first attracted to the bandaged hand, and I forced him to show it to me. What I saw made me, a medical man of many years' standing, grow sick with loathing, and the story I was forced to listen to was infinitely more frightful than I could have believed possible. It has tempted me to doubt the Eternal Goodness which can permit nature to offer such hideous possibilities; and if you had not with your own eyes seen the end, I should have said to you—disbelieve it all. I have not, I think, many more weeks to live, but you are young, and may forget all this.
"JOSEPH HABERDEN, M.D."

In the course of two or three months I heard that Dr. Haberden had died at sea shortly after the ship left England.

XÉLUCHA

by M. P. Shiel

"He goeth after her . . . and knoweth not . . ."

[FROM A DIARY]

THREE days ago! by heaven, it seems an age. But I am shaken—my reason is debauched. A while since, I fell into a momentary coma precisely resembling an attack of *petit mal*. "Tombs, and worms, and epitaphs"—that is my dream. At my age, with my physique, to walk staggery, like a man stricken! But all that will pass: I must collect myself—my reason is debauched. Three days ago! it seems an age! I sat on the floor before an old cista full of letters. I lighted upon a packet of Cosmo's. Why, I had forgotten them! they are turning sere! Truly, I can no more call myself a young man. I sat reading, listlessly, rapt back by memory. To muse is to be lost! of *that* evil habit I must wring the neck, or look to perish. Once more I threaded the mazy sphere-harmony of the minuet, reeled in the waltz, long pomps of candelabra, the noonday of the bacchanal, about me. Cosmo was the very tsar and maharajah of the Sybarites! the Priap of the *détraqués!* In every unexpected alcove of the Roman Villa was a couch, raised high, with necessary foot-stool, flanked and canopied

153

with *mirrors* of clarified gold. Consumption fastened upon him; reclining at last at table, he could, till warmed, scarce lift the wine! his eyes were like two fat glow-worms, coiled together! they seemed haloed with vaporous emanations of phosphorus! Desperate, one could see, was the secret struggle with the Devourer. But to the end the princely smile persisted calm; to the end—to the last day—he continued among that comic crew unchallenged choragus of all the rites, I will not say of Paphos, but of Chemos! and Baal-Peor! Warmed, he did not refuse the revel, the dance, the darkened chamber. It was utterly black, rayless; approached by a secret passage; in shape circular; the air hot, haunted always by odours of balms, bdellium, hints of dulcimer and flute; and radiated round with a hundred thick-strewn ottomans of Morocco. Here Lucy Hill stabbed to the heart Caccofogo, mistaking the scar of his back for the scar of Soriac. In a bath of malachite the Princess Egla, waking late one morning, found Cosmo lying stiffly dead, the water covering him wholly.

"But in God's name, Mérimée!" (so he wrote), "to think of Xélucha dead! Xélucha! Can a moon-beam, then, perish of suppurations? Can the rainbow be eaten by worms? Ha! ha! ha! laugh with me, my friend: '*elle dérangera l'Enfer*'! She will introduce the *pas de tarantule* into Tophet! Xélucha, the feminine Xélucha recalling the splendid harlots of history! Weep with me—manat rara meas lacrima per genas! expert as Thargelia; cultured as Aspatia; purple as Semiramis. She comprehended the human tabernacle, my friend, its secret springs and tempers, more intimately than any *savant* of Salamanca who breathes. *Tarare*—but Xélucha is not dead! Vitality is not mortal; you cannot wrap flame in a shroud. Xélucha! where then is she? Translated, perhaps—rapt to a constellation like the daughter of Leda. She journeyed to Hindostan, accompanied by the train and appurtenance of a Begum, threatening descent upon the Emperor of Tartary. I spoke of the desolation of the West; she kissed me, and promised return. Mentioned you, too, Mérimée—'her Conqueror'—'Mérimée, Destroyer of Woman.' A breath from the conservatory rioted among the ambery whiffs of her forelocks, sending it singly a-wave over that thulite tint you know. Costumed cap-à-pie, she had, my friend, the dainty little completeness of a daisy mirrored bright in the eye of the browsing ox. A simile of Milton had for years, she said, inflamed the lust of her Eye: 'The barren plains of Sericana, where Chineses drive with sails and wind their cany wagons light.' I, and the Sabæans, she assured me, wrongly considered Flame the whole of being; the other half of things being Aristotle's quintessential light. In the Ourania Hierarchia and the Faust-book you meet a completeness: burning Seraph, Cherub full of eyes. Xélucha combined them. She would reconquer the Orient for Dionysius, and return. I heard of her blazing at Delhi; drawn in a chariot by lions. Then this rumour—probably false. Indeed, it comes from a source somewhat turgid. Like Odin, Arthur, and the rest, Xélucha—will reappear."

Soon subsequently, Cosmo lay down in his balneum of malechite, and slept, having drawn over him the water as a coverlet. I, in England, heard little of Xélucha: first that she was alive, then dead, then alighted at old Tadmor in the Wilderness, Palmyra now. Nor did I greatly care, Xélucha having long since turned to apples of Sodom in my mouth. Till I sat by the cista of letters and re-read Cosmo, she had for some years passed from my active memories.

The habit is now confirmed in me of spending the greater part of the day in sleep, while by night I wander far and wide through the city under the sedative influence of a tincture which has become necessary to my life. Such an existence of shadow is not without charm; nor, I think, could many minds be steadily subjected to its conditions without elevation, deepened awe. To travel alone with the Primordial cannot but be solemn. The moon is of the hue of the glow-worm; and Night of the sepulchre. Nux bore not less Thanatos than Hupuos, and the bitter tears of Isis redundulate to a flood. At three, if a cab rolls by, the sound has the augustness of thunder. Once, at two, near a corner, I came upon a priest, seated, dead, leering, his legs bent. One arm, supported on a knee, pointed with rigid accusing forefinger obliquely upward. By exact observation, I found that he indicated Betelgeux, the star "*a*" which shoulders the wet sword of Orion. He was hideously swollen, having perished of dropsy. Thus in all Supremes is a *grotesquerie*; and one of the sons of Night is—Buffo.

In a London square deserted, I should imagine, even in the day, I was aware of the metallic, silvery-clinking approach of little shoes. It was three in a heavy morning of winter, a day after my rediscovery of Cosmo. I had stood by the railing, regarding the clouds sail as under the sea-legged pilotage of a moon wrapped in cloaks of inclemency. Turning, I saw a little lady, very gloriously dressed. She had walked straight to me. Her head was bare, and crisped with the amber stream which rolled lax to a globe, kneaded thick with jewels, at her nape. In the redundance of her décolleté development, she resembled Parvati, mound-hipped love-goddess of the luscious fancy of the Brahmin.

She addressed to me the question:

"What are you doing there, darling?"

Her loveliness stirred me, and Night is *bon camarade*. I replied:

"Sunning myself by means of the moon."

"All that is borrowed lustre," she returned, "you have got it from old Drummond's *Flowers of Sion*."

Looking back, I cannot remember that this reply astonished me, though it should—of course—have done so. I said:

"On my soul, no; but you?"

"You might guess whence *I* come!"

"You are dazzling. You come from Paz."

"Oh, farther than that, my son! Say a subscription ball in Soho."

"Yes? . . . and alone? in the cold? on foot . . . ?"

"Why, I am old, and a philosopher. I can pick you out riding Andromeda yonder from the ridden Ram. They are in error, M'sieur, who suppose an atmosphere on the broad side of the moon. I have reason to believe that on Mars dwells a race whose lids are transparent like glass; so that the eyes are visible during sleep; and every varying dream moves imaged forth to the beholder in tiny panorama on the limpid iris. You cannot imagine me a mere *fille*! To be escorted is to admit yourself a woman, and that is improper in Nowhere. Young Eos drives an *équipage à quatre*, but Artemis 'walks' alone. Get out of my borrowed light in the name of Diogenes! I am going home."

"Near Piccadilly."

"But a cab?"

"No cabs for *me*, thank you. The distance is a mere nothing. Come."

We walked forward. My companion at once put an interval between us, quoting from the *Spanish Curate* that the open is an enemy to love. The Talmudists, she twice insisted, rightly held the hand the sacredest part of the person, and at that point also contact was for the moment interdict. Her walk was extremely rapid. I followed. Not a cat was anywhere visible. We reached at length the door of a mansion in St. James's. There was no light. It seemed tenantless, the windows all uncurtained, pasted across, some of them, with the words, To Let. My companion, however, flitted up the steps, and, beckoning, passed inward. I, following, slammed the door, and was in darkness. I heard her ascend, and presently a region of glimmer above revealed a stairway of marble, curving broadly up. On the floor where I stood was no carpet, nor furniture: the dust was very thick. I had begun to mount when, to my surprise, she stood by my side, returned; and whispered:

"To the very top, darling."

She soared nimbly up, anticipating me. Higher, I could no longer doubt that the house was empty but for us. All was a vacuum full of dust and echoes. But at the top, light streamed from a door, and I entered a good-sized oval saloon, at about the centre of the house. I was completely dazzled by the sudden resplendence of the apartment. In the midst was a spread table, square, opulent with gold plate, fruit dishes; three ponderous chandeliers of electric light above; and I noticed also (what was very *bizarre*) one little candlestick of common tin containing an old soiled curve of tallow, on the table. The impression of the whole chamber was one of gorgeousness not less than Assyrian. An ivory couch at the far end was made sun-like by a head-piece of chalcedony forming a sea for the sport of emerald ichthyotauri. Copper hangings, panelled with mirrors in iasperated crystal, corresponded with a dome of flame and copper; yet this latter, I now remember, produced upon my glance an impression of actual grime. My companion reclined on a small Sigma couch, raised high to the table-level in the Semitic manner, visible to her saffron slippers of satin. She pointed me a seat opposite. The incongruity of its presence in the middle of this arrogance of pomp so tickled me, that no power could have kept me from a smile: it was a grimy chair, mean, all wood, nor was I long in discovering one leg somewhat shorter than its fellows.

She indicated wine in a black glass bottle, and a tumbler, but herself made no pretence of drinking or eating. She lay on hip and elbow, *petite*, resplendent, and looked gravely upward. I, however, drank.

"You are tired," I said, "one sees that."

"It is precious little than *you* see!" she returned, dreamy, hardly glancing.

"How! your mood is changed, then? You are morose."

"You never, I think, saw a Norse passage-grave?"

"And abrupt."

"Never?"

"A passage-grave? No."

"It is worth a journey! They are circular or oblong chambers of stone, covered by great earthmounds, with a 'passage' of slabs connecting them with the outer air. All round the chamber the dead sit with head resting upon the bent knees, and consult together in silence."

"Drink wine with me, and be less Tartarean."

"You certainly seem to be a fool," she replied with perfect sardonic iciness. "Is it not, then, highly romantic? They belong, you know, to the Neolithic age. As the teeth fall, one by one, from the lipless mouths—they are caught by the lap. When the lap thins—they roll to the floor of stone. Thereafter, every tooth that drops all round the chamber sharply breaks the silence."

"Ha! ha! ha!"

"Yes. It is like a century-slow, circularly-successive dripping of slime in some cavern of the far subterrene."

"Ha! ha! This wine seems heady! They express themselves in a dialect largely dental."

"The Ape, on the other hand, in a language wholly guttural."

A town-clock tolled four. Our talk was holed with silences, and heavy-paced. The wine's yeasty exhalation reached my brain. I saw her through mist, dilating large, uncertain, shrinking again to dainty compactness. But amorousness had died within me.

"Do you know," she asked, "what has been discovered in one of the Danish *Kjökkenmöddings* by a little boy? It was ghastly. The skeleton of a huge fish with human——"

"You are most unhappy."

"Be silent."

"You are full of care."

"I think you a great fool."

"You are racked with misery."

"You are a child. You have not even an instinct of the meaning of the word."

"How! Am I not a man? I, too, miserable, careful?"

"You are not, really, *anything*—until you can create."

"Create what?"

"Matter."

"That is foppish. Matter cannot he created, nor destroyed."

"Truly, then, you must be a creature of unusually weak intellect. I see that now. Matter does not exist, then, there is no such thing, really—it is an appearance, a spectrum—every writer not imbecile from Plato to Fichte has, voluntary or involuntary, proved that for good. To create it is to produce an impression of its reality upon the senses of others; to destroy it is to wipe a wet rag across a scribbled slate."

"Perhaps. I do not care. Since no one can do it"

"No one? You are mere embryo——"

"Who then?"

"*Anyone*, whose power of Will is equivalent to the gravitating force of a star of the First Magnitude."

"Ha! ha! ha! By heaven, you choose to be facetious. Are there then wills of such equivalence?"

"There have been three, the founders of religions. There was a fourth: a cobbler of Herculaneum, whose mere volition induced the cataclysm of Vesuvius in 79, in direct opposition to the gravity of Sirius. There are more fames than *you* have ever sung, you know. The greater number of disembodied spirits, too, I feel certain——"

"By heaven, I cannot but think you full of sorrow! Poor wight! come, drink with me. The wine is thick and boon. Is it not Setian? It makes you sway and swell before me, I swear, like a purple cloud of evening——"

"But you are mere clayey ponderance!—I did not know that!—you are no companion! your little interest revolves round the lowest centres."

"Come—forget your agonies——"

"What, think you, is the portion of the buried body first sought by the worm?"

"The eyes! the eyes!"

"You are *hideously* wrong—you are so *utterly* at sea——"

"My God!"

She had bent forward with such rage of contradiction as to approach me closely. A loose gown of amber silk, wide-sleeved, had replaced her ball attire, though at what opportunity I could not guess; wondering, I noticed it as she now placed her palms far forth upon the table. A sudden wafture as of spice and orange-flowers, mingled with the abhorrent faint odour of mortality over-ready for the tomb, greeted my sense. A chill crept upon my flesh.

"You are so *hopelessly* at fault——"

"For God's sake——"

"You are so *miserably* deluded! Not the eyes *at all!*"

"Then, in heaven's name, what?"

Five tolled from a clock.

"*The Uvula!* the soft drop of mucous flesh, you know, suspended from the palate above the glottis. They eat through the face-cloth and cheek, or crawl by the lips through a broken tooth, filling the mouth. They make straight for it. It is the *deliciæ* of the vault."

At her horror of interest I grew sick, at her odour, and her words. Some unspeakable sense of insignificance, of debility, held me dumb.

"You say I am full of sorrows. You say I am racked with woe; that I gnash with anguish. Well, you are a mere child in intellect. You use words without realization of meaning like those minds in what Leibnitz calls 'symbolical consciousness.' But suppose it were so——"

"It is so."

"You know nothing."

"I see you twist and grind. Your eyes are very pale. I thought they were hazel. They are of the faint bluishness of phosphorus shimmerings seen in darkness."

"That proves nothing."

"But the 'white' of the sclerotic is dyed to yellow. And you look inward. Why do you look so palely inward, so woe-worn, upon your soul? Why can you speak of nothing but the sepulchre, and its rottenness? Your eyes seem to me wan with centuries of vigil, with mysteries and millenniums of pain."

"Pain! but you know so *little* of it! you are wind and words! of its philosophy and *rationale* nothing!"

"Who knows?"

"I will give you a hint. It is the sub-consciousness in conscious creatures of Eternity, and of eternal loss. The least prick of a pin not Pæan and Æsculapius and the powers of heaven and hell can utterly heal. Of an everlasting loss of pristine wholeness the conscious body is sub-conscious, and 'pain' is its sigh at the tragedy. So with all pain—greater, the greater the loss. The hugest of losses is, of course, the loss of Time. If you lose that, any of it, you plunge at once into the transcendentalisms, the infinitudes, of Loss; if you lose *all of it*——"

"But you so wildly exaggerate! Ha! ha! You rant, I tell you, of commonplaces with the woe——"

"Hell is where a clear, untrammelled Spirit is sub-conscious of lost Time; where it boils and writhes with envy of the living world; hating it for ever, and all the sons of Life!"

"But curb yourself! Drink—I implore—I *implore*—for God's sake—but *once*——"

"To *hasten* to the snare—*that* is woe! to drive your ship upon the *lighthouse* rock—that is Marah! To wake, and feel it irrevocably true that you went after her—*and the dead were there*—and her guests were in the depths of hell—*and you did not know it*!—though you *might* have. Look out upon the houses of the city this dawning day: not one, I tell you, but in it haunts some soul—walking up and down the old theatre of its little Day—goading imagination by a thousand childish tricks, vraisemblances—elaborately duping itself into the momentary fantasy *that it still lives*, that the chance of life is not for ever and for ever lost—yet riving all the time with under-memories of the wasted Summer, the lapsed brief light between the two eternal glooms—riving I say and shriek to you!—riving, *Mérimée, you destroying fiend*——"

She had sprung—*tall* now, she seemed to me—between couch and table.

"Mérimée!" I screamed,——"*my* name, harlot, in your maniac mouth! By God, woman, you terrify me to death!"

I too sprang, the hairs of my head catching stiff horror from my fancies.

"Your name? Can you imagine me ignorant of your name, or anything concerning you? Mérimée! Why, did you not sit yesterday and read of me in a letter of Cosmo's?"

"Ah-h . . ." hysteria bursting high in sob and laughter from my arid lips—"Ah! ha! ha! Xélucha! My memory grows palsied and grey, Xélucha! pity me—my walk is in the very valley of shadow!—senile and sere!—observe my hair, Xélucha, its grizzled growth—trepidant, Xélucha, clouded—I am not the man you knew, Xélucha, in the palaces—of Cosmo! You are Xélucha!"

"You rave, poor worm!" she cried, her face contorted by a species of malicious contempt. "Xélucha died of cholera ten years ago at Antioch. I wiped the froth from her lips. Her nose underwent a green decay beforc burial. So far sunken into the brain was the left eye——"

"You are—*you are Xélucha!*" I shrieked; "voices now of thunder howl it within my consciousness—and by the holy God, Xélucha, though you blight me with the breath of the hell you are, I shall clasp you, living or damned——"

I rushed toward her. The word "Madman!" hissed as by the tongues of ten thousand serpents through the chamber, I heard; a belch of pestilent corruption puffed poisonous upon the putrid air; for a moment to my wildered eyes there seemed to rear itself, swelling high to the roof, a formless tower of ragged cloud, and before my projected arms had closed upon the very emptiness of insanity, I was tossed by the operation of some Behemoth potency far-circling backward to the utmost circumference of the oval, where, my head colliding, I fell, shocked, into insensibility.

When the sun was low toward night, I lay awake, and listlessly observed the grimy roof, and the sordid chair, and the candlestick of tin, and the bottle of which I had drunk. The table was small, filthy, of common deal, uncovered. All bore the appearance of having stood there for years. But for them, the room was void, the vision of luxury thinned to air. Sudden memory flashed upon me. I scrambled to my feet, and plunged and tottered, bawling, through the twilight into the street.

THE FACE OF THE MONK

by Robert Hichens

I

"NO, it will not hurt him to see you," the doctor said to me; "and I have no doubt he will recognise you. He is the quietest patient I have ever had under my care—gentle, kind, agreeable, perfect in conduct, and yet quite mad. You know him well?"

"He was my dearest friend," I said. "Before I went out to America three years ago we were inseparable. Doctor, I cannot believe that he is mad, he—Hubert Blair—one of the cleverest young writers in London, so brilliant, so acute! Wild, if you like, a libertine perhaps, a strange mixture of the intellectual and the sensual—but mad! I can't believe it!"

"Not when I tell you that he was brought to me suffering from acute religious mania?"

"Religious! Hubert Blair!"

"Yes. He tried to destroy himself, declaring that he was unfit to live, that he was a curse to some person unknown. He protested that each deed of his affected this unknown person, that his sins were counted as the sins of another, and that this other had haunted him—would haunt him for ever."

The doctor's words troubled me.

"Take me to him," I said at last. "Leave us together."

It was a strange, sad moment when I entered the room in which Hubert was sitting. I was painfully agitated. He knew me, and greeted me warmly. I sat down opposite to him.

✳

There was a long silence. Hubert looked away into the fire. He saw, I think, traced in scarlet flames, the scenes he was going to describe to me; and I, gazing at him, wondered of what nature the change in my friend might be. That he had changed since we were together three years ago was evident, yet he did not look mad. His dark, clean-shaven young face was still passionate. The brown eyes were still lit with a certain devouring eagerness. The mouth had not lost its mingled sweetness and sensuality. But Hubert was curiously transformed. There was a dignity, almost an elevation, in his manner. His former gaiety had vanished. I knew, without words, that my friend was another man—very far away from me now. Yet once we had lived together as chums, and had no secrets the one from the other.

At last Hubert looked up and spoke.

"I see you are wondering about me," he said.

"Yes."

"I have altered, of course—completely altered."

"Yes," I said, awkwardly enough. "Why is that?"

I longed to probe this madness of his that I might convince myself of it, otherwise Hubert's situation must for ever appal me.

He answered quietly, "I will tell you—nobody else knows—and even you may—"

He hesitated, then he said:—

"No, you will believe it."

"Yes, if you tell me it is true."

"It is absolutely true.

"Bernard, you know what I was when you left England for America—gay, frivolous in my pleasures, although earnest when I was working. You know how I lived to sound the depths of sensation, how I loved to stretch all my mental and physical capacities to the snapping-point, how I shrank from no sin that could add one jot or tittle to my knowledge of the mind of any man or woman who interested me. My life seemed a full life then. I moved in the midst of a thousand intrigues. I strung beads of all emotions upon my rosary, and told them until at times my health gave way. You remember my recurring periods of extraordinary and horrible mental depression—when life was a demon to me, and all my success in literature less than nothing; when I fancied myself hated, and could believe I heard phantom voices abusing me. Then those fits passed away, and once more I lived as ardently as ever, the most persistent worker, and the most persistent excitement-seeker in London.

"Well, after you went away I continued my career. As you know, my success increased. Through many sins I had succeeded in diving very deep into human hearts of men and women. Often I led people deliberately away from innocence in order that I might observe the gradual transformation of their natures. Often I spurred them on to follies that I might see the effect our deeds have upon our faces—the seal our actions set upon our souls. I was utterly unscrupulous, and yet I thought myself good-hearted. You remember that my servants always loved me, that I attracted people. I can say this to you. For some time my usual course was not stayed. Then—I recollect it was in the middle of the London season—one of my horrible fits of unreasonable melancholy swept over me. It stunned my soul like a heavy blow. It numbed me. I could not go about. I could not bear to see anybody. I could only shut myself up and try to reason myself back into my usual gaiety and excitement. My writing was put aside. My piano was locked. I tried to read, but even that solace was denied to me. My attention was utterly self-centred, riveted upon my own condition.

"Why, I said to myself, am I the victim of this despair, this despair without a cause? What is this oppression which weighs me down without reason? It attacks me abruptly, as if it were sent to me by some power, shot at me like an arrow by an enemy hidden in the dark. I am well—I am gay. Life is beautiful and wonderful to me. All that I do interests me. My soul is full of vitality. I know that I have troops of friends, that I am loved and thought of by many people. And then suddenly the arrow strikes me. My soul is wounded and sickens to death. Night falls over me, night so sinister that I shudder when its twilight comes. All my senses faint within me. Life is at once a hag, weary, degraded, with tears on her cheeks and despair in her hollow eyes. I feel that I am deserted, that my friends despise me, that the world hates me, that I am less than all other men—less in powers, less in attraction—that I am the most crawling, the most grovelling of all the human species, and that there is no one who does not know it. Yet the doctors say I am not physically ill, and I know that I am not mad. Whence does this awful misery, this unmeaning, causeless horror of life and of myself come? Why am I thus afflicted?

"Of course I could find no answer to all these old questions, which I had asked many times before. But this time, Bernard, my depression was more lasting, more overwhelming than usual. I grew terribly afraid of it. I thought I might be driven to suicide. One day a crisis seemed to come. I dared no longer remain alone, so I put on my hat and coat, took my stick, and hurried out, without any definite intention. I walked along Piccadilly, avoiding the glances of those whom

I met. I fancied they could all read the agony, the degradation of my soul. I turned into Bond Street, and suddenly I felt a strong inclination to stop before a certain door. I obeyed the impulse, and my eyes fell on a brass plate, upon which was engraved these words:—

Vane.

Clairvoyant.

11 till 4 daily.

"I remember I read them several times over, and even repeated them in a whisper to myself. Why? I don't know. Then I turned away, and was about to resume my walk. But I could not. Again I stopped and read the legend on the brass plate. On the right-hand side of the door was an electric bell. I put my finger on it and pressed the button inwards. The door opened, and I walked, like a man in a dream, I think, up a flight of narrow stairs. At the top of them was a second door, at which a maidservant was standing.

"'You want to see Mr. Vane, sir?'

"'Yes. Can I?'

"'If you will come in, sir, I will see.'

"She showed me into a commonplace, barely-furnished little room, and, after a short period of waiting, summoned me to another, in which stood a tall, dark youth, dressed in a gown rather like a college gown. He bowed to me, and I silently returned the salutation. The servant left us. Then he said:—

"'You wish me to exert my powers for you?'

"'Yes.'

"'Will you sit here?'

"He motioned me to a seat beside a small round table, sat down opposite to me, and took my hand. After examining it through a glass, and telling my character fairly correctly by the lines in it, he laid the glass down and regarded me narrowly.

"'You suffer terribly from depression,' he said.

"'That is true.'

"He continued to gaze upon me more and more fixedly. At length he said:—

"'Do you know that everybody has a companion?'

"'How—a companion?'

"'Somebody incessantly with them, somebody they cannot see.'

"'You believe in the theory of guardian angels?'

"'I do not say these companions are always guardian angels. I see your companion now, as I look at you. His face is by your shoulder.'

"I started, and glanced hastily round; but, of course, could see nothing.

"'Shall I describe him?'

"'Yes,' I said.

"'His face is dark, like yours; shaven, like yours. He has brown eyes, just as brown as yours are. His mouth and his chin are firm and small, as firm and small as yours.'

"'He must be very like me.'

"'He is. But there is a difference between you.'

"'What is it?'

"'His hair is cut more closely than yours, and part of it is shaved off.'

"'He is a priest, then?'

"'He wears a cowl. He is a monk.'

"'A monk! But why does he come to me?'

"'I should say that he cannot help it, that he is your spirit in some former state. Yes'—and he stared at me till his eyes almost mesmerised me—'you must have been a monk once.'

"'I—a monk! Impossible! Even if I have lived on earth before, it could never have been as a monk.'

"'How do you know that?'

"'Because I am utterly without superstitions, utterly free from any lingering desire for an ascetic life. That existence of silence, of ignorance, of perpetual prayer, can never have been mine.'

"'You cannot tell,' was all his answer.

II

"When I left Bond Street that afternoon I was full of disbelief. However, I had paid my half-guinea and escaped from my own core of misery for a quarter of an hour. That was something. I didn't regret my visit to this man Vane, whom I regarded as an agreeable charlatan. For a moment he had interested me. For a moment he had helped me to forget my useless wretchedness. I ought to have been grateful to him. And, as always, my soul regained its composure at last. One morning I awoke and said to myself that I was happy. Why? I did not know. But I got up. I was able to write once more. I was able to play. I felt that I had friends who loved me and a career before me. I could again look people in the face without fear. I could even feel a certain delightful conceit of mind and body. Bernard, I was myself. So I thought, so I knew. And yet, as days went by, I caught myself often thinking of this invisible, tonsured, and cowled companion of mine, whom Vane had seen, whom I did not see. Was he indeed with me? And, if so, had he thoughts, had he the holy thoughts of a spirit that has renounced the world and all fleshly things? Did he still keep that cloistered nature which is at home with silence, which aspires, and prays, and lives for possible eternity, instead of for certain time? Did he still hold desolate vigils? Did he still scourge himself along the thorny paths of faith? And, if he did, how must he regard me?

"I remember one night especially how this last thought was with me in a dreary house, where I sinned, and where I dissected a heart.

"And I trembled as if an eye was upon me. And I went home.

"You will say that my imagination is keen, and that I gave way to it. But wait and hear the end.

"This definite act of mine—this, my first conscious renunciation—did not tend, as you might suppose, to the peace of my mind. On the contrary, I found myself angry, perturbed, as I analysed the cause of my warfare with self. I have naturally a supreme hatred of all control. Liberty is my fetish. And now I had offered a sacrifice to a prisoning unselfishness, to a false god that binds and gags its devotees. I was angry, and I violently resumed my former course. But now I began to be ceaselessly companioned by uneasiness, by a furtive cowardice that was desolating. I felt that I was watched, and by some one who suffered when I sinned, who shrank and shuddered when I followed where my desires led.

"It was the monk.

"Soon I gave to him a most definite personality. I endowed him with a mind and with moods. I imagined not only a heart for him, but a voice, deep with a certain ecclesiastical beauty, austere, with a note more apt for denunciation than for praise. His face was my own face, but with an expression not mine, elevated, almost fanatical, yet nobly beautiful; praying eyes— and mine were only observant; praying lips—and mine were but sensitively sensual. And he was haggard with abstinence, while I—was I not often haggard with indulgence? Yes, his face was mine, and not mine. It seemed the face of a great saint who might have been a great sinner. Bernard, that is the most attractive face in all the world. Accustoming myself thus to a thought-companion, I at length—for we men are so inevitably materialistic—embodied him, gave to him hands,

172

feet, a figure, all—as before, mine, yet not mine, a sort of saintly replica of my sinfulness. For do not hands, feet, figure cry our deeds as the watchman cries the hour in the night?

"So, I had the man. There he stood in my vision as you are now.

"Yes, he was there; but only when I sinned.

"When I worked and yielded myself up to the clear assertion of my intellect, when I fought to give out the thoughts that lingered like reluctant fish far down in the deep pools of my mind, when I wrestled for beauty of diction and for nameless graces of expression, when I was the author, I could not see him.

"But when I was the man, and lived the fables that I was afterwards to write, then he was with me. And his face was as the face of one who is wasted with grey grief.

"He came to me when I sinned, as if by my sins I did him grave injury. And, allowing my imagination to range wildly, as you will say, I grew gradually to feel as if each sin did indeed strike a grievous blow upon his holy nature.

"This troubled me at last. I found myself continually brooding over the strange idea. I was aware that if my friends could know I entertained it, they would think me mad. And yet I often fancied that thought moved me in the direction of a sanity more perfect, more desirable than my sanity of self-indulgence. Sometimes even I said to myself that I would reorganise my life, that I would be different from what I had been. And then, again, I laughed at my folly of the imagination, and cursed that clairvoyant of Bond Street, who made a living by trading upon the latent imbecility of human nature. Yet, the desire of change, of soul-transformation, came and lingered, and the vision of the monk's worn young face was often with me. And whenever, in my waking dreams, I looked upon it, I felt that a time might come when I could pray and weep for the wild catalogue of my many sins.

"Bernard, at last the day came when I left England. I had long wished to travel. I had grown tired of the hum of literary cliques, and the jargon of that deadly parasite called 'modernity.' Praise fainted, and lay like a corpse before my mind. I was sick of gaiety. It seemed to me that London was stifling my powers, narrowing my outlook, barring out real life from me with its moods and its fashions, and its idols of the hour, and its heroes of a day, who are the traitors of the day's night.

"So I went away.

"And now I come to the part of my story that you may find it hard to believe. Yet it is true.

"One day, in my wanderings, I came to a monastery. I remember the day well. It was an afternoon of early winter, and I was *en route* to a warm climate. But to gain my climate, and snatch a vivid contrast such as I love, I toiled over a gaunt and dreary pass, presided over by heavy, beetling-browed mountains. I rode upon a mule, attended only by my manservant and by a taciturn guide who led a baggage-mule. Slowly we wound, by thin paths, among the desolate crags, which sprang to sight in crowds at each turn of the way, pressing upon us, like dead faces of Nature, the corpses of things we call inanimate, but which had surely once lived. For the earth is alive, and gives life. But these mountains were now utterly dead. These grey, petrified countenances of the hills subdued my soul. The pattering shuffle of the mules woke an occasional echo, and even an echo I hated. For the environing silence was immense, and I wished to steep myself in it. As we still ascended, in the waste winter afternoon, towards the hour of twilight, snow—the first snow of the season—began to fall. I watched the white vision of the flakes against the grey vision of the crags, and I thought that this path, which I had cho-

sen as my road to Summer, was like the path by which holy
men slowly gain Paradise, treading difficult ways through life
that they may attain at last those eternal roses which bloom
beyond the granite and the snows. Up and up I rode, into
the clouds and the night, into the veil of the world, into the
icy winds of the heights. An eagle screamed above my head,
poised like a black shadow in the opaque gloom. That flying
life was the only life in this waste.

"And then my mule, edging ever to the precipice as a man
to his fate, sidled round a promontory of rock and set its feet
in snow. For we had passed the snow-line. And upon the snow
lay thin spears of yellow light. They streamed from the lattices
of the monastery which crowns the very summit of the pass.

III

"At this monastery I was to spend the night. The good monks
entertain all travellers, and in summer-time their hospitalities
are lavishly exercised. But in winter, wanderers are few, and
these holy men are left almost undisturbed in their meditative
solitudes. My mule paused upon a rocky plateau before the
door of the narrow grey building. The guide struck upon the
heavy wood. After a while we were admitted by a robed figure,
who greeted us kindly and made us welcome. Within, the
place was bare and poor enough, but scrupulously clean. I was
led through long, broad, and bitterly cold corridors to a big
chamber in which I was to pass the night. Here were ranged
in a row four large beds with white curtains. I occupied one
bed, my servant another. The rest were untenanted. The walls
were lined with light wood. The wooden floor was uncarpet-
ed. I threw open the narrow window. Dimly I could see a
mountain of rocks, on which snow lay in patches, towering
up into the clouds in front of me. And to the left there was

a glimmer of water. On the morrow, by that water, I should ride down into the land of flowers to which I was bound. Till then I would allow my imagination to luxuriate in the bleak romance of this wild home of prayer. The pathos of the night, shivering in the snow, and of this brotherhood of aspiring souls, detached from the excitement of the world for ever, seeking restlessly their final salvation day by day, night by night, in clouds of mountain vapour and sanctified incense, entered into my soul. And I thought of that imagined companion of mine. If he were with me now, surely he would feel that he had led me to his home at length. Surely he would secretly long to remain here.

"I smiled, as I said to myself—'Monk, tomorrow, if, indeed, you are fated to be my eternal attendant, you must come with me from this cold station of the cross down into the sunshine, where the blood of men is hot, where passions sing among the vineyards, where the battle is not of souls but of flowers. Tomorrow you must come with me. But tonight be at peace!'

"And I smiled to myself again as I fancied that my visionary companion was glad.

"Then I went down into the refectory.

"That night, before I retired to my room of the four beds, I asked if I might go into the chapel of the monastery. My request was granted. I shall never forget the curious sensation which overtook me as my guide led me down some steps past a dim, little, old, painted window set in the wall, to the chapel. That there should be a church here, that the deep tones of an organ should ever sound among these rocks and clouds, that the Host should be elevated and the censer swung, and litanies and masses be chanted amid these everlasting snows, all this was wonderful and quickening to me. When we reached the chapel, I begged my kind guide to leave me for a while. I longed to meditate alone. He left me, and instinctively I sank down upon my knees.

"I could just hear the keening of the wind outside. A dim light glimmered near the altar, and in one of the oaken stalls I saw a bent form praying. I knelt a long time. I did not pray. At first I scarcely thought definitely. Only, I received into my heart the strange, indelible impression of this wonderful place; and, as I knelt, my eyes were ever upon that dark praying figure near to me. By degrees I imagined that a wave of sympathy flowed from it to me, that in this monk's devotions my name was not forgotten.

"'What absurd tricks our imaginations can play us!' you will say.

"I grew to believe that he prayed for me, there, under the dim light from the tall tapers.

"What blessing did he ask on me? I could not tell; but I longed that his prayer might be granted.

"And then, Bernard, at last he rose. He lifted his face from his hands and stood up. Something in his figure seemed so strangely familiar to me, so strangely that, on a sudden, I longed, I craved to see his face.

"He seemed about to retreat through a side door near to the altar; then he paused, appeared to hesitate, then came down the chapel towards me. As he drew near to me—I scarcely knew why—but I hid my face deep in my hands, with a dreadful sense of overwhelming guilt which dyed my cheeks with blood. I shrank—I cowered. I trembled and was afraid. Then I felt a gentle touch on my shoulder. I looked up into the face of the monk.

"Bernard, it was the face of my invisible companion—it was my own face.

"The monk looked down into my eyes searchingly. He recoiled.

"'*Mon démon!*' he whispered in French. '*Mon démon!*'

"For a moment he stood still, like one appalled. Then he turned and abruptly quitted the chapel.

"I started up to follow him, but something held me back. I let him go, and I listened to hear if his tread sounded upon the chapel floor as a human footstep, if his robe rustled as he went.

"Yes. Then he was, indeed, a living man, and it was a human voice which had reached my ears, not a voice of imagination. He was a living man, this double of my body, this antagonist of my soul, this being who called me demon, who fled from me, who, doubtless, hated me. He was a living man.

"I could not sleep that night. This encounter troubled me. I felt that it had a meaning for me which I must discover, that it was not chance which had led me to take this cold road to the sunshine. Something had bound me with an invisible thread, and led me up here into the clouds, where already I—or the likeness of me—dwelt, perhaps had been dwelling for many years. I had looked upon my living wraith, and my living wraith had called me demon.

"How could I sleep?

"Very early I got up. The dawn was bitterly cold, but the snow had ceased, though a coating of ice covered the little lake. How delicate was the dawn here! The gathering, growing light fell upon the rocks, upon the snow, upon the ice of the lake, upon the slate walls of the monastery. And upon each it lay with a pretty purity, a thin refinement, an austerity such as I had never seen before. So, even Nature, it seemed, was purged by the continual prayers of these holy men. She, too, like men, has her lusts, and her hot passions, and her wrath of warfare. She, too, like men, can be edified and tended into grace. Nature among these heights was a virgin, not a wanton, a fit companion for those who are dedicated to virginity.

"I dressed by the window, and went out to see the entrance of the morning. There was nobody about. I had to find my own way. But when I had gained the refectory, I saw a monk standing by the door.

"It was my wraith waiting for me.

"Silently he went before me to the great door of the building. He opened it, and we stepped out upon the rocky plateau on which the snow lay thickly. He closed the door behind us, and motioned me to attend him among the rocks till we were out of sight of the monastery. Then he stopped, and we faced one another, still without a word, the grey light of the wintry dawn clothing us so wearily, so plaintively.

"We gazed at each other, dark face to dark face, brown eyes to brown eyes. The monk's pale hands, my hands, were clenched. The monk's strong lips, my lips, were set. The two souls looked upon each other, there, in the dawn.

"And then at last he spoke in French, and with the beautiful voice I knew.

"'Whence have you come?' he said.

"'From England, father.'

"'From England? Then you live! you live. You are a man, as I am! And I have believed you to be a spirit, some strange spirit of myself, lost to my control, interrupting my prayers with your cries, interrupting my sleep with your desires. You are a man like myself?'

"He stretched out his hand and touched mine.

"'Yes; it is indeed so,' he murmured.

"'And you,' I said in my turn, 'are no spirit. Yet, I, too, believed you to be a wraith of myself, interrupting my sins with your sorrow, interrupting my desires with your prayers. I have seen you. I have imagined you. And now I find you live. What does it mean? For we are as one and yet not as one.'

"'We are as two halves of a strangely-mingled whole,' he answered. 'Do you know what you have done to me?'

"'No, father.'

"'Listen,' he said. 'When a boy I dedicated myself to God. Early, early I dedicated myself, so that I might never know sin. For I had heard that the charm of sin is so great and so terrible that, once it is known, once it is felt, it can never be forgotten. And so it can make the holiest life hideous with its memories. It can intrude into the very sanctuary like a ghost, and murmur its music with the midnight mass. Even at the elevation of the Host will it be present, and stir the heart of the officiator to longing so keen that it is like the Agony of the Garden, the Agony of Christ. There are monks here who weep because they dare not sin, who rage secretly like beasts—because they will not sin.'

"He paused. The grey light grew over the mountains.

"'Knowing this, I resolved that I would never know sin, lest I, too, should suffer so horribly. I threw myself at once into the arms of God. Yet I have suffered—how I have suffered!'

"His face was contorted, and his lips worked. I stood as if under a spell, my eyes upon his face. I had only the desire to hear him. He went on, speaking now in a voice roughened by emotion:

"'For I became like these monks. You'—and he pointed at me with outstretched fingers—'you, my wraith, made in my very likeness, were surely born when I was born, to torment me. For, while I have prayed, I have been conscious of your neglect of prayer as if it were my own. When I have believed, I have been conscious of your unbelief as if it were my own. Whatever I have feebly tried to do for God, has been marred and defaced by all that you have left undone. I have wrestled with you; I have tried to hold you back; I have tried to lead you with me where I want to go, where I must go. All these years I have tried, all these years I have striven. But it has seemed as if God did not choose it. When you have been sinning, I have been agonising. I have lain upon the floor of my cell in the night, and I have torn at my evil heart. For—sometimes—I have longed—how I have longed!—to sin your sin.'

"He crossed himself. Sudden tears sprang into his eyes.

180

"'I have called you my demon,' he cried. 'But you are my cross. Oh, brother, will you not be my crown?'

"His eyes, shadowed with tears, gazed down into mine. Bernard, in that moment, I understood all—my depression, my unreasoning despair, the fancied hatred of others, even my few good impulses, all came from him, from this living holy wraith of my evil self.

"'Will you not be my crown?' he said.

"Bernard, there, in the snow, I fell at his feet. I confessed to him. I received his absolution.

"And, as the light of the dawn grew strong upon the mountains, he, my other self, my wraith, blessed me."

※

There was a long silence between us. Then I said:—

"And now?"

"And now you know why I have changed. That day, as I went down into the land of the sunshine, I made a vow."

"A vow?"

"Yes; to be his crown, not his cross. I soon returned to England. At first I was happy, and then one day my old evil nature came upon me like a giant. I fell again into sin, and, even as I sinned, I saw his face looking into mine, Bernard, pale, pale to the lips, and with eyes—such sad eyes of reproach! Then I thought I was not fit to live, and I tried to kill myself. They saved me, and brought me here."

"Yes; and now, Hubert?"

"Now," he said, "I am so happy. God surely placed me here where I cannot sin. The days pass and the nights, and they are stainless. And he—he comes by night and blesses me. I live for him now, and see always the grey walls of his monastery, his face which shall, at last, be completely mine."

✳

"Good-bye," the doctor said to me as I got into the carriage to drive back to the station. "Yes, he is perfectly happy, happier in his mania, I believe, than you or I in our sanity."

I drove away from that huge home of madness, set in the midst of lovely gardens in a smiling landscape, and I pondered those last words of the doctor's:—

"You and I—in our sanity."

And, thinking of the peace that lay on Hubert's face, I compared the so-called mad of the world with the so-called sane—and wondered.

THE STOLEN BODY

by H. G. Wells

M R. BESSEL was the senior partner in the firm of Bessel, Hart, and Brown, of St. Paul's Churchyard, and for many years he was well known among those interested in psychical research as a liberal-minded and conscientious investigator. He was an unmarried man, and instead of living in the suburbs, after the fashion of his class, he occupied rooms in the Albany, near Piccadilly. He was particularly interested in the questions of thought transference and of apparitions of the living, and in November, 1896, he commenced a series of experiments in conjunction with Mr. Vincey, of Staple Inn, in order to test the alleged possibility of projecting an apparition of one's self by force of will through space.

Their experiments were conducted in the following manner: At a pre-arranged hour Mr. Bessel shut himself in one of his rooms in the Albany and Mr. Vincey in his sitting-room in Staple Inn, and each then fixed his mind as resolutely as possible on the other. Mr. Bessel had acquired the art of self-hypnotism, and, so far as he could, he attempted first to hypnotise himself and then to project himself as a "phantom of the living" across the intervening space of nearly two miles into Mr. Vincey's apartment. On several evenings this was tried without any satisfactory result, but on the fifth or sixth occasion Mr. Vincey did actually see or imagine he saw an apparition of Mr. Bessel standing in his room. He states that the appearance, although brief, was very vivid and real. He noticed that Mr. Bessel's face was white and his expression anxious, and, moreover, that his hair was disordered. For a moment Mr. Vincey, in spite of his state of expectation, was too surprised to speak or move, and in that moment it seemed to him as though the figure glanced over its shoulder and incontinently vanished.

It had been arranged that an attempt should be made to photograph any phantasm seen, but Mr. Vincey had not the instant presence of mind to snap the camera that lay ready on the table beside him, and when he did so he was too late. Greatly elated, however, even by this partial success, he made a note of the exact time, and at once took a cab to the Albany to inform Mr. Bessel of this result.

He was surprised to find Mr. Bessel's outer door standing open to the night, and the inner apartments lit and in an extraordinary disorder. An empty champagne magnum lay smashed upon the floor; its neck had been broken off against the inkpot on the bureau and lay beside it. An octagonal occasional table, which carried a bronze statuette and a number of choice books, had been rudely overturned, and down the primrose paper of the wall inky fingers had been drawn, as it seemed for the mere pleasure of defilement. One of the delicate chintz curtains had been violently torn from its rings and thrust upon the fire, so that the smell of its smouldering filled the room. Indeed the whole place was disarranged in the strangest fashion. For a few minutes Mr. Vincey, who had entered sure of finding Mr. Bessel in his easy chair awaiting him, could scarcely believe his eyes, and stood staring helplessly at these unanticipated things.

Then, full of a vague sense of calamity, he sought the porter at the entrance lodge. "Where is Mr. Bessel?" he asked.

"Do you know that all the furniture is broken in Mr. Bessel's room?" The porter said nothing, but, obeying his gestures, came at once to Mr. Bessel's apartment to see the state of affairs. "This settles it," he said, surveying the lunatic confusion. "I didn't know of this. Mr. Bessel's gone off. He's mad!"

He then proceeded to tell Mr. Vincey that about half an hour previously, that is to say, at about the time of Mr. Bessel's apparition in Mr. Vincey's rooms, the missing gentleman had rushed out of the gates of the Albany into Vigo Street, hatless and with disordered hair, and had vanished into the direction of Bond Street. "And as he went past me," said the porter, "he laughed—a sort of gasping laugh, with his mouth open and his eyes glaring—I tell you, sir, he fair scared me!—like this."

According to his imitation it was anything but a pleasant laugh. "He waved his hand, with all his fingers crooked and clawing—like that. And he said, in a sort of fierce whisper, 'LIFE!' Just that one word, 'LIFE!'"

"Dear me," said Mr. Vincey. "Tut, tut," and "Dear me!" He could think of nothing else to say. He was naturally very much surprised. He turned from the room to the porter and from the porter to the room in the gravest perplexity. Beyond his suggestion that probably Mr. Bessel would come back presently and explain what had happened, their conversation was unable to proceed. "It might be a sudden toothache," said the porter, "a very sudden and violent toothache, jumping on him suddenly-like and driving him wild. I've broken things myself before now in such a case . . ." He thought. "If it was, why should he say 'LIFE' to me as he went past?"

Mr. Vincey did not know. Mr. Bessel did not return, and at last Mr. Vincey, having done some more helpless staring, and having addressed a note of brief inquiry and left it in a conspicuous position on the bureau, returned in a very perplexed frame of mind to his own premises in Staple Inn. This affair had given him a shock. He was at a loss to account for Mr. Bessel's conduct on any sane hypothesis. He tried to read, but he could not do so; he went for a short walk, and was so preoccupied that he narrowly escaped a cab at the top of Chancery Lane; and at last—a full hour before his usual time—he went to bed. For a considerable time he could not sleep because of his memory of the silent confusion of Mr. Bessel's apartment, and when at length he did attain an uneasy slumber it was at once disturbed by a very vivid and distressing dream of Mr. Bessel.

He saw Mr. Bessel gesticulating wildly, and with his face white and contorted. And, inexplicably mingled with his appearance, suggested perhaps by his gestures, was an intense fear, an urgency to act. He even believes that he heard the voice of his fellow experimenter calling distressfully to him, though at the time he considered this to be an illusion. The vivid impression remained though Mr. Vincey awoke. For a space he lay awake and trembling in the darkness, possessed with that vague, unaccountable terror of unknown possibilities that comes out of dreams upon even the bravest men. But at last he roused himself, and turned over and went to sleep again, only for the dream to return with enhanced vividness.

He awoke with such a strong conviction that Mr. Bessel was in overwhelming distress and need of help that sleep was no longer possible. He was persuaded that his friend had rushed out to some dire calamity. For a time he lay reasoning vainly against this belief, but at last he gave way to it. He arose, against all reason, lit his gas, and dressed, and set out through the deserted streets—deserted, save for a noiseless policeman or so and the early news carts—towards Vigo Street to inquire if Mr. Bessel had returned.

But he never got there. As he was going down Long Acre some unaccountable impulse turned him aside out of that street towards Covent Garden, which was just waking to its nocturnal activities. He saw the market in front of him—a queer effect of glowing yellow lights and busy black figures. He became aware of a shouting, and perceived a figure turn the corner by the hotel and run swiftly towards him. He knew at once that it was Mr. Bessel. But it was Mr. Bessel transfigured. He was hatless and dishevelled, his collar was torn open, he grasped a bone-handled walking-cane near the ferrule end, and his mouth was pulled awry. And he ran, with agile strides, very rapidly. Their encounter was the affair of an instant. "Bessel!" cried Vincey.

The running man gave no sign of recognition either of Mr. Vincey or of his own name. Instead, he cut at his friend savagely with the stick, hitting him in the face within an inch of the eye. Mr. Vincey, stunned and astonished, staggered back, lost his footing, and fell heavily on the pavement. It seemed to him that Mr. Bessel leapt over him as he fell. When he looked again Mr. Bessel had vanished, and a policeman and a number of garden porters and salesmen were rushing past towards Long Acre in hot pursuit.

With the assistance of several passers-by—for the whole street was speedily alive with running people—Mr. Vincey struggled to his feet. He at once became the centre of a crowd greedy to see his injury. A multitude of voices competed to re-assure him of his safety, and then to tell him of the behaviour of the madman, as they regarded Mr. Bessel. He had suddenly appeared in the middle of the market screaming "LIFE! LIFE!" striking left and right with a blood-stained walking-stick, and dancing and shouting with laughter at each successful blow. A lad and two women had broken heads, and he had smashed a man's wrist; a little child had been knocked insensible, and for a time he had driven every one before him, so furious and resolute had his behaviour been. Then he made a raid upon a coffee stall, hurled its paraffin flare through the window of the post office, and fled laughing, after stunning the foremost of the two policemen who had the pluck to charge him.

Mr. Vincey's first impulse was naturally to join in the pursuit of his friend, in order if possible to save him from the violence of the indignant people. But his action was slow, the blow had half stunned him, and while this was still no more than a resolution came the news, shouted through the crowd, that Mr. Bessel had eluded his pursuers. At first Mr. Vincey could scarcely credit this, but the universality of the report, and presently the dignified return of two futile policemen, convinced him. After some aimless inquiries he returned towards Staple Inn, padding a handkerchief to a now very painful nose.

He was angry and astonished and perplexed. It appeared to him indisputable that Mr. Bessel must have gone violently mad in the midst of his experiment in thought transference, but why that should make him appear with a sad white face in Mr. Vincey's dreams seemed a problem beyond solution. He racked his brains in vain to explain this. It seemed to him at last that not simply Mr. Bessel, but the order of things must be insane. But he could think of nothing to do. He shut himself carefully into his room, lit his fire—it was a gas fire with asbestos bricks—and, fearing fresh dreams if he went to bed, remained bathing his injured face, or holding up books in a vain attempt to read, until dawn. Throughout that vigil he had a curious persuasion that Mr. Bessel was endeavouring to speak to him, but he would not let himself attend to any such belief.

About dawn, his physical fatigue asserted itself, and he went to bed and slept at last in spite of dreaming. He rose late, unrested and anxious, and in considerable facial pain. The morning papers had no news of Mr. Bessel's aberration—it had come too late for them. Mr. Vincey's perplexities, to which the fever of his bruise added fresh irritation, became at last intolerable, and, after a fruitless visit to the Albany, he went down to St. Paul's Churchyard to Mr. Hart, Mr. Bessel's partner, and, so far as Mr. Vincey knew, his nearest friend.

He was surprised to learn that Mr. Hart, although he knew nothing of the outbreak, had also been disturbed by a vision, the very vision that Mr. Vincey had seen—Mr. Bessel, white and dishevelled, pleading earnestly by his gestures for help. That was his impression of the import of his signs. "I was just going to look him up in the Albany when you arrived," said Mr. Hart. "I was so sure of something being wrong with him."

As the outcome of their consultation the two gentlemen decided to inquire at Scotland Yard for news of their missing friend. "He is bound to be laid by the heels," said Mr. Hart. "He can't go on at that pace for long." But the police authorities had not laid Mr. Bessel by the heels. They confirmed Mr. Vincey's overnight experiences and added fresh circumstances, some of an even graver character than those he knew—a list of smashed glass along the upper half of Tottenham Court Road, an attack upon a policeman in Hampstead Road, and an atrocious assault upon a woman. All these outrages were committed between half-past twelve and a quarter to two in the morning, and between those hours—and, indeed, from the very moment of Mr. Bessel's first rush from his rooms at half-past nine in the evening—they could trace the deepening violence of his fantastic career. For the last hour, at least from before one, that is, until a quarter to two, he had run amuck through London, eluding with amazing agility every effort to stop or capture him.

But after a quarter to two he had vanished. Up to that hour witnesses were multitudinous. Dozens of people had seen him, fled from him or pursued him, and then things suddenly came to an end. At a quarter to two he had been seen running down the Euston Road towards Baker Street, flourishing a can of burning colza oil and jerking splashes of flame therefrom at the windows of the houses he passed. But none of the policemen on Euston Road beyond the Waxwork Exhibition, nor any of those in the side streets down which he must have passed had he left the Euston Road, had seen anything of him. Abruptly he disappeared. Nothing of his subsequent doings came to light in spite of the keenest inquiry.

Here was a fresh astonishment for Mr. Vincey. He had found considerable comfort in Mr. Hart's conviction: "He is bound to be laid by the heels before long," and in that assurance he had been able to suspend his mental perplexities. But any fresh development seemed destined to add new impossibilities to a pile already heaped beyond the powers of his acceptance. He found himself doubting whether his memory might not have played him some grotesque trick, debating whether any of these things could possibly have happened; and in the afternoon he hunted up Mr. Hart again to share the intolerable weight on his mind. He found Mr. Hart engaged with a well-known private detective, but as that gentleman accomplished nothing in this case, we need not enlarge upon his proceedings.

All that day Mr. Bessel's whereabouts eluded an unceasingly active inquiry, and all that night. And all that day there was a persuasion in the back of Vincey's mind that Mr. Bessel sought his attention, and all through the night Mr. Bessel with a tear-stained face of anguish pursued him through his dreams. And whenever he saw Mr. Bessel in his dreams he also saw a number of other faces, vague but malignant, that seemed to be pursuing Mr. Bessel.

It was on the following day, Sunday, that Mr. Vincey recalled certain remarkable stories of Mrs. Bullock, the medium, who was then attracting attention for the first time in London. He determined to consult her. She was staying at the house of that well-known inquirer, Dr. Wilson Paget, and Mr. Vincey, although he had never met that gentleman before, repaired to him forthwith with the intention of invoking her help. But scarcely had he mentioned the name of Bessel when Doctor Paget interrupted him. "Last night—just at the end," he said, "we had a communication."

He left the room, and returned with a slate on which were certain words written in a handwriting, shaky indeed, but indisputably the handwriting of Mr. Bessel!

"How did you get this?" said Mr. Vincey. "Do you mean—?"

"We got it last night," said Doctor Paget. With numerous interruptions from Mr. Vincey, he proceeded to explain how the writing had been obtained. It appears that in her seances, Mrs. Bullock passes into a condition of trance, her eyes rolling up in a strange way under her eyelids, and her body becoming rigid. She then begins to talk very rapidly, usually in voices other than her own. At the same time one or both of her hands may become active, and if slates and pencils are provided they will then write messages simultaneously with and quite independently of the flow of words from her mouth. By many she is considered an even more remarkable medium than the celebrated Mrs. Piper. It was one of these messages, the one written by her left hand, that Mr. Vincey now had before him. It consisted of eight words written disconnectedly: "George Bessel . . . trial excavn . . . Baker Street . . . help . . . starvation." Curiously enough, neither Doctor Paget nor the two other inquirers who were present had heard of the disappearance of Mr. Bessel—the news of it appeared only in the evening papers of Saturday—and they had put the message aside with many others of a vague and enigmatical sort that Mrs. Bullock has from time to time delivered.

When Doctor Paget heard Mr. Vincey's story, he gave himself at once with great energy to the pursuit of this clue to the discovery of Mr. Bessel. It would serve no useful purpose here to describe the inquiries of Mr. Vincey and himself; suffice it that the clue was a genuine one, and that Mr. Bessel was actually discovered by its aid.

He was found at the bottom of a detached shaft which had been sunk and abandoned at the commencement of the work for the new electric railway near Baker Street Station. His arm and leg and two ribs were broken. The shaft is protected by a hoarding nearly 20 feet high, and over this, incredible as it seems, Mr. Bessel, a stout, middle-aged gentleman, must have scrambled in order to fall down the shaft. He was saturated in colza oil, and the smashed tin lay beside him, but luckily the flame had been extinguished by his fall. And his madness had passed from him altogether. But he was, of course, terribly enfeebled, and at the sight of his rescuers he gave way to hysterical weeping.

In view of the deplorable state of his flat, he was taken to the house of Dr. Hatton in Upper Baker Street. Here he was subjected to a sedative treatment, and anything that might recall the violent crisis through which he had passed was carefully avoided. But on the second day he volunteered a statement.

Since that occasion Mr. Bessel has several times repeated this statement—to myself among other people—varying the details as the narrator of real experiences always does, but never by any chance contradicting himself in any particular. And the statement he makes is in substance as follows.

In order to understand it clearly it is necessary to go back to his experiments with Mr. Vincey before his remarkable attack. Mr. Bessel's first attempts at self-projection, in his experiments with Mr. Vincey, were, as the reader will remember, unsuccessful. But through all of them he was concentrating all his power and will upon getting out of the body—"willing it with all my might," he says. At last, almost against expectation, came success. And Mr. Bessel asserts that he, being alive, did actually, by an effort of will, leave his body and pass into some place or state outside this world.

The release was, he asserts, instantaneous. "At one moment I was seated in my chair, with my eyes tightly shut, my hands gripping the arms of the chair, doing all I could to concentrate my mind on Vincey, and then I perceived myself outside my body—saw my body near me, but certainly not containing me, with the hands relaxing and the head drooping forward on the breast."

Nothing shakes him in his assurance of that release. He describes in a quiet, matter-of-fact way the new sensation he experienced. He felt he had become impalpable—so much he had expected, but he had not expected to find himself enormously large. So, however, it would seem he became. "I was a great cloud—if I may express it that way—anchored to my body. It appeared to me, at first, as if I had discovered a greater self of which the conscious being in my brain was only a little part. I saw the Albany and Piccadilly and Regent Street and all the rooms and places in the houses, very minute and very bright and distinct, spread out below me like a little city seen from a balloon. Every now and then vague shapes like drifting wreaths of smoke made the vision a little indistinct, but at first I paid little heed to them. The thing that astonished me most, and which astonishes me still, is that I saw quite distinctly the insides of the houses as well as the streets, saw little people dining and talking in the private houses, men and women dining, playing billiards, and drinking in restaurants and hotels, and several places of entertainment crammed with people. It was like watching the affairs of a glass hive."

Such were Mr. Bessel's exact words as I took them down when he told me the story. Quite forgetful of Mr. Vincey, he remained for a space observing these things. Impelled by curiosity, he says, he stooped down, and, with the shadowy arm he found himself possessed of, attempted to touch a man walking along Vigo Street. But he could not do so, though his finger seemed to pass through the man. Something prevented his doing this, but what it was he finds it hard to describe. He compares the obstacle to a sheet of glass.

"I felt as a kitten may feel," he said, "when it goes for the first time to pat its reflection in a mirror." Again and again, on the occasion when I heard him tell this story, Mr. Bessel returned to that comparison of the sheet of glass. Yet it was not altogether a precise comparison, because, as the reader will speedily see, there were interruptions of this generally impermeable resistance, means of getting through the barrier to the material world again. But, naturally, there is a very great difficulty in expressing these unprecedented impressions in the language of everyday experience.

A thing that impressed him instantly, and which weighed upon him throughout all this experience, was the stillness of this place—he was in a world without sound.

At first Mr. Bessel's mental state was an unemotional wonder. His thought chiefly concerned itself with where he might be. He was out of the body—out of his material body, at any rate—but that was not all. He believes, and I for one believe also, that he was somewhere out of space, as we understand it, altogether. By a strenuous effort of will he had passed out of his body into a world beyond this world, a world undreamt of, yet lying so close to it and so strangely situated with regard to it that all things on this earth are clearly visible both from without and from within in this other world about us. For a long time, as it seemed to him, this realisation occupied his mind to the exclusion of all other matters, and then he recalled the engagement with Mr. Vincey, to which this astonishing experience was, after all, but a prelude.

He turned his mind to locomotion in this new body in which he found himself. For a time he was unable to shift himself from his attachment to his earthly carcass. For a time this new strange cloud body of his simply swayed, contracted, expanded, coiled, and writhed with his efforts to free himself, and then quite suddenly the link that bound him snapped. For a moment everything was hidden by what appeared to be whirling spheres of dark vapour, and then through a momentary gap he saw his drooping body collapse limply, saw his lifeless head drop sideways, and found he was driving along like a huge cloud in a strange place of shadowy clouds that had the luminous intricacy of London spread like a model below.

But now he was aware that the fluctuating vapour about him was something more than vapour, and the temerarious excitement of his first essay was shot with fear. For he perceived, at first indistinctly, and then suddenly very clearly, that he was surrounded by FACES! that each roll and coil of the seeming cloud-stuff was a face. And such faces! Faces of thin shadow, faces of gaseous tenuity. Faces like those faces that glare with intolerable strangeness upon the sleeper in the evil hours of his dreams. Evil, greedy eyes that were full of a covetous curiosity, faces with knit brows and snarling, smiling lips; their vague hands clutched at Mr. Bessel as he passed, and the rest of their bodies was but an elusive streak of trailing darkness. Never a word they said, never a sound from the mouths that seemed to gibber. All about him they pressed in that dreamy silence, passing freely through the dim mistiness that was his body, gathering ever more numerously about him. And the shadowy Mr. Bessel, now suddenly fear-stricken, drove through the silent, active multitude of eyes and clutching hands.

So inhuman were these faces, so malignant their staring eyes, and shadowy, clawing gestures, that it did not occur to Mr. Bessel to attempt intercourse with these drifting creatures. Idiot phantoms, they seemed, children of vain desire, beings unborn and forbidden the boon of being, whose only expressions and gestures told of the envy and craving for life that was their one link with existence.

It says much for his resolution that, amidst the swarming cloud of these noiseless spirits of evil, he could still think of Mr. Vincey. He made a violent effort of will and found himself, he knew not how, stooping towards Staple Inn, saw Vincey sitting attentive and alert in his arm-chair by the fire.

And clustering also about him, as they clustered ever about all that lives and breathes, was another multitude of these vain voiceless shadows, longing, desiring, seeking some loophole into life.

For a space Mr. Bessel sought ineffectually to attract his friend's attention. He tried to get in front of his eyes, to move the objects in his room, to touch him. But Mr. Vincey remained unaffected, ignorant of the being that was so close to his own. The strange something that Mr. Bessel has compared to a sheet of glass separated them impermeably.

And at last Mr. Bessel did a desperate thing. I have told how that in some strange way he could see not only the outside of a man as we see him, but within. He extended his shadowy hand and thrust his vague black fingers, as it seemed, through the heedless brain.

Then, suddenly, Mr. Vincey started like a man who recalls his attention from wandering thoughts, and it seemed to Mr. Bessel that a little dark-red body situated in the middle of Mr. Vincey's brain swelled and glowed as he did so. Since that experience he has been shown anatomical figures of the brain, and he knows now that this is that useless structure, as doctors call it, the pineal eye. For, strange as it will seem to many, we have, deep in our brains—where it cannot possibly see any earthly light—an eye! At the time this, with the rest of the internal anatomy of the brain, was quite new to him. At the sight of its changed appearance, however, he thrust forth his finger, and, rather fearful still of the consequences, touched this little spot. And instantly Mr. Vincey started, and Mr. Bessel knew that he was seen.

And at that instant it came to Mr. Bessel that evil had happened to his body, and behold! a great wind blew through all that world of shadows and tore him away. So strong was this persuasion that he thought no more of Mr. Vincey, but turned about forthwith, and all the countless faces drove back with him like leaves before a gale. But he returned too late. In an instant he saw the body that he had left inert and collapsed—lying, indeed, like the body of a man just dead—had arisen, had arisen by virtue of some strength and will beyond his own. It stood with staring eyes, stretching its limbs in dubious fashion.

For a moment he watched it in wild dismay, and then he stooped towards it. But the pane of glass had closed against him again, and he was foiled. He beat himself passionately against this, and all about him the spirits of evil grinned and pointed and mocked. He gave way to furious anger. He compares himself to a bird that has fluttered heedlessly into a room and is beating at the window-pane that holds it back from freedom.

And behold! the little body that had once been his was now dancing with delight. He saw it shouting, though he could not hear its shouts; he saw the violence of its movements grow. He watched it fling his cherished furniture about in the mad delight of existence, rend his books apart, smash bottles, drink heedlessly from the jagged fragments, leap and smite in a passionate acceptance of living. He watched these actions in paralysed astonishment. Then once more he hurled himself against the impassable barrier, and then with all that crew of mocking ghosts about him, hurried back in dire confusion to Vincey to tell him of the outrage that had come upon him.

But the brain of Vincey was now closed against apparitions, and the disembodied Mr. Bessel pursued him in vain as he hurried out into Holborn to call a cab. Foiled and terror-stricken, Mr. Bessel swept back again, to find his desecrated body whooping in a glorious frenzy down the Burlington Arcade . . . .

And now the attentive reader begins to understand Mr. Bessel's interpretation of the first part of this strange story. The being whose frantic rush through London had inflicted so much injury and disaster had indeed Mr. Bessel's body, but it was not Mr. Bessel. It was an evil spirit out of that strange world beyond existence, into which Mr. Bessel had so rashly ventured. For twenty hours it held possession of him, and for all those twenty hours the dispossessed spirit-body of Mr. Bessel was going to and fro in that unheard-of middle world of shadows seeking help in vain. He spent many hours beating at the minds of Mr. Vincey and of his friend Mr. Hart. Each, as we know, he roused by his efforts. But the language that might convey his situation to these helpers across the gulf he did not know; his feeble fingers groped vainly and powerlessly in their brains. Once, indeed, as we have already told, he was able to turn Mr. Vincey aside from his path so that he encountered the stolen body in its career, but he could not make him understand the thing that had happened: he was unable to draw any help from that encounter. . . .

All through those hours the persuasion was overwhelming in Mr. Bessel's mind that presently his body would be killed by its furious tenant, and he would have to remain in this shadow-land for evermore. So that those long hours were a growing agony of fear. And ever as he hurried to and fro in his ineffectual excitement, innumerable spirits of that world about him mobbed him and confused his mind. And ever an envious applauding multitude poured after their successful fellow as he went upon his glorious career.

For that, it would seem, must be the life of these bodiless things of this world that is the shadow of our world. Ever they watch, coveting a way into a mortal body, in order that they may descend, as furies and frenzies, as violent lusts and mad, strange impulses, rejoicing in the body they have won. For Mr. Bessel was not the only human soul in that place. Witness the fact that he met first one, and afterwards several shadows of men, men like himself, it seemed, who had lost their bodies even it may be as he had lost his, and wandered, despairingly, in that lost world that is neither life nor death. They could not speak because that world is silent, yet he knew them for men because of their dim human bodies, and because of the sadness of their faces.

But how they had come into that world he could not tell, nor where the bodies they had lost might be, whether they still raved about the earth, or whether they were closed forever in death against return. That they were the spirits of the dead neither he nor I believe. But Doctor Wilson Paget thinks they are the rational souls of men who are lost in madness on the earth.

At last Mr. Bessel chanced upon a place where a little crowd of such disembodied silent creatures was gathered, and thrusting through them he saw below a brightly-lit room, and four or five quiet gentlemen and a woman, a stoutish woman dressed in black bombazine and sitting awkwardly in a chair with her head thrown back. He knew her from her portraits to be Mrs. Bullock, the medium. And he perceived that tracts and structures in her brain glowed and stirred as he had seen the pineal eye in the brain of Mr. Vincey glow. The light was very fitful; sometimes it was a broad illumination, and sometimes merely a faint twilight spot, and it shifted slowly about her brain. She kept on talking and writing with one hand. And Mr. Bessel saw that the crowding shadows of men about him, and a great multitude of the shadow spirits of that shadowland, were all striving and thrusting to touch the lighted regions of her brain. As one gained her brain or another was thrust away, her voice and the writing of her hand changed. So that what she said was disorderly and confused for the most part; now a fragment of one soul's message, and now a fragment of another's, and now she babbled the insane fancies of the spirits of vain desire. Then Mr. Bessel understood that she spoke for the spirit that had touch of her, and he began to struggle very furiously towards her. But he was on the outside of the crowd and at that time he could not reach her, and at last, growing anxious, he went away to find what had happened meanwhile to his body. For a long time he went to and fro seeking it in vain and fearing that it must have been killed, and then he found it at the bottom of the shaft in Baker Street, writhing furiously and cursing with pain. Its leg and an arm and two ribs had been broken by its fall. Moreover, the evil spirit was angry because his time had been so short and because of the painmaking violent movements and casting his body about.

And at that Mr. Bessel returned with redoubled earnestness to the room where the séance was going on, and so soon as he had thrust himself within sight of the place he saw one of the men who stood about the medium looking at his watch as if he meant that the séance should presently end. At that a great number of the shadows who had been striving turned away with gestures of despair. But the thought that the séance was almost over only made Mr. Bessel the more earnest, and he struggled so stoutly with his will against the others that presently he gained the woman's brain. It chanced that just at that moment it glowed very brightly, and in that instant she wrote the message that Doctor Wilson Paget preserved. And then the other shadows and the cloud of evil spirits about him had thrust Mr. Bessel away from her, and for all the rest of the séance he could regain her no more.

So he went back and watched through the long hours at the bottom of the shaft where the evil spirit lay in the stolen body it had maimed, writhing and cursing, and weeping and groaning, and learning the lesson of pain. And towards dawn the thing he had waited for happened, the brain glowed brightly and the evil spirit came out, and Mr. Bessel entered the body he had feared he should never enter again. As he did so, the silence—the brooding silence—ended; he heard the tumult of traffic and the voices of people overhead, and that strange world that is the shadow of our world—the dark and silent shadows of ineffectual desire and the shadows of lost men—vanished clean away.

He lay there for the space of about three hours before he was found. And in spite of the pain and suffering of his wounds, and of the dim damp place in which he lay; in spite of the tears—wrung from him by his physical distress—his heart was full of gladness to know that he was nevertheless back once more in the kindly world of men.

TRANSMIGRATION

by Dora Sigerson Shorter

I

MANY men have tasted Hell some moments of their lives—a Hell of their own making, perhaps; but I, oh God! I have been in the Hell of the damned.

I cannot remember my father or my mother; oh, wretched that I am! Had I either to love one whom no man loves? No, I cannot remember. My memory goes back three months—no further. Every day I live those three months over and over again.

I had too much money when I came of age. I knew not how to use it. I threw it here and there, ever indulging in my own pleasure. Playing in the world till the dust of it rose up and clouded my eyes—till the hand of innocence I held in mine was changed for the hand of sin.

Playing in a world that I was sent to work in, I forgot I had a soul or that there was a God who had given it to me. I played until my selfish indulgences brought upon me the sickness of death. And then my three months of Hell commenced. Unloved, unfriended, I tossed upon my bed, blaspheming a God I did not believe in, swearing I would not die. Shrieking in my terror of that Hell, I felt myself approaching a Hell I had so often scoffed at. I heard my screams re-echo through the empty house, unreplied to, making my desolation complete. Then I lay still, gasping on my bed; so would my prayers soar up to Heaven, I thought, unanswered, unheard. But stay! a step on the stairs—nearer, nearer; the door has opened, and a man stands upon the threshold. Oh, eyes that beamed peace and love, you saved me from Heaven's vengeance for the moment—at what a cost! He came forward into the room when he saw me, and I thought for an instant it was an angel sent to comfort my misery.

"I heard you call," he said; "and, fearing you were ill, I entered. I am your neighbour, my latch-key fits your door. You must pardon my coming, but, thinking you were ill—and alone——"

"I am alone," I said—"alone, alone, deserted alike by God and man. Body and soul I am alone, and sick unto death."

"Despair not, my friend," said he. "I will attend you; you are sick, and morbid from being left alone. Rouse yourself, and I will try and help."

"Help me! no man can help me; I have helped no man. Unless you can give me another life to live with the knowledge I have of this."

"My dear friend, God alone can do that," his voice went on soothingly; "but you are truly sorry for your past?"

"Man," I cried, "there are no such things as death-bed repentances. Death is ever beside us a yawning precipice; as we walk along its edge we *know* that it is there. We look at the sky above it, at the flowers by its brink, but we never look at it; we turn our heads away, but we know that it is there. We feel the chill of it in the heat of the sun. We see its shadow on the petals of the flowers. We know that a false step, a stumble, and we are gone, plunged into Eternity in a moment. We say that sometime this path must come to an end, as we but follow it to our extermination, and when we see before us the black doors of death, *then* will we lay aside our flowers, and still our songs and laughter. And Heaven will pity our prayers and sighs. Talk not to me of such repentances; I believe them not, nor you, nor any man."

"You are very ill," the stranger said, as I raved on.

"I will not die, I must live, though Heaven itself has shut its gates upon me. Hell—if such is my destination—must give me a year of life. I say, I will not die." A strange strength seemed to flow through my veins. I raised myself on my elbow. The stranger was standing at my bedside looking with divine pity at my convulsed face.

"You," I said. Oh, the horror of it! "You must die, you with your life of purity behind you; death should have no fears for you. The gates of Heaven are open for you; give me your body, your life, and let me live."

"Friend," he said, as though humouring me, "I cannot die; I have a mother who is old and requires my care, and a child, a darling little child."

"You must die!" I cried again. "I will care for your mother and child. You must die and let me live—I say, I will not die."

"You are very ill," was all he said, laying his hand upon my brow. And then, I know not how it came to pass, whether my cry to Heaven or Hell had been answered, or, whatever it was, by some great effort of my will, but *I stood by the bed looking down at my own sleeping body*. I dashed across the room to the glass. It was the stranger it reflected back—yes, the same high forehead, with fair, wavy hair, the same large, dreamy eyes; but his soul, ah! his soul lay sleeping in that motionless form upon the bed. I turned and left the haunted room, living, living, living!

II

Living, living—oh, the joy of it! I had died and was born again. How it came about, what cared I? "Who," I thought, as I bounded down the stairs, "so fortunate as I?" What man or woman thinking over the past has not said—"Oh, could I but live my life over again, I would not have done this thing or that"? And I, with my evil past laid out before me, could live it again, casting out the weeds and cultivating the trodden flowers; with nothing to hinder me, not even the sensual flesh that lay upstairs, a prison-house for the spirit of that good man whose body I was inhabiting and whose life I proposed to live.

I closed the door of my own house and went up the tiny garden to the next; as I did so, I heard the patter of little feet and a childish voice calling, "Here's papa! Here's papa!"

I opened the door and took the little darling into my arms. Never had I felt such happiness as when the innocent parted lips met mine and the soft baby-hands went round my neck. I stood still to take in the joy of it, but the child drew back in my arms and for a moment she sat quite quiet, and then she struggled until I had to let her down.

"It's not my papa!" she sobbed, running into the little sitting-room. "Oh, gran'ma, 'tis not my own papa!"

Mechanically I hung my hat upon the rack in the hall and followed the child. The room was small, but very bright and cosy; an old lady was seated in an arm-chair before the blazing fire; one withered hand was laid caressingly upon the golden head of the little girl, the other shaded her eyes as she anxiously watched the door. When I entered she smiled and turned to the weeping child.

"Why, what ailed you, darling? Look, Rosy, it is your own papa."

Rosy looked up through her tears, and, seeing me standing in the full glare of the lamp and fire, ran to me again. I sat down in a low chair opposite the old woman, and the little child climbed on to my knees.

"It's my dood papa," she said, laying her wet cheek against mine.

For an hour I sat thus tasting for the first time the joy of a home, and listening to the old woman as she told me tales of her son's youth—my youth now.

For some time she rambled on, in the fashion of the old, and at last for very joy I laughed aloud, waking the child, who had fallen asleep in my arms.

"Will you take her up to bed, Gilbert," said her grandmother; "she sat up for you that you might put her to sleep tonight."

I raised the child in my arms, the pretty little babe with her soft curls falling across her face, and she laid her drowsy head upon my shoulder. I pressed her with joy to my breast as I turned up the narrow, dark stairs; at my movement she sat up suddenly and pushed me from her with both her tiny hands. Oh, wonderful instinct of the child that in the light beheld her father, but in darkness knew me for a stranger!

"You're not my papa! Oh, I want papa!"

"Hush, hush!" I whispered; "I am your papa."

"You're not, you're not!" and she beat upon my breast with both her tiny fists.

"Give me my own papa, you bad, bad man!"

Then a great fury seized me, and I held her over the banisters.

"Call me your father, or I let you go."

"No, no; I want my own papa!"

"Call me your father, or I let you go."

"I want my dood papa!"

I did not mean it, Heaven knows I did not mean it, but my fingers loosed their hold. I shook the little hands from their terrified grasp upon my coat. The hall echoed the screams of a child and a sickening thud on the flags beneath. A terrible laugh followed, a laugh that might have come from the lowest pits of Hell. Was it I who uttered it? I looked into the hall beneath me. A trembling old woman knelt there, and, at her side, a servant with a lighted candle, but their white faces were not turned to the motionless body at their feet, but towards me, unspeaking, as though they were frozen by some terrible sight or sound. Had a devil entered into the body of Gilbert Graham during the time my spirit was passing from my own to it—a devil who, making me work its will, thus laughed in its hideous triumph. Surely devils were many round my bed when I lay dying. Its power had left me now, and I went, in bitter remorse, to the little child.

"She slipped from my arms," I whispered. "She slipped, mother."

She answered me nothing; but, as I raised the senseless babe, the servant sobbed, "Oh, Master Gilbert, we thought the shock had sent you mad!"

I laid the child upon the sofa, while the girl ran for a doctor. I stood as though stunned until he came, watching him then in a dream as he examined the soft limbs of the poor babe, and he shook his head as he arose.

"I am sorry to have to tell you that if she lives she will be a cripple all her life."

"Tell my mother," I whispered. I was not the one to tell her this.

"I am sorry," he said; "I am very sorry, Madam."

"Hush!" the old woman answered; "hush! You will waken her."

"She may never waken," he whispered "Bear up, dear Madam."

"Hush!" the old woman said again, touching the golden curls that were stained with blood. "Hush! The fairies have come to her and laid red poppies in her hair."

And thus had I fulfilled my trust to care for his mother and child—one a cripple or dead, the other a muttering idiot.

I had launched my new life, and the waters that bore it were red human blood; but who or what was the dread pilot that guided it?

III

I stole out into the dimly lighted street. Of what use was I at home?

The little child still lingered. The old woman was still happy in her ignorance, babbling of fairies and red poppies. My hands were the fairies that had laid those terrible flowers on her babe's fair head, the sleep-giving poppies on her eyes.

The paper-boys were shouting in my ears as I passed, but I paid no attention to them. Their "terrible tragedies" could not equal mine; their cries of "Murder!" woke no horror in my heart; they only cried aloud the word that echoed there. I dare not think of the imprisoned soul that lay as dead in my room—the only one who sought me out in my hour of death's despair. My horrible cries, that had frightened the very servants from my house, but hastened his feet to my side; and now he slept, a thin wall between him and the reward I had given him—a ruined home.

Oh, how could I hear the city noises and a thousand cries within my breast—a thousand little hands beating upon my heart, "Give back! give back!"

And so I strode through the damp fog, caring not, thinking not where I was going. At last a bright light flashed in my eyes, and I started as though awaking. Before me was a lighted doorway, and above it, in the light of the lamp, hung a board, and upon it in red letters the word "Billiards." The place was a gambling-hell. I had known it but too well in the old days. I gazed about, half-hearing some one speaking, and saw a young man before me, his face flushed and his eyelids drooping.

"I could not help it, Graham; indeed I could not! I tried to keep away because of my promise to you and for my mother's sake."

His promise to me! I almost laughed aloud. Yes, I knew that boyish, effeminate face. It had been often opposite to me at the gambling-table inside. I had seen it grow white and tortured as the game went on. I had made its hairless lips grow sweet in a smile, or quiver pathetically like a girl's, by the turn of my hand; I had lured him on night after night with a hope I held between my fingers. His promise to me! I had forgotten. Something evil was rising in my heart. I felt it would claim my lips if I did not speak. I seized his arm.

"Go home," I said; "heed not what I may say to you after this, heed not what I may seem to you. The most beautiful statue is but hollow and moulded in common clay. The tiger's claws are soft as a lady's cheek, but they will tear you to pieces if you trust them. The moth sees the candle's flame, and, thinking it fair, he dies. I am not as you think——"

"I do not know what you mean, Graham. If you mean this den has any fairness for me, it is not so, unless it be the fascination of the bird to the serpent's eye."

"Leave me!" I cried despairingly, for devils' words were rising to my lips; and as he did not heed me, I turned and spoke them.

"Come in with me," I said, and laughed. "Come in with me, and I shall see fair play."

"With you!" He started. "With you, Graham! you who have preached of its dangers to me and its temptations and wickedness; you to whom I looked to save me from where it will lead me. Oh, Graham! I could laugh, 'tis so absurd!"

"I'll see fair play," I said again; "besides, you could not break yourself of the habit so easily and abruptly—I will wean you from it by degrees."

I took his arm, and we passed inside. No one took any notice of me when we entered, but they all gathered around my companion.

"Why, Varen, we thought you were going to leave us?"

"Did you hear of the discovery in Harrington Street last night? Poor Bulger! You remember Bulger, don't you? You lost a cool hundred to him one night here over the cards, eh? Got a cataleptic fit, they say; most interesting case. Went home in a most distressing state of mind the other night, commenced shouting like the devil, frightened the servant out of her wits and out of the house—says she hid in a doorway till dawn, afraid to go back; then she screwed up her courage and stole to the house; finding no answer to her knocks, and being unable to open the door, became alarmed, started for the police-station, and returned with some of the force. One got into the house by a low window and opened the door to the rest; they found poor Bulger lying on his bed—they thought—dead as a herring, but the doctors say 'tis a most interesting case of catalepsy."

I listened without speaking. "What a queer old world it is!" I thought; "we must have a name for everything, no matter how wonderful, or where would our doctors and men of science be? Nothing is left to the God who designed the whole. Our beliefs are superstitions, we laugh them away; we would explain the very law of life itself."

A hand was laid upon my arm.

"Play a game of cards, Graham? The fellows are asking me."

"No, no; this is no place for you—for me. Come out of it quickly."

But the men surrounded us.

"You are not going yet? just one game, then?"

Fool that I was, I complied, and took my seat at the table. They thought I was a "green one," as was evident from their surprised looks when I swept up their little pile of silver at the end of the first game.

"You would think it was old Bulger himself," I heard one say; "he seems to have his accursed luck."

One game led to another; my companion's face grew pale; some demon arose within me, and I took a pleasure in its paleness.

Why is it innocence attracts the guilty so? Behind the bar connected with this card-room there was a young girl serving. I heard men make rude jests that brought the colour to her cheeks; she would hang her head if they called her endearing names, and the angry tears would spring to her eyes: she would shake off their hands with passion. For this girl they would leave their billiards and their cards to watch the red and white fly to her face; and now, when they speak to her, she answers their jests with similar ones; she answers their calls with a simper; she courts their caresses and their company; she is no longer attractive to them—she is one of themselves.

Why did I not pick out my prey among those evil, coarse faces—why did I seek to destroy the one exception? I know not; life preys upon that which is weaker than itself, not that which is its equal.

I swept pile after pile of silver into my pockets, Varen's white face growing whiter and whiter. At last he started to his feet—

"I'm cleared out—I have only a shilling left; I'm going home."

"Put it down," I said to him. "Why, man, you may win a pile on it yet. Finish this round, anyway."

Sullenly he sat down again and took up his cards.

I let him win game after game, and when he rose to depart he had won back a third of his losses.

"I'll come again tomorrow night and win the rest," he said, with a smile.

Why follow the downfall of that young life? Night after night we met in the same place, I hastening away from the ceaseless crying of a little, suffering child, calling for the father I had robbed her of; he from the complaints of a broken-hearted mother, powerless to draw her only son from the snare I had set for him. Night after night I robbed him of his earnings, leaving him to win back a third, to lure him with a hope, never to be fulfilled, that the next time he might win a fortune.

Paler each night grew the young face, shabbier the clothes, thinner the hands that grasped the cards so eagerly. Now he spoke no word of greeting to me; only his eyes revealed his thoughts: therein I could see the light of hope gleam faintly each night, fading, fading to give place to despair, returning again as the closing hours approached and the waiter's voice warned us it was time to stop.

One night Varen came hastily in, staggering as though he were drunk. Flinging himself down in a chair, he took his cards. There was no hope in his eyes; I saw only terrible anguish and despair. On one sleeve of his shabby coat I saw a broad band of crape.

He played wildly—and won. I had slain my devil; he won again; I was glad. I saw his silver flow back to him; I was happy for the first time in many a weary hour. "I shall no longer be his curse," I thought; "through me he shall win back his fortune, his mother's blessing, his lost youth. I shall restore all."

A cry recalled me. I had been dreaming. I gazed around bewildered; the candles were spluttering in their sockets, and on the side of one was a great roll of wax. It was turned towards Varen—I had heard old wives call it a winding-sheet.

The dust of the day before lay white on the sideboard and table, disturbed only where the cards fell and by the track of our fingers. The dawn was creeping through the half-closed shutters of the window, making our faces grey and ghastly in the two lights.

Young Varen was staring at me with mad eyes, and on the table at my side lay a heap of silver. It was I who had been winning.

Varen leaned across the table and gazed into my face.

"Are you a man," he said, "or are you a devil?"

I did not answer, but that terrible thing within me broke into a laugh. The men beside me started in horror as the sound came forth and echoed round the room as though a demon were in each corner to repeat it.

Varen's hand went to his breast.

"Devil in the shape of a man," he said, "your work is done! Crudest of enemies in the guise of a friend! You won my trust and led me to this. What is pure, since you I believed so pure are as you are? What is the reward of love, since you I have loved reward me so? Through your aid I was fighting the old life from me, and rising to honour and esteem, to the knowledge of a mother's proud heart. And through your aid I fell to meanness and disgrace, to see a mother robbed of her necessaries, and worse—to lose her son's love and care and to die broken-hearted alone. Your hand had saved me from the precipice of Hell, and your hand it is that flings me into its hottest fire. Finish, then, your devil's work, for I dare not!"

He drew a pistol from his breast and handed it to me. I felt the cold steel in my hand, and saw the horrified looks of the men around us; they seemed powerless to cry out or interrupt us; before me the ghastly face of young Varen. A wild rage rose up in my heart; I panted like a mad dog, and foam fell from my mouth. I tried to pray, but could not.

A pistol-shot rang through the room, and the white face before me vanished. There was hot blood upon my hands; a terror seized me—what had I done? Hands were upon my shoulders. But I escaped them. I flew down the creaking stairs. People were shouting. Steps were coming after me. I flung wide the door and flew wildly, blindly, down the street. Feet were repeating the echo of mine. People were calling "Murder! murder!" Windows were flung open, men joined in the chase. People were calling "Murder!"—and my hands were red with blood. Ha! the well-known door—it was my own; *his* latch-key opened it. I let myself in and flew upstairs; there was a light in my old room; a nurse sat nodding over the fire. I saw my old form lying motionless upon the bed. I sprang to its side. Voices were calling at the hall-door—men were breaking it in. They had tracked me.

I seized the hand that lay upon the counterpane; a shudder ran through it. Steps were at the door, "Murder" ran through the house. There was a moment of nothingness and I woke.

It was all a terrible dream; I lay upon my own bed. The kind neighbour, hearing my cry, had called in to see if I needed anything; he was looking down with pity in his eyes, his hands cooling mine—he had dipped them in water. No! it was blood, BLOOD! and the room rang with the cries of "MURDERER!" I started up; they were putting manacles on his wrists. He was stunned, he knew not what to say; he answered not their insinuations, but passed his manacled hands now and again across his eyes, like a man who had been long sleeping.

A terrible laugh sounded round the room; it seemed to float through the doorway, and we heard it echo down the house, fading away into stillness. I tried to rise and speak, but fell back unconscious.

IV

I awoke to misery and despair. Lying still a moment, to gather my thoughts together, I heard some persons talking at the head of my bed. It was the nurse and a couple of men, doctors I soon knew them to be. They were talking excitedly, but in subdued voices; I heard every word distinctly: "Graham is to be hanged for the murder of young Varen." I started up, gazing at them in agony.

"He did not do it. I, and I alone, am guilty."

They had started back when I moved, in astonishment; but when I spoke they came beside me, trying to soothe me and make me lie down and rest again. To rest! O Heaven! there was no more rest for me in this world.

I told them I would explain, but they would not let me speak. I heard them whisper of my most extraordinary case. They thought I had gained consciousness while they were speaking of Graham, and, hearing their words at that critical moment, took the idea into my head that I had committed the crime.

"Let me go!" I moaned; "let me go!"

But they held me down in their cruel kindness till I had to do their bidding from very weakness.

But when the night came on, and when the old nurse was nodding in her chair, I arose in the darkness and went from the house. Up and down the streets I wandered till dawn grew grey, but no dawn arose in my heart, only black night for ever. Through the streets, never stopping, I walked till the sun grew hot and bright, and people crowded out into the pathways. I bought a paper from a newsvendor, and read the trial of Gilbert Graham. It was nearly over; all the evidence was against him. He had nothing to say for himself; once he spoke to ask if he might see his little child, and he was told she was dead. They said he seemed stunned, or as though in a dream. I read no more.

When the court was opened, and the trial came on again, I hid myself among the crowd that attended it. I saw the prisoner at the bar; he was not pale; a colour tinged his cheeks. He seemed as if he were asleep. I do not think he heard anything of what was going on. Witness after witness came to condemn him. I could not bear it. I put myself forward as a witness for the defence. They allowed me into the box. I tried to tell my story, but they would not listen to me; some laughed; some pitied me; but they would not let me speak.

"Will you not hear me?" I cried. "You cannot understand, but do not laugh; there are so many things men know nothing of, but do not scorn them because you do not understand them. Can you know what gives life to the smallest insect living on this earth? Can you explore a step beyond the grave? You cannot. I alone am guilty of this murder; by my own act, or by the act of Heaven or Hell, I know not."

A gentleman rose in the court; he sent a message to the Judge, whispered to a constable, and I was dragged out of the house. I heard a murmur of excited voices and a whisper.

"'Tis that poor fellow Bulger; they say his brain is turned since he had his cataleptic attack."

I was forced along by my doctor, his arm linked in mine. Calling a cab, he put me inside, and was about to follow, when a friend of his came up and spoke to him.

"Oh, yes," he answered, "I thought I'd find him there. He woke to consciousness just as Dr. Gill and myself were speaking of young Varen's death, and he seemed to get it into his head that he was the murderer. He escaped from the house last night, but from his ravings I thought it probable I should find him at court today."

I heard no more. Silently opening the door furthest from the speaker, I slipped out, and in the dusk of the evening made my escape.

How the night passed I know not, but, when the light came, I had but one thought: to seek out Graham and beg his forgiveness. Again I bought a morning paper, and read the finish of the trial. Graham was condemned to death.

After a day's wandering, or maybe more—I knew nothing of time in those blank hours—I found out the prison where he lay awaiting his doom, and craved admittance, saying I was a particular friend—a friend!

They let me see him for a moment, but he did not know me. He even smiled when I asked his forgiveness; even he would not believe me.

"I do not understand it at all," he said, laying his head on his hand wearily. "I cannot think, I cannot even feel these last few days," and then raised his head and gazed at me eagerly. "Do you know anything of my mother?"

I did not know of her, and turned away my face.

"I had a child!" he cried. "Oh, tell me of my little child!"

"Do you not remember?—she is dead," I told him, weeping.

He leaned his head upon his hand again. "I had forgotten."

He spoke no more to me, and I was taken out of the place. "He will forgive me tomorrow," I said.

But, hidden away in a low lodging-house, I was too ill to stir for many days; then early one morning I found myself at the prison door again; it opened for me readily, and when it closed I found myself confronted by my doctor and some of his friends.

"I thought our patient would turn up sooner or later," he said. "How fortunate you should choose the time we are here!"

"I will go anywhere you will if you but let me see him once again," I cried; "only once till he forgives me. Let me go! I must!" I cried, fighting them. "I cannot live unless I get his pardon."

"You cannot see him," they said.

"But I will—I must!"

"You cannot—he was hanged this morning at seven."

PLAYING WITH FIRE

by Arthur Conan Doyle

I cannot pretend to say what occurred on the 14th of April last at No. 17, Badderly Gardens. Put down in black and white, my surmise might seem too crude, too grotesque, for serious consideration. And yet that something did occur, and that it was of a nature which will leave its mark upon every one of us for the rest of our lives, is as certain as the unanimous testimony of five witnesses can make it. I will not enter into any argument or speculation. I will only give a plain statement, which will be submitted to John Moir, Harvey Deacon, and Mrs. Delamere, and withheld from publication unless they are prepared to corroborate every detail. I cannot obtain the sanction of Paul Le Duc, for he appears to have left the country.

It was John Moir (the well-known senior partner of Moir, Moir, and Sanderson) who had originally turned our attention to occult subjects. He had, like many very hard and practical men of business, a mystic side to his nature, which had led him to the examination, and eventually to the acceptance, of those elusive phenomena which are grouped together with much that is foolish, and much that is fraudulent, under the common heading of spiritualism. His researches, which had begun with an open mind, ended unhappily in dogma, and he became as positive and fanatical as any other bigot. He represented in our little group the body of men who have turned these singular phenomena into a new religion.

Mrs. Delamere, our medium, was his sister, the wife of Delamere, the rising sculptor. Our experience had shown us that to work on these subjects without a medium was as futile as for an astronomer to make observations without a telescope. On the other hand, the introduction of a paid medium was hateful to all of us. Was it not obvious that he or she would feel bound to return some result for money received, and that the temptation to fraud would be an over-powering one? No phenomena could be relied upon which were produced at a guinea an hour. But, fortunately, Moir had discovered that his sister was mediumistic—in other words, that she was a battery of that animal magnetic force which is the only form of energy which is subtle enough to be acted upon from the spiritual plane as well as from our own material one. Of course, when I say this, I do not mean to beg the question; but I am simply indicating the theories upon which we were ourselves, rightly or wrongly, explaining what we saw. The lady came, not altogether with the approval of her husband, and though she never gave indications of any very great psychic force, we were able, at least, to obtain those usual phenomena of message-tilting which are at the same time so puerile and so inexplicable. Every Sunday evening we met in Harvey Deacon's studio at Badderly Gardens, the next house to the corner of Merton Park Road.

Harvey Deacon's imaginative work in art would prepare anyone to find that he was an ardent lover of everything which was *outré* and sensational. A certain picturesqueness in the study of the occult had been the quality which had originally attracted him to it, but his attention was speedily arrested by some of those phenomena to which I have referred, and he was coming rapidly to the conclusion that what he had looked upon as an amusing romance and an after-dinner entertainment was really a very formidable reality. He is a man with a remarkably clear and logical brain—a true descendant of his ancestor, the well-known Scotch professor—and he represented in our small circle the critical element, the man who has no prejudices, is prepared to follow facts as far as he can see them, and refuses to theorise in advance of his data. His caution annoyed Moir as much as the latter's robust faith amused Deacon, but each in his own way was equally keen upon the matter.

And I? What am I to say that I represented? I was not the devotee. I was not the scientific critic. Perhaps the best that I can claim for myself is that I was the dilettante man about town, anxious to be in the swim of every fresh movement, thankful for any new sensation which would take me out of myself and open up fresh possibilities of existence. I am not an enthusiast myself, but I like the company of those who are. Moir's talk, which made me feel as if we had a private pass-key through the door of death, filled me with a vague contentment. The soothing atmosphere of the séance with the darkened lights was delightful to me. In a word, the thing amused me, and so I was there.

It was, as I have said, upon the 14th of April last that the very singular event which I am about to put upon record took place. I was the first of the men to arrive at the studio, but Mrs. Delamere was already there, having had afternoon tea with Mrs. Harvey Deacon. The two ladies and Deacon himself were standing in front of an unfinished picture of his upon the easel. I am not an expert in art, and I have never professed to understand what Harvey Deacon meant by his pictures; but I could see in this instance that it was all very clever and imaginative, fairies and animals and allegorical figures of all sorts. The ladies were loud in their praises, and indeed the colour effect was a remarkable one.

"What do you think of it, Markham?" he asked.

"Well, it's above me," said I. "These beasts—what are they?"

"Mythical monsters, imaginary creatures, heraldic emblems—a sort of weird, bizarre procession of them."

"With a white horse in front!"

"It's not a horse," said he, rather testily—which was surprising, for he was a very good-humoured fellow as a rule, and hardly ever took himself seriously.

"What is it, then?"

"Can't you see the horn in front? It's a unicorn. I told you they were heraldic beasts. Can't you recognize one?"

"Very sorry, Deacon," said I, for he really seemed to be annoyed.

He laughed at his own irritation.

"Excuse me, Markham!" said he; "the fact is that I have had an awful job over the beast. All day I have been painting him in and painting him out, and trying to imagine what a real live, ramping unicorn would look like. At last I got him, as I hoped; so when you failed to recognise it, it took me on the raw."

"Why, of course it's a unicorn," said I, for he was evidently depressed at my obtuseness. "I can see the horn quite plainly, but I never saw a unicorn except beside the Royal Arms, and so I never thought of the creature. And these others are griffins and cockatrices, and dragons of sorts?"

"Yes, I had no difficulty with them. It was the unicorn which bothered me. However, there's an end of it until to-morrow." He turned the picture round upon the easel, and we all chatted about other subjects.

Moir was late that evening, and when he did arrive he brought with him, rather to our surprise, a small, stout Frenchman, whom he introduced as Monsieur Paul Le Duc. I say to our surprise, for we held a theory that any intrusion into our spiritual circle deranged the conditions, and introduced an element of suspicion. We knew that we could trust each other, but all our results were vitiated by the presence of an outsider. However, Moir soon reconciled us to the innovation. Monsieur Paul Le Duc was a famous student of occultism, a seer, a medium, and a mystic. He was travelling in England with a letter of introduction to Moir from the President of the Parisian brothers of the Rosy Cross. What more natural than that he should bring him to our little séance, or that we should feel honoured by his presence?

He was, as I have said, a small, stout man, undistinguished in appearance, with a broad, smooth, clean-shaven face, remarkable only for a pair of large, brown, velvety eyes, staring vaguely out in front of him. He was well dressed, with the manners of the gentleman, and his curious little turns of English speech set the ladies smiling. Mrs. Deacon had a prejudice against our researches and left the room, upon which we lowered the lights, as was our custom, and drew up our chairs to the square mahogany table which stood in the centre of the studio. The light was subdued, but sufficient to allow us to see each other quite plainly. I remember that I could even observe the curious, podgy little square-topped hands which the Frenchman laid upon the table.

"What a fun!" said he. "It is many years since I have sat in this fashion, and it is to me amusing. Madame is medium. Does madame make the trance?"

"Well, hardly that," said Mrs. Delamere. "But I am always conscious of extreme sleepiness."

"It is the first stage. Then you encourage it, and there comes the trance. When the trance comes, then out jumps your little spirit and in jumps another little spirit, and so you have direct talking or writing. You leave your machine to be worked by another. Hein? But what have unicorns to do with it?"

Harvey Deacon started in his chair. The Frenchman was moving his head slowly round and staring into the shadows which draped the walls.

"What a fun!" said he. "Always unicorns. Who has been thinking so hard upon a subject so bizarre?"

"This is wonderful!" cried Deacon. "I have been trying to paint one all day. But how could you know it?"

"You have been thinking of them in this room."

"Certainly."

"But thoughts are things, my friend. When you imagine a thing you make a thing. You did not know it, *hein?* But I can see your unicorns because it is not only with my eye that I can see."

"Do you mean to say that I create a thing which has never existed by merely thinking of it?"

"But certainly. It is the fact which lies under all other facts. That is why an evil thought is also a danger."

"They are, I suppose, upon the astral plane?" said Moir.

"Ah, well, these are but words, my friends. They are there—somewhere—everywhere—I cannot tell myself. I see them. I could touch them."

"You could not make us see them."

"It is to materialise them. Hold! It is an experiment. But the power is wanting. Let us see what power we have, and then arrange what we shall do. May I place you as I wish?"

"You evidently know a great deal more about it than we do," said Harvey Deacon; "I wish that you would take complete control."

"It may be that the conditions are not good. But we will try what we can do. Madame will sit where she is, I next, and this gentleman beside me. Meester Moir will sit next to madame, because it is well to have blacks and blonds in turn. So! And now with your permission I will turn the lights all out."

"What is the advantage of the dark?" I asked.

"Because the force with which we deal is a vibration of ether and so also is light. We have the wires all for ourselves now—*hein?* You will not be frightened in the darkness, madame? What a fun is such a séance!"

At first the darkness appeared to be absolutely pitchy, but in a few minutes our eyes became so far accustomed to it that we could just make out each other's presence—very dimly and vaguely, it is true. I could see nothing else in the room—only the black loom of the motionless figures. We were all taking the matter much more seriously than we had ever done before.

"You will place your hands in front. It is hopeless that we touch, since we are so few round so large a table. You will compose yourself, madame, and if sleep should come to you you will not fight against it. And now we sit in silence and we expect——*hein?*"

So we sat in silence and expected, staring out into the blackness in front of us. A clock ticked in the passage. A dog barked intermittently far away. Once or twice a cab rattled past in the street, and the gleam of its lamps through the chink in the curtains was a cheerful break in that gloomy vigil. I felt those physical symptoms with which previous séances had made me familiar—the coldness of the feet, the tingling in the hands, the glow of the palms, the feeling of a cold wind upon the back. Strange little shooting pains came in my forearms, especially as it seemed to me in my left one, which was nearest to our visitor—due no doubt to disturbance of the vascular system, but worthy of some attention all the same. At the same time I was conscious of a strained feeling of expectancy which was almost painful. From the rigid, absolute silence of my companions I gathered that their nerves were as tense as my own.

And then suddenly a sound came out of the darkness—a low, sibilant sound, the quick, thin breathing of a woman. Quicker and thinner yet it came, as between clenched teeth, to end in a loud gasp with a dull rustle of cloth.

"What's that? Is all right?" someone asked in the darkness.

"Yes, all is right," said the Frenchman. "It is madame. She is in her trance. Now, gentlemen, if you will wait quiet you will see something, I think, which will interest you much."

Still the ticking in the hall. Still the breathing, deeper and fuller now, from the medium. Still the occasional flash, more welcome than ever, of the passing lights of the hansoms. What a gap we were bridging, the half-raised veil of the eternal on the one side and the cabs of London on the other. The table was throbbing with a mighty pulse. It swayed steadily, rhythmically, with an easy swooping, scooping motion under our fingers. Sharp little raps and cracks came from its substance, file-firing, volley-firing, the sounds of a fagot burning briskly on a frosty night.

"There is much power," said the Frenchman. "See it on the table!"

I had thought it was some delusion of my own, but all could see it now. There was a greenish-yellow phosphorescent light—or I should say a luminous vapour rather than a light—which lay over the surface of the table. It rolled and wreathed and undulated in dim glimmering folds, turning and swirling like clouds of smoke. I could see the white, square-ended hands of the French medium in this baleful light.

"What a fun!" he cried. "It is splendid!"

"Shall we call the alphabet?" asked Moir.

"But no—for we can do much better," said our visitor. "It is but a clumsy thing to tilt the table for every letter of the alphabet, and with such a medium as madame we should do better than that."

"Yes, you will do better," said a voice.

"Who was that? Who spoke? Was that you, Markham?"

"No, I did not speak."

"It was madame who spoke."

"But it was not her voice."

"Is that you, Mrs. Delamere?"

"It is not the medium, but it is the power which uses the organs of the medium," said the strange, deep voice.

"Where is Mrs. Delamere? It will not hurt her, I trust."

"The medium is happy in another plane of existence. She has taken my place, as I have taken hers."

"Who are you?"

"It cannot matter to you who I am. I am one who has lived as you are living, and who has died as you will die."

We heard the creak and grate of a cab pulling up next door. There was an argument about the fare, and the cabman grumbled hoarsely down the street. The green-yellow cloud still swirled faintly over the table, dull elsewhere, but glowing into a dim luminosity in the direction of the medium. It seemed to be piling itself up in front of her. A sense of fear and cold struck into my heart. It seemed to me that lightly and flippantly we had approached the most real and august of sacraments, that communion with the dead of which the fathers of the Church had spoken.

"Don't you think we are going too far? Should we not break up this séance?" I cried.

But the others were all earnest to see the end of it. They laughed at my scruples.

"All the powers are made for use," said Harvey Deacon. "If we can do this, we *should* do this. Every new departure of knowledge has been called unlawful in its inception. It is right and proper that we should inquire into the nature of death."

"It is right and proper," said the voice.

"There, what more could you ask?" cried Moir, who was much excited. "Let us have a test. Will you give us a test that you are really there?"

"What test do you demand?"

"Well, now—I have some coins in my pocket. Will you tell me how many?"

"We come back in the hope of teaching and of elevating, and not to guess childish riddles."

"Ha, ha, Meester Moir, you catch it that time," cried the Frenchman. "But surely this is very good sense what the Control is saying."

"It is a religion, not a game," said the cold, hard voice.

"Exactly—the very view I take of it," cried Moir. "I am sure I am very sorry if I have asked a foolish question. You will not tell me who you are?"

"What does it matter?"

"Have you been a spirit long?"

"Yes."

"How long?"

"We cannot reckon time as you do. Our conditions are different."

"Are you happy?"

"Yes."

"You would not wish to come back to life?"

"No—certainly not."

"Are you busy?"

"We could not be happy if we were not busy."

"What do you do?"

"I have said that the conditions are entirely different."

"Can you give us no idea of your work?"

"We labour for our own improvement and for the advancement of others."

"Do you like coming here tonight?"

"I am glad to come if I can do any good by coming."

"Then to do good is your object?"

"It is the object of all life on every plane."

"You see, Markham, that should answer your scruples."

It did, for my doubts had passed and only interest remained.

"Have you pain in your life?" I asked.

"No; pain is a thing of the body."

"Have you mental pain?"

"Yes; one may always be sad or anxious."

"Do you meet the friends whom you have known on earth?"

"Some of them."

"Why only some of them?"

"Only those who are sympathetic."

"Do husbands meet wives?"

"Those who have truly loved."

"And the others?"

"They are nothing to each other."

"There must be a spiritual connection?"

"Of course."

"Is what we are doing right?"

"If done in the right spirit."

"What is the wrong spirit?"

"Curiosity and levity."

"May harm come of that?"

"Very serious harm."

"What sort of harm?"

"You may call up forces over which you have no control."

"Evil forces?"

"Undeveloped forces."

"You say they are dangerous. Dangerous to body or mind?"

"Sometimes to both."

There was a pause, and the blackness seemed to grow blacker still, while the yellow-green fog swirled and smoked upon the table.

"Any questions you would like to ask, Moir?" said Harvey Deacon.

"Only this—do you pray in your world?"

"One should pray in every world."

"Why?"

"Because it is the acknowledgment of forces outside ourselves."

"What religion do you hold over there?"

"We differ exactly as you do."

"You have no certain knowledge?"

"We have only faith."

"These questions of religion," said the Frenchman, "they are of interest to you serious English people, but they are not so much fun. It seems to me that with this power here we might be able to have some great experience—*hein?* Something of which we could talk."

"But nothing could be more interesting than this," said Moir.

"Well, if you think so, that is very well," the Frenchman answered, peevishly. "For my part, it seems to me that I have heard all this before, and that tonight I should weesh to try some experiment with all this force which is given to us. But if you have other questions, then ask them, and when you are finish we can try something more."

But the spell was broken. We asked and asked, but the medium sat silent in her chair. Only her deep, regular breathing showed that she was there. The mist still swirled upon the table.

"You have disturbed the harmony. She will not answer."

"But we have learned already all that she can tell—*hein?* For my part I wish to see something that I have never seen before."

"What then?"

"You will let me try?"

"What would you do?"

"I have said to you that thoughts are things. Now I wish to *prove* it to you, and to show you that which is only a thought. Yes, yes, I can do it and you will see. Now I ask you only to sit still and say nothing, and keep ever your hands quiet upon the table."

The room was blacker and more silent than ever. The same feeling of apprehension which had lain heavily upon me at the beginning of the séance was back at my heart once more. The roots of my hair were tingling.

"It is working! It is working!" cried the Frenchman, and there was a crack in his voice as he spoke which told me that he also was strung to his tightest.

The luminous fog drifted slowly off the table, and wavered and flickered across the room. There in the farther and darkest corner it gathered and glowed, hardening down into a shining core—a strange, shifty, luminous, and yet non-illuminating patch of radiance, bright itself, but throwing no rays into the darkness. It had changed from a greenish-yellow to a dusky sullen red. Then round this centre there coiled a dark, smoky substance, thickening, hardening, growing denser and blacker. And then the light went out, smothered in that which had grown round it.

"It has gone."

"Hush—there's something the room."

We heard it in the corner where the light had been, something which breathed deeply and fidgeted in the darkness.

"What is it? Le Duc, what you have done?"

"It is all right. No harm will come." The Frenchman's voice was treble with agitation.

"Good heavens, Moir, there's a large animal in the room. Here it is, close by my chair! Go away! Go away!"

It was Harvey Deacon's voice, and then came the sound of a blow upon some hard object. And then . . . And then . . . how can I tell you what happened then?

Some huge thing hurtled against us in the darkness, rearing, stamping, smashing, springing, snorting. The table was splintered. We were scattered in every direction. It clattered and scrambled amongst us, rushing with horrible energy from one corner of the room to another. We were all screaming with fear, grovelling upon our hands and knees to get away from it. Something trod upon my left hand, and I felt the bones splinter under the weight.

"A light! A light!" someone yelled.

"Moir, you have matches, matches!"

"No, I have none. Deacon, where are the matches? For God's sake, the matches!"

"I can't find them. Here, you Frenchman, stop it!"

"It is beyond me. Oh, *mon Dieu*, I cannot stop it. The door! Where is the door?"

My hand, by good luck, lit upon the handle as I groped about in the darkness. The hard-breathing, snorting, rushing creature tore past me and butted with a fearful crash against the oaken partition. The instant that it had passed I turned the handle, and next moment we were all outside, and the door shut behind us. From within came a horrible crashing and rending and stamping.

"What is it? In Heaven's name, what is it?"

"A horse. I saw it when the door opened. But Mrs. Delamere——?"

"We must fetch her out. Come on, Markham; the longer we wait the less we shall like it."

He flung open the door and we rushed in. She was there on the ground amidst the splinters of her chair. We seized her and dragged her swiftly out, and as we gained the door I looked over my shoulder into the darkness. There were two strange eyes glowing at us, a rattle of hoofs, and I had just time to slam the door when there came a crash upon it which split it from top to bottom.

"It's coming through! It's coming!"

"Run, run for your lives!" cried the Frenchman.

Another crash, and something shot through the riven door. It was a long white spike, gleaming in the lamplight. For a moment it shone before us, and then with a snap it disappeared again.

"Quick! Quick! This way!" Harvey Deacon shouted. "Carry her in! Here! Quick!"

We had taken refuge in the dining-room, and shut the heavy oak door. We laid the senseless woman upon the sofa, and as we did so, Moir, the hard man of business, drooped and fainted across the hearthrug. Harvey Deacon was as white as a corpse, jerking and twitching like an epileptic. With a crash we heard the studio door fly to pieces, and the snorting and stamping were in the passage, up and down, up and down, shaking the house with their fury. The Frenchman had sunk his face on his hands, and sobbed like a frightened child.

"What shall we do?" I shook him roughly by the shoulder. "Is a gun any use?"

"No, no. The power will pass. Then it will end."

"You might have killed us all—you unspeakable fool—with your infernal experiments."

"I did not know. How could I tell that it would be frightened? It is mad with terror. It was his fault. He struck it."

Harvey Deacon sprang up. "Good heavens!" he cried.

A terrible scream sounded through the house.

"It's my wife! Here, I'm going out. If it's the Evil One himself I am going out!"

He had thrown open the door and rushed out into the passage. At the end of it, at the foot of the stairs, Mrs. Deacon was lying senseless, struck down by the sight which she had seen. But there was nothing else.

With eyes of horror we looked about us, but all was perfectly quiet and still. I approached the black square of the studio door, expecting with every slow step that some atrocious shape would hurl itself out of it. But nothing came, and all was silent inside the room. Peeping and peering, our hearts in our mouths, we came to the very threshold, and stared into the darkness. There was still no sound, but in one direction there was also no darkness. A luminous, glowing cloud, with an incandescent centre, hovered in the corner of the room. Slowly it dimmed and faded, growing thinner and fainter, until at last the same dense, velvety blackness filled the whole studio. And with the last flickering gleam of that baleful light the Frenchman broke into a shout of joy.

"What a fun!" he cried. "No one is hurt, and only the door broken, and the ladies frightened. But, my friends, we have done what has never been done before."

"And as far as I can help," said Harvey Deacon, "it will certainly never be done again."

And that was what befell on the 14th of April last at No. 17 Badderly Gardens. I began by saying that it would seem too grotesque to dogmatise as to what it was which actually did occur; but I give my impressions, our impressions (since they are corroborated by Harvey Deacon and John Moir), for what they are worth. You may, if it pleases you, imagine that we were the victims of an elaborate and extraordinary hoax. Or you may think with us that we underwent a very real and a very terrible experience. Or perhaps you may know more than we do of such occult matters, and can inform us of some similar occurrence. In this latter case a letter to William Markham, 146m, The Albany, would help to throw a light upon that which is very dark to us.

ONLY A DREAM

by H. Rider Haggard

FOOTPRINTS—footprints—the footprints of one dead. How ghastly they look as they fall before me! Up and down the long hall they go, and I follow them. Pit, pat they fall, those unearthly steps, and beneath them starts up that awful impress. I can see it grow upon the marble, a damp and dreadful thing.

Tread them down; tread them out; follow after them with muddy shoes, and cover them up. In vain. See how they rise through the mire! Who can tread out the footprints of the dead?

And so on, up and down the dim vista of the past, following the sound of the dead feet that wander so restlessly, stamping upon the impress that will not be stamped out. Rave on, wild wind, eternal voice of human misery; fall, dead footsteps, eternal echo of human memory; stamp, miry feet; stamp into forgetfulness that which will not be forgotten.

And so on, on to the end.

Pretty ideas these for a man about to be married, especially when they float into his brain at night like ominous clouds into a summer sky, and he is going to be married tomorrow. There is no mistake about it—the wedding, I mean. To be plain and matter-of-fact, why there stand the presents, or some of them, and very handsome presents they are, ranged in solemn rows upon the long table. It is a remarkable thing to observe when one is about to make a really satisfactory marriage how scores of unsuspected or forgotten friends crop up and send little tokens of their esteem. It was very different when I married my first wife, I remember, but then that match was not satisfactory—just a love-match, no more.

There they stand in solemn rows, as I have said, and inspire me with beautiful thoughts about the innate kindness of human nature, especially the human nature of our distant cousins. It is possible to grow almost poetical over a silver teapot when one is going to be married tomorrow. On how many future mornings shall I be confronted with that teapot? Probably for all my life; and on the other side of the teapot will be the cream jug, and the electro-plated urn will hiss away behind them both. Also the chased sugar basin will be in front, full of sugar, and behind everything will be my second wife.

"My dear," she will say, "will you have another cup of tea?" and probably I shall have another cup.

Well, it is very curious to notice what ideas will come into a man's head sometimes. Sometimes something waves a magic wand over his being, and from the recesses of his soul dim things arise and walk. At unexpected moments they come, and he grows aware of the issues of his mysterious life, and his heart shakes and shivers like a lightning-shattered tree. In that drear light all earthly things seem far, and all unseen things draw near and take shape and awe him, and he knows not what is true and what is false, neither can he trace the edge that marks off the Spirit from the Life. Then it is that the footsteps echo, and the ghostly footprints will not be stamped out.

Pretty thoughts again! and how persistently they come! It is one o'clock and I will go to bed. The rain is falling in sheets outside. I can hear it lashing against the window panes, and the wind wails through the tall wet elms at the end of the garden. I could tell the voice of those elms anywhere; I know it as well as the voice of a friend. What a night it is; we sometimes get them in this part of England in October. It was just such a night when my first wife died, and that is three years ago. I remember how she sat up in her bed.

"Ah! those horrible elms," she said; "I wish you would have them cut down, Frank; they cry like a woman," and I said I would, and just after that she died, poor dear. And so the old elms stand, and I like their music. It is a strange thing; I was half broken-hearted, for I loved her dearly, and she loved me with all her life and strength, and now—I am going to be married again.

"Frank, Frank, don't forget me!" Those were my wife's last words; and, indeed, though I am going to be married again tomorrow, I have not forgotten her. Nor shall I forget how Annie Guthrie (whom I am going to marry now) came to see her the day before she died. I know that Annie always liked me more or less, and I think that my dear wife guessed it. After she had kissed Annie and bid her a last good-bye, and the door had closed, she spoke quite suddenly: "There goes your future wife, Frank," she said; "you should have married her at first instead of me; she is very handsome and very good, and she has two thousand a year; *she* would never have died of a nervous illness." And she laughed a little, and then added:

"Oh, Frank dear, I wonder if you will think of me before you marry Annie Guthrie. Wherever I am I shall be thinking of you."

And now that time which she foresaw has come, and Heaven knows that I have thought of her, poor dear. Ah! those footsteps of one dead that will echo through our lives, those woman's footprints on the marble flooring which will not be stamped out. Most of us have heard and seen them at some time or other, and I hear and see them very plainly

236

tonight. Poor dead wife, I wonder if there are any doors in the land where you have gone through which you can creep out to look at me tonight? I hope that there are none. Death must indeed be a hell if the dead can see and feel and take measure of the forgetful faithlessness of their beloved. Well, I will go to bed and try to get a little rest. I am not so young or so strong as I was, and this wedding wears me out. I wish that the whole thing were done or had never been begun.

What was that? It was not the wind, for it never makes that sound here, and it was not the rain, since the rain has ceased its surging for a moment; nor was it the howling of a dog, for I keep none. It was more like the crying of a woman's voice; but what woman can be abroad on such a night or at such an hour—half-past one in the morning?

There it is again—a dreadful sound; it makes the blood turn chill, and yet has something familiar about it. It is a woman's voice calling round the house. There, she is at the window now, and rattling it, and, great heavens! she is calling me.

"Frank! Frank! Frank!" she calls.

I strive to stir and unshutter that window, but before I can get there she is knocking and calling at another.

Gone again, with her dreadful wail of "Frank! Frank!" Now I hear her at the front door, and, half mad with a horrible fear, I run down the long, dark hall and unbar it. There is nothing there—nothing but the wild rush of the wind and the drip of the rain from the portico. But I can hear the wailing voice going round the house, past the patch of shrubbery. I close the door and listen. There, she has got through the little yard, and is at the back door now. Whoever it is, she must know the way about the house. Along the hall I go again, through a swing door, through the servants' hall, stumbling down some steps into the kitchen, where the embers of the fire are still alive in the grate, diffusing a little warmth and light into the dense gloom.

Whoever it is at the door is knocking now with her clenched hand against the hard wood, and it is wonderful, though she knocks so low, how the sound echoes through the empty kitchens.

※

There I stood and hesitated, trembling in every limb; I dared not open the door. No words of mine can convey the sense of utter desolation that overpowered me. I felt as though I were the only living man in the whole world.

"*Frank! Frank!*" cries the voice with the dreadful familiar ring in it. "Open the door; I am so cold. I have so little time."

My heart stood still, and yet my hands were constrained to obey. Slowly, slowly I lifted the latch and unbarred the door, and, as I did so, a great rush of air snatched it from my hands and swept it wide. The black clouds had broken a little overhead, and there was a patch of blue, rain-washed sky with just a star or two glimmering in it fitfully. For a moment I could only see this bit of sky, but by degrees I made out the accustomed outline of the great trees swinging furiously against it, and the rigid line of the coping of the garden wall beneath them. Then a whirling leaf hit me smartly on the face, and instinctively I dropped my eyes on to something that as yet I could not distinguish—something small and black and wet.

"What are you?" I gasped. Somehow I seemed to feel that it was not a person—I could not say, *Who* are you?

"Don't you know me?" wailed the voice, with the far-off familiar ring about it. "And I mayn't come in and show myself. I haven't the time. You were so long opening the door, Frank, and I am so cold—oh, so bitterly cold! Look there, the moon is coming out, and you will be able to see me. I suppose that you long to see me, as I have longed to see you."

As the figure spoke, or rather wailed, a moonbeam struggled through the watery air and fell on it. It was short and shrunken, the figure of a tiny woman. Also it was dressed in black and wore a black covering over the whole head, shrouding it, after the fashion of a bridal veil. From every part of this veil and dress the water fell in heavy drops.

The figure bore a small basket on her left arm, and her hand—such a poor thin little hand—gleamed white in the moonlight. I noticed that on the third finger was a red line, showing that a wedding-ring had once been there. The other hand was stretched towards me as though in entreaty.

All this I saw in an instant, as it were, and as I saw it, horror seemed to grip me by the throat as though it were a living thing, for as the voice had been familiar, so was the form familiar, though the churchyard had received it long years ago. I could not speak—I could not even move.

"Oh, don't you know me yet?" wailed the voice; "and I have come from so far to see you, and I cannot stop. Look, look," and she began to pluck feverishly with her poor thin hand at the black veil that enshrouded her. At last it came off, and, as in a dream, I saw what in a dim frozen way I had expected to see—the white face and pale yellow hair of my dead wife. Unable to speak or to stir, I gazed and gazed. There was no mistake about it, it was she, ay, even as I had last seen her, white with the whiteness of death, with purple circles round her eyes and the grave-cloth yet beneath her chin. Only her eyes were wide open and fixed upon my face; and a lock of the soft yellow hair had broken loose, and the wind tossed it.

"You know me now, Frank—don't you, Frank? It has been so hard to come to see you, and so cold! But you are going to be married tomorrow, Frank; and I promised—oh, a long time ago—to think of you when you were going to be married wherever I was, and I have kept my promise, and I have come from where I am and brought a present with me. It was bitter to die so young! I was so young to die and leave you, but I had to go. Take it—take it; be quick, I cannot stay any longer. *I could not give you my life, Frank, so I have brought you my death—take it!*"

The figure thrust the basket into my hand, and as it did so the rain came up again, and began to obscure the moonlight.

"I must go, I must go," went on the dreadful, familiar voice, in a cry of despair. "Oh, why were you so long opening the door? I wanted to talk to you before you married Annie; and now I shall never see you again—never! never! *never!* I have lost you for ever! ever! *ever!*"

As the last wailing notes died away the wind came down with a rush and a whirl and the sweep as of a thousand wings, and threw me back into the house, bringing the door to with a crash after me.

I staggered into the kitchen, the basket in my hand, and set it on the table. Just then some embers of the fire fell in, and a faint little flame rose and glimmered on the bright dishes on the dresser, even revealing a tin candlestick, with a box of matches by it. I was well-nigh mad with the darkness and fear, and, seizing the matches, I struck one, and held it to the candle. Presently it caught, and I glanced round the room. It was just as usual, just as the servants had left it, and above the mantelpiece the eight-day clock ticked away solemnly. While I looked at it it struck two, and in a dim fashion I was thankful for its friendly sound.

Then I looked at the basket. It was of very fine white plaited work with black bands running up it, and a chequered black-and-white handle. I knew it well. I have never seen another like it. I bought it years ago at Madeira, and gave it to my poor wife. Ultimately it was washed overboard in a gale in the Irish Channel. I remember that it was full of newspapers and library books, and I had to pay for them. Many and many is the time that I have seen that identical basket standing there on that very kitchen table, for my dear wife always used it to put flowers in, and the shortest cut from that part of the garden where her roses grew was through the kitchen. She used to gather the flowers, and then come in and place her basket on the table, just where it stood now, and order the dinner.

All this passed through my mind in a few seconds as I stood there with the candle in my hand, feeling indeed half dead, and yet with my mind painfully alive. I began to wonder if I had gone asleep, and was the victim of a nightmare. No such thing. I wish it had only been a nightmare. A mouse ran out along the dresser and jumped on to the floor, making quite a crash in the silence.

What was in the basket? I feared to look, and yet some power within me forced me to it. I drew near to the table and stood for a moment listening to the sound of my own heart. Then I stretched out my hand and slowly raised the lid of the basket.

"I could not give you my life, so I have brought you my death!" Those were her words. What could she mean—what could it all mean? I must know or I would go mad. There it lay, whatever it was, wrapped up in linen.

Ah, heaven help me! It was a small bleached human skull!

A dream! After all, only a dream by the fire, but what a dream! And I am to be married tomorrow.

Can I be married tomorrow?

A DIALOGUE OF VISION

by Florence Farr

REBECCA: I love everything Egyptian and I have seen many visions; I wish you would help me to see visions of Egypt.

Widow: I will do what I can. Here is a real Egyptian talisman. Can you see anything if you hold it in your hand?

Rebecca (after a short pause): It is the furnace of Set-Hor. I pass into it. I am between two eternities. I see worlds breaking like bubbles. I come to a region of awful cold; there are pyramidal blocks of ice in a polar sea.

Widow: Yes.

Rebecca: A great galley approaches. In it is an immensely old man. He holds up a circle with seven rings on it. He says it represents the etherial invisible worlds that are attracted by the moon. He is covered with fishes' scales, which he says are symbols of sovereignty. When the seven worlds were more material he controlled them. At one time he had complete control over the solar forces, but the sun got strength and consumed his worlds, and they melted away from material sight. They are pleasant dwelling places for the wandering thoughts of men, and full of immeasurable wisdom. It is aeons of time since any of the human race have penetrated to this region. The earth, when he knew it, was mere star dust. When worlds were making he and the great solar influence then under his rule played at ball with them.

Widow: They are, I suppose, the Beings who, some say, flung worlds to each other across the spaces. I am afraid I have not helped you to see a characteristic *Egyptian* Vision. Shall we try another symbol?

Rebecca: Do let us. I see so easily with you. (*The widow gave her another talisman.*) Oh, now I see a wonderful chamber, the top is like vernis martin. Coiled green serpents form a lamp hanging from the ceiling. The lights are in flowers made of green chrysoprase, of ruby, of yellow chrysolite, of sapphire and diamond. An ancient Chaldean sage, in a red robe, sits under the green serpents. He sits cross-legged, and the serpents whisper to him and connect him with the five lamps of the soul. The sage says the lamps are influences surrounding the soul.

Widow: I think I can explain them; they are the moods of Nature; the green and white are the outward and inward rush of multiplicity, and the red and blue the outward and inward rush of unity; and the serpents are the mystical paths by which we connect ourselves with those moods.

Rebecca: The green light is wonder and fear and vision; the red light is the fire of the intelligence and devours all things but itself; the yellow light is the light which foresees the future; the blue light is the knowledge of the inmost meanings of the present, and is immortal; the white light is the knowledge of past tradition and ritual; it attracts gods as prayer attracts them.

Widow: This is an interesting vision; I will ask another seeress about it.

Rebecca: It is puzzling to me because I know nothing of occult systems.

Seeress (after she has visualised the scene): The green lamp is the exterior life-principle, and is manifested by most healthy people as energy and readiness to take up ideas and carry out plans. The ruby lamp is an absorbing passion; it manifests when some fixed idea gains possession of the soul, and when its whole energies are turned into one deep channel from which it seems impossible to escape. It is an intense fervour of devotion which makes it feed upon itself until it is burnt out. The pale yellow crystal lamp is the interpreter of wisdom; it is the revealer of the interior divine light to the mortal soul. The diamond light is the interior light peopled with Driving Forces and energies which the ancients called gods, bright iridescent beings who have no part in the life of the flesh. The sapphire light is that still more interior world which strips itself of diversity and desire and lives in the clearest etheric region as pure consciousness.

Widow: Then may we take it that the five lights are the moods of the soul induced by contact with the moods of time such as of heat and cold, dawn and sunset?

Seeress: Yes, and with the moods of space also—the solid, liquid, fiery, gaseous and etheric.

Rebecca: The Chaldean has risen. He is wise but not benevolent. He will show me no more unless I follow him into a horrible dark cavern.

Widow: That is enough. We will leave the vision. Repeat the formula I gave you and return.

(*A few days later.*)

Widow: The black cavern you feared was a strangely interesting place. It was the Symbolic Well of Truth, the Truth that kills out all desire for life.

Rebecca: I felt it was terrible.

Widow (quoting): "Who shall look upon Jehovah's face and live?" Our seeress had a vision of the pythoness sitting in her cavern. Around her were the five birds of Egypt, the goose, the flamingo, the hoopoe, the hawk and the heron. They represented the Lord of changing life; the Lady of Single purpose; That which sees the wide fields; the Dreamer and the Cataclysm; they are the rulers of the five moods you saw symbolised as lamps. Now let us see what you get with another talisman.

Rebecca: I see a hawk hovering over Mount Horeb. There is an immensely old man who tells me he is the solar influence which superseded the most ancient solar worship of the red dragon with seven heads and ten horns.

Widow: I wonder if that means a time when there was nothing of our universe but a fiery cloud? Ask to see the school of mystics who are supposed to have lived in this region long before the time of Moses.

Rebecca: I see a rock, like a human head; within it is a shrine with the image of an eye on a single square pillar. Priests dressed in black wind round it continually. Their work is to worship the unsleeping eye; the community is very small; each priest has been selected and made to feel that he must leave everything else in order to join the fraternity. The priests were often entranced for long periods and entombed; the hibernation caused a complete change in the brother who underwent it; he became immensely powerful and in turn communicated a kind of human power to stones and herbs; a human consciousness was communicated to the different kingdoms of nature. The black-robed priests died or were killed when their time came, but two in violet were stable magical forms which were inhabited by a series of souls. Golden radiations came from their heads and sounds like those of stringed instruments. The pillar of the earth stands in the midst of their dominion, and round it the priests of harvests and famines and the priests of floods and rains are disposed. The priests hold these offices after 700 years of initiation.

Widow: This seems to be a vision of the co-operation of human consciousness and natural forces in the primeval world.

Rebecca: I see bay trees growing from the tombs of the sepultured monks; they are symbols of the triumph of life; their leaves and berries give power over the shades of the dead and over all the terrors of the soul. The Horeb priests help the unhappy dead. The two priests in violet especially ruled in the twilight regions.

Widow: Take the hands of the priests.

Rebecca: They have crowned me with bay leaves so that I may have no fear of death. I see the souls like outlines in light, they are throwing up their hands with little tapers, reaching to something above them. There I see souls sitting in the flowers of lotuses with light shining and curling round them in strange convolutions. These are saviours of the earth, they walk in the midst of us but we cannot see them unless our hearts are open. They touch us then and that is the beginning of knowledge and initiation.

Widow: Can you see the effect of the touch?

Rebecca: Healing first, then gradual dissolution, the heart opens more and more and the man fades until there is nothing left but a flaming heart, an ecstasy of fervour. There are many shades who long for extinction; they drift through the void and must be helped; otherwise they would become like a heap of ashes instead of part of the fiery consciousness which is their destiny.

Widow: Suppose the ego becomes a heap of ashes, what then?

Rebecca: The ego that fails makes no difference to the consciousness of the whole. You cannot lose consciousness because all the filaments of life are so interwoven that whether the nucleus ego is merged in the fire or not, yet its filaments remain intertwined with other egos. It is just as if there were a great network of light and each knot were an ego, yet the string goes through countless other knots and the little charred patch makes very little difference in reality. I see consciousness as a great network with stars and planets worked into it and the whole palpitates as waves of Breath pass through and through it, making it quicken and die alternately. The source of this breath is what we call God. The antithesis is black, and out of the blackness the souls seem to pour. I see a great black image; there are five kinds of souls—glorious souls, living, actively teaching souls, inspired souls, human souls and animal souls. They pour like sparks from the different parts of the body of the image. The blackness blindly manufactures these different degrees of soul. They are all red and fiery because they are to burn out the unconscious blackness. The white world of the gods seems quite separate from this black ignorance and red struggle. The gods combine and work out beautiful patterns with no flaw in them; they are white as impalpable snow, and each part moulds itself consciously into beautiful shining shapes. The whole place is a wonder, and sounds of great harmonies like the Eroica Symphony seem to sweep through it.

Widow: Are there no human beings there?

Rebecca: No. Human beings have always the red mark of blood on them like a bird's foot; the greatest human power is in a mixing of the black, the red, and the white natures.

Widow: You are speaking in the symbolism of the alchemists, and of Jacob Böhme.

Rebecca: I see a track of the red footprints of birds, leading to a wonderful sun; flights and flights of heavy bodied birds fly in circles round it. I count seven flights. In the sun is a cauldron where the black and white natures are melted. The pathway of red footprints means blood sacrifice, threefold renunciation, three passions for stripping the soul naked of its ignorance and illusions. One passion is love of the mystical sun. One is the passion for shining wisdom and one is a passion for energetic action. The gods never follow those paths. They are only for souls incarnate. Incarnation means a fusion of worldstuff and consciousness. In a god's consciousness nothing exists because everything subsists. It is impossible to *be conscious* of omniscience because it *is* omniscience. So that in our sense a god is unconscious.

Widow: What happens when a god becomes conscious in our sense?

Rebecca: The god is limited for the time being in order to manifest; but he does not forget his godhead and his power, as the human souls forget their power when they are manifested. A god uses limitation as we use a chariot, not as we use our bodies, identifying ourselves with them. The earth is self-forgetful also like a human soul; but round it there are seven luminous worlds which are informed by radiations from the divine state, who guard it during its period of forgetfulness.

Widow: Then the emanations are not pure divinity?

Rebecca: No, they are seven great Beings who have passed through the fusion in the cauldron. They are great Powers partaking of the red and black natures as well as of the white.

Widow: It sounds like the Indian idea of the Seven Rishis who are guardians of the earth,

Rebecca: I know nothing of that. I can only tell you what I see.

Widow: Can you see what happens to an individual soul?

Rebecca: At first it seems like one of the heat sparks I saw streaming from the blackness some time ago. It gives form to the blackness and gathers it together. It seems to be making universes. I see suns with hundreds of planets streaming round them. These sparks seem to be the cause of this. They palpitate in the centres and rush inwards and outwards as if they were weaving a cosmos. Everything gets dark. Now I see one spark. It is a human soul, I think; but not an individual quite; it is surrounded with colours. The colours are influences left by other human souls. Human souls are all making colours, they seem to do nothing else, that is, during manifestation in a body. The forms of bodies keep changing but the colour accumulates and gets more and more powerful. When persons die their forms divide into five, and are quite separated from the living people; but they leave their colour with the living people, and it twines itself into the living, and influences them for a long time. I see all the results of life symbolised by different colours. There are horrid devouring colours, dark and ugly; they deteriorate and obsess; but they are simply human emanations, not devils or anything of that sort. How careful one ought to be not to leave ugly colours behind one! Ugliness drags the life out of the living, just as beauty gives them life. Beautiful colours seem almost godlike. They are beneficent and helpful.

Widow: Have they any lasting connection with the souls who created them?

Rebecca: No, the dead are quite absorbed in an interior world. I see them, as I said, in five parts. First there is their link with life which is just a red geometrical symbol or seal, more or less perfect in shape; secondly, a wanderer who seems to watch for a signal; thirdly an enraptured being, sitting at the feet of an embodied wisdom. It is shown to me like this but I may not see the true form. The fourth being is superhuman and never incarnates; but is the source of the beneficent beings I saw as the most beautiful colours he'ping the living. Only geniuses among men can leave this highest kind of influence with the living. That part is what is sometimes called the Christ or Buddha in us. It gives impulses to the sacrifice of the intellect and perceptions. Beyond it is the happy being which is just like a star singing for joy; at least that is the only way I can express it. It belongs to the white world which never knows sorrow, and only touches the black and the red worlds when they have attained perfection.

Widow: Then people who think they can communicate with the dead are really communicating with the impression the dead person has left upon them, that is what influence is at bottom?

Rebecca: Yes, the form leaves a photograph behind it. That is why spiritualistic communications are generally so extraordinarily uninteresting. Very few of us can make beautiful pictures of our friends; we can only get distorted and badly focussed photographs.

Widow: Which part of you is it that sees visions?

Rebecca: It seems to me it is the wandering watchman, the second stratum of the soul. In life I see the soul arranged in concentric layers round the ethereal starry part which is the innermost soul of joy, which sometimes gives a little beauty to an artist's work. Next to the innermost is the part that does what it thinks right, the sense of duty and sacrifice to an idea. The third part receives ideas, eats them as it were, the second digests them. All the time you are struggling to argue about pros and cons you are functioning in the outermost crust, which always wants to solidify changeable things; it is fundamentally perverse.

A WEIRD EXPERIENCE

by Zuresta

WHEN I first saw Honoria Westcar I thought she was the prettiest woman I had ever met. Her eyes and hair were dark and her colour a rich carmine, while the rest of her complexion was of a creamy tint. She had winning ways, and I was altogether charmed with her.

Her visit was professional. She told me she would be much pleased to come and see me again, on her return from an operatic tour, which was to extend for some months; she had a fine voice and was singing in grand opera.

I neither heard from her nor saw her for over a year. I often remarked to my companion with whom I live: "I wonder what has become of pretty Miss Westcar?"

One day a visitor was ushered into my consulting-room. I could not recognize her in the least. She said—

"Don't you know me? I am Miss Westcar."

I started. Changed isn't the word, she was simply a wreck.

Her lovely colour had gone, the creamy tint of her complexion had become a dirty drab, quantities of deep furrows and wrinkles marred the former smoothness of her skin, her beautiful dark eyes were dull and sunken with deep circles beneath them. Instead of a girl of twenty-six to twenty-seven which I knew her to be, she looked like a haggard old woman of seventy. I could only gaze at her in amazement.

"Have you been ill?" I asked at length.

"Oh, no," she replied. "I have gone in for spiritualism and have had some very strange happenings."

"Indeed," I said, vaguely uncomfortable.

She told me thirteen was her lucky number. She always did everything in thirteens. She had repeatedly found mysterious presents put in her work-basket when no one had been near the room, and once a golden horseshoe was dropped in front of her on the table without visible hands. I let her ramble on, for I could hardly credit these, to me, foolish stories.

Meanwhile she had edged quite close to me and took my hand in both hers. "You comfort me so," she remarked, as she held it tightly clasped and every now and then rubbed her fingers up and down my arm.

For a while I took no heed, and then a most peculiar sensation came over me and I felt myself getting pale and faint. I noticed her colour was gradually returning and I grew every moment fainter and fainter. My friend at this moment came into the room, and, seeing how tired I was, insisted on my having some lunch and going to lie down. In fact, she had almost to turn Miss Westcar out of the room, so reluctant was she to go. As she said good-bye she remarked: "I shall be with you in spirit."

(I may mention I have a very bright colour which hardly ever fades, even in illness.)

I went to lie down, being thoroughly exhausted. I had hardly lain ten minutes when a most excruciating pain shot through me, as though body and soul were being violently wrenched asunder, and I lay still and rigid on the bed.

When I opened my eyes I found, to my surprise, I was not in my own room at all. It was quite unfamiliar to me and was furnished with six chairs and a sofa all covered in dingy green rep, faded rep curtains hung before the windows, which, though it was summer time, were closed and the curtains drawn across.

I was seated in a high-backed oak chair, one of the only things of value in the room.

A fair man, thin and with a deathly white complexion stood on one side. His eyes were close set and of a hard cold steel blue; his face was adorned with a blond moustache and beard, but the little I could see of the mouth was cruel. Miss Westcar stood on the opposite side to him.

"Have you locked the door?" she asked anxiously; "it would be awkward if we are disturbed."

"No one will come, we are alone in the house; I have seen to that. Yes, this is just the subject we need. We both want a fresh supply of ozone, shall I call it? I am glad you secured her"; and he laughed cynically.

"I hardly thought I should, but she is evidently sympathetic."

"All the better for us. Let us waste no more time." I could not move hand or foot, and yet with the horror of the whole thing, I tried to scream for help, but I was voiceless. Miss Westcar approached me and opened my dress at the neck.

"Yes," he said gloatingly, "she has a fine throat and neck. Will you begin?"

"Very well." She took one of the instruments and punctured my neck. She then started to suck where she had made the incision. In a very short time her face became a glow of colour; a glass was opposite me and I saw myself become whiter than I ever remember.

"That's enough," he said; "it's my turn now."

He started to do the same in two or three places, lower down in my neck, and, oh! the sickening sense of repulsion I felt when his lips touched my bare skin.

"Oh," he remarked with a ghoulish smile, "this is something like; it gives one new life. You must visit her again in a day or two." He made another puncture and again applied his lips, and I could neither speak nor move. When I looked at him he had a fine, fresh colour and appeared ten years younger.

"I think that's enough for today. Release her or she won't be any use for some days, and she is too good a subject to lose." Then they went through some incantations with the chafing dish and burnt some powders which gave out a greenish-blue flame, and I knew no more till I found myself undergoing the same horrible pain as before.

I had no idea how long I had been abstracted, but my friend told me I had been in a death-like trance for two hours, and nothing could rouse me.

She now brought me a cup of strong tea, and, though I was very white and shaken, that revived me somewhat.

I should have thought the whole was a ghastly dream had I not, when undressing that night, noticed five or six punctures on my neck and throat like the prick of a needle or pin; then I knew it had really happened.

Two days after she called and was admitted without my knowledge, and before I could prevent her had seized my hand and begun fondling it as before. I snatched it away, but not before the mischief was done, for that day again I had the same attack, though not quite so long nor so violent.

Both again punctured me and pressed their lips to my neck and throat, but whether they were disturbed in their unholy work or had had enough, I cannot say, I was released under the hour.

The next time she came, a few days later, hoping, I suppose, to renew supplies, she was told I was not at home, nor would anything induce me to see her again. Though she called frequently, she was never admitted, and I never saw her again.

But the extraordinary part of this horrible, and I venture to say unique experience, happened quite four or five years later. A lady who is a very good medium herself came to spend an evening, and I related these facts to her.

"Oh, yes," she exclaimed, "I know that room quite well and Honoria Westcar. The man you describe is, or was, her fiancé; they both went in strongly for black magic. The last time I saw them they were absolute wrecks."

HOW SOMETHING CAME FROM SOMEWHERE

by Evelyn Underhill

Une pratique, même superstitieuse, même insensée, est efficace, parce que c'est un réalisation de la volonté.
—Éliphas Lévi: *Rituel de la Haute Magie.*

WITHIN the bookshop a dusty darkness was made noticeable by the existence of one low-lying patch of light. At 10 p.m. business hours were long over, and the place revenged itself upon intrusion by the uncanny air of peopled solitude, the suggestion that all trespassers will be prosecuted with circumstances of occult terror, which lurks in empty houses, deep forests, and solitary shrines. Commerce was cast out, and seven other devils took her place.

A woman stood within the patch of light, and also within a small circle which she had traced with charcoal upon the imperfectly scrubbed floor. She seemed a healthy and a solid woman: body and brain well balanced, soul asleep. She was studying a stained and coarsely-printed duodecimo which lay upon the desk beside her. It was a rare old English translation of the "Grand Grimoire," which, having recently been rebacked with new brown morocco by strenuous and unsympathetic hands, was now kept open with difficulty by a heavy stamp-moistener and two bulldog letter-clips.

The light was produced by two candles of that brownish-yellow wax which Catholics always burn about the biers of their dead. Since the agents of death and birth are always one, it is hardly strange that these should be the lights assigned by antique tradition to help the incoming of another life. The candles stood upon the floor; with the spot on which the woman was, they marked the points of a triangle which had been carefully drawn within the charcoal ring. Hence they at once proclaimed themselves as instruments of ceremony, not of illumination; belonging rather to the saucerful of incense, the little pan of charcoal that stood on the gas-stove, than to the daily apparatus of ledger, order-book, and publishers' catalogues which crowded the neighbouring desk.

A small mirror hung high up between the book-shelves. It was tilted forward, giving an excellent view of the floor. The flames of the candles were reflected in it: two shining points, exhibiting with a horrible thoroughness the vast and lonely dusk in which they shone. Thus seen, winking and glittering out of the greyness, they seemed intimately, unpleasantly alive; and Constance Tyrrel, in spite of a sound classical education, and much inherited and carefully fostered common sense, felt them to be watchful personalities, companions full of eerie suggestion, poisoning her essential solitude by their hint of terrible companionship.

She began, instinctively, to calculate the shortest possible time in which her present business could be done; then, detecting in this operation the first symptom of oncoming panic, she deliberately looked away from the mirror, and again forced her attention to the Grimoire and to the grotesque and varied objects which were ranged upon her desk ready for use.

There was a piece of cardboard, on which the Pentagram, the Tetragrammaton, and the Caduceus had been traced in coloured inks according to the recipe of Éliphas Lévi. Symbols in outline are seldom impressive, and I am afraid that this talisman had failed to affect her imagination as it should. She hung it upon her breast with a piece of string; and, noting the effect, wondered whether this were or were not the ancestor of the scapular. There was also a forked hazel twig, its tips covered with little thimbles of steel: the magician's wand. She took it in her hand; and, staying always within the circle, reached out for the pan of charcoal and placed it on the ground before her. The childishness of these proceedings would have amused her had it not been for the intense silence, the loneliness of the book-shop, its dim uncertain corners, and the horrible impression of looking out into infinite and cruel darkness—only possible to those who stand in a restricted patch of light—which she received when she raised her eyes from the ground. This darkness was made the more hateful by its very incompleteness; by the radiant mirror which swam out of it, reflecting the two candle flames, like the glowing eyes of some vigilant animal eternally imprisoned in its depths. Now and then she heard footsteps in the street; the rattle and hoot of a motor, the barking of dogs. These noises reminded her that she was shut in with another world, another century, where she could claim no aid but that afforded by her own curiosity and courage.

She took a little incense from her saucer, and threw it on the charcoal. The perfumed smoke ascended in a thick white cloud, veiling the disconcerting mirror and the surrounding bookshelves, inappropriately filled with county histories, educational works, and cheap reprints. It placed itself between Constance and the objects of her daily toil; shut her more closely with her undertaking. She was in the midst of it now: this visible sign of transcendental ambitions assured her of that. Its scent in her nostrils assured her, too, of the solemnities of the undertaking. It lapped her in the atmosphere of ceremony, opened vistas of dream. She turned with a new confidence to the Grimoire, and began to read aloud the Ritual of Conjuration. It was her first attempt to force the lock of that Door which has no key.

"'Ego Constantia conjuro te per Deum vivum, per Deum verum, per Deum sanctum et regnantem.'"

She said it bravely: yet in the very act of reading her judgment sat aloof. It refused to capitulate before the fragrance, the darkness, the amazing phrases. It reminded her that the thing was silly, whilst her imagination murmured that the words were at any rate stupendous. She read them—the long elaborate spell—in the high-pitched, shaky, and shame-stricken voice of one who rehearses some pretentious piece of rhetoric alone, and dreads the mortification of being overheard. Also, to speak clearly seemed almost an acknowledgment that there was, after all, something present to which she could speak: it was an act which peopled the dusky corners of the shop with terrible presences. She shivered a little, and forgot to attribute her discomfort to self-suggestion or over-stimulated nerves. She kept her eyes fixed upon the Grimoire, lest they should meet in the mirror the reflection of some life other than their own. With each fresh phase of the strange chant, the majestic appeal to invisible peoples, intangible powers, the suspicion that this life awaited the opening of her eyes increased.

"'Te exorciso ut nunc et sine mora appareas mihi juxta circulum pulchrâ et honestâ, animæ et corporis forma.'"

She paused. She wondered whether she really desired this terrific result: conceived its possibility. The smoke had cleared a little, and she could detect the opposite side of the shop and the glint of some unpleasant scarlet bindings; standard English novelists in half-roan with deckled edge. Everything was very quiet. Her nervousness had passed away. Nothing happened.

Constance discovered herself to be disappointed. She believed nothing, and was therefore the more ready to believe anything; having all the transcendental curiosity of the true materialist. Her present undertaking was either perilous or absurd. She was not disposed to take either of these risks for nothing. Her fighting instincts were aroused. If success were possible, she would not forego it. Hence the last clauses of the incantation came from her lips with an imperious ring which was appropriate enough to that superb procession of Divine names by which the student of magic really compels himself to exaltation, whilst he purports to be compelling the spirits of the air.

> "'Per nomina maxima Dei deorum Dominus
>   dominatium, Adonay Tetragrammaton Jehovah!
>   *O Theos Athanatos!*
> Ischyros Hagios, Pentagrammaton Shadday
>   *O Theos Athanatos!*
> Tetragrammaton Adonay, Ischyros Athanatos, Shadday!
> Cados, Eloy, Hagios!
>   *O Theos A thanatos!*
> Adonay! Adonay! Adonay!'"

The final phrases echoed through the empty shop in a wild, an appealing cry which she hardly recognized as her own. Thus recited, fresh from the book, by one who knew nothing of its cipher, the necessity of discovering the truly secret words beneath their concealing signs, it would have sounded absurd enough in the ears of a professional occultist; but on this woman's lips it was at once a prayer and a command. She perceived for the first time why it was that these eccentric substantives were known as Words of Power. Their curious rhythms rose, as it were, to waves—inexorable waves of sound—which battered the cliff of uncreated things. As she ceased, she realized that she was intensely fatigued: the over-powering fatigue of a person who has worked beyond her strength, and feels every limb to be invaded by the languors of her brain. It seemed to her, too, that the shop had become very cold. Evidently a gusty wind had arisen outside, and found its way under the ill-fitting door; for the two candle flames flickered suddenly, as if blown sharply towards her, then righted themselves and burned steadily again. Nothing happened.

At the ending of the evocation, said the Grimoire, if the spirit which is conjured by the Magus still fails to appear, the operator will place the steel tips of his wand upon the burning brazier, and make the last and most violent assault upon the unseen world; the mighty and primitive spell called the Clavicle of Solomon. "And be ye not afraid," adds the rubric, "though ye shall hear the loud cries and groans of the spirits who are now being forced to appear within the circle of earth."

Constance had read these directions and this warning with some amusement during her furtive studies of the occult. Upon a sunny afternoon in early spring, in the interval of serving a lady addicted to the literature of the Higher Health and a curate who wished to read Pierre Louys for reasons unconnected with French prose, she had found its careful encouragements quaint and delightful. Now, oddly enough, she turned at once, though with a certain tremulousness, to look for the page upon which the strange syllables of the Clavicle were drawn within their encompassing sign. She did it naturally and inevitably; as if it were now impossible to abandon this adventure whilst any path remained untried.

But as she searched by the feeble light of her candles, the tightly-bound leaves of the little book escaped from fingers which were no longer very steady in their grasp. It shut itself with a snap, and she caught sight between two fly-leaves of a tiny slip of paper, so thin that a breath was needed to disengage it from the page on which it lay. There were on it a few lines of faded writing and many curious signs.

In her rather hasty collation of the Grimoire she had not seen this paper. Now, because she was eager and somewhat disheartened by her non-success, wide-eyed towards all chances of adventure, she took it from its place, held it to the light, and deciphered with difficulty the opening words

"Lo, my beloved son and very dear disciple, I bequeath to thee this Grimoire, the companion of my labours, wherein are faithfully set forth the true Rituals of Magic, together with all things needful for the prosecution of that most divine experiment on which thou art set: to wit, the Word, the Sign, and the Way. Guard well that secret knowledge, remembering the four oaths of thy initiation: to Dare; to Will, to Learn, and to Conceal. But as to this book, have no fear lest the profane and those unlearned in Philosophie discover aught therein, since, even as the Ark within the Temple, all truth here dwells behind a veil; which veil the priests of the Hidden Wisdom alone may pass. . . ." Here followed three lines of Cabalistic figures, which Constance could not read. At the side there was a gloss in tiny writing: "*Nota.*—Take heed that thou dost not forget to sing rightly, and according to the manner of the adepts, these most powerful and all-holy Names of God, and the great Key of Solomon, our Master; for it is very certain that upon the due observance of this matter the whole virtue of thy evocation doth depend."

She replaced the paper in the Grimoire, feeling herself to be little enlightened; for she had no knowledge of that right singing of the adepts which it held essential to the work. However, she turned to the Clavicle, and laid the metal tips of her wand upon the brazier carefully and efficiently, as if she were busied over some intricate operation of cookery; as accurate in her ritual actions as any priest before the altar of his God. She glanced at the mirror, and saw reflected in it her own face. The candles lit it from below, casting peculiar shadows upon the eye-sockets and chin. It seemed a stranger's face: white, peering, curious, and amazed. The contours which gave to it its workaday expression of responsibility and common sense had disappeared.

She began to read; and now, to her amazement, a third and almost horrible change came over her voice. It was no longer the shamefaced muttering thing of a person who suspects her own absurdity; had no more the sharp pitch of overstrung but undefeated nerves. Constance was now impelled to chant, in a loud tone and with a grave intense and crescent determination, the strange old Hebrew spell. The words drew from her—she knew not for what reason—a long and rhythmic cry; a wailing music, with curious ululative prolongations of the vowel sounds. It came from some obscure corner of her spirit, which thus found for the first time a language suited to its needs. She had ceased to be self-conscious, and was far away from the bookshop; her whole will pressing against the barriers of an experience which, as she had gradually and automatically come to believe, was close to her hand. And as the walls of Jericho fell before the persistent trumpets, so under the assault of her cry this barrier seemed to tremble.

"Therefore appear, lest I continue to torment thee with the Words of Power of the great Solomon thy master."

The stream of strange and twisted syllables, the unearthly wailing song, the rhythms which made no appeal to the ear of sense, rose and lifted her with them; then gathered the whole strength of her spirit for the supreme statement of exalted and illuminated will: "Messias Soter Emanuel Sabaoth Adonay, to adorn et invoco."

Her eyes were upon the mirror as she ended; and still it reflected her own strained face, but no other. There was no hand laid on her shoulder, no veiled form.

But there was surely something in the mirror which she had not seen before. She saw a tiny disturbance on the ground, close beyond the edge of the charcoal ring; as if the draught that blew beneath the door had disturbed a little pile of dust. It rose in the air a little way, and hung there like a cloud. The thing was natural enough, for there is always plenty of dust in a bookshop. Nevertheless, the small movement in the dusk had jogged Constance's weary nerves. She watched it, fascinated, longing all the while to look away; and as she watched a fresh wave of overmastering fatigue came on her, and with it, of course, a sudden gust of fear. She knew that, in the impossible event of a spiritual manifestation, she had but to conquer her will, to lay her hand upon the pentagram, and command the Presence to obey, not to intimidate, its conjurer; but it takes great confidence in the unseen to attribute to supernatural causes a phenomenon which may well have been produced by a draughty door. She stared, and struggled with a rising pulse and feelings of great discomfort in the throat.

Meanwhile, the little column of dust rose with a curious spiral motion, as if it were impelled from within. It hung in the air; a grey, faint, cobwebby thing. And then she heard the crying of a sad and frightened voice, which said:

"Ah, what has happened? I am caught! I cannot get away!" And again an inarticulate cry, that came in a rising cadence of anguish and dread.

She exclaimed: "My God! What is it? What have I done?"

The sound of her own voice, harsh and uncertain, convinced her that the other voice had not been heard by the outward ear.

She turned from the mirror, and looked with horror at the floor. The column of dust had disappeared. The candles burned clearly in the dusk.

Then she remembered that she was quite alone: that there was nothing more to do, nothing that she could do. It was late, and she longed to be away. She went to the back of the shop, and switched on the electric light. It seemed an almost impious proceeding after all that had passed; but the nice commonplace click and the immediate radiance comforted her. She extinguished her ceremonial candles, packed away wand, pentagram, and incense in her little leather bag, and carefully rubbed the circle from the floor. The physical exercise restored her to a sense of her own largeness, healthiness, and solidity. She forgot the imaginary voice, and remembered the real world.

She left the bookshop, locking the door behind her. She held the keys, for Mr. Lambton was of a slothful disposition, and left his manager as many responsibilities as he could. She was glad to be out in the air again, and looked forward to a brisk walk through lighted streets. At this moment the mud and motor-omnibuses, the drizzling rain that fell, were familiar and delightful things; freckles on the beloved face of life.

There was a dead kitten in the gutter; a little bag of fur. She stepped back when she saw it, and crossed the road lower down. She was not a squeamish woman, but this was hardly the moment for dead things. It was evidently true, as Éliphas Lévi had said, and the best modern occultists agreed, that magical operations did have some curious effect upon the mind. She could not recover her normal poise; things wore an unusual air, and she was an alien amongst them. She decided that she would go to bed early; she was not in the mood for sitting alone that night.

She had yet to realize that she would never be alone any more.

THE SOUL-HUNTER[1]

by Aleister Crowley

I BOUGHT his body for ten francs. Months before I had bought his soul, bought it for the first glass of the poison—the first glass of the new series of horrors since his discharge, cured—cured!—from the "retreat." Yes, I tempted him, I, a doctor! Bound by the vows—faugh! I needed his body! His soul? pah! but an incident in the bargain. For soul is but a word, a vain word—a battlefield of the philosopher fools, the theologian fools, since Anaximander and Gregory Nanzianus. A toy. But the consciousness? That is what we mean by *soul*, we others. That then must live somewhere. But is it, as Descartes thought, atomic? or fluid, now here, now there? Or is it but a word for the totality of bodily sense? As Weir Mitchell supposed. Well, we should see. I would buy a brain and hunt this elusive consciousness. Just so, luck follows skill; the brain of Jules Foreau was the very pick of the world's brains. The most self-conscious man in Europe! Intellectual to an incredible point, introspective beyond the Hindus, *and* with the fatal craving which made him mine. Jules Foreau, you might have been a statesman; you became a sot—but you shall make the name of Doctor Arthur Lee famous for ever, and put an end

---

1 Unpublished pages from the diary of Dr. Arthur Lee—"the Montrouge Vampire."

to the great problem of the ages. Aha, my friend, how mad of me to fill my diary with this cheap introspective stuff! I feel somehow that the affair will end badly. I am writing my *defence*. Certainly that excuses the form. A jury can never understand plain facts—the cold light of science chills them; they need eloquence, sentiment. . . . Well, I must pay a lawyer for that, if trouble should really arise. How should it? I have made all safe—trust me!

I gave him the drug yesterday. The atropine was a touch of almost superhuman cleverness; the fixed, glassy stare deader than death itself. I complied with the foolish formulæ of the law; in three hours I had the body in my laboratory. In the present absurd state of the law there is really nobody trustworthy in a business of this sort. *Tant pis!* I must cook my own food for a month or so. For no doubt there will be a good deal of noise. No doubt a good deal of noise. I must risk that. I dare not touch anything but the brain; it might vitiate the whole experiment. Bad enough this plaster of Paris affair. You see a healthy man of thirteen stone odd in his prime will dislike any deep interference with his brain—resent it. Chains are useless; nothing keeps a man still. Bar anæsthesia. And anæsthesia is the one thing barred. He must feel, he must talk, he must be as normal as possible. So I have simply built his neck, shoulders, and arms into plaster. He can yell and he can kick. If it does him any good he is welcome. So—to business.

10.30. A.M. He is decidedly under the new drug—η''; yet he does not move. He takes longer to come back to life than I supposed.

10.40. Warmth to extremities. Inhalations of λ. He cannot speak yet, I think. The glare of his eyes is not due to hate, but to the atropine.

10.45. He has noticed the plaster arrangement and the nature of the room. I think he guesses. A gurgle. I light a cigarette and put it in his mouth. He spits it out. He seems hardly to understand my good-humour.

10.47. The first word—"What is it, you devil?" I show him the knife, *et cetera*, and urge him to keep calm and self-collected.

10.50. A laugh, not too nervous. A good sigh. "By George, you amuse me!" Then with a sort of wistful sigh, "I thought you just meant to poison me in some new patent kind of way." Bad; he wants to die. Must cheer him up.

11.00. I have given my little scientific lecture. The patient unimpressed. The absinthe has damaged his reasoning faculty. He cannot see the *a priori* necessity of the experiment. Strange!

11.10. Lord, how funny!—he thinks I may be mad, and is trying all the old dodges to "humour" me! I must sober him.

11.15. Sobered him. Showed him his own cranium—he had never missed it, of course. Yet the fact seemed to surprise him. Important, though, for my thesis. Here at least is one part of the body whose absence in nowise diminishes the range of the sensorium—soul—what shall we call it? "x." Some important glands, of course, rule a man's whole life. Others again—what use is a lymphatic to the soul? To "x."? Well, we must deal with the glands in detail, at the fountain-head, in the brain.

11.20. My writing seems to irritate him. Daren't give drugs. He flushes and pales too easily. Absence of skull? Now, a little cut and tie—and we shall see. N.B.—To keep this record very distinct from the pure surgery of the business.

11.22. A concentrated, sustained yell. It has quite shaken me. I never heard the like. "All out" too, as we used to say on the Cam; he's physically exhausted—*e.g.*, has stopped kicking. Legs limp as possible. Pure funk; I never hurt him.

11.25. A most curious thing: I feel an intense dislike of the man coming over me; and, with an almost insane fascination, the thought, "Suppose I were to kiss him?" Followed by a shiver of physical loathing and disgust. Such thoughts have no business here at all. To work.

12.0. I want a drink; there are most remarkable gaps in the consciousness—not implying unconsciousness. I am inclined to think that what we call continuous pain is a rhythmic beat, frequency of beat less than one in sixty. The shrieks are simply heartbreaking.

12.5. Silence, more terrible than the yells. Afraid I had an accident. He smiles, reassures me. Speaks—"Look here, doctor, enough of this fooling; I'm annoyed with you, really don't know why—and I yell because I know it worries you. But listen to this: under the drug I really died, though you thought I was simulating death. On the contrary, it is now that I am simulating life." There seemed to me, and still seems, some essential absurdity in these words; yet I could not refute him. I opened my mouth and closed it. The voice went on: "It follows that your whole experiment is a childish failure." I cut him short; this time I found words. "You forget your position," I said hotly. "It is against all precedent for the vivisectee to abuse his master. Ingrate!" So incensed was I that I strode angrily to the operating-chair and paralysed the ganglia governing the muscles of speech. Imagine my surprise when he proceeded, entirely incommoded: "On the contrary, it is you who are dead, Arthur Lee." The voice came from behind me, from far off. "Until you die you never know it, but you have been dead all along." My nerve is clearly gone; this must be a case of pure hallucination. I begin to remember that I am alone—alone in the big house with the . . . patient. Suppose I were to fall ill? . . . Was this thought written in my face? He laughed harsh and loud. Disgusting beast!

12.15. A pretty fool I am, tying the wrong nerve. No wonder he could go on talking! A nasty slip in such an experiment as this. Must check the whole thing through again. . . .

1.0. O.K. now. Must get some lunch. Oddly enough, I am pretty sure he was telling the truth. He feels no pain, and only yells to annoy me.

2.10. Excellent! I suppress all the senses but smell, and give him his wife's handkerchief. He bubbles over with amorous drivel; I should love to tell him what she died of, and who. . . . A curious trait, that last remark. Why do I *dislike* the man? I used to get on A1 with him. (N.B. to stitch eyelids with silk. Damn the glare.)

2.20. Theism! The convolution with the cause-idea lying too close to the convolution with the fear-idea. And imagination at work on the nexus! About 24 μ between Charles Bradlaugh and Cardinal Newman!

2.50. So for faith and doubt? Sceptical criticism of my whole experiment boils up in me. What is "normality"? Even so, what possible relation is there between things and the evidence of them recorded in the brain? Evidence of something, maybe. A thermometer chart gives a curve; yet the mercury has only moved up and down. What about the time dimension? But it

270

is not a dimension; it is only a word to explain multiplicity of sensation. Words! words! words! This is the last straw. There is no conceivable standard whereby we may measure anything whatever; and it is useless to pretend there is.

3.3. In short, we are all mad. Yet all this is but the expression of the doubt-stop in the human organ. Let me pull out his faith-stop!

4.45. Done; the devil's own job. He seems to be a Pantheist Antinomian with leanings towards Ritualism. Not impressive. My observation-stop (= my doubt-stop nearly) is full out. (Funny that we should fall into the old faculty jargon.) Perhaps if one's own faith-stop were out there would be a fight; if one's reception-of-new-ideas-stop, a conversion.

5.12. I only wish I had two of them to test the "tuning-up" theory of Collective Hallucination and the like. Out of the question; we must wait for Socialism. But enough for the day is the research thereof. I've matter for a life's work already.

7.50. An excellent scratch dinner—none too soon. Turtle soup, potted char, Yorkshire pie, Stilton, burgundy. Better than nothing. Tomorrow the question of putrefactive changes in the limbs and their relation to the brain.

3.1. Planted bacilli in left foot. Will leave him to sleep. No difficulty there; the brute's as tired as I am. Too tired to curse. I recited "Abide with Me" throughout to soothe him. Some lines distinctly humorous under the circumstances. Will have a smoke in the study and check through the surg. record. Too dazed to realise everything, but I am assuredly an epoch. Whaur's your Robbie Pasteur noo?

12.20. A.M. So I've been on a false trail all day! The course of the research has let right away fromthe "*x*-hunt." The byways have obscured the main road. Valuable though; very very valuable. In the morning success. Bed!

12.30. Yells and struggles again when I went in to say good-night. As I had carefully paralysed *all* sensory avenues (to ensure perfect rest), how was he aware of my presence? The memory of the scented handkerchief, too, very strong; talked a lot of his wife, thinking here with him. Pah! what beasts some men must be! Disgusting fellow! I'm no prude either! If ever I do a woman I'll stop the Filth-gutter. *Ce serait trop.*

12.40. Maybe he did *not* know of my presence; merely re-membered me. He has cause. How much there is in one's mind of the merely personal idea of scoring off the bowlers. And every man is a bats-man in a world of bowlers. Like that leg-cricket game, what did we call it? Oh! bed, bed!

5.0. Patient seriously ill; plaster irks breathing; all sorts of troubles expected and unexpected. Putrefaction of left foot well advanced: promises well for the day's work if I can check collapse.

5.31. Patient very much better; paralysed motor ganglia; safe to remove plaster. Too much time wasted on these foolish mechanical details of life when one is looking for the Master of the Machine.

6.12. Patient in excellent fettle; now to find "*x*"—the soul!

11.55. Worn out; no "*x*" yet. Patient well, normal; have checked shrieks, ingenious dodge.

2.15. No time for food; brandy. Patient fighting fit. No "*x*."

3.1. *Dead!!!* No cause in the world—I must have cut right into the "*x*," the soul. The meningeal——

[Dr. Lee's diary breaks off abruptly at this point. His researches were never published. It will be remembered that he was convicted of causing the death of his mistress, Jeannette Pheyron, under mysterious circumstances, some six months after the date of the above. The surgical record referred to has not been found.—Editor.]

THE THREE WORMS

by Edward Storer

IN the great vault is a coffin. In the coffin is the corpse of a
very beautiful woman. The vault is deep under the ground
and very still. Above its bricks is a layer of earth, and if any
sound at all percolates into this chamber of death, it is only
the delicate tremor and rustle of things growing, of the grass
seed pushing its tiny way through the mould, to break at
the last into its narrow slip of bright green flame. This, and
the weak whisper of trailing rose-roots in whose brown and
ugly stems glow such a tender sap and noiseless fervour of
exquisite perfume. At intervals, maybe, this dark blue silence
is wounded by strange creakings and indescribably tremors:
noises that are really the wastings and settlings of decaying
bone and flesh, just as if Death were feasting his lips at last
with murderous kisses on the flesh of his latest mistress in
the secret peace of his terrible bridal chamber. All around the
vault are hung great blue-black carpets of shadow, and the
floor is damp, and wriggling with the spawn of low life.

Let us look into the coffin of the beautiful dead woman,
look into it as we would have strangers look into our own
with the child eyes of fancy and imagination, rather than with
the cold and scaly eyes of knowledge.

Only to vulgar and brutish eyes is there any horror, for the sweet process of life is at work in every cell and particle of the dead. Truly, there is no such thing as death. Lips grown tired of speech, and outhonied of the honey of all kisses fade and whisper away into something else. The crude utterances of human language fail them, and they win instead the subtle perfumed conversation of flowers and vegetation. Thus their dust comes to lie about a rose-root, and with the lovely chemistry of earth they tremble back to the surface once more as crinkled and crimson perfume, or a frail flutter of yellow longing. Like flags, like tender waving pennons or messengers of hope and greeting from those beleaguered ones dissolving in the fastnesses of earth.

Every rose, every lily is a message from our dead: a sigh or a smile: something simple like the daisy from a simple heart, something of weird and oppressive beauty from some poet's brain, like the passion flower or the fuchsia.

In the coffin of the beautiful dead woman, there are three worms, sweet, clean, wavy, little maggots that will one day carry all the charm and delight of the dead back into the world again, will quicken and nourish seeds and roots, so that in the pink glamour of an April almond tree, the glory of the dead woman's hair shall be returned again.

One of these creatures is poised over her mouth, which again, to vulgar in unseeing eyes, looks ugly, though it is really more beautiful now than ever it was, for it is quick with frail seeds of countless existences, and is become a very factory and warehouse of Life Itself.

Another worm is coming out of the dead right eye of the woman, coiled, as it were, like a little pink amethyst from the stuff of her brain. And yet another peers from the mysterious citadel of her heart, which like a faded and extinguished censer, rusts in the decadence of its scented memories.

The three worms dispose themselves and begin to talk.

The little worm which is issuing from her mouth begins:

"I am her mouth, her beautiful mouth, that sweet frail chalice where her soul delighted to dissolve itself and to lie. That mouth of hers, so nervous, so intimately sensible, that it is pleasant to think of it as the fragile rim of the holy and wonderful amphora of her strange exultant being.

"I am—since I was fed on them—all that litany of kisses which passion flung like a storm of wet rose-leaves on to her mouth—am, am I not?—all those dreams and pale blue shimmering fantasies that love drew like mists out of the hearts of all her lovers to expire in the stained fervour of an instant's rapture.

"I am—forgive it to me!—all the lies which floated from her lips as sweetly as caresses, all those lies which fled like arrows barbed with gall into the ravished brains of her adorers. One I sent to America, and another to pick out the green glint of Death's eye in the lustre of a glass of poison. I tore husband from wife with my wingèd scented words, redolent of the very nudity and flesh of love, yellow, crocus-tinted, opalescent, murderously sweet.

"I pricked the souls of little children with the crystal toys of speech that fell from the melting coral of my curvèd lips.

"I was East and West, and North and South, and sun and moon, and shuddering flight of stars to more than one, and it seems to me, as one of her heirs and sons, that she was not a good woman.

"I fear she was bad, for from me were twisted such devious messages, such various, unalike reports, that yes and no became counters of speech almost indistinguishable to my thinking. Once, I remember, there trickled from me a vagrant little flow of words, so bitter and so inviting, so poisonous and yet so intoxicating, that the soul for whom they were meant held up the silver goblets of hearing for its own destruction with trembling, greedy hands, covetous and anxious, hungry and afraid. her voice that purled and rippled and sang through me—ah! it was like a kiss caged in her throat, and to hear it made a man a father in longing. There are voices like that, and when men hear them, they live a lifetime in an instant, mate, rear children, are widowed, or have their eyes closed for them for the last time by these women whose souls they thus secretly and inviolately espouse."

After a little silence the worm which issued from her eyes then spoke:

"I am her eyes, and she was bad, bad as her mouth says. Some of that mouth's warm tribute came indeed to me, and I was shut from seeing with the close lips of men beating time to the superb madness of their love music and rhythmic kisses. And I saw—O what I saw!—mountains that bowed to her, and stringed necklaces of stars that flashed in ecstasy on Eternity's bosom from the very sight of her. Seas over which she passed on a sensuous errand as live and tremulous as the heave of their own great hearts—heaves that are the world's sighs for the little brood that teases it, and festers the green and waving glory of its skin and hair.

"Much have I looked upon—I, the now crawling, damp and sightless evidence of her sight.

"I am her eyes.

"Empires shone in me: suns set, moons arose, and were drowned like lovely naiads in the waters of the sky. I knew wild flowers so beautiful, that one dared not touch them lest their beauty start to mere ugly life.

"I am that quiver of fragile and delicious expectation that shone in the virgin eyes of her when . . . O happy hour!

"I am that greediness, that terrible woman's greediness, fierce as drought, relentless as Death, which devours its own portion in the feast of life.

"And I too, like her mouth, witness to it that she was evil. The senses are the person in so much as they are the sweet janitors to all that come and go. Through our five portals life only flows, and the flavour of its tides is with us always. I sit in judgment on myself—I where the world could gather itself in one, little, humble, focus-point of curiosity and peep into the garden of her soul—I—where seas could be held calm and captive in a little pool of blue—I—who could consume mountains in a flash, and devour the dawn, I who could bit the moon trail her white limbs for my pleasure through the windy bagnios of the sky.

"I sit in judgment and condemn, for often I was a sword when Truth was a little child, and the breasts of my beauty I gave to Worthlessness in the stinking lupanars of Treachery and Deceit.

"Brothers, like the afterlight of day, I the light of her life consort with the shadows of evening, and I say it softly, gently, ever as Spring's flying feet touch with unaccustomed primroses the wood, I say it—She was bad."

Then the third worm, which came from the woman's heart, turned to the other two, and said:

"I am her heart . . . her beautiful, beautiful heart.

"What do you know of the deeds of the Queen who were never in her council chamber?

"When you were bold, I was perhaps afraid, and when you exulted, there was I know not what trouble of sadness throbbing within me. All that you were I sustained: all your pleasure stirred through me, and you but harvested that which I sowed.

"When you were all aflame, it was I who lit you, and you could not even be sad without me.

"Not less tender than the inviting curl—like a curled and fluffy feather of coral—with which you who were her lips made welcome to some man, was the slow hypnotic wave of my thurible with whose essence I drenched ever cell of her body. I say that she was good, for she was human and she loved, oh! so sweetly, so delicately, so tenderly.

"What you did, you, her lips, her eyes and her other senses, was but to make vain effigies of our interior delight, to shatter in the broken shards of translation the mysterious silent beauty of the vase itself.

"I, the woman's heart of her, was like to a cave where thousands of voices of unborn children cried softly in the dark, where one felt their outstretching hands in pale and piteous appeal, as one may hear the early lilies break through the encompassing earth. In me were the seed of kisses that could only burst to flower in a hundred years to come.

"I am her heart, her ordinary, commonplace woman's heart. Commonplace! Ah! nothing is so mysterious as the commonplace, for it is only Subtlety sleeping and holding its hands a little while. A country clod is more interesting than the most awake and magnetic of geniuses, even as the veiled and cloistered odours of Spring with which one knows the earth is tingling in Winter are more delirious and exciting than the naked bosoms of May.

"Will you believe me, that, but I know not what exquisite contradiction, the sweetest kiss was ever a pang to her, and yielding was only less terrible than denial?

"On my small insistent beat have lain heads that were heavy with great dreams: men of action and men of fancy who loved her and were loved, it may be, a little of her too. I have been the couch of treaties and the pillow of financial strifes, and on me much uncoined gold has slept through dreamless transparent nights.

"Once a poet received her favours, and his head, bowed and weighted with its spongy amorphous magic, rested on me like a honeycomb, all giddy and vibrant with perfume and emotion.

"And once an old mother's head, gray and weary with its long rolling down the years, found on me the unexpected peace and happiness of the old. For the old are so lonely, and no one is their friend. . . . So, my brothers, I give you the key of all her secrets except that secret which she shares with Time and herself.

"I can make all plain except my own mystery, which is the tragedy of everyone, worm, or man, or God.

"Blaspheme no more in such childish, imitative fashion! You are nearer the world than I, and its weak vanity has stained you. The eye looks at the world, and the world looks at the eye, and though each learns from the other, it is not often an even bargain and exchange. . . ."

Then, as the heart-worm ceased to speak, the other two, the eye-worm and the mouth-worm, drew closer to where during all his talking they had been magnetically moved. And all those years which they had passed unconsciously as the lips or the eyes of a woman became suddenly revealed, most vividly different to them.

They could not speak, the two detractors, for they had learnt the wisdom and merit of sin. They knew that good and evil are the same thing, that in a world of illusion he who has the most illusions is the richest man, that to be wise unto ignorance is the fairest counsel, that they knew nothing and yet all, that . . .

And the heart-worm, whose judgment and reasonings had been so readily accepted by the others, grew in his turn a sceptic, since faith cannot live without doubt, and truth is only co-existent with untruth, as day with night, as life with death, as, O beloved! my heart with thine, as vain and coloured chatterings like this with noble and inviolate silence.

CASTING THE RUNES

by M.R. James

April 15th, 190—.

DEAR SIR,—I am requested by the Council of the —— Association to return to you the draft of a paper on *The Truth of Alchemy*, which you have been good enough to offer to read at our forthcoming meeting, and to inform you that the Council do not see their way to including it in the programme.

I am,

Yours faithfully,

—— *Secretary.*

✳

April 18th.

Dear Sir,—I am sorry to say that my engagements do not permit of my affording you an interview on the subject of your proposed paper. Nor do our laws allow of your discussing the matter with a Committee of our Council, as you suggest. Please allow me to assure you that the fullest consideration was given to the draft which you submitted, and that it was not declined without having been referred to the judgment of a most competent authority. No personal question (it can hardly be necessary for me to add) can have had the slightest influence on the decision of the Council.

Believe me (*ut supra*).

✳

April 20th.

The Secretary of the —— Association begs respectfully to inform Mr. Karswell that it is impossible for him to communicate the name of any person or persons to whom the draft of Mr. Karswell's paper may have been submitted; and further desires to intimate that he cannot undertake to reply to any further letters on this subject.

✳

"And who *is* Mr. Karswell?" inquired the Secretary's wife. She had called at his office, and (perhaps unwarrantably) had picked up the last of these three letters, which the typist had just brought in.

"Why, my dear, just at present Mr. Karswell is a very angry man. But I don't know much about him otherwise, except that he is a person of wealth, his address is Lufford Abbey, Warwickshire, and he's an alchemist, apparently, and wants to tell us all about it; and that's about all—except that I don't want to meet him for the next week or two. Now, if you're ready to leave this place, I am."

"What have you been doing to make him angry?" asked Mrs. Secretary.

"The usual thing, my dear, the usual thing: he sent in a draft of a paper he wanted to read at the next meeting, and we referred it to Edward Dunning—almost the only man in England who knows about these things—and he said it was perfectly hopeless, so we declined it. So Karswell has been pelting me with letters ever since. The last thing he wanted was the name of the man we referred his nonsense to; you saw my answer to that. But don't you say anything about it, for goodness' sake."

"I should think not, indeed. Did I ever do such a thing? I do hope, though, he won't get to know that it was poor Mr. Dunning."

"Poor Mr. Dunning? I don't know why you call him that; he's a very happy man, is Dunning. Lots of hobbies and a comfortable home, and all his time to himself."

"I only meant I should be sorry for him if this man got hold of his name, and came and bothered him."

"Oh, ah! yes. I dare say he would be poor Mr. Dunning then."

✳

The Secretary and his wife were lunching out, and the friends to whose house they were bound were Warwickshire people. So Mrs. Secretary had already settled it in her own mind that she would question them judiciously about Mr. Karswell. But she was saved the trouble of leading up to the subject, for the hostess said to the host, before many minutes had passed, "I saw the Abbot of Lufford this morning." The host whistled. "*Did* you? What in the world brings him up to town?" "Goodness knows; he was coming out of the British Museum gate as I drove past." It was not unnatural that Mrs. Secretary should inquire whether this was a real Abbot who was being spoken of. "Oh no, my dear: only a neighbour of ours in the country who bought Lufford Abbey a few years ago. His real name is Karswell." "Is he a friend of yours?" asked Mr.

Secretary, with a private wink to his wife. The question let loose a torrent of declamation. There was really nothing to be said for Mr. Karswell. Nobody knew what he did with himself: his servants were a horrible set of people; he had invented a new religion for himself, and practised no one could tell what appalling rites; he was very easily offended, and never forgave anybody: he had a dreadful face (so the lady insisted, her husband somewhat demurring); he never did a kind action, and whatever influence he did exert was mischievous. "Do the poor man justice, dear," the husband interrupted. "You forget the treat he gave the school children." "Forget it, indeed! But I'm glad you mentioned it, because it gives an idea of the man. Now, Florence, listen to this. The first winter he was at Lufford this delightful neighbour of ours wrote to the clergyman of his parish (he's not ours, but we know him very well) and offered to show the school children some magic-lantern slides. He said he had some new kinds, which he thought would interest them. Well, the clergyman was rather surprised, because Mr. Karswell had shown himself inclined to be unpleasant to the children—complaining of their trespassing, or something of the sort; but of course he accepted, and the evening was fixed, and our friend went himself to see that everything went right. He said he never had been so thankful for anything as that his own children were all prevented from being there: they were at a children's party at our house, as a matter of fact. Because this Mr. Karswell had evidently set out with the intention of frightening these poor village children out of their wits, and I do believe, if he had been allowed to go on, he would actually have done so. He began with some comparatively mild things. Red Riding Hood was one, and even then, Mr. Farrer said, the wolf was so dreadful that several of the smaller children had to be taken out: and he said Mr. Karswell began the story by producing a noise like a wolf howling in the distance, which was the most gruesome thing he had ever heard. All the slides he showed, Mr. Farrer said, were most clever; they were absolutely realistic, and where he had got them or how he worked them he could not imagine. Well, the show went on, and the stories kept on becoming a little more terrifying each time, and the children were mesmerized into complete silence. At last he produced a series which represented a little boy passing through his own park—Lufford, I mean—in the evening. Every child in the room could recognize the place from the pictures. And this poor boy was followed, and at last pursued and overtaken, and either torn in pieces or somehow made away with, by a horrible hopping creature in white, which you saw first dodging about among the trees, and gradually it appeared more and more plainly. Mr. Farrer said it gave him one of the worst nightmares he ever remembered, and what it must have meant to the children doesn't bear thinking of. Of course this was too much, and he spoke very sharply indeed to Mr. Karswell, and said it couldn't go on. All *he* said was: 'Oh, you think it's time to bring our little show to an end and send them home to their beds? *Very* well!' And then, if you please, he switched on another slide, which showed a great mass of snakes, centipedes, and disgusting creatures with wings, and somehow or other he made it seem as if they were climbing out of the picture and getting in amongst the audience; and this was accompanied by a sort of dry rustling noise which sent the children nearly mad, and of course they stampeded. A good many of them were rather hurt in getting out of the room, and I don't suppose one of them closed an eye that night. There was the most dreadful trouble in the village afterwards. Of course the mothers threw a good part of the blame on poor Mr. Farrer, and, if they could have got past the gates, I believe the fathers would have broken every window in the Abbey. Well, now, that's Mr. Karswell: that's the Abbot of Lufford, my dear, and you can imagine how we covet *his* society."

"Yes, I think he has all the possibilities of a distinguished criminal, has Karswell," said the host. "I should be sorry for anyone who got into his bad books."

"Is he the man, or am I mixing him up with someone else?" asked the Secretary (who for some minutes had been wearing the frown of the man who is trying to recollect something). "Is he the man who brought out a *History of Witchcraft* some time back—ten years or more?"

"That's the man; do you remember the reviews of it?"

"Certainly I do; and what's equally to the point, I knew the author of the most incisive of the lot. So did you: you must remember John Harrington; he was at John's in our time."

"Oh, very well indeed, though I don't think I saw or heard anything of him between the time I went down and the day I read the account of the inquest on him."

"Inquest?" said one of the ladies. "What has happened to him?"

"Why, what happened was that he fell out of a tree and broke his neck. But the puzzle was, what could have induced him to get up there. It was a mysterious business, I must say. Here was this man—not an athletic fellow, was he? and with no eccentric twist about him that was ever noticed—walking home along a country road late in the evening—no tramps about—well known and liked in the place—and he suddenly begins to run like mad, loses his hat and stick, and finally shins up a tree—quite a difficult tree—growing in the hedgerow: a dead branch gives way, and he comes down with it and breaks his neck, and there he's found next morning with the most dreadful face of fear on him that could be imagined. It was pretty evident, of course, that he had been chased by something, and people talked of savage dogs, and beasts escaped out of menageries; but there was nothing to be made of that. That was in '89, and I believe his brother Henry (whom I remember as well at Cambridge, but *you* probably don't) has been trying to get on the track of an explanation ever since. He, of course, insists there was malice in it, but I don't know. It's difficult to see how it could have come in."

After a time the talk reverted to the *History of Witchcraft.* "Did you ever look into it?" asked the host.

"Yes, I did," said the Secretary. "I went so far as to read it."

"Was it as bad as it was made out to be?"

"Oh, in point of style and form, quite hopeless. It deserved all the pulverizing it got. But, besides that, it was an evil book. The man believed every word of what he was saying, and I'm very much mistaken if he hadn't tried the greater part of his receipts."

"Well, I only remember Harrington's review of it, and I must say if I'd been the author it would have quenched my literary ambition for good. I should never have held up my head again."

"It hasn't had that effect in the present case. But come, it's half-past three; I must be off."

On the way home the Secretary's wife said, "I do hope that horrible man won't find out that Mr. Dunning had anything to do with the rejection of his paper." "I don't think there's much chance of that," said the Secretary. "Dunning won't mention it himself, for these matters are confidential, and none of us will for the same reason. Karswell won't know his name, for Dunning hasn't published anything on the same subject yet. The only danger is that Karswell might find out, if he was to ask the British Museum people who was in the habit of consulting alchemical manuscripts: I can't very well tell them not to mention Dunning, can I? It would set them talking at once. Let's hope it won't occur to him."

However, Mr. Karswell was an astute man.

✳

This much is in the way of prologue. On an evening rather later in the same week, Mr. Edward Dunning was returning from the British Museum, where he had been engaged in Research, to the comfortable house in a suburb where he lived alone, tended by two excellent women who had been long with him. There is nothing to be added by way of description of him to what we have heard already. Let us follow him as he takes his sober course homewards.

A train took him to within a mile or two of his house, and an electric tram a stage farther. The line ended at a point some three hundred yards from his front door. He had had enough of reading when he got into the car, and indeed the light was not such as to allow him to do more than study the advertisements on the panes of glass that faced him as he sat. As was not unnatural, the advertisements in this particular line of cars were objects of his frequent contemplation, and, with the possible exception of the brilliant and convincing dialogue between Mr. Lamplough and an eminent K.C. on the subject of Pyretic Saline, none of them afforded much scope to his imagination. I am wrong: there was one at the corner of the car farthest from him which did not seem familiar. It was in blue letters on a yellow ground, and all that he could read of it was a name—John Harrington—and something like a date. It could be of no interest to him to know more; but for all that, as the car emptied, he was just curious enough to move along the seat until he could read it well. He felt to a slight extent repaid for his trouble; the advertisement was *not* of the usual type. It ran thus: "In memory of John Harrington, F.S.A., of The Laurels, Ashbrooke. Died Sept. 18th, 1889. Three months were allowed."

The car stopped. Mr. Dunning, still contemplating the blue letters on the yellow ground, had to be stimulated to rise by a word from the conductor. "I beg your pardon," he said, "I was looking at that advertisement; it's a very odd one, isn't it?" The conductor read it slowly. "Well, my word," he said, "I never see that one before. Well, that is a cure, ain't it? Someone bin up to their jokes 'ere, I should think." He got out a duster and applied it, not without saliva, to the pane and then to the outside. "No," he said, returning, "that ain't no transfer; seems to me as if it was reg'lar in the glass, what I mean in the substance, as you may say. Don't you think so, sir?" Mr. Dunning examined it and rubbed it with his glove, and agreed. "Who looks after these advertisements, and gives leave for them to be put up? I wish you would inquire. I will just take a note of the words." At this moment there came a call from the driver: "Look alive, George, time's up." "All right, all right; there's somethink else what's up at this end. You come and look at this 'ere glass." "What's gorn with the glass?" said the driver, approaching. "Well, and oo's 'Arrington? What's it all about?" "I was just asking who was responsible for putting the advertisements up in your cars, and saying it would be as well to make some inquiry about this one." "Well, sir, that's all done at the Company's orfice, that work is: it's our Mr. Timms, I believe, looks into that. When we put up tonight I'll leave word, and per'aps I'll be able to tell you to-morrer if you 'appen to be coming this way."

This was all that passed that evening. Mr. Dunning did just go to the trouble of looking up Ashbrooke, and found that it was in Warwickshire.

Next day he went to town again. The car (it was the same car) was too full in the morning to allow of his getting a word with the conductor: he could only be sure that the curious advertisement had been made away with. The close of the day brought a further element of mystery into the transaction.

He had missed the tram, or else preferred walking home, but at a rather late hour, while he was at work in his study, one of the maids came to say that two men from the tramways was very anxious to speak to him. This was a reminder of the advertisement, which he had, he says, nearly forgotten. He had the men in—they were the conductor and driver of the car—and when the matter of refreshment had been attended to, asked what Mr. Timms had had to say about the advertisement. "Well, sir, that's what we took the liberty to step round about," said the conductor. "Mr. Timm's 'e give William 'ere the rough side of his tongue about that: 'cordin' to 'im there warn't no advertisement of that description sent in, nor ordered, nor paid for, nor put up, nor nothink, let alone not bein' there, and we was playing the fool takin' up his time. 'Well,' I says, 'if that's the case, all I ask of you, Mr. Timms,' I says, 'is to take and look at it for yourself,' I says. 'Of course if it ain't there,' I says, 'you may take and call me what you like.' 'Right,' he says, 'I will': and we went straight off. Now, I leave it to you, sir, if that ad., as we term 'em, with 'Arrington on it warn't as plain as ever you see anythink—blue letters on yeller glass, and as I says at the time, and you borne me out, reg'lar in the glass, because, if you remember, you recollect of me swabbing it with my duster." "To be sure I do, quite clearly— well?" "You may say well, I don't think. Mr. Timms he gets in that car with a light—no, he telled William to 'old the light outside. 'Now,' he says, 'where's your precious ad. what we've 'eard so much about?' ''Ere it is,' I says, 'Mr. Timms,' and I laid my 'and on it." The conductor paused.

"Well," said Mr. Dunning, "it was gone, I suppose. Broken?"

"Broke!—not it. There warn't, if you'll believe me, no more trace of them letters—blue letters they was—on that piece o' glass, than—well, it's no good *me* talkin'. *I* never see such a thing. I leave it to William here if—but there, as I says, where's the benefit in me going on about it?"

"And what did Mr. Timms say?"

"Why 'e did what I give 'im leave to—called us pretty much anythink he liked, and I don't know as I blame him so much neither. But what we thought, William and me did, was as we seen you take down a bit of a note about that—well, that letterin'———"

"I certainly did that, and I have it now. Did you wish me to speak to Mr. Timms myself, and show it to him? Was that what you came in about?"

"There, didn't I say as much?" said William. "Deal with a gent if you can get on the track of one, that's my word. Now perhaps, George, you'll allow as I ain't took you very far wrong tonight."

"Very well, William, very well; no need for you to go on as if you'd 'ad to frog's-march me 'ere. I come quiet, didn't I? All the same for that, we 'adn't ought to take up your time this way, sir; but if it so 'appened you could find time to step round to the Company's orfice in the morning and tell Mr. Timms what you seen for yourself, we should lay under a very 'igh obligation to you for the trouble. You see it ain't bein' called—well, one thing and another, as we mind, but if they got it into their 'ead at the orfice as we seen things as warn't there, why, one thing leads to another, and where we should be a twelvemunce 'ence—well, you can understand what I mean."

Amid further elucidations of the proposition, George, conducted by William, left the room.

The incredulity of Mr. Timms (who had a nodding acquaintance with Mr. Dunning) was greatly modified on the following day by what the latter could tell and show him; and any bad mark that might have been attached to the names of William and George was not suffered to remain on the Company's books; but explanation there was none.

Mr. Dunning's interest in the matter was kept alive by an incident of the following afternoon. He was walking from his club to the train, and he noticed some way ahead a man with a handful of leaflets such as are distributed to passers-by by agents of enterprising firms. This agent had not chosen a very crowded street for his operations: in fact, Mr. Dunning did not see him get rid of a single leaflet before he himself reached the spot. One was thrust into his hand as he passed: the hand that gave it touched his, and he experienced a sort of little shock as it did so. It seemed unnaturally rough and hot. He looked in passing at the giver, but the impression he got was so unclear that, however much he tried to reckon it up subsequently, nothing would come. He was walking quickly, and as he went on glanced at the paper. It was a blue one. The name of Harrington in large capitals caught his eye. He stopped, startled, and felt for his glasses. The next instant the leaflet was twitched out of his hand by a man who hurried past, and was irrecoverably gone. He ran back a few paces, but where was the passer-by? and where the distributor?

It was in a somewhat pensive frame of mind that Mr. Dunning passed on the following day into the Select Manuscript Room of the British Museum, and filled up tickets for Harley 3586, and some other volumes. After a few minutes they were brought to him, and he was settling the one he wanted first upon the desk, when he thought he heard his own name whispered behind him. He turned round hastily, and in doing so, brushed his little portfolio of loose papers on to the floor. He saw no one he recognized except one of the staff in charge of the room, who nodded to him, and he proceeded to pick up his papers. He thought he had them all, and was turning to begin work, when a stout gentleman at the table behind him, who was just rising to leave, and had collected his own belongings, touched him on the shoulder, saying, "May I give you this? I think it should be yours," and handed him a missing quire. "It is mine, thank you," said Mr. Dunning. In another moment the man had left the room.

Upon finishing his work for the afternoon, Mr. Dunning had some conversation with the assistant in charge, and took occasion to ask who the stout gentleman was. "Oh, he's a man named Karswell," said the assistant; "he was asking me a week ago who were the great authorities on alchemy, and of course I told him you were the only one in the country. I'll see if I can't catch him: he'd like to meet you, I'm sure."

"For heaven's sake don't dream of it!" said Mr. Dunning, "I'm particularly anxious to avoid him."

"Oh! very well," said the assistant, "he doesn't come here often: I dare say you won't meet him."

More than once on the way home that day Mr. Dunning confessed to himself that he did not look forward with his usual cheerfulness to a solitary evening. It seemed to him that something ill-defined and impalpable had stepped in between him and his fellow-men—had taken him in charge, as it were. He wanted to sit close up to his neighbours in the train and in the tram, but as luck would have it both train and car were markedly empty. The conductor George was thoughtful, and appeared to be absorbed in calculations as to the number of passengers. On arriving at his house he found Dr. Watson, his medical man, on his doorstep. "I've had to upset your household arrangements, I'm sorry to say, Dunning. Both your servants *hors de combat*. In fact, I've had to send them to the Nursing Home."

"Good heavens! what's the matter?"

"It's something like ptomaine poisoning, I should think: you've not suffered yourself, I can see, or you wouldn't be walking about. I think they'll pull through all right."

"Dear, dear! Have you any idea what brought it on?"

"Well, they tell me they bought some shell-fish from a hawker at their dinner-time. It's odd. I've made inquiries, but I can't find that any hawker has been to other houses in the street. I couldn't send word to you; they won't be back for a bit yet. You come and dine with me tonight, anyhow, and we can make arrangements for going on. Eight o'clock. Don't be too anxious."

The solitary evening was thus obviated; at the expense of some distress and inconvenience, it is true. Mr. Dunning spent the time pleasantly enough with the doctor (a rather recent settler), and returned to his lonely home at about 11.30. The night he passed is not one on which he looks back with any satisfaction. He was in bed and the light was out. He was wondering if the charwoman would come early enough to get him hot water next morning, when he heard the unmistakable sound of his study door opening. No step followed it on the passage floor, but the sound must mean mischief, for he knew that he had shut the door that evening after putting his papers away in his desk. It was rather shame than courage that induced him to slip out into the passage and lean over the banister in his nightgown, listening. No light was visible; no further sound came: only a gust of warm, or even hot air played for an instant round his shins. He went back and decided to lock himself into his room. There was more unpleasantness, however. Either an economical sub-urban company had decided that their light would not be required in the small hours, and had stopped working, or else something was wrong with the meter; the effect was in any case that the electric light was off. The obvious course was to find a match, and also to consult his watch: he might as well know how many hours of discomfort awaited him. So he put his hand into the well-known nook under the pillow: only, it did not get so far. What he touched was, according to his account, a mouth, with teeth, and with hair about it, and, he declares, not the mouth of a human being. I do not think it is any use to guess what he said or did; but he was in a spare room with the door locked and his ear to it before he was clearly conscious again. And there he spent the rest of a most miserable night, looking every moment for some fumbling at the door: but nothing came.

The venturing back to his own room in the morning was attended with many listenings and quiverings. The door stood open, fortunately, and the blinds were up (the servants had been out of the house before the hour of drawing them down); there was, to be short, no trace of an inhabitant. The watch, too, was in its usual place; nothing was disturbed, only the wardrobe door had swung open, in accordance with its confirmed habit. A ring at the back door now announced the charwoman, who had been ordered the night before, and nerved Mr. Dunning, after letting her in, to continue his search in other parts of the house. It was equally fruitless.

The day thus begun went on dismally enough. He dared not go to the Museum: in spite of what the assistant had said, Karswell might turn up there, and Dunning felt he could not cope with a probably hostile stranger. His own house was odious; he hated sponging on the doctor. He spent some little time in a call at the Nursing Home, where he was slightly cheered by a good report of his housekeeper and maid. Towards lunch-time he betook himself to his club, again experiencing a gleam of satisfaction at seeing the Secretary of the Association. At luncheon Dunning told his friend the more material of his woes, but could not bring himself to speak of those that weighed most heavily on his spirits. "My poor dear man," said the Secretary, "what an upset! Look here: we're alone at home, absolutely. You must put up with us. Yes! no excuse: send your things in this afternoon." Dunning was unable to stand out: he was, in truth, becoming acutely anxious, as the hours went on, as to what that night might have waiting for him. He was almost happy as he hurried home to pack up.

His friends, when they had time to take stock of him, were rather shocked at his lorn appearance, and did their best to keep him up to the mark. Not altogether without success: but, when the two men were smoking alone later, Dunning became dull again. Suddenly he said, "Gayton, I believe that alchemist man knows it was I who got his paper rejected." Gayton whistled. "What makes you think that?" he said. Dunning told of his conversation with the Museum assistant, and Gayton could only agree that the guess seemed likely to be correct. "Not that I care much," Dunning went on, "only it might be a nuisance if we were to meet. He's a bad-tempered party, I imagine." Conversation dropped again; Gayton became more and more strongly impressed with the desolateness that came over Dunning's face and bearing, and finally—though with a considerable effort—he asked him point-blank whether something serious was not bothering him. Dunning gave an exclamation of relief. "I was perishing to get it off my mind," he said. "Do you know anything about a man named John Harrington?" Gayton was thoroughly startled, and at the moment could only ask why. Then the complete story of Dunning's experiences came out—what had happened in the tramcar, in his own house, and in the street, the troubling of spirit that had crept over him, and still held him; and he ended with the question he had begun with. Gayton was at a loss how to answer him. To tell the story of Harrington's end would perhaps be right; only, Dunning was in a nervous state, the story was a grim one, and he could not help asking himself whether there were not a connecting link between these two cases, in the person of Karswell. It was a difficult concession for a scientific man, but it could be eased by the phrase "hypnotic suggestion." In the end he decided that his answer tonight should be guarded; he would talk the situation over with his wife. So he said that he had known Harrington at Cambridge, and believed he had died suddenly in 1889, adding a few details about the man and his published work. He did talk over the matter with Mrs. Gayton, and, as he had anticipated, she leapt at once to the conclusion which had been hovering before him. It was she who reminded him of the surviving brother, Henry Harrington, and she also who suggested that he might be got hold of by means of their hosts of the day before. "He might be a hopeless crank," objected Gayton. "That could be ascertained from the Bennetts, who knew him," Mrs. Gayton retorted; and she undertook to see the Bennetts the very next day.

It is not necessary to tell in further detail the steps by which Henry Harrington and Dunning were brought together.

The next scene that does require to be narrated is a conversation that took place between the two. Dunning had told Harrington of the strange ways in which the dead man's name had been brought before him, and had said something, besides, of his own subsequent experiences. Then he had asked if Harrington was disposed, in return, to recall any of the circumstances connected with his brother's death. Harrington's surprise at what he heard can be imagined: but his reply was readily given.

"John," he said, "was in a very odd state, undeniably, from time to time, during some weeks before, though not immediately before, the catastrophe. There were several things; the principal notion he had was that he thought he was being followed. No doubt he was an impressionable man, but he never had had such fancies as this before. I cannot get it out of my mind that there was ill-will at work, and what you tell me about yourself reminds me very much of my brother. Can you think of any possible connecting link?"

"There is just one that has been taking shape vaguely in my mind. I've been told that your brother reviewed a book very severely not long before he died, and just lately I have happened to cross the path of the man who wrote that book in a way he would resent."

"Don't tell me the man was called Karswell."

"Why not? that is exactly his name."

Henry Harrington leant back. "That is final to my mind. Now I must explain further. From something he said, I feel sure that my brother John was beginning to believe—very much against his will—that Karswell was at the bottom of his trouble. I want to tell you what seems to me to have a bearing on the situation. My brother was a great musician, and used to run up to concerts in town. He came back, three months before he died, from one of these, and gave me his programme to look at—an analytical programme: he always kept them. 'I nearly missed this one,' he said. 'I suppose I must have dropped it: anyhow, I was looking for it under my seat and in my pockets and so on, and my neighbour offered me his: said "might he give it me, he had no further use for it," and he went away just afterwards. I don't know who he was—a stout, clean-shaven man. I should have been sorry to miss it; of course I could have bought another, but this cost me nothing.' At another time he told me that he had been very uncomfortable both on the way to his hotel and during the night. I piece things together now in thinking it over. Then, not very long after, he was going over these pro-grammes, putting them in order to have them bound up, and in this particular one (which by the way I had hardly glanced at), he found quite near the beginning a strip of paper with some very odd writing on it in red and black—most carefully done—it looked to me more like Runic letters than anything else. 'Why,' he said, 'this must belong to my fat neighbour. It looks as if it might be worth returning to him; it may be a copy of something; evidently someone has taken trouble over it. How can I find his address?' We talked it over for a little and agreed that it wasn't worth advertising about, and that my brother had better look out for the man at the next concert, to which he was going very soon. The paper was lying on the book and we were both by the fire; it was a cold, windy summer evening. I suppose the door blew open, though I didn't notice it: at any rate a gust—a warm gust it was—came quite suddenly between us, took the paper and blew it straight into the fire: it was light, thin paper, and flared and went up the chimney in a single ash. 'Well,' I said, 'you can't give it back now.' He said nothing for a minute: then rather crossly, 'No, I can't; but why you should keep on saying so I don't know.' I remarked that I didn't say it more than once. 'Not more than four times, you mean,' was all he said. I remember all that very clearly, without any good reason; and now to come to the point. I don't know if you looked at that book of Karswell's which my unfortunate brother reviewed. It's not likely that you should: but I did, both before his death and after it. The first time we made game of it together. It was written in no style at all—split infinitives, and every sort of thing that makes an Oxford gorge rise. Then there was nothing that the man didn't swallow: mixing up classical myths, and stories out of the *Golden Legend* with reports of savage customs of today—all very proper, no doubt, if you know how to use them, but he didn't: he seemed to put the *Golden Legend* and the *Golden Bough* exactly on a par, and to believe both: a pitiable exhibition, in short. Well, after the misfortune, I looked over the book again. It was no better than before, but the impression which it left this time on my mind was different. I suspected—as I told you—that Karswell had borne ill-will to my brother, even that he was in some way responsible for what had happened; and now his book seemed to me to be a very sinister performance indeed. One chapter in particular struck me, in which he spoke of 'casting the Runes' on people, either for the purpose of gaining their affection or of getting them out of the way—perhaps more especially the latter: he spoke of all this in a way that really seemed to me to imply actual knowledge. I've not time to go into details, but the upshot is that I am pretty sure from information received that the civil man at the concert was Karswell: I suspect—I more than suspect—that the paper was of importance: and I do believe that if my brother had been able to give it back, he might have been alive now. Therefore, it occurs to me to ask you whether you have anything to put beside what I have told you."

By way of answer, Dunning had the episode in the Manuscript Room at the British Museum to relate. "Then he did actually hand you some papers; have you examined them? No? because we must, if you'll allow it, look at them at once, and very carefully."

They went to the still empty house—empty, for the two servants were not yet able to return to work. Dunning's portfolio of papers was gathering dust on the writing-table. In it were the quires of small-sized scribbling paper which he used for his transcripts: and from one of these, as he took it up, there slipped and fluttered out into the room with uncanny quickness, a strip of thin light paper. The window was open, but Harrington slammed it to, just in time to intercept the paper, which he caught. "I thought so," he said; "it might be the identical thing that was given to my brother. You'll have to look out, Dunning; this may mean something quite serious for you."

A long consultation took place. The paper was narrowly examined. As Harrington had said, the characters on it were more like Runes than anything else, but not decipherable by either man, and both hesitated to copy them, for fear, as they confessed, of perpetuating whatever evil purpose they might conceal. So it has remained impossible (if I may anticipate a little) to ascertain what was conveyed in this curious message or commission. Both Dunning and Harrington are firmly convinced that it had the effect of bringing its possessors into very undesirable company. That it must be returned to the source whence it came they were agreed, and further, that the only safe and certain way was that of personal service; and here contrivance would be necessary, for Dunning was known by sight to Karswell. He must, for one thing, alter his appearance by shaving his beard. But then might not the blow fall first? Harrington thought they could time it. He knew the date of the concert at which the "black spot" had been put on his brother: it was June 18th. The death had followed on Sept. 18th. Dunning reminded him that three months had been mentioned on the inscription on the car-window. "Perhaps," he added, with a cheerless laugh, "mine may be a bill at three months too. I believe I can fix it by my diary. Yes, April 23rd was the day at the Museum; that brings us to July 23rd. Now, you know, it becomes extremely important to me to know anything you will tell me about the progress of your brother's trouble, if it is possible for you to speak of it." "Of course. Well, the sense of being watched whenever he was alone was the most distressing thing to him. After a time I took to sleeping in his room, and he was the better for that: still, he talked a great deal in his sleep. What about? Is it wise to dwell on that, at least before things are straightened out? I think not, but I can tell you this: two things came for him by post during those weeks, both with a London postmark, and addressed in a commercial hand. One was a woodcut of Bewick's, roughly torn out of the page: one which shows a moonlit road and a man walking along it, followed by an awful demon creature. Under it were written the lines out of the 'Ancient Mariner' (which I suppose the cut illustrates) about one who, having once looked round—

walks on,
And turns no more his head,
Because he knows a frightful fiend
Doth close behind him tread.

The other was a calendar, such as tradesmen often send. My brother paid no attention to this, but I looked at it after his death, and found that everything after Sept. 18 had been torn out. You may be surprised at his having gone out alone the evening he was killed, but the fact is that during the last ten days or so of his life he had been quite free from the sense of being followed or watched."

The end of the consultation was this. Harrington, who knew a neighbour of Karswell's, thought he saw a way of keeping a watch on his movements. It would be Dunning's part to be in readiness to try to cross Karswell's path at any moment, to keep the paper safe and in a place of ready access.

They parted. The next weeks were no doubt a severe strain upon Dunning's nerves: the intangible barrier which had seemed to rise about him on the day when he received the paper, gradually developed into a brooding blackness that cut him off from the means of escape to which one might have thought he might resort. No one was at hand who was likely to suggest them to him, and he seemed robbed of all initiative. He waited with inexpressible anxiety as May, June, and early July passed on, for a mandate from Harrington. But all this time Karswell remained immovable at Lufford.

At last, in less than a week before the date he had come to look upon as the end of his earthly activities, came a telegram: "Leaves Victoria by boat train Thursday night. Do not miss. I come to you tonight. Harrington."

He arrived accordingly, and they concocted plans. The train left Victoria at nine and its last stop before Dover was

Croydon West. Harrington would mark down Karswell at Victoria, and look out for Dunning at Croydon, calling to him if need were by a name agreed upon. Dunning, disguised as far as might be, was to have no label or initials on any hand luggage, and must at all costs have the paper with him.

Dunning's suspense as he waited on the Croydon platform I need not attempt to describe. His sense of danger during the last days had only been sharpened by the fact that the cloud about him had perceptibly been lighter; but relief was an ominous symptom, and, if Karswell eluded him now, hope was gone: and there were so many chances of that. The rumour of the journey might be itself a device. The twenty minutes in which he paced the platform and persecuted every porter with inquiries as to the boat train were as bitter as any he had spent. Still, the train came, and Harrington was at the window. It was important, of course, that there should be no recognition: so Dunning got in at the farther end of the corridor carriage, and only gradually made his way to the compartment where Harrington and Karswell were. He was pleased, on the whole, to see that the train was far from full.

Karswell was on the alert, but gave no sign of recognition. Dunning took the seat not immediately facing him, and attempted, vainly at first, then with increasing command of his faculties, to reckon the possibilities of making the desired transfer. Opposite to Karswell, and next to Dunning, was a heap of Karswell's coats on the seat. It would be of no use to slip the paper into these—he would not be safe, or would not feel so, unless in some way it could be proffered by him and accepted by the other. There was a handbag, open, and with papers in it. Could he manage to conceal this (so that perhaps Karswell might leave the carriage without it), and then find and give it to him? This was the plan that suggested itself. If he could only have counselled with Harrington! but that could not be. The minutes went on. More than once

Karswell rose and went out into the corridor. The second time Dunning was on the point of attempting to make the bag fall off the seat, but he caught Harrington's eye, and read in it a warning. Karswell, from the corridor, was watching: probably to see if the two men recognized each other. He returned, but was evidently restless: and, when he rose the third time, hope dawned, for something did slip off his seat and fall with hardly a sound to the floor. Karswell went out once more, and passed out of range of the corridor window. Dunning picked up what had fallen, and saw that the key was in his hands in the form of one of Cook's ticket-cases, with tickets in it. These cases have a pocket in the cover, and within very few seconds the paper of which we have heard was in the pocket of this one. To make the operation more secure, Harrington stood in the doorway of the compartment and fiddled with the blind. It was done, and done at the right time, for the train was now slowing down towards Dover.

In a moment more Karswell re-entered the compartment. As he did so, Dunning, managing, he knew not how, to suppress the tremble in his voice, handed him the ticket-case, saying, "May I give you this, sir? I believe it is yours." After a brief glance at the ticket inside, Karswell uttered the hoped-for response, "Yes, it is; much obliged to you, sir," and he placed it in his breast pocket.

Even in the few moments that remained—moments of tense anxiety, for they knew not to what a premature finding of the paper might lead—both men noticed that the carriage seemed to darken about them and to grow warmer; that Karswell was fidgety and oppressed; that he drew the heap of loose coats near to him and cast it back as if it repelled him; and that he then sat upright and glanced anxiously at both. They, with sickening anxiety, busied themselves in collecting their belongings; but they both thought that Karswell was on the point of speaking when the train stopped at Dover Town.

It was natural that in the short space between town and pier they should both go into the corridor.

At the pier they got out, but so empty was the train that they were forced to linger on the platform until Karswell should have passed ahead of them with his porter on the way to the boat, and only then was it safe for them to exchange a pressure of the hand and a word of concentrated congratulation. The effect upon Dunning was to make him almost faint. Harrington made him lean up against the wall, while he himself went forward a few yards within sight of the gangway to the boat, at which Karswell had now arrived. The man at the head of it examined his ticket, and, laden with coats, he passed down into the boat. Suddenly the official called after him, "You, sir, beg pardon, did the other gentleman show his ticket?" "What the devil do you mean by the other gentleman?" Karswell's snarling voice called back from the deck. The man bent over and looked at him. "The devil? Well, I don't know, I'm sure," Harrington heard him say to himself, and then aloud, "My mistake, sir; must have been your rugs! ask your pardon." And then, to a subordinate near him, "'Ad he got a dog with him, or what? Funny thing: I could 'a' swore 'e wasn't alone. Well, whatever it was, they'll 'ave to see to it aboard. She's off now. Another week and we shall be gettin' the 'oliday customers." In five minutes more there was nothing but the lessening lights of the boat, the long line of the Dover lamps, the night breeze, and the moon.

Long and long the two sat in their room at the "Lord Warden." In spite of the removal of their greatest anxiety, they were oppressed with a doubt, not of the lightest. Had they been justified in sending a man to his death, as they believed they had? Ought they not to warn him, at least? "No," said Harrington; "if he is the murderer I think him, we have done no more than is just. Still, if you think it better—but how and where can you warn him?" "He was booked to Abbeville only," said Dunning. "I saw that. If I wired to the hotels there in Joanne's Guide, 'Examine your ticket-case, Dunning,' I should feel happier. This is the 21st: he will have a day. But I am afraid he has gone into the dark." So telegrams were left at the hotel office.

It is not clear whether these reached their destination, or whether, if they did, they were understood. All that is known is that, on the afternoon of the 23rd, an English traveller, examining the front of St. Wulfram's Church at Abbeville, then under extensive repair, was struck on the head and instantly killed by a stone falling from the scaffold erected round the north-western tower, there being, as was clearly proved, no workman on the scaffold at that moment: and the traveller's papers identified him as Mr. Karswell.

Only one detail shall be added. At Karswell's sale a set of Bewick, sold with all faults, was acquired by Harrington. The page with the woodcut of the traveller and the demon was, as he had expected, mutilated. Also, after a judicious interval, Harrington repeated to Dunning something of what he had heard his brother say in his sleep: but it was not long before Dunning stopped him.

THE MIDDLE AGE

by G.M. Irvine

THE DOCTOR had just left, and for this I was indeed truly thankful. He bored me with his long-winded sentences and jaw-breaking words in an attempt to reassure my people, not only as regarded the prospects of my recovery, but also with reference to his own indisputable claim to the position of high-water mark in the realm of scientific knowledge and skill.

I could hear him delaying outside the door to expatiate on a crisis, and wondered whether he was concerned with home politics or more serious international relations. Mingled with the talk of crisis there frequently recurred reference to the ninth day. My head ached to such a degree that I was unable to make out distinctly whether we were in the ninth day of a prolonged crisis, or within nine days of it, or had got nine days beyond it.

At length, however, I knew he had gone and taken his troublesome, critical atmosphere with him; for I heard my mother, on entering the room, express the wish that the man of crisis would not boast so extensively of the superhuman efforts he had to make in order to overtake his work, and keep pace with the rapidly growing confidence which the public placed in his skill.

Gradually light dawned on me, and I saw clearly that this Doctor had for nine days to run after distant, fleeing patients, whom I could discern at varying distances almost to the horizon. He ran strong and well, his long hair—I believe he seldom found time to have it cut, and then only in a great hurry had the mere ends removed—streaming in the breeze, his tall hat involuntarily, and frock coat voluntarily discarded in his anxiety to overtake his prey.

Three days he ran, and as he stopped to draw a deep breath or two and mop his perspiring brow, with a shiver and much chattering of teeth I drew a broad black line across the country at that point. No sooner had this been done than he darted forward for other three days, and again rested a moment while I shivered and drew the second black line. On and on he hurried until he had become almost a speck, and at the end of the ninth day disappeared over the sky-line, holding on by the coat-tail of the last retreating patient—slower than the others, though apparently no less eager to escape.

He had been quite right, I saw; in nine days he had secured one patient, and in nine more would probably secure another, and so on. But why this nineness of all things? I bethought me of the properties of the repeating decimal, but could derive no clue to a solution of the difficulty therefrom. "The ninth day," a voice said close beside me. "Oh, this nineification of time! I must and will find out the secret of it," I said to myself, as I left the house bent on solving the question.

Outside, where there should have been the darkness of night, three luminant figures of 3, placed at the corners of a large equilateral triangle, cast beams of blue, red and white light in all directions. At the examination, which I just then remembered I had to attend, a knowledge of the occult properties of the figure nine was required, and this, I knew, was contained in a Sanskrit work lately prescribed for the third professional examination. The three examiners with one voice put the question to me at three o' clock, when the clock stood still, just as it had completed the third stroke of the hour, and the examiners fell into three separate sleeps, the coming and going of their breath sounding as double, and their snores as single cycles of three. I tried to solve the question, gazing on the clock and listening to the threefold snore in turn for inspiration. It was of no use, so I determined to slip out of the room in order to find a copy of the Sanskrit book and make up the subject, knowing that the examiners could not stir for three times three hundred years, and in that time I should have returned to my place replete with Eastern lore.

Outside it was night, though the town was lighted up in ghostly manner by the three lights of three. The wind was bitingly cold and the ground crisp with frost, so that I greatly regretted having come out with no clothing on. Approaching the park, by which I had thought to take a near-cut to the centre of the city, I found on the entrance gate a notice to the effect that the way was closed at 9 p.m., and opened at 9 a.m. Policeman No. 999 told me it was 900 yards from the corner where I stood to the public library, which, however, he said was closed for repairs for nine days, and that in any case it always closed at 9 p.m. I told him this was unreasonable, but he refused to admit it, and when I became excited ordered me to move on, which I would not do, but waxed very wroth. "Know you not," I cried, "that the very secret of the numbers on your collar—dog's collar as it is—awaits solution? Let me pass, or by heaven———" We closed, and it was instantly plain he was no match for me; I threw him easily, hampered as he was by clothes, but he rose again breathing vengeance and hissing his murderous hate into my face as we again grappled. The struggle was longer this time, but the result infinitely more disastrous to the guardian of the peace; gradually his hold relaxed under the overpowering grasp of my unconquerable arms, until at last, disengaging myself, I lifted his limp form and flung it with much violence across the street, full against the houses on the opposite side. His clothing fell half-way like the wads of a discharged cartridge, and his body met the wall just beside a door, where it made a horrid mark of three bent limbs, somewhat like the coat-of-arms of Manxland, and above it stood out the three figures of 9 which had been the official number on his uniform. "Great heavens!" I thought, "he is dead and will be recognised by his number." At any rate, the thought consoled me that he had been unreasonable and the aggressor, also that no one had seen me, and even if they had I could not be recognised by my clothing; "true," I thought, "there is a mole on my left shoulder," and I put up my right hand to cover it.

A grinning death's head here looked over my shoulder and whispered into my ear: "guilty man, flee until the ninth aeon." And I fled through the city, noiselessly save for my panting breath and the wild beatings of my heart, which were like the pulsations of a mighty locomotive. And ever behind was heard the rustle of the cerecloth garments of the owner of the death's head, mingled with the rattle of dry bones. "Until the ninth aeon," he muttered, flitting along apparently close behind me, though I dared not look round to see how closely he followed.

Onward we pressed through and beyond the city, out into the open plain where at some distance I saw clumps of ever-green here and there. The voice behind whispered "ware ambush;" but I could not understand, and even if I had there was an irresistible impulse driving me on. Presently I noticed the glint of shining armour in one of the copses, and almost simultaneously heard a hurried short command at which there rode out from behind it two bodies of horsemen—each a company of ten—one taking up a position on my front, the other cutting off my retreat. Resplendent in the light of the "Threes" they sat, perfect pictures of gallant knighthood as they wheeled into line. At this I wondered, and would have fled in vague terror had not a number of footmen, armed with pikes, rushed straight on me from the cover with evident intent to bear me down. I faced the footmen and death boldly with extended chest, head held high in disdain for their utmost. Already a sharp pike had pricked me, and almost penetrated my chest wall on the right side, when the death's head whispered "hold your breath." Blindly obeying I did so, and at the word "Excalibur," whispered over my shoulder, a sword flashing in the light of the "Threes" stood in the air ready to my hand. The man whose pike had almost entered my right lung, pushed with all his might, twisting and pushing in turn, but all without result; as well might he have sought to pierce the finest chain mail with a cabbage stalk. The hair on his head stood on end dislodging his casque as he looked up and saw me grasp the flashing sword, the next instant he was out clean in two about midway; the upper half stood brandishing its arms like a bust of evil and of murderous hate newly overcast with abject terror; the lower half, deprived of all power of expression, except through its legs, fled to the coppice, followed by the other terror-stricken pikemen. With a wild yell of triumph I shouted: "ha! ha! poltroons, murderous, caitiff knaves, death is on my side! Excalibur!" Here, looking round, I beheld the two bodies of horsemen in full flight in opposite directions, but pursued them not.

Often had I wished to reform the world of the Middle Age, and here I had now been granted a glorious opportunity not to be let slip. On I went for many miles until a strong and wonderfully beautiful castle rose in view. Smaller bodies of horsemen hurried towards it on my approach and in front stood the serried ranks of knighthood gaily caparisoned in full armour, apparently expecting and awaiting my approach. There was evident perturbation, much hurrying to and fro, and shouting of words of command. Right and left the horsemen divided and took up positions, one half on my right and the other on my left. "Stand still," said the voice, "and await their evil machinations." I did so, and behold now I saw the attendants of each company lighting a fire on which they proceeded to pile huge bundles of damp hay, so that clouds of heavy, acrid smoke soon began to float over the space separating us. Did they intend advancing on me under cover of these smoke clouds? "Oh, evil murderers," I cried, "I wait no longer," and with this prepared to march into the smoke. "Stand still," said the voice, "and do not cough; the moment thou coughest thou shalt surely die, and the enemy know this." On came the smoke until it surrounded me closely and finally completely enveloped me. Oh heavens! Oh Excalibur! I could no longer refrain from coughing, but even as I started to draw a quick breath with a view to driving quietly some of the smoke from my lungs a lance point darting out of the bluish cloud pierced my right side; holding the cough still in incompletion I brought down my trusty sword in the direction of the lance shaft, and straightway a gaudy knight rolled out of the smoke to my very feet.

But what was I to do with the remains of this horrid cough? It would out, and they, hearing, would wound me again, perhaps unto death. I tried artfully to grind out the descending part of the cough slowly, softly, and in imitation of a snatch of a war-song, and for a moment looked to be succeeding, when suddenly I was pierced in the right side from before and behind by several lances, some of which went right through. Nine shafts and nine points I counted in front, and saw that it was impossible, transfixed as I was, to fall to the ground though mightily desiring it. Gazing on the lances, I saw that they had all passed above the dome of the liver, and knew that I might yet survive if the attack were not renewed.

Presently the smoke began to roll back and the knights with it, having rudely withdrawn their weapons, whereupon I fell to the ground exhausted. The voice said "the attack is over," and in an instant, busy, unseen hands were engaged in healing my wounds with the softness and warmth of a wizard cure, after which I rose completely healed and ready for the fray.

Advancing on the castle I saw the last of the horsemen disappear into it, saw the draw-bridge rise and the portcullis fall. Boldly I stood before the gate and called on the stronghold to surrender, but my only answer was a shower of sharpest arrows from the battlements; many of these pierced my right side causing quite as much pain as I withdrew them in handfuls as they had done on entering. I recalled how a mighty ancient hero had been vulnerable in the heel only, and reflected on the accuracy of the marksman who had picked him off. These bowmen, too, had their hands guided by the devil, who appeared to have spent most of his energy in securing accuracy of aim, there being not enough left to supply the necessary strength of flight. But they were numerous and persistent, and in the end might prevail. I placed my hand over the spot, but the arrow heads slipped between my fingers. Something had to be done immediately in order to put an end to this state of matters, so I called aloud on the castle to surrender, raising my sword with the vague intention of attacking single-handed, when to my astonishment the assiduous bowmen suddenly desisted and the draw-bridge was being lowered; across the bridge there advanced towards me an old, lame man. My soul was filled with sorrow as I recognised the great Sir Walter Scott in the person of this man. "What," I cried, "thou, Sir Walter, the envoy of this ruffianly band of marauders? Would heaven it were otherwise! Now, indeed, do I see with what tinsel glitter of spurious virtue and valour thy pen was used to cover over this shameful age of misnamed chivalry, this Middle Age, this ugly scar of vice on the fair face of time, the age when honour slept, when the noble courage of man in the daylight of former times degenerated into the fearful crouching ambush of the beast of prey by night. Thou, the envoy from this mephitic pit of perfidy! Ah me, Sir Walter!"

My voice trembled and failed me at the sight of the old man weeping with head bent low. "Hear me," he pleaded, stretching forth his left hand towards me; "but hear me, thou hero of the more modern time. I, too, had almost lived to discard my idol; indeed I had taken a first step in giving to the world a history of Napoleon, when the rude hand of death hurried me off, and here since then I have been condemned to companionship of these, shut up in this castle, the home of knights once noble on earth, but now doomed to defeat without end at the hands of heroes of a nobler time, who come this way every ninth year, and none more terrible than thou—the bare knight of the naked sword—whose coming has long been expected with fear and trembling. Oh, spare us; add not to the already intolerable miseries, never-ending, which we here are destined to endure."

"Spare us, oh most gallant knight of the bare skin," said a voice, and looking round I beheld a tall thin man in tight-fitting, parti-coloured dress, a pointed cap adorned with bells on his head, advancing towards us, whirling and pirouetting on his toes after the manner of an harlequin. Passing quite close to me in his mad career, with a grinning leer on his face, he suddenly flung a handful of brownish, ill-odoured powder full in my face, whereupon I coughed violently, irresistibly, and at the Sir Walter's right hand, which had remained hidden in his tunic all this time, quick as lightning flashed forth to plunge a long dagger straight through my right side. upon same moment in his "Oh, god of poets and novelists," I groaned as I fell, "to what depths has sunk this thy handi-work; surely the hand which dared to indite such malignity against the great Napoleon dead—against Napoleon, the hero of his time, spotless as an angel compared with this armoured knightly scum—has been justly condemned to an eternity of vice, ever more and more decadent, in company with the cowardly and now despised objects of his former hero-worship."

Falling into a swoon, I must have been a long time oblivious to everything when a footfall close by caused me to look up, and my eyes fell on a tall, spare knight, heavily armoured and of noble bearing, who approached me on foot. His visor was up so that I could see his keen, dark eye flash vengeance as he shook his mailed fist towards the castle and looked on me prostrate in turn. "Come hither, Sancho," he called out to his portly attendant, "my medicaments are here required forthwith for this foully treated knight."

In a trice he was bending over me, and by the prick of a tiny needle in my arm immediately relieved me of all pain from my recent wound. When I had sat up he placed a small shield, which seemed to be made of paper covered on one side with a yellow substance, very cold at first but growing in a few minutes very hot, over my vulnerable spot. "Now," said he, "thou art safe from pike, lance, and sword of these recreant knights, from sharpest arrow of base retainer. Every ninth year come I, the knight Don Quixote, to this land of the border, where all things ever struggle to be what they had failed to be on earth. These knights strove on earth to accomplish nought but evil, and here are destined to aim until the ninth aeon at the accomplishment of evil unattainable; whilst I, who had been thwarted in my nobler designs on earth by these, and such as these, have been appointed along with others to return every ninth year, in order to overthrow these wicked men and thwart them in their foul designs. "But, Sir Knight," he continued, looking on me curiously, "I do not know thee. Art thou one of the noble few who approach this land of the Border from the further side, as once I did myself, to do deeds of mighty daring? To such, if such thou art, this is in truth a land of disenchantment. Here to the eye of the good and brave the tinsel glitter of the caitiff is torn away, and he is seen at length clad in the real baseness of his nature. What idols of generous youth are broken to pieces on the way through this borderland! Truly it is a land of disenchantment."

Here he drew his sword, motioning me to take mine from the ground, which I gladly did. Then turning to his attendant he addressed to him these words of command: "Wind, Sancho, wind me thy bugle in the ear of this den of thieves that they may come forth at the end of the ninth year;" and Sancho did as he was ordered three times, again and yet again three times; at the end of the ninth bugle note the draw-bridge fell, and a troop of armoured knights issued forth in all their bravery only to cower right and left, the weapons shaking in their hands the while, at the sight of the noble Don and of myself whom they had thought dead.

Nine days and nights the battle raged unceasingly. Many a headless trunk rushed aimlessly to and fro, obstructing those whom they would willingly aid; many a trunkless head impotently glowered from the ground, the battle-cry cut short in their throats. When the last knight had been disarmed, we paused to take a copious draught of wine from the skin brought to us by the admiring and faithful Sancho, for my thirst, at least, was great.

The Spanish Knight then leading the way, we entered the empty sounding castle, crossed the courtyard, and by a winding stone stair found our way to a bare comfortless apartment, the floor of which was strewn with rushes. Here, on a stone bench in the window, sat Sir Walter Scott with writing material on his knees, and weeping bitterly. "Poor old man" said I, turning to the great Don, who also looked on him in pity. "Aye," said he in reply, "he has indeed touched the lowest depth of misery in futile, earnest repentance. Eight times outside these walls have I shattered his idols of the former time; eight times now have I found him thus. Nine times have I been deputed to immolate these sycophants and cowardly knaves for the purification of this great man greatly deluded, and now the eighth has just been completed with your assistance. Cervantes, away far off in the Beyond, awaits with eagerness the ninth immolation and this man's release from the borderland of uncertainty."

"Ah, me!" moaned Sir Walter, "I had refrained from violence for almost nine years, when this nobly unclad knight appeared, armed with a magic sword, and I was tempted to undertake his life with a view to save this miserable, woestricken place—the abode of futile violence and oppression. This last wrong, expiable and irreparable for nine years, dooms me to a ninth period of probation, during which I must live in constant dread of lapsing into violence, even as now on the very last day of the ninth year—all these nine years must I live, wondering how soon and in what shape the irresistible temptation to violence and wrong will present itself, unless by pardon of this Knight freely given."

"If lack of my forgiveness," quoth I earnestly, "be indeed all that stands between thee, Sir Walter, and deliverance from this evil place, I freely and gladly give it, seeing, as I do, that the dastardly deed has been the cause of greater violence to the better nature within thee than it has been to me." At this the great writer ceased weeping and held his breath, looking expectantly, though doubtfully, towards Don Quixote, who smiled as he spoke thus:

"The noblest deed done by this Knight of the 'bare skin' is this, that he has given thee his pardon freely; and as I was empowered on this condition to take thee with me, I now gladly invite thee to come to the Beyond—to the land of perfect knightly deeds, and perfect power to portray them. Lucky for thee, Sir Walter, this Knight chanced this way—lucky in that thou hast wounded the truest friend."

Refusing to go to the Beyond, though I earnestly entreated, I took leave of the two and set out for home. Being overpowered by fatigue, I fell by the roadside into a deep and dreamless sleep, out of which I arose refreshed, to find that I had returned to earth and was being nursed back to health and strength out of the wounds and weakness resulting from the part I had taken in the recent overthrow of the stronghold of Medævalism.

ABOUT THE AUTHORS

"A.E." was the pseudonym employed by George William Russell (1867-1935), an Irish writer, artist, and editor who edited *The Irish Homestead* for many years before editing *The Irish Statesman*. A friend of both W. B. Yeats, with whom he helped found the Dublin Lodge of the Theosophical Society, and James Joyce (the latter placed him in his novel Ulysses), he did much to promote the work of Irish writers. His pseudonym was derived from the word ÆON, which he intended to have printed on the title page of his first book of poetry *Homeward Songs by the Way* (1894), but the printer mistakenly made it simply Æ. His writings, noteworthy among these being *The Candle of Vision* (1920), were influenced by various revelations he was subject to during states of meditation. "The Story of the Star" first appeared in the August 15, 1894 issue of *The Irish Theosophist*.

H.P. BLAVATSKY (1831-1891) was a Russian-born author who, at the age of eighteen, left home to travel the world. According to her, while in London in 1851, she met a master of ancient wisdom by the name of Morya, who instructed her to voyage to Tibet where she would be trained by various spiritual adepts. Later, in 1875, in New York, she co-founded the Theosophical Society. In 1877 she published the occult work *Isis Unveiled*, and would go on to publish many articles and books. "Karmic Visions" originally appeared under the pseudonym of "Sanjna" in the June 15, 1888 issue of *Lucifer*, the famous London-based Theosophical Monthly which she herself edited.

CHARLES E. BENHAM (1860-1929) was a journalist who for many years edited the *Essex County Standard*. A keen scientific amateur, he invented the Benham's top, which was designed with black and white patterns but which created the illusion of colour when spun. He wrote a number of books, including *William Gilbert of Colchester: A Sketch of his Magnetic philosophy* (1902) and published a translation of Joseph Serre'sP*Au large!*, titled *The Broad View: Outline of a Method of Universal Conciliation and Comprehensive Thought* (1927). He was involved with the Christo-Theosophical Society, delivering at least one lecture at their Bloomsbury Square address on "The Symphalmograph and its Teaching," and he contributed pieces to both *Light* and *Lucifer*, the latter periodical being where "Was He Mad?" originally appeared, the story spanning the November 15, 1888 and the December 15, 1888 issues.

ALEISTER CROWLEY (1875-1947), one of the most important English occultists, joined the Hermetic Order of the Golden Dawn in 1898, before becoming the founder and prophet of the religion of Thelema, and later the founder of the A∴A∴ magical organization. A prolific writer, he published numerous volumes, which included poetry, fiction, essays and instructions. In 1909 he started to put out a biannual periodical, billed as the "Official Organ of the A∴A∴" called *The Equinox: The Review of Scientific Illuminism*, the March 1910 issue being that from which "The Soul Hunter" is taken.

ARTHUR CONAN DOYLE (1859-1930) was a British writer and physician. A practising spiritualist, he attended *séances*, visited mediums and searched for poltergeists. In 1889, he became a founding member of the Hampshire Society for Psychical Research, in 1893 joined the London-based Society for Psychical Research, and thereafter joined the Ghost Club, which was involved in paranormal investigations. Though most famed for his Sherlock Holmes stories, he wrote a large amount of other work, including *The New Revelation* (1918), *The Vital Message* (1919), and *The History of Spiritualism* (1926). "Playing with Fire" was originally published in the March 1900 issue of *The Strand Magazine*.

HELEN FAGG was active in London Theosophical circles in the 1880s and 1890s, but aside from that very little about her is known. She made several contributions to *Lucifer*, the March 15, 1888 issue of which contained "Zarina!"

FLORENCE FARR (1860-1917) was a British actress and writer. She was initiated into the Isis-Urania Temple of the Order of the Golden Dawn in London by W. B. Yeats in July 1890, and later, in 1894, became Praemonstratrix of the temple, and then in 1897 Chief Adept in Anglia, that is to say, the leader of the English branch of the Order. Due to various fractures within the Order, however, she separated herself from it and joined the Theosophical Society of London. A deep scholar, she wrote a number of works on occult subjects, including, under the pseudonym S.S.D.D., *Egyptian Magic* (1896), and, together with Olivia Shakespeare, the plays *The Shrine of the Golden Hawk and The Beloved of Hathor* (1902). "A Dialogue of Vision" first appeared in the September 1906 issue of *The Theosophical Review*.

LETTICE GALBRAITH is an author of which very little is known, outside of the fact that she published stories in various periodicals, her writing career culminating in the release of her two collections, *Pretty Miss Allington and Other Tales* (1893) and *New Ghost Stories* (1893), the latter volume being that from which "In the Séance Room" is taken.

H. RIDER HAGGARD (1856-1925) was an English barrister, politician, and writer. His interest in the occult began as a young man, when he was studying in London and became immersed in spiritualist circles and attended *séances*. A good deal of his work was informed by the occult, including the novel *She: A History of Adventure* (1886), *The Ancient Allan* (1920), and *Heu-Heu* (1924). "Only a Dream" originally appeared in 1905 in *Harry Furniss's Christmas Annual* under the title "A Wedding Gift," but was reprinted under the title used in the present anthology in *Smith and the Pharaohs and Other Tales* (1920).

ROBERT HICHENS (1864-1950) was an English man of letters who published a great many volumes of fiction, a good portion of these, such as *Flames* (1897), and the short story collection *Bye-Ways* (1897), from which "The Face of the Monk" is taken, being heavily informed by his interest in the occult.

G.M. Irvine was an Irish doctor responsible for several books, including two of fiction: *The Lion's Whelp* (1910), and a volume of short stories supposedly written by a Dr. Semel Bis via telepathic communication titled *In the Valley of Vision* (1911), the latter volume being that from which "The Middle Age" is taken.

M.R. JAMES (1862-1936) was an English author, medievalist scholar and provost of King's College, Cambridge, and of Eton College, as well as being Vice-Chancellor of the University of Cambridge. Though best remembered for his ghost stories, he also wrote numerous scholarly works, many of which were descriptive catalogues of manuscripts held in the various libraries of the colleges of the University of Cambridge. His studies undoubtedly informed his fictional works, many of which deal with the occult. "Casting the Runes" is taken from the collection *More Ghost Stories* (1911).

ANNA KINGSFORD (1846-1888), was the second woman in Britain to obtain a degree in medicine, managing to do so without experimenting on a single animal. In 1866 she published anonymously a volume of poetry titled *River Reeds*, and in 1875, as Mrs. Algernon Kingsford, *Rosamunda the Princess, and Other Tales*. A vegetarian and animal rights advocate, she was vice president of the Vegetarian Society. In 1873 she began an association with the occultist and writer Edward Maitland which resulted in the anonymously published volume of correspondence *The Key of Creeds* (1875), and subsequently the volume of lectures *The Perfect Way; or, Finding the Christ* (1882). Keenly interested in Buddhism, ancient Egyptian religion, and a "restoration" of Christianity, she became president of the London Lodge of the Theosophical Society in 1883. Subject to visions and illuminations, both in and out of sleep, she produced, under the latter influence, *Dreams and Dream Stories* (1888), from which "The Enchanted Woman" is taken.

ARTHUR MACHEN (1863-1947), was a Welsh author widely considered to be one of the greatest practitioners of supernatural fiction in the English language. A somewhat ambivalent member of the Hermetic Order of the Golden

Dawn, he was extremely well versed in occultism in its various manifestations, that knowledge informing much of his best writing, including *The Great God Pan* (1894), *The White People* (1904), and *The Three Impostors* (1895), this latter volume being that from which "The Novel of the White Powder" is taken.

WILLIAM SHARP (1855-1905), who also wrote under the name of his alter-ego "Fiona Macleod," was a Scottish writer of broad range and ability, his work encompassing poetry, non-fiction, and fiction. He was a member of the Hermetic Order of the Golden Dawn and also engaged with W. B. Yeats in psychic experiments and assisted him in his endeavours to gain rituals for the Celtic Mystical Order. "The Last Quest" is taken from the collection *Vistas* (1894).

M.P. SHIEL (1865-1947), was born on the island of Montserrat in the West Indies, and educated in Barbados, but at the age of twenty moved to England where he began to make a living as a man of letters, producing an abundance of translations, serialized novels, and short stories, many of which had occult themes. "Xélucha" is taken from the collection *Shapes in the Fire* (1896).

DORA SIGERSON SHORTER (1866-1918) was born in Dublin to the author and physician George Sigerson and the author Hester Varian, and was the wife of the journalist Clement Shorter. A sculptor of note and an important part of the Irish Literary Revival, she was the author of a number of volumes of both poetry and prose, including *The Fairy Changeling and Other Poems* (1898), and *The Father Confessor: Stories of Death and Danger* (1900), the latter volume being that from which "Transmigration" is taken.

EDWARD STORER (1880-1944) was an English writer, translator and poet. One of the creators and first proponents of imagism, he outlined his views in an essay appended to his poetry collection *Mirrors of Illusion* (1908). It is not entirely clear where he met Aleister Crowley, but the latter included "The Three Worms" in the September 1910 issue of *The Equinox*.

EVELYN UNDERHILL (1875-1941) was an English author of over thirty books, almost all mystical in nature, which she published both under her own name and the pseudonym "John Cordelier". She was a close friend of Arthur Machen, to whom, along with his wife Purefoy, she dedicated her novel *A Column of Dust* (1909), from which "How Something came from Somewhere" is taken.

H. G. WELLS (1866-1946) was a writer who, though he practised many genres, is best remembered for his ground-breaking science fiction novels, which included *The Island of Doctor Moreau* (1896) and *The Invisible Man* (1897). Though not an occultist, he did take an academic interest in the subject, as is in evidence in his many supernatural stories, which include "The Stolen Body" which was originally published in the November 1898 issue of *The Strand Magazine*.

"X.L." was the pseudonym of Julian Osgood Field (1852-1925), who, though born in the United States, lived in London and Paris for the majority of his life, most, if not all of his work, being published in England. An intimate of the future King Edward VII of Great Britain, and an associate of many others in high society, he led a life beyond any legal means that were at his disposal and, it seems, made use of means that were less than legal, being jailed in 1901 for three months for forgery, and in 1908 for eighteen months for conspiring to defraud a wealthy lady of her riches. In Paris he had a large circle of acquaintances, including those which Huysmans based his *Là-Bas* on. "Aut Diabolus Aut Nihil," first published in the October 1888 issue of *Blackwood's Magazine*, is said to have described practices by Osgood's personal friends, though the latter made a point of denying it in his introduction to *Aut Diabolus Aut Nihil and Other Stories*, when the tale was reprinted in the much longer version that is included in the present volume.

"ZURESTA" was the pseudonym of I. B. Prangley, the London-based author of various books on tarot and palmistry, of which she (the "I." stood for Ida) was likely a practitioner, possibly working from her home on Edgware Road, and possibly also working under the title of Madame Chira, a pseudonym which was said to have been hers and under which was published *Fortune Telling by Cards, Describing how Cards are "read" by Persons Professing to tell Fortunes by their Aid* (1901). She made several contributions to the *Occult Review*, of which "A Weird Experience" is one, having been published in the August 1908 issue of that journal.

A PARTIAL LIST OF SNUGGLY BOOKS

MAY ARMAND BLANC *The Last Rendezvous*
G. ALBERT AURIER *Elsewhere and Other Stories*
CHARLES BARBARA *My Lunatic Asylum*
S. HENRY BERTHOUD *Misanthropic Tales*
LÉON BLOY *The Tarantulas' Parlor and Other Unkind Tales*
ÉLÉMIR BOURGES *The Twilight of the Gods*
CYRIEL BUYSSE *The Aunts*
JAMES CHAMPAGNE *Harlem Smoke*
FÉLICIEN CHAMPSAUR *The Latin Orgy*
BRENDAN CONNELL *Metrophilias*
BRENDAN CONNELL *Unofficial History of Pi Wei*
BRENDAN CONNELL (editor)
    The World in Violet: An Anthology of EnglishDecadent Poetry
RAFAELA CONTRERAS *The Turquoise Ring and Other Stories*
DANIEL CORRICK (editor)
    Ghosts and Robbers: An Anthology of German Gothic Fiction
ADOLFO COUVE *When I Think of My Missing Head*
QUENTIN S. CRISP *Aiaigasa*
LUCIE DELARUE-MARDRUS *The Last Siren and Other Stories*
LADY DILKE *The Outcast Spirit and Other Stories*
CATHERINE DOUSTEYSSIER-KHOZE *The Beauty of the Death Cap*
ÉDOUARD DUJARDIN *Hauntings*
BERIT ELLINGSEN *Now We Can See the Moon*
ERCKMANN-CHATRIAN *A Malediction*
ALPHONSE ESQUIROS *The Enchanted Castle*
ENRIQUE GÓMEZ CARRILLO *Sentimental Stories*
DELPHI FABRICE *Flowers of Ether*
DELPHI FABRICE *The Red Sorcerer*
DELPHI FABRICE *The Red Spider*
BENJAMIN GASTINEAU *The Reign of Satan*
EDMOND AND JULES DE GONCOURT *Manette Salomon*
REMY DE GOURMONT *From a Faraway Land*
REMY DE GOURMONT *Morose Vignettes*
GUIDO GOZZANO *Alcina and Other Stories*
GUSTAVE GUICHES *The Modesty of Sodom*
EDWARD HERON-ALLEN *The Complete Shorter Fiction*
EDWARD HERON-ALLEN *Three Ghost-Written Novels*
RHYS HUGHES *Cloud Farming in Wales*
J.-K. HUYSMANS *The Crowds of Lourdes*
J.-K. HUYSMANS *Knapsacks*
COLIN INSOLE *Valerie and Other Stories*
JUSTIN ISIS *Pleasant Tales II*

www.ingramcontent.com/pod-product-compliance
Lightning Source LLC
Chambersburg PA
CBHW050521110726
47899CB00005B/1539